HOLLYWOOD LEGENDS
BOOK TWO

Dreaming
WITH MY EYES
WIDE OPEN

MARY J. WILLIAMS

About the Author

Want to know how to motivate yourself to write a book? Have your favorite football team lose the Super Bowl. On the last play. With an interception. The next day I was so depressed I tuned out all media. No TV, no internet, no newspapers — nothing. And I started to write. I'm still writing. As you can see, a little motivation can do wonders. Football will play a big part in my next series of books due out next year. And since I'm writing the ending? No interceptions. Guaranteed. Happy reading everyone.

How to Get in Touch

Please visit me at these sites, sign up for my newsletter or leave a message.

http://www.maryjwilliams.net/home.html
https://www.facebook.com/pages/Mary-J-Williams/1561851657385417
https://twitter.com/maryjwilliams05
https://www.pinterest.com/maryj0675/
https://instagram.com/2015romance/
https://www.goodreads.com/author/show/5648619.Mary_J_Williams

More Books by Mary J. Williams

Harper Falls Series
If I Loved You
If Tomorrow Never Comes
If You Only Knew
If I Had You (Christmas in Harper Falls)

Hollywood Legends Series
Dreaming With a Broken Heart

Contents

To My Sister Ivy
With All My Love

Prologue

NATE LANDIS NEVER thought much about the way he looked. Women seemed to like his face. That was genetics. He was the son of Hollywood royalty. Alone, they turned heads. Together, they dazzled. It made sense that they would pass some of that on.

Nate took it in stride. He was strong. Healthy. His body was trained to do what he wanted it to do, under what could only be called extreme situations. He ate right, worked hard, and played harder.

At some point, his lifestyle would catch up with him. Age would take care of that. Right now, he was in his prime. If he wanted to scale a mountain, that's what he did. Jump from a plane? A piece of cake. Race car driving. Deep sea diving. You name it; Nate was the first one in line.

When he was three years old, his mother called him her little daredevil. Fearless, she swore he gave her wrinkles for worrying what he would get into next. Nate would always laugh, peering closely at Callie Flynn's flawless complexion. What wrinkles? In her fifties, she was, and would always be, one of the movie industry's great beauties. Nothing he or his brothers did could alter that.

As Nate stepped to the edge of the cliff, he didn't think about the two-hundred-foot drop. He'd jumped from higher than this. It was what he did. And he did it better than anyone else. For some reason, today he thought about his mother.

Callie never discouraged him from pursuing danger, even though Nate knew she wished he had chosen a safer way to make a living. She didn't say so, but he knew she worried about his safety. It didn't stop him — he seldom thought about it. Until today. As he waited for the director to signal the camera was rolling, for the first time Nate let himself worry about his mother's reaction if something happened to him.

He shook off the morbid thought. Now wasn't the time. He needed to focus. Ninety-nine percent of the time, if something went wrong, it was due to a loss of focus. Nate took a deep breath. He cleared his mind. Three flashes of light. That was his signal. He squared his shoulders, coiled his body. And jumped.

Nate Landis was a stuntman. Some might say it was his calling. If a director needed it done big and done right, that person called him. Nate loved his job.

He let his body relax as he sailed through the air. The count in his head was precise. If he pulled the ripcord too soon, the shot would be ruined. Too late, he risked ending up a pile of broken bones.

Nate planned every stunt. He worked out the timing, the logistics, and the angles. He never let anyone perform a stunt unless he tested it. Over and over again. He refused to rush. Anxious directors. Bottom-line producers. Some tried to push him into cutting corners.

Few things made Nate lose his temper. His brother Garrett claimed Nate had the longest, slowest burning fuse in history. But he had his hot buttons. Endangering himself and his crew was one of them. Last year, a director, trying to save time, ran a stunt when Nate was away from the set. Poorly conceived and executed, two stuntmen went to the hospital with second-degree burns.

Todd Winesap went to the hospital with a broken jaw and a tarnished reputation.

It took a lot to make Nate mad. But watch out when it happened.

Nate ran the count through his head. Eight, nine, ten. He gave the cord a firm, steady pull. Smooth as glass, the chute opened. Even so, he traveled at a high speed. The parachute was safety measure number one. Number two was the large, air-filled target waiting below.

Having done this stunt hundreds of times, Nate knew what to expect and how it should feel. And he knew when something was wrong.

The air bag, that Nate had personally supervised the placement of, wasn't where it was supposed to be. He didn't have the time to wonder how that had happened. If he didn't act fast, he wouldn't be around to beat the shit out of the asshole responsible.

Grabbing the guide strings, Nate pulled a hard right with all his considerable strength — and prayed.

Chapter One

HOLLYWOOD WAS AN unforgiving town with a long memory. Drugs could be forgiven. Drunk driving. Spousal abuse. Those things could be forgiven. In the movie industry, your worth was measured by one thing — box office returns. Three strikes, you're out.

Early in his career, Caleb Landis knew the meaning of holding on by his fingertips. He was young, inexperienced, and hungry. That meant working all the angles. No one opened any doors for a dirt-poor would-be producer. That was fine with him. He had no problem barreling his way in. His take no prisoners attitude earned him respect. And enemies.

Hard work. Long hours. Sacrifice. Eventually, it paid off. Caleb's career spanned over four decades. He had money and power. The shelves of his office were lined with every award the industry could give him.

When a movie had the name Landis attached to it, the world knew they were getting quality.

Sitting back, Caleb looked around the table with pride. His family. That was his greatest accomplishment. The fame and money meant nothing compared to the joy of knowing the most important people in the world surrounded him. The people he loved. The people who loved him.

It all started and ended with his Callie.

Screen goddess to the world. To him, protector of his heart.

He had no doubt the first time he saw her. He knew she was the woman he wanted to spend his life with. She was the only woman he would ever love. Their life hadn't been the fairy tale some people made it out to be. They had their ups and downs. But through it all, one thing never changed. Their unshakable love.

His beautiful wife had given him four strong, healthy sons. Men a father could be proud of.

Wyatt was the oldest. Like Caleb, a producer. The difference was *he* trusted his gut. If a project felt right, he fought until he got it made. Wyatt was a thinker. His first concern was the bottom line. They had squared off more than once about artistry versus the almighty dollar.

The end was always the same. He and Wyatt were different enough that butting heads was inevitable. They had enough similarities to put those differences aside. The most important thing was the movie. Together they made art — and money.

Caleb's gaze moved to the other side of the table. The laugh he heard was a deeper version of his sweet Callie's. It made him smile. Colton. The youngest of his four boys. He was the only one to follow his mother's lead, stepping in front of the camera to make his mark. And what a mark it was going to be.

Colt had a face the camera loved. The first offer to put him in the movies came when he was only a year old. The offers kept coming. Callie didn't want any of her sons to be *child stars*. Caleb agreed.

Growing up was hard enough. In Beverly Hills, the temptations were magnified. Caleb and Callie did their best to give their children as normal a childhood as possible. Family dinners. Game night. Backyard barbecues. If that childhood included trips to Cannes and vacations on private yachts, so what? This was their version of normal. It wasn't perfect. But then, what was?

Colton was one of the biggest movie stars in the world. In public, that meant screaming fans and preferential treatment. At dinner with his family, he was expected to set the table and dry the dishes. It was true when he was ten. It was true now, even if his last movie *did* break box office records.

Then there was Garrett. Caleb sat back smiling when he heard his middle son complaining to his mother.

"What is the world coming to when a man's family takes sides against him?"

"First, Jade is your family. And ours." Callie patted Jade's hand. "Second. She's right. You're wrong. End of discussion."

"Hey." Garrett looked at the two women. His mother on his right. The love of his life on his left. There was no rock. No hard place. With a snap of his fingers, there would be a thousand men lined up to take his place. He was no fool. He knew he had it good. "I give up," he said, wisely conceding the point.

Dazzled by Jade's smile, Garrett melted. He tucked a lock of her long, silky red hair behind her ear. The unconsciously intimate gesture had his parents smiling with approval.

"A wise decision, son." Caleb nodded at Garrett with a wink. "When you realize your lady is the brains in the relationship, the sailing will be much smoother."

"Where are you on *Exile*?"

Garrett and Jade were just back from Vancouver where he had finished principal shooting on his current film. His last project had garnered him an Oscar nomination for best director. Caleb believed this one would win his son the statue.

"I'm in the studio next week. The soundtrack needs some tweaking, but the composer assures me it will be ready."

"It better be," Wyatt added. "The Los Angeles Philharmonic doesn't come cheap. You have them for a week. That's all the budget will allow. After that, I'll take it out of your salary."

"It's my own fault for working with family," Garrett sighed. "I could knock any other producer on his ass if he talked to me like that. Mommy would have a fit if I bruised her baby's face."

"Jade, you're marrying an idiot."

"Pardon my French in advance, Mom." Garrett gave Wyatt the finger, and then added, "Fuck you, Wyatt."

"Nice mouth, brother. You might think about washing it out with soap before kissing your woman." Out of Callie's sight, Wyatt flipped Garrett the bird.

"I just brushed. How about kissing me instead?"

"Nate!"

Callie was across the room in a flash. Instead of jumping into his arms, as was her custom, she held back. She knew the doctor said Nate's ribs were healed, but she was his mother. The thought of causing him the slightest pain was unthinkable.

"Where's your sling?"

"Gone for good. Thank God."

Nate's left arm was still in a cast. With little effort, he used his right to swing Callie in a circle. The comforting scent of roses and vanilla drifted around him. As always, it took him back to his childhood when she would tuck him in at night. Burying his face in her hair, he breathed deeply.

Mother. Love. Safety. From the time he was born, she had steered him with a gentle yet firm hand. There was a fine line between controlling and supportive. Callie Flynn showed her sons by example that a woman could thrill the world with her acting and still be the best mother anyone could ask for. Nate affectionately kissed the top of her head. What would he have done without this woman?

"We didn't think you were going to make it." Callie took his good hand, leading him to the table. "Sit. I'll get you a plate. I swear, since the accident you've wasted away to nothing."

Colt snorted in disbelief. "How can you tell? The man is a freaking brick wall."

"Callie's right." Jade smiled at Nate. "You look thinner."

"I knew the woman couldn't keep her eyes off me. Tell me you've finally realized you picked the wrong brother."

"One more word and I'll forget you're my twin." Garrett turned to

Jade. "I always felt sorry for him. I got the looks, the brains, and the charm. And Nate got the...? What did Nate get?"

"The ability to kick your ass?" Nate flexed his impressive biceps. "And more women than even Colton could handle."

"Hey," Colt interjected. "That's my reputation as a man-whore you're besmirching. What would the tabloids say if word got out that my brother was getting more women than I was?"

"Don't listen to him, Colt." Garrett loved jabbing at his twin. Just as Nate loved returning the favor. The sport never grew old. "He overcompensated for his shortcomings by living in the gym. I suppose some women find brawn over brains attractive."

"More than a few."

"Enough." Callie chuckled. She had heard this banter for years. "You," she said to Nate, "stop talking — eat. And you," she looked at Garrett. "Leave your brother in peace for five minutes."

Thanking her with a smile, Nate took the plate from his mother. It overflowed with roast beef, mashed potatoes, fresh green beans, all drowned in rich, brown gravy. Adding three fresh baked rolls from the basket on the table, Nate was a happy man.

The truth was, since the accident on the movie set last month, he hadn't been himself. It would be different if he could work. Keeping busy was the best way to calm his mind and body. Unfortunately, the injuries he had sustained kept him sidelined.

Too much time on his hands. Too much time to think about what had gone wrong. The botched stunt could have ended in tragedy. Thanks to his quick reflexes, physical strength, and determination not to end up in a heap of mangled bones, Nate walked away with a few cracked ribs and a broken arm. The only reason he stayed the night in the hospital was to appease his mother. The doctor assured her Nate didn't have a concussion. Callie didn't want to take any chances. One night of observation was a small price to pay for his mother's peace of mind.

It didn't hurt that his nurse was a curvy brunette with warm, soft hands.

"I know that smile." Wyatt shook his head. "Which conquest are you thinking about now?"

"You wouldn't give me such a hard time if you were getting laid more often." Remembering where he was, Nate gave his mother a repentant grin. "Sorry."

"Your brother's love life is his own business," Callie said firmly.

"Thank you." Wyatt gave Nate a *take that* glare.

"Though…"

"Ah, crap." Wyatt's head fell forward, his chin hitting his chest.

"Come on, Wyatt," Garrett laughed with delight. "Every man lives to have his mother discuss his sex life."

"There will be no discussion," Callie assured her oldest. "I'm just saying. Once you've been sexually active, going cold turkey isn't healthy for the mind or body."

"Thanks for not talking about it," Wyatt mumbled.

"I have a friend whose daughter would be perfect."

"Callie,"

Everyone at the table recognized that tone in Caleb's voice. The boys had heard it often when growing up. Better than a raised hand, it had the ability to keep them on the straight and narrow. He rarely used that deep, in charge, producer's voice with his wife. When he did, she knew she crossed the line into an area he didn't approve of. Sometimes she listened; sometimes she barreled ahead. Today, she silently conceded that her husband was right.

"Fine."

Callie patted Wyatt's hand. Looking deep into his eyes, she saw the lingering pain that he never seemed to completely shake. A bad marriage that ended in his wife's death wasn't something he could easily get over. Questions about whether the car crash had been accidental or deliberate still lingered. He carried around the guilt even though the marriage had ended well before Stephanie's death.

Nate decided it was time to throw his big brother a lifeline. They gave each other a ton of grief, but when it came down to it, the four of them were the other's best friends.

"I finally tracked down the witness."

"What?" Callie's expressive eyes widened. "When? Why didn't you say something sooner? What did he say?"

"Breathe, Mom."

Nate took a bite of potato. Mmm. Food always tasted better at his mother's table surrounded by family. Nate was not a solitary person by nature. Since the accident, he had been spending too much time alone. Between recovering and trying to figure out what went wrong, there hadn't been a lot of time to be social. It was time to change that.

"Well?" Callie demanded.

"Brett Walcott."

"Right," Garrett nodded. "The assistant to an assistant. He left word with you that he saw something. Then he disappeared."

"I had that stunt set up exactly right. Between the time it took to get to the top of the cliff and when I jumped, something happened."

"It had to be during the delay." Wyatt's people had investigated. Right after Nate left the set, a fire broke out in one of the trailers. It turned out to be minor and luckily, no one was hurt, but it had the entire crew scrambling for almost an hour.

Nate had his own helpers whose job it was to keep the status quo on all equipment until the stunt was finished. They admitted to leaving the airbag unattended while they helped with the fire. As a result, someone had time to make a small puncture at the base of the bag.

The leak was slow but effective. As Nate approached from above, it appeared the bag had been moved. In reality, the loss of air pressure gave it that appearance. If Nate hadn't been able to muscle his chute and land as close to the center as possible, chances were, he wouldn't have been here to tell the tale. The bounce he took that landed him on the hard ground was bad, resulting in relatively minor injuries. His quick reflexes and some luck had spoiled someone's deadly plans.

Finding a witness had been almost impossible. Nate trusted his crew. They were lured away like everyone else. The only person willing to talk called Nate the day after he left the hospital.

Brett Walcott was so low on the movie set ladder that Nate didn't recognize his name. Assistant was pushing it. He was a gopher. He fetched coffee, jackets, lip balm. Whatever was needed, he was the man who made the run. It wasn't a well-paying job.

So when Brett saw his opportunity, he took it. He claimed to know who punctured the bag, and was willing to share the information with Nate. For a price.

Nate had been around. He knew the drill. Brett agreed to meet him the next day. Nate agreed to bring twenty thousand dollars. It was a small price to pay; he would have doled out twice that amount to discover who wanted him dead.

With Garrett along for backup, Nate drove to the drop-off spot in East Los Angeles. It was too much like something out of a bad action flick for Nate's taste, but he wasn't in a position to complain.

They sat for three hours before finally giving up. Either Brett had second thoughts or someone got to him first.

"Where has the weasel been hiding?"

"In plain sight." Nate set his fork on the now empty plate. "He's been getting a tan in a high-end Mexican resort."

"You're kidding?" Wyatt exchanged amazed looks with Garrett and Caleb. "All this time? How did you find out?"

"A few days ago, I called Jack."

"Damn," Wyatt said. "H&W Security is getting a lot of our money lately."

As far as the Landis family was concerned, H&W could do no wrong. The bodyguard their old friend Jack Winston sent to protect Jade had been worth every penny. She was safe and the danger that had plagued her for years was behind her. After that, Garrett wouldn't begrudge Jack anything.

"Turns out I should have called him right away. He turned it over to Alex Fleming, who tracked Walcott down in a matter of hours. The fool was spreading cash around like there was no tomorrow. That kind of behavior gets people talking."

"I assume you've booked a flight," Wyatt said. "I'm going with you."

"I appreciate it, but there's no need." Nate laughed, shaking his head. "Our buddies at H&W provide an all-inclusive service. As we speak, Brett Walcott is on his way back to the States."

"How did they manage that?"

"I didn't ask, Dad. I was so happy with the results, I figured Jack and Alex could keep their trade secrets to themselves. I do know it involved Jack piloting a plane in and out of Mexico." Nate sat back. He was full. With family. And he would soon have the answers he needed. "I will be heading to Spokane in the morning. Jack flew straight to Harper Falls. He didn't want to take a chance on having a run-in with LAX security."

"Want some company?"

All eyes turned to Jade.

"Excuse me?" Garrett asked.

"What? I thought it would be a good chance to visit Sable."

"Ah," Colt smiled thoughtfully. "The lovely bodyguard. Maybe—"

"No." Nate shook his head, frowning at his younger brother. "You and your libido are staying put." When he turned to Jade, his tone was softer. "I plan on being in and out, honey. No time for social niceties."

"I trust Jack and his crew to have your back." Wyatt frowned. "I wonder if this is the best way to handle it."

"If you mean the police? They haven't been interested, Wyatt. As far as they're concerned, this was an accident."

"But now you have a witness." Callie was for anything that kept her family out of danger. "What will you do with him?"

"There's plenty of undeveloped ground on the mountain behind H&W headquarters," Garrett said helpfully.

"You could bury the body with little chance of detection."

"Ha, ha. You boys missed your calling as stand-up comedians."

Even knowing it would garner him a dirty look, Caleb couldn't help joining in.

"As long as you're at it, I have an investor I wouldn't mind chucking down a deep hole."

"That's where they get it," Callie told Jade, ignoring her husband. "Come and help me with dessert."

"What are we having?" Nate called out.

"*Jade and I* are sharing some strawberry cheesecake. If you're lucky, we'll leave you some crumbs."

Cheesecake was Nate's favorite.

"Don't worry, son. I know for a fact that your mother had Lorena make an extra for you to take home."

The family's long-time cook made the best desserts in the world. Nate wouldn't argue if one ended up in his refrigerator.

"Hey!" Colton protested.

Nate swung his cast from side to side, a *poor me* expression on his face.

"I don't remember special desserts when I broke my leg skiing."

"That's because you moved back here. Mom and Lorena waited on your pathetic ass night and day."

Colt grinned at Nate. "Mmm. One of the best months of my life. All the food I could eat served by two beautiful, loving women. In my mind, that's what heaven will be like."

"You live in heaven twenty-four-seven, little brother. Women are lined up for miles for the honor of doing your dirty laundry." Garrett grimaced. "I lived with your slovenly ways for sixteen years. No one, no matter how smitten, should have to deal with your foul socks. I swear those things stood up by themselves."

"Look who's talking." Colt turned to Wyatt. "Remember the summer Garrett decided to *get back to nature*? In other words, he didn't shower for a month. Dad finally held him down while Nate sprayed him with a hose."

Nate listened with half an ear while his brothers entertained each other with stories of their youth. His mind was already on his trip north. Now that he was so close to finding out the truth, he wished he had booked an earlier flight.

"Nathaniel."

"Hmm?" The use of his full name got Nate's attention. "Did you need something, Dad?"

"Funny you should ask." Caleb stood, gesturing for Nate to follow.

"Come to my office. I have something I want you to see. By the time we're done, your mother should have calmed down enough to share some of that cheesecake."

Nate followed his father down the hall. The door at the end had always been Caleb's domain. Callie fiddled and decorated the rest of the house to her liking, but this one room was off limits. She was welcome to visit, but every inch was sacrosanct. Hands off. No exceptions. Caleb allowed the housekeeper cleaning access once a week. That was as far as his concessions went.

When they were little, Caleb would let his boys crawl around on the floor to their hearts' content. He liked having the toddlers nearby. Nate remembered using his father as a jungle gym, Caleb's patience infinite. One of the many ways the big, boisterous man showed his love. He taught by example the proper way to show affection.

One day, Nate thought, if he were blessed enough to have children, he already knew how to be a man they could look up to. His father showed him — every day of his life.

"Have a look at this."

Caleb took a letter from the top drawer of his desk. Sitting, he waited while Nate read the two pages. When he had finished, he looked up with a puzzled frown.

"Have I ever met Chuck Chamberlin?"

"No. He was a roustabout on a few of my early films. By the time you and your brothers came along, Chuck was married and living in Montana."

"But you've kept in touch?" Nate handed back the letter.

"Off and on."

Caleb sat back. Absently, he tapped one long finger against his chin. Nate recognized it as a gesture his father made when he was thinking.

"It sounds like your old friend is in a bind. I admire the nerve of his daughter. Her father is in over his head and she contacts one of the biggest movie producers in Hollywood to bail him out?"

"*One* of the most successful?"

Amused, Nate glanced at the rows of awards on the shelves behind his father. "I'm not giving your ego an unneeded boost, Pops."

"Ah, children." Caleb's over-exaggerated sigh made it clear he had chosen the right side of the camera. He was wise to leave the acting to Callie and Colt.

"Paige is worried about her father. I can't blame her for reaching out to the only person she thought might help. Wouldn't you do the same?"

Nate had to concede the point. If his parents were in a bind, Nate would track down God if he thought it would help.

"Like I said, I admire her nerve." Nate tapped his chin, unconsciously echoing his father's gesture. "This movie her father is making. She says he's wanted to do it for years. Did he ever mention wanting to direct?"

"This is Hollywood, Nate. Everybody wants to direct."

"I don't. Neither do Wyatt or Colt."

Caleb chuckled. "The exceptions that prove the rule. Add your mother and me to that list and you have most of the Landis clan. Wonderful anomalies."

"But this Chamberlin guy. Where was his ambition when he worked here?"

"There are different kinds of ambition, Nate. Chuck found Hollywood exciting. But his dream was to make enough money to go back to his hometown and take over the family ranch. And that's what he did."

"What do you think changed? The daughter's letter isn't exactly packed full of details."

"Which is why I called her last week. She seems genuine, Nate."

"You mean she isn't using an obscure connection to get a little free advice?"

"The thought crossed my mind." One didn't survive in Hollywood as long as he had without developing a thick skin and a nose for bullshit. It was possible that Paige Chamberlin wasn't what she seemed, but Caleb didn't think so. She came across as a daughter at her wits' end. She was worried about her father. She waited as long as she could before contacting him. He was the last resort that she hated to use. The fact that she had, spoke louder than words.

"Chuck's wife died two years ago. According to Paige, he's been a little depressed. Understandable. I think he's afraid of losing his daughter, too. The movie isn't just his vanity project. It's a way of keeping Paige close."

"Jesus, Dad."

"I know… it sounds messed up."

"No." Nate tried to think of a way of putting it that wouldn't come across as judgmental, but came up empty. "Okay, yes. It sounds a little twisted. Hell, for all we know, it's a lot twisted."

"I don't think so." Caleb shook his head. "I honestly believe he's a lonely man who's worried his daughter will move away, get married, have children, and he won't be around to watch them grow up."

"Is that what she said?"

"Paige painted a picture of a man who has gotten in over his head. She didn't say it, but I think she's afraid he'll crash and burn. Personally and financially."

"All to keep his daughter down on the ranch? That's some job of reading between the lines, Dad."

"I put myself in his shoes."

"Come on." Nate wasn't buying it. "You wouldn't have stopped us from leaving Los Angeles if it was what we wanted."

"I was lucky enough that it was never an issue. And, there are four of you. Chuck only has Paige."

"Speaking of." Nate absently scratched at the edge of his cast. Three more weeks and the damn thing came off. It couldn't happen soon enough. "What's her part in all this? She would have to be dense not to see through her father's motives. She's what?"

"Twenty-five. She was little late finishing college. When her mother got sick, she took time off to nurse her at home."

"Admirable."

"From what Chuck has said over the years, the girl is a pistol. Smart as a whip and doesn't take shit from anyone."

"Except her father, apparently." Nate settled back in his chair. "What's the deal, Dad? Why are you telling me all of this?"

"Your mother and I had planned on taking some time to go up and help out."

"On a rag-tag film with no budget?" Nate laughed at the thought. "Callie Flynn and Caleb Landis? In the middle of nowhere? Doing what?"

"Whatever needs doing. You think your mother and I are above that? Drop the attitude, Nate. Snobbery doesn't suit you."

"It's not snobbery," Nate protested. When his father leveled him with a long look, Nate sighed. "Okay. Maybe it is. A little. You have to admit, it is a bit... unexpected."

"Yes." Caleb nodded. "Callie and I were looking forward to getting away from the city. And the idea of leaving the big budgets and special effects behind held some appeal."

"If you say so."

Nate couldn't picture his parents in the wilds of Montana. Yes, they came from poor backgrounds. They had worked damn hard to get where they were. The pampered lifestyle they now lived was well deserved. It had been a long time since either had to go for more than a day without hot running water and someone to cook their meals.

Could they do it? Nate had no doubt. Why would they want to? Even for an old friend.

"Wait," Nate suddenly realized what his father was saying. "You say it *held* some appeal. You aren't going?"

"Your mother was offered a movie with Meryl Streep and Helen Mirren."

"Wow."

"Exactly. She couldn't turn down an opportunity that is unlikely to come along again. And since I'll be producing, we can't get away."

"That's too bad for your friend, but maybe this will bring him to his senses."

"Too late." Caleb shrugged. "He's already sunk most of his money into the project. No backing out."

"Then send him a few bucks. I'm sure he'd appreciate it." Nate grinned. "Who knows, it could become a box office sleeper and you'll be glad you were in on the ground floor."

"Oh, I'm sending money. And you."

Nate sat up straight, his chin practically on the floor. "Say again?"

Chapter Two

NATE WATCHED AS the Bitterroot Mountains spread out below in a glorious vista of colors.

Greens, blues, browns. September was waning, bringing a hint of the coming change of seasons. It was a sight to see.

Nate was fortunate to have traveled all over the world. Seen every continent. Since he was a small child, his parents took him and his brothers on their movie sets.

Morocco. India. Bangladesh. Brazil. Australia. Japan.

The list went on and on.

As an adult, his job gave him the chance to see those same places and more through different eyes. What he appreciated as a boy was different now that he was a man. Nate still felt a rush every time he encountered a new culture.

His need to explore and drink in the differences from his everyday life in Los Angeles was as strong as when he and his brothers ran up and down the streets of Nairobi, chased by their harried bodyguards. It wasn't an easy task to keep track of four active, inquisitive boys.

It seemed impossible to believe, but with all the traveling he had done, this was his first trip to Montana. If what he saw from the seat in Jack Winston's private plane were any indication, it wouldn't be his last.

"How you doing?"

Jack didn't have to raise his voice. Nate sat next to him in the cockpit of the plane. If given a choice, Nate always rode in that spot. The view was better up here. And as a pilot himself, he liked to be near the controls. Just in case.

"Good."

Jack laughed. He was a big man. Almost as tall as Nate. He had earned a full-ride football scholarship and most people assumed he would ride that to a career in the NFL. He was that good. However, what most people didn't know was that Jack's real passion was computers. More accurately, creating cutting-edge software with his best friend, Drew Harper.

"I'm sorry Brett Walcott turned out to be a bust."

"There was no way for you to know that the weasel lied through his teeth the entire time." Nate tried to relax his shoulders. They had been in a perpetual knot since he met with Walcott. He went in expecting answers, but ended up coming out with more questions.

"It's embarrassing. And frustrating." Nate took his eyes off the scenery. "Walcott is hardly the sharpest tool in the box. Yet he managed to convince me he saw who sabotaged my jump."

"Don't beat yourself up." Jack banked the plane to the left. "He managed to bilk the guilty party out of a sizable chunk of cash. Walcott isn't smart, but he is wily."

"Wily. Good word."

The situation played out with so many convenient twists and turns, Nate would have sworn they were in the middle of a Lifetime TV movie.

First the fire on the set that drew everyone away from the airbag. Then a puncture that created a leak not meant to be detected until it was too late. Luckily for Nate, it was a *very* slow leak.

A non-witness who took advantage of the situation to fill his pockets. Somehow, the perpetrator found out Walcott was going to talk.

To keep his identity hidden, the mystery person paid out double what Nate agreed upon. In the end, neither needed to bother. Walcott hadn't seen anything.

"If he hadn't been drunk off his ass when we found him, we would have questioned him in Mexico and saved us all a lot of wasted time. Being in a foreign country, we thought it best to pour him into the plane and head for the border."

"You did the right thing, Jack. Walcott was a bust. No one could have anticipated that."

"The police—" Jack nodded when he heard Nate snort. "I know. They aren't going to bother. Now if you had died, it would be another story."

"Sorry to disappoint so many people, but I prefer the way it turned out."

"Me too, buddy. We'll keep looking. Though to be honest, I'm not sure what to look for. You can't think of anyone who wants you dead? A disgruntled husband?"

"I stay away from married women."

Like men, women lied about those things. Nate found that out the hard way when he was still wet behind the ears. Since then, he never let his dick get in the way of common sense. He liked women. He *loved* sex. Being straight, he couldn't have one without the other.

However, he never let himself get carried away. Losing himself for a few hours in the arms of a soft, sweet-smelling woman was one of his all-time favorite things. Losing his mind over that woman? When that day came, he would know he was a goner. Like his father. Like Garrett. Only one thing made the Landis men's brains turn to mush. Love.

Nate happily played the field. However, he knew when the right woman came along he wouldn't hesitate. He was fortunate to have seen what a loving relationship looked like. He grew up watching two people who *liked* each other. Openly affectionate and over thirty years together, they couldn't keep their hands off one another.

It was inspiring and a little daunting. Nate knew what he wanted. Finding it wasn't as easy.

"What about that director you punched?" Jack interrupted his thoughts, pulling him back to the discussion. "From what I hear, he tried to get you blackballed."

"Tried and failed."

"Right." Jack shot Nate a look. "I know murder is extreme, but Hollywood is an extreme place."

"Hardy Thomas isn't capable of killing anything but a good script." Nate couldn't stand the man and the feeling was mutual. "It's been five years, Jack. Revenge might be best served cold, but…"

"This would be an icicle. I get it." Jack adjusted his sunglasses before hitting a switch on the control panel. "Like I said, we'll keep looking. Now buckle up. We'll be landing soon."

PAIGE CHAMBERLIN watched the plane circle the small airport. She tapped her foot with impatience.

"Easy. I know you want everything done yesterday, Paige. That plane will get here when it gets here. Not even you can make it descend faster by the sheer force of your will."

Paige didn't answer. She and Lottie Craig had known each other all their lives. In a small town like Basic, Montana you had few options when it came to friends your own age. Luckily, the two of them hit it off when they were in diapers and had been thick as thieves ever since.

She was nervous. Paige was not a shrinking violet. Her method of getting something done was to plow forward with blinders on. If she took the time to worry about what was going on around her, the chances were the distractions would slow her down. Or worse — knock her out of the game altogether.

From the time Paige learned to walk without assistance, she had continued on that way. Asking for help didn't come easily. Her father would shake his head when she insisted that if she found a solution to a problem on her own, the victory would be that much sweeter.

That need to be self-sufficient had her stomach in a knot. The hardest thing she had ever done was write that letter to Caleb Landis asking for his advice.

Paige rarely found herself at her wits' end, but dealing with her father had become impossible. He looked like the same man she loved and respected above all others. Tall, wiry, with the same blond hair and brown eyes he had passed on to her.

This man she had breakfast with and worked beside every day looked like Chuck Chamberlin. It was when he opened his mouth that Paige could have sworn someone else had replaced him.

Her responsible, salt of the earth father… God, she hated to even think it. He had mortgaged the ranch to the hilt so he could make a movie.

If it weren't so alarming, Paige would have found the idea hysterical.

She knew their friends and neighbors thought Chuck Chamberlin had gone off the deep end. Basic, Montana was having a good laugh at her father's expense and Paige knew it was up to her to stop the insanity before it went any further.

"Here it comes."

Paige stood, arms crossed, feet firmly planted as the sleek plane touched down. When she wrote to Caleb Landis, the best she had hoped for was a letter in return. If she were lucky, it would contain something that would snap her father out of the fantasy world he had entered.

When Caleb called her, Paige couldn't believe it wasn't a joke. *The* Caleb Landis? Every time her father mentioned his Hollywood days, Paige took it with a grain of salt. After speaking with Caleb, she realized her father hadn't exaggerated. He had friends in the movie industry. Big, powerful, influential friends.

That fact was driven home even harder when Caleb offered to show up in person. With his glamorous wife. Paige was still letting the idea sink in when there was a change in plans. Caleb was sending one of his sons.

Paige didn't know what she thought about that, but she wasn't in the position to decline the offer.

The Landis brothers. If their parents were Hollywood royalty, each of them was a crown prince. Even in Basic, Montana, they had the internet. The money, the beautiful women. The brothers lived life in the fast lane.

Paige shook her head. Good luck finding that in Basic. Her only consoling thought was, *at least Caleb didn't send the movie star.*

It was wait and see time as to whether Nate Landis turned out to be any help.

The plane taxied to a stop. Paige didn't have to look at Lottie to know what she was doing. A man was about to descend onto the tarmac. A single man. New blood. Lottie had a pose designed for just such an occasion. One hand on her nicely curved hip. Sizable breasts pushed forward. A come-hither smile on her face.

Paige thought it was ridiculous. On the other hand? Lottie dated. Paige didn't. There was probably something to Lottie's methods, but Paige found the idea of corkscrewing herself into an unnatural position, just to attract a man, exhausting.

Not that she had a lot to put on display — especially in comparison to Lottie.

Her friend was blessed with tits and ass. Paige got her mother's legs. Given a choice, ninety-nine percent of the men she knew picked Lottie's natural charms over her own. Ninety-nine percent of the time, Paige was just fine with that.

"Oh. My. God." Lottie breathed the words like a prayer. "Would you look at them, Paige?"

That was all Paige could do. It wasn't often she saw men that looked like the two who stepped out of the plane. Never in person — and certainly never together.

It was hard to know where to look. Tall and dark, they dazzled equally. Strong thighs in faded denim and muscled arms encased in soft cotton t-shirts. And those chests. Wide and well defined. Oh. My. God. That was putting it mildly.

"Which one is yours 'cause I'm happy with the leftovers?"

It took Paige a second to answer. She swallowed, trying to moisten her dry mouth.

"Neither is *mine*, Lottie. If you want to know which one is Nate Landis, he's on the right. With the cast."

And the swagger. The picture on her computer hadn't done him justice. As he drew closer, Paige wondered if superheroes really existed, because this man had the body of one.

"I'll offer to kiss it and make it better," Lottie sighed. "I wonder who his pretty friend is?"

"Down girl, he's married."

"How do you know?"

"Wedding ring."

"Well, crap, crap, and more crap." Lottie slumped for a second. Paige always did have eyes like a hawk. "How about the other one?"

"He isn't married."

Encouraged, Lottie's chest puffed out again. "You say you aren't interested?"

"No."

"I wonder what color his eyes are behind those sunglasses. I hope they're blue. I do love a dark-haired, blue-eyed man."

Paige remembered the picture of him and his brothers. "They're blue. And by the look of that smile he's sending you, I'd say he'll be easy pickings."

Paige didn't know why she felt a wave of disappointment. Men always noticed Lottie. The long, chestnut hair. The easy smile. The killer curves. Why should Nate Landis be any different? Why should she care?

Because, the little voice in her head taunted. *For the first time in a long time, you wanted a man to notice you first.*

"NOW THAT IS what I call a welcoming committee."

Jack laughed. He was married to the most beautiful, desirable woman in the world, but that didn't stop him from taking an appreciative look around every now and then.

"Who knew what Montana grew on this side of the Bitterroots? What's your pleasure? Curvy brunettes or leggy blondes?"

If Jack had asked that question when they were up in the air, Nate would have unequivocally answered curves all the way. But as they approached the two women, he couldn't look away from the honey-haired beauty. Something about the way she stood with her arms crossed over her chest, her chin stuck out, practically dared someone to take a swipe at it. Nate guessed that person would soon regret the impulse.

"Welcome to Basic, Mr. Landis. I'm Paige Chamberlin."

Nice words, he thought, shaking her proffered hand. However, when she said them through gritted teeth, they lost some of their warmth. Paige Chamberlin may have been the one to reach out to his father, but it appeared she wasn't happy to have the son as a substitute.

Nate didn't know how he felt about that. Being a reluctant participant in this venture, he expected Paige to be grateful for his assistance. He promised his father that he would take stock of the situation and help in any way possible. Caleb didn't ask very much of his sons. When he did, they took it seriously.

Nate wasn't thrilled to be here. Paige wasn't thrilled to have him. Since they were doing this for their fathers, they didn't have a choice. For the time being, they were stuck with each other.

Behind the shield of his sunglasses, he gave her another look. Up close, the view was even better. Her face wasn't beautiful in the classic sense. Nate preferred a woman with character. What looked good on a glossy magazine cover didn't always transfer well to real life. What looked perfect on paper often turned out to be cold, shallow, and uninteresting.

No one would ever call Paige Chamberlin's face boring. Lively. Vibrant. Expressive as hell. Nate wondered if she realized how much a person could see in those deep chocolate-colored eyes of hers? Her stance said, *Warning — tough girl ahead.* Her eyes showed a touch of vulnerability that reached something inside Nate.

Always the champion of the underdog, glimpsing behind the mask that Paige presented made him wonder what else she was hiding.

Time to readjust his thinking. A trip that had seemed like an obligation had taken a sudden and interesting turn. The last thing Nate had expected to find in Basic, Montana was a sexy, interesting woman. A week or two getting to know Paige? Maybe coaxing her into his bed? Or hers? Or both?

Nate liked Montana more and more by the second.

"Throttle back on the wolf grin," Jack whispered. "If I can read your thoughts, imagine what the ladies are thinking."

"This lady thinks it's fine and dandy."

Lottie slowly straightened, pretending to smooth the front of her shirt. It was her experience that if she could draw a man's attention to her chest, the rest was a piece of cake. A little flirtation. A few drinks. It didn't always end with sex. However, in the case of Nate Landis, Lottie couldn't wait to see that long, muscled body stretched out underneath her.

"No offense," Jack said. "But you have ears like a bat."

"I consider it a compliment." For a second, Lottie forgot this one had a wife. She bit her bottom lip. Another surefire attention-getter. "Paige tells me your friend is Nate Landis. I'm Lottie. Who are you?"

"Jack Winston." Jack shook the brunette's hand. When she moved a little closer, he held up his hand, wiggling the finger with the ring firmly in place. "And happily married."

"Oops," Lottie's laugh was light and good-natured. "My mistake. Paige already told me you were off limits. I was so dazzled by that killer smile, I forgot."

"Lottie, you are a born heartbreaker." Jack appreciated a person who could flirt one second and take rejection with ease the next. "Miss Chamberlin?"

"Yes."

"It's been a pleasure to meet you and your friend." Jack shook her hand. "A few years ago, I would have happily stayed for a few days to see the sights." Jack winked at Lottie. "But those days are in the past. I need to do a check of the plane then it's back home."

"Thanks for the lift, Jack. Excuse me for a minute, ladies."

Nate walked Jack back to the plane.

"I know it's turned into a brick wall, but if anything turns up in the investigation?"

"You'll be the first to know. And Nate?"

"Ya?"

"Keep your powder dry."

"What the hell does that mean?"

"I think I'm mixing up my sayings." Jack shook his head and shrugged. "Rose is a big old movie fan. I think it was a Revolutionary War thing."

"Okay." Nate's look made it clear he had no idea what that had to do with anything.

"Let me simplify. Watch your back." Jack reached into the cockpit, coming back with a list of things he had to check before taking off again. "It's possible that the attempt on your life was a one-time thing. Somebody saw their chance and gave into temptation. Or..."

"Okay. I get it."

Nate sighed. It wasn't as though the thought hadn't entered his mind. Somebody wanted him dead and he was still breathing. It was part of the reason he gave in so easily to his father's request. If he was a target, he wanted to be far away from his family.

"If you need anything, don't hesitate to call. You know how much Drew and I love an excuse to take our babies up."

H&W owned five planes ranging in size from a two-seater to one that could fly them and fifty friends and family anywhere in the world. "I'll keep it in mind." Nate gave Jack a friendly slap on the back. "Thanks again."

"Ready?"

Nate lifted his duffle bag into the back of an old Ford. His eye told him late sixties to early seventies. For its age, the truck was in amazing condition. The shine on what looked to be the original paint job gleamed with a spotless luster in the afternoon sun.

"Is this yours?"

"It is now," Paige said as she opened the driver's side door. "My grandfather bought it new. He passed it on to my father and my father on to me." She gave him a steady look. "Not exactly what you're used to."

Was that a jab? Nate considered it as he held the passenger door for Lottie. Letting her climb into the cab, he followed close behind. *It felt like one.*

Never afraid to ask a question, no matter how awkward, Nate decided it would be better to get all the cards on the table.

"You think I'm a pampered Hollywood trust fund baby?"

"I think you've led a privileged life."

"I won't deny my parents' money and position allowed my brothers and me to enjoy the good things in life."

Nate stretched his arm with the cast along the top of the bench seat. His fingers were close enough to brush Paige's hair if the impulse should arise. Or give it a firm tug. Right now, he didn't know which would be more satisfying.

"I'll bet you have all kinds of interesting stories about your movie star friends."

Lottie turned a dazzling smile on Nate. The effect was completely wasted. Nate's attention was focused on the woman shifting the truck into third.

"I'll bet I've roughed it in the wild twice as many times as you have."

"Probably." Paige gave him a quick, sneering glance. "The difference is I can't call for a limo to pick me up when I get bored. When _you_ rough it, you're on vacation. This is my life. Sun up to sun up."

"Snob."

"Jerk."

"Bitch."

"Damn straight. And proud of it."

Lottie's head whipped back and forth, eyes wide with confusion. She didn't know what had gotten into Paige. The last time she was this rude was... well, Lottie couldn't remember when it had happened. Certainly not to a stranger. One who was here to help her. As for Nate Landis. His smile was still as charming as when he got off the plane. However, there was something in his voice. Not anger. More of an edge.

Lottie hated tension. She grew up in a household that always seemed to be one step away from all-out warfare. Smoothing over a tense situation was her specialty.

Before Lottie could intervene, she heard a snicker from Paige.

"Well, damn." Nate grinned. "She has a sense of humor."

Paige sent him another look, this time with a slight smile and sparkling eyes. "On occasion. How about you, Hollywood? Can you laugh at yourself?"

"On occasion," Nate shot back. For good measure, he gave her hair a gentle tug. "Blondie."

Lottie almost slapped herself on the forehead. So that was it. Paige wasn't pissed off at Nate. She was attracted to him. And if her instincts were right, Nate was attracted right back.

Instead of lamenting the loss, Lottie silently rejoiced. It had been a long time since Paige met a man who interested her. Her best friend wasn't in the middle of a sexual dry spell. It was a certified drought. If she didn't get laid soon, her vagina would dry up and blow away.

Nate would have his work cut out for him. Paige wasn't a push over. If he wanted her, he would have to work for it.

Out of the corner of her eye, Lottie gave his long, muscular body another once over. From the tips of his scuffed work boots to the top of that dark, wavy hair, Nate Landis would make any woman's mouth water. Paige wouldn't be immune to that sexy smile and bright blue eyes. Getting her to admit it was another matter.

Lottie mentally rubbed her hands together in anticipation. She didn't know who would win the battle of wills. But for Paige's sake, she rooted for the Hollywood hunk.

Chapter Three

THE CHAMBERLIN RANCH had been in the family for close to a hundred years.

Paige's great-great-grandfather came to Montana to work in the copper mines. He didn't make a fortune by most estimation. However, for an Irish immigrant who came to America with little more than the clothes on his back, having enough money to buy a few acres of land was exactly what he dreamed of.

Cyrus Chamberlin wasn't afraid to work hard. He started small. Two head of cattle turned into four. Then ten. Soon, he purchased more land and more cattle. In time, he sold beef to the very mine owners he once worked for.

The Double C Ranch never became a huge moneymaking enterprise. Some years were better than others. They survived the Depression. Heavily fluctuating cattle prices. More often than not, they were cash poor and land rich.

When Paige's father was born, there were already two brothers ahead of him. He loved Montana. He loved his home. It was his dream to run the Double C. Turn its fortunes around. He had ideas that he knew would work.

However, he understood that as the youngest, he was never going to get the chance to put those ideas to use. So he moved to California where he hoped he could find work. In his mind, Chuck pictured himself working the land. He was an outdoor person. He didn't want to be trapped all day with four walls surrounding him.

He fell into the movie business. A friend of a friend set him up with a one-day gig moving scenery. It meant joining a union. Once he had his card, Chuck soon had more work than he could handle. He was reliable, fast, and did the job right the first time. He made a reputation for himself and, as a result, was paid well.

It wasn't the glamorous end of the business. Not by any stretch of the imagination. He was a grunt. One who was known by sight by the biggest of the big.

Chuck had a nice nest egg put aside when he received a call that would change his life. His brothers had been killed when their truck went off the road, flipping several times. Neither wore a seatbelt. Both had been drinking.

Since his brothers never married, the ranch went to him.

It was hard to be happy when the fulfillment of his dream came at such a heavy price, with no family left and a heavily mortgaged ranch. After such a long time, Chuck hadn't known what he would feel when he stepped onto the familiar Double C soil.

It took only seconds to find out. For the first time in ten years, Chuck Chamberlin was home.

Everything he had learned in Hollywood came in handy. The main house was a mess. Calling it rundown was being kind. Chuck didn't mind. He rolled up his sleeves and got to work.

Winter would be on him before he knew it. He hadn't been gone so long that he didn't remember what it was like when the heavy snow hit. The roof needed repairs before anything else. When that was done, Chuck fixed the sagging back porch, the front entryway. It seemed like there was an endless list.

Chuck tackled every task with happy gusto. When the first snowflake fell, the outside was ready. With only a few head of cattle to tend, he spent the next few months making the inside of the house shine like it did when he was a small boy.

There was no time to be lonely. Or so he thought. It was a bitterly cold day in early January when his isolation hit him. The snow piled up. He made a run into Basic once a month to replenish his supplies, but other than that, human contact was non-existent.

Chuck was almost at his wits' end when an angel came calling.

Erin Wakes was the new schoolteacher in Basic. A Southern girl, she wasn't used to snow of any kind. Her first Montana winter had come as a shock. On weekends, she liked to visit the families of her students. An icy patch of road and a large snow bank proved providential.

Chuck's was the nearest house. When the pretty, rosy-cheeked blonde knocked on his door, it was love at first sight. For them both.

Though she had never hammered a single nail, Erin began spending her weekends helping Chuck fix up the house. She was a fast learner. By spring, her stamp was in every room from the paint color on the walls to the fabric hanging at every window.

In June, when Chuck carried his new bride over the gleaming threshold, it wasn't his house. It was theirs.

Erin was his helpmate in everything he did. He shared his dream to raise horses instead of cattle and soon it was her dream too. Separately, they had always been determined, capable people. Together, nothing could stop them.

For the next thirty years, that remained true. Chuck and Erin grew their fledgling business slowly but surely. They bought horses at bargain basement prices. They came cheap because they were considered misfits. Too small. Too slow. Untrainable.

What other people saw as a problem, Chuck and Erin saw as a challenge. They were seldom wrong. Chuck knew horseflesh — one of the many things he learned while in California.

It turned out Erin was the one with *the touch*. She shied away from terms like *horse whisperer*. She called it common sense. Yes, she talked to them. However, they didn't talk back. It was instinct and trust that allowed her to get so much out of the horses no one else wanted.

Soon, they made a good living selling the animals to the proper owner. Erin insisted on making sure there was a proper fit before they exchanged money. She took pride in what they did. That included her care and love for each and every horse.

It took five years to pay off the debt Chuck had inherited. The business grew to a comfortable size. They weren't rich, but they wanted for nothing. A healthy, bundle of energy only added to their happiness. Their beloved daughter had her father's brown eyes and love of the land. She inherited her mother's honey-blond hair and her way with horses.

For thirty years, it was a near perfect life.

That life changed forever when Erin was diagnosed with an aggressive form of liver cancer. A year later, she was gone.

Chuck Chamberlin had lost his anchor. His partner. The love of his life. Paige helped. If it weren't for her, he wouldn't have gotten out of bed each morning. For those first few months, all he wanted to do was curl up and forget the world existed. For him, without Erin, it didn't.

Going through the motions became a habit. He would smile when it was appropriate — even laugh on occasion. He showered. Ate three meals a day. Worked. At the end of the day, he crawled back into the bed he had shared with his wife and tried to pretend she would be there when he woke up in the morning.

After a while, the pretending became easier. The pain lessened. The hole that Erin's death left in his heart didn't go away, but Chuck wasn't constantly aware of it.

That should have been a good thing. The passing of the crippling grief should have made life easier. Instead, it sent Chuck into a state of panic.

If he stopped thinking about Erin every second of every day, that meant she was slipping away from him. He needed something to bring her close again. That was when he hit on the idea of making Erin's movie.

Before Erin met Chuck, she wasn't just a teacher. She was a writer. A closet novelist who never had the time or courage to follow her dream. She shared her secret with Chuck because they shared everything. They were just married. The house and business needed their full attention.

Erin thought Chuck had forgotten her confession until one day when she was four months pregnant with Paige; he presented his wife with an electric typewriter. Now was the time. It was November. She would soon be too far along to do anything but stay in the house and nest. Why not take the opportunity to finally turn that dream into a reality.

Later, Erin would refer to that time as her winter of discontent. Writing didn't come naturally to her. She knew what she wanted to say. The story had simmered in her brain for years. Getting it from her thoughts to her fingers wasn't as easy as she imagined it would be.

The idea to make it a screenplay instead of a novel came one evening when Chuck told her stories about his old Hollywood friends. He would often amuse her with outrageous stories. They were over the top. If Chuck hadn't sworn on his mother's grave that they were one hundred percent true, Erin would have thought he was the fiction writer in the family.

On a snowy night, curled up together in front of the fire, Erin realized her story was meant to be a visual experience. She had struggled to express her thoughts on paper without realizing they needed to be seen, not read.

With Chuck's full support, Erin switched gears. She read several books about screenplay writing, absorbing the process like an eager sponge. Soon she wrote with abandon. Ideas and words flowed from her like water. Erin had found her medium of expression.

By March, when Erin was round and ready to pop, her screenplay was finished. And so was she.

The screenplay was decent. With some time and a lot of polish, she might elevate it to not bad. The problem was she didn't want to spend any more time on it or any other writing project.

The process was excruciating. The entire time she typed, all Erin wanted was to get outside. Horses were her passion — not stringing words together. She would always be grateful to her husband, her pregnancy, and a long winter. She found out her dream had changed.

Erin Chamberlin was not a writer. Finding that out didn't make her sad. It was a relief. She would never lament what might have been. With no regrets, she put the screenplay into a box and stored it in the attic.

As far as Chuck knew, Erin never again gave the screenplay more than a passing thought. She had been happy with him, their daughter, and using her magic on the dozens of horses that came and went over the years.

If life had been kinder, someday one of their descendants would find the screenplay long after he and Erin were gone. A funny piece of nostalgia.

However, Erin was gone. Taken from him much too soon. That screenplay was a part of her. A part he could hold in his hands.

When Chuck scoured the attic, searching for the long-forgotten screenplay, he didn't have a plan beyond reading it again. When he found it in an unmarked box in the back corner, he felt like he had uncovered a priceless treasure.

It was only as he read the words that Erin had spent hours crafting that the germ of an idea began to form. He could follow through on the dream she put aside. Her words the way she saw them. Up on the screen for the world to see.

Erin's name in bold letters. A permanent tribute. A love letter from him to the woman who had changed his life for the better.

Chuck started the project in secret. He didn't want to face the inevitable questions or deal with any negativity and doubts. Especially from Paige.

He knew she worried about him. Paige was a loving, caring daughter. Strong. Independent. She grew up running free on the ranch. Her mother had called her a beautiful soul. He called her stubborn and opinionated. She was used to doing things her own way.

A perfect example was when Erin was diagnosed with terminal

cancer. Paige was in Illinois attending Northwestern University on a full scholarship. Three months to go and she would have her Bachelor's degree in business.

Their girl had her mother's way with horses. Where she got her head for finance, neither of her parents knew. Paige saw a bright future ahead. They would branch out. Expand.

College wasn't necessary for that. Paige was smart enough to learn everything she needed to know without traveling halfway across the country. Furthering her education wasn't about expanding her brain. It was about seeing something outside of Montana.

Basic was home. She loved it there. However, Paige had always had a wandering heart. She didn't have to tell her parents. They knew she was restless. Like Paige, they saw college as a way for her to decide if she wanted to settle down on the Double C.

Chuck and Erin wanted their only child to be happy. Going away to college was the perfect way to explore a different way of life. *Many* different ways of life. If Paige decided Montana was what she wanted, they would welcome her back with open arms. If her future was someplace else, so be it. They wouldn't lose their girl simply because she was no longer down the hall.

Dreams were funny things. Chuck's had always been on the ranch. Hollywood was a detour. When he came back, he appreciated his home that much more. Erin's dreams shifted over the years. Writer. Teacher. Horsewoman. She happily left the first two behind, adding wife and mother along the way.

Paige had always been a wildcard. She spoke of spending her life on the Double C, but her yearning to see the world warred with the rural life she would have if she chose Montana.

Erin's cancer put a halt to everyone's dreams. Their world became rooted in a tragic reality no one could ignore.

Paige insisted on leaving school to help take care of her mother. Erin didn't want her to leave school when she was so close to finishing. When it came to a battle of wills, it was no contest. Paige was on the first flight home.

Erin could have put up more of an argument except for one thing. She and Paige knew her time was limited. They wanted to spend it together. It was a beautifully tragic and bittersweet year. They spent it as a loving family.

When Erin couldn't fight any longer and the time came for her to let go, Paige and Chuck were by her side, holding her hand.

Chuck broke. Paige became stronger. Not that she didn't miss her mother. She did. Every day. But unlike Chuck, Paige looked at life with a new sense of urgency. Her mother's death taught her that tomorrow wasn't a given. There were no guarantees, no matter your age.

Paige didn't return to school. Over the next year, between working hard on the Double C and researching the best way to build up the business, she completed her degree online.

Chuck was glad Paige kept busy — that she had a vision for the future. It wasn't until the haze of grief lifted that he began to wonder if she was working for the right reason. Was she entrenching herself on the ranch for him and for her mother's memory? If Erin were still with them, would Paige's choice have been Montana?

All these worries and questions spurred Chuck on. He would make Erin's movie. Once he had all the details smoothed out, it would be something he and Paige could work on together. They could reconnect.

A few months into the project, he finally shared what he was doing with Paige. To say that she was surprised was putting it mildly.

"You've been doing what?"

"Putting together the funding to make a movie," Chuck said.

It was such a matter of fact statement. Like saying it looks like rain. Paige stared at her father for a moment trying to decide if she heard him correctly or if he was going out of his mind.

They were having breakfast, as they did most mornings, before heading out to do the chores. Chuck had his usual coffee and cold cereal. A habit no amount of tempting from his wife and daughter could break. The only exceptions were Christmas morning and his birthday. On those occasions, he sat with the family for a feast of Erin's choosing.

"How long has this been going on?"

"A month." Chuck shrugged. "Or two. I found that old script your mother wrote. It's good, Paige. Better than she ever let herself believe."

Trying to wrap her mind around her father's words, Paige sipped her hot chocolate. Two months. That was about the time she had noticed a change in her father. Livelier. The word that popped into her head. After almost two years of going through the motions, she had been relieved to see glimpses of the man he was before her mother's death.

Now Paige found out the change wasn't a simple progression past his grief, it was caused by a crazy scheme. *Finance a movie? What the hell?*

Paige didn't say that to her father. She tempered her words. It appeared he was in the early stages of his plan. Not too late to scrap it altogether.

"Mom's script." Paige vaguely remembered hearing about it. "Have you found investors?"

"It's been slow going," Chuck admitted. "I tried some of my old Hollywood connections."

"And." Paige mentally crossed her fingers that her father's *connections* turned him down flat.

"There wasn't a lot of interest."

"That's to be expected. You've been away from the industry for a long time. And even then…"

"Even then I wasn't anything but a glorified gopher."

"I didn't mean that."

"I'm not embarrassed, Paige. I served an important function." Chuck smiled when he thought back. "Those bigwigs had no idea how important. Without people like me, a movie would grind to a halt in no time. They had the money and the ideas. However, the little things make it all run. The toilet paper alone. There were times when every actor wanted a different kind. Can you imagine? If the leading lady didn't have the made-in-Europe, triple-ply, double-quilted to wipe her pampered backside, good luck getting her on set for her love scene."

"Who knew that toilet paper ruled the movies?"

Paige loved her father's stories. Even the ones she had heard a thousand times. They fascinated her as a child, filling her head with ideas. Dreams. As she grew older, she put those dreams aside for a more practical life. She was happy with her life. What they did on the ranch was grounded in reality — not fancy. Something her father needed to be reminded of.

"It's probably for the best, Dad. Making a movie, even one on a shoestring budget takes time and know-how. We have neither."

"What's time?" Chuck dismissed the notion with a wave of his hand. "You need to loosen the reins a little, Paige. Ambition is fine, but your mother always made time for fun."

"I have fun," Paige mumbled defensively.

"When was the last time you went out with... anyone?"

"Lottie and I do things all the time."

"Getting coffee in Basic with your best friend doesn't count."

"You think making a movie is the answer to my social woes?"

"I think it will be *fun*. For both of us."

For the first time, what her father said began to sink in. He needed this. Maybe it was his way of staying connected with his wife and moving on at the same time. It was hard to argue with that.

Then there was the other part of it. *Fun*. Paige wondered when she had become such a stick in the mud? She knew the answer. Her mother's death had hit her hard. In trying to make the most of the time she had, Paige had lost sight of everything except work. If it didn't involve the ranch and horses, she wasn't interested.

Paige let the idea of a movie flow over her.

She had the business in a good place. A *very* good place. Every horse on the ranch was spoken for. Paige had plans to expand next year. She wanted to add on to the stables. Make the corral bigger. That meant hiring extra help. At the moment, they had one full-time employee and three part-timers. If her vision became a reality, those numbers would grow a little each year.

If her father wanted to play for a few months, now was the best time he could have chosen.

Paige was about to tell him that she was on board when her father dropped his bombshell.

"I've decided to finance the movie myself."

"*Are you out of your mind?*"

"Watch your tone, young lady."

"This isn't your daughter speaking, *Chuck*."

"You're afraid I'll lose the ranch."

"The thought had crossed my mind." Paige set the cocoa aside. With her stomach in a knot, the sweet hot chocolate no longer held any appeal. "Not that I have any legal say. Technically, I work for you. The ranch is yours to do whatever you want with."

"Low blow, Paige." Chuck leveled a steady look toward her. "The Double C is your legacy. I might be the legal owner, but we are equal partners in every other way."

"Then don't do this, Dad."

"It's already done."

"What?" Paige felt the knot turn into a fiery ball of anxiety. "Exactly *what* is done?"

"I've mortgaged half of the land. The house and all the buildings aren't included."

And that makes it okay? Paige wanted to shout. The land that the horses ran free on? Where, as a child, *she* ran free?

"That can't be enough money. Even a do-it-yourself production costs several million dollars."

Even as she said the words, Paige wondered at the amount. *Millions.* She dealt in thousands of dollars. When she occasionally reached into the tens of thousands, her palms would sweat. Her father wasn't batting an eye.

"It is an all-volunteer cast and crew. I promised them screen credits and a percentage of the profits."

"Profits? You expect to make a profit? And who have you recruited?"

"Like I said before, this is for fun." Chuck patted her hand. He put his bowl in the dishwasher before rinsing out his cup and setting it beside the half-full coffee pot. He would use both later in the morning when he came in from feeding the stock. "As for who is on board? Myra Winslow is doing the catering. She has a small part, too. Then there's Sonny Dawson. He can fix anything with an engine. That's bound to come in handy. I thought he would be good for the grandfather. He has experience in local theater."

"He played Santa Claus at the high school pageant, Dad. No lines."

Chuck shrugged. "Hence the grandfather. He only has a line. It will all work out. You'll see."

"I suppose I should be grateful you told me about it before you started production."

"Don't be snarky, Paige. I'm telling you now." Chuck kissed her forehead before grabbing his jacket from the peg by the door. "We'll go over everything after dinner." He reached for the door. "And Paige."

"Yes."

"It will all work out. Trust me."

Trust me.

Paige had trusted her father all her life. Without reservation. She wanted to trust him this time. However, with so much on the line, she decided she needed some help knocking sense into her father's head. That was why she wrote to Caleb Landis. It had been a long shot.

Instead of a calming influence, what had she gotten? Not only hadn't the legendary Hollywood producer discouraged Chuck, he gave him money. Then to top it off, he sent his son.

Paige shifted the truck into second gear. She had dropped Lottie off before heading back to the ranch. Her passenger seemed content to ride in silence. Strange. She imagined all Hollywood types to be talkative. And their favorite subject of conversation — themselves.

Nate Landis wasn't conforming to her ideas. But it was early.

"How much of this belongs to your family?"

"As far as the eye can see. And beyond. It isn't big by some standards, but it suits our needs." At least it was theirs for now. After her father was finished, who knew what would be left.

"This is beautiful country. Living at the base of the Bitterroots. All that open, undeveloped area. You're very lucky to have all this."

There was nothing condescending in Nate's tone. Why Paige expected it, she couldn't say. From the moment she found out about his impending arrival, she had been on edge. Now that he was here, Nate Landis posed a different problem than she had anticipated.

She wanted him. Plain, simple, unadulterated lust.

Paige couldn't remember the last time she felt this kind of instant attraction. Oh, when she was a teenager gushing over the latest heartthrob's music video. But that didn't count. At fourteen, she wouldn't have known what to do with one of those boys if he had magically appeared before her.

She was well past the age where she had figured it out. She knew exactly what she would like to do to Nate. Over and over again.

Sneaking a quick look, she almost sighed aloud. No one should be that good looking. Not that looks mattered. She could ignore the muscles and the chiseled jawline. They were a nice bonus. Her problem was that Nate Landis practically oozed sex appeal.

The man smelled good enough to eat. Clean and masculine. That was it. Good Lord. He wasn't wearing expensive cologne. It was straightforward soap and something that was uniquely Nate. Bottle *that* and you could make a fortune.

On top of everything else happening, she would be dealing with sexual frustration. Nate was not for her, even short-term.

First, he was attracted to Lottie and the feeling was mutual. That signaled off limits in big neon letters. Second, he wasn't here to give her a tumble. Nate's father sent him to help, not to scratch an itch she hadn't known she possessed until he stepped off that plane. Third, in spite of the instant attraction, something about him rubbed her the wrong way.

Nate Landis, with his confident swagger and scuffed boots, was *too* casual about his appeal. He had to know that he was sex walking, yet there he sat. Cool and relaxed. It pissed her off. And knowing it was irrational pissed her off even more.

Layer upon layer of frustration with no end in sight.

"Excuse me?"

"I didn't say anything."

"You were muttering something under your breath, and then you gave a long sigh." Nate pulled down his sunglasses, his eyes meeting hers. "Something is wrong. Want to share?"

"Blue eyes."

"Excuse me?"

"You have blue eyes."

So blue. Like the clear mountain lake on the Double C. She swam in that lake every summer. Just as she swam in his eyes right now. With effort, Paige broke away, shifting her gaze back to the road before she drove into the ditch. Dangerous. That's what he was. It was something she would have to keep reminding herself.

"And yours are brown. Like rich, dark chocolate."

"No."

"You've lost me again," Nate chuckled. "No what?"

"Do not flirt with me. You see this." Paige motioned over her body with her hand. "This is off limits. I don't know what you're used to, but around here you get one woman at a time."

"And you are one woman."

Nate's voice lowered. Deep and a little husky. The sound shot straight into Paige's bloodstream, causing her pulse to throb. Along with certain other parts of her body.

"Lottie is my best friend."

"I figured."

"Well, there you go."

The woman was confusing as hell. Nate looked out the window, a grin plastered on his face. Confusing and fascinating. She seemed to think her friend had dibs on him. Normally, the sweet, curvy Lottie would have been right up his alley. However, the long-legged blond made him think of a soft bed and those legs wrapped around him — hour after hour.

Paige Chamberlin was a little prickly, but she had a sense of humor. He liked a woman who could laugh at herself. With that long, honey-blond hair and full mouth, she was just the right combination to keep him interested while he was in Montana.

There was only one problem — a big one. She was the daughter of his father's friend. A man who would be his host for as long as he was here. There were rules about this kind of thing. Nothing written in stone, but rules nonetheless.

Nate wasn't a rutting boar. He was capable of keeping his dick in his pants. But oh, Lordy. He shook his head when he glanced at those long legs. This was a temptation he didn't want to resist.

"I read the script."

Paige gave him a surprised glance.

"Where did you get a copy?"

"When Dad called your father to tell him I'd be coming, Chuck expressed me a copy."

"And?"

"You want me to say it stinks, don't you? It would be easier to talk your father into shutting down production if it's badly written." Nate laughed when he saw guilt flash across Paige's face.

"There's a reason my mother only wrote the one thing. She found out she wasn't cut out for it."

"According to your father, she decided it didn't make her happy. That isn't the same thing as not being good at it." Unconsciously, Nate scratched at the edge of his cast.

"True," Paige conceded. "Then tell me. What did you think of it?"

"Other than being a little rough in patches, it's pretty good. Readable. Your mother had a unique voice, Paige. I was impressed."

Paige had the overwhelming desire to cry. It wasn't fair! Her mother should be hearing this. She deserved to know that her screenplay was good. A unique voice. That was her mother to a T.

The fates that decided who lived a long, healthy life and who died much too soon were evil in their capriciousness.

Erin Chamberlin was the anchor of her family. Loved. Respected. She helped her community and was a good friend. She wasn't a saint, thank goodness. Her bawdy sense of humor precluded that classification. However, she was the best person Paige had ever known.

God, she missed her mother.

"Are you all right?"

"I'm fine." Paige turned her head, wiping at the tear on her cheek. "I got something in my eye."

"Paige…"

"I don't want your sympathy, Hollywood."

"We'll have to work on the nickname. I'm the least *Hollywood* person you'll ever meet."

"Mmm."

Paige kept her opinion on that subject open. So far, she would agree. Dressed like a regular person. He hadn't balked at her mode of transportation. Then again, she had known him a grand total of one hour. She liked him. The attraction she felt was off the charts.

Wait and see, Paige. She could almost hear her mother's voice telling her not to jump either way. *Conclusions*, she used to say, *are best kept at the end of the story.*

Paige didn't know how it would end with Nate, but she was willing to give it more time. He might surprise her.

Perhaps you'll surprise yourself. Paige smiled. Her mother had always given the best advice. This time? She definitely would have to *wait and see.*

"We're about five minutes from the house. Dad will be—"

Her words trailed off when to her surprise, she found that Nate had fallen asleep. Boom. He hadn't seemed tired. Relaxed, yes. But sleepy?

Paige shook her head, chuckling quietly. Nate must be one of those people who could sleep anywhere. He was lucky. Personally, if she didn't have a soft bed and her favorite pillow, she tossed and turned all night. It made camping out difficult even though she loved lying under the stars. Getting any rest was another matter. Nate would probably drop off in a heartbeat.

She could add that to the *reasons he pissed her off* list. Except in all fairness, that was her failing, not his. Paige might be looking for the negative when it came to her passenger, but her innate fairness wouldn't let her purposely stack the deck against him.

The truck hit an unexpectedly large pothole, causing Paige's shoulder to slam into the door. Thank goodness for seat belts or the bounce would have caused her to hit her head on the roof of the cab. She glanced at Nate.

"Sorry. I'm usually better at avoiding those."

No response. Not only could Nate fall asleep at the drop of a hat, once he was out? He stayed out. Interesting. Paige laughed aloud. She wondered what it took to rouse the big man.

"I like that sound."

Startled, Paige whipped her head around.

"I thought you were sleeping."

"I was." Nate stretched, every muscle in his long body rippling. "Your laugh woke me up."

"You're kidding. I hit a hole back there that rattled my teeth and you didn't stir. I hardly made a sound."

"My sleeping habits are... unusual."

"How unusual?"

Paige suddenly pictured Nate walking around in the middle of the night. Asleep. Naked. That couldn't be all bad. *No.* There was something slightly perverted in the idea of watching a man who wasn't in the erotic loop with you. If she ever saw Nate without his clothes, she wanted him fully conscious.

"I'm not a good sleeper when I'm alone."

"That shouldn't be difficult. Between the way you look and your family name, women must pop out at every corner."

"You like the way I look?"

Of course, that was what Nate zoomed in on. The man was a born flirt. Normally, Paige would simply ignore him. Even in the wilds of Montana, she had learned how to handle *interested* men. Sometimes she was interested back. That made things easy. When she wasn't, and the man wouldn't take no for an answer, she used her sharp tongue to cut him down to size. On rare occasions, a knee to the balls never failed to get her point across.

Nate was different. She couldn't flirt back. He seemed to like when she gave him verbal grief. And as for his balls? Right now, he was a guest that she was responsible for. The good hostess in her didn't think hobbling a man was the proper way to make him feel welcome.

Not rising to his bait seemed the safest way to handle him. For now. If she ever decided he was getting to be a problem, jabbing his hanging appendages was always an option she could fall back on.

"My dad will be your only sleep buddy option at the ranch. You will have to work that one out between you."

Nate turned back to the scenery. There was another option. The prickly Paige. He wondered if her thorns were as tough as she tried to make out. Grinning, Nate crossed his arms. He didn't know if he would be here days or weeks. When the trip started, Nate hoped the problem had an easy solution that would put him back in Los Angeles by Saturday.

The more he was around Paige, the less he worried about that timetable. She interested him. More than any woman in a long time. The countryside was beautiful and so was the woman next to him. He could think of worse ways to spend the time until his cast came off and he could get back to work.

Montana and Paige. Untamed. Nate couldn't wait to start his exploration.

Chapter Four

"IT WAS GOOD of your father to send you, Nate."

"He and my mother wanted to be here. When they get a break in shooting Mom's movie, they'll take a few days and come up."

"They will?"

Nate gave Paige a slow smile. "You need to rethink your idea of Hollywood. If you had a friend who needed your help, what would you do?"

Help, of course. Paige understood what Nate was saying. Friends were friends, wherever they lived. Still...

"Your parents aren't the neighbors down the road, Nate."

"They could be."

When Paige gave him a *give me a break* look, Nate's grin got bigger. "I don't deny that Callie Flynn and Caleb Landis are different. What I'm saying is that they still think like the people they were before all the fame and fortune. Small town values don't wash away in the California rain."

"I didn't think it rained in California."

"Smartass."

Chuck watched the rapid fire, back and forth banter with amused bewilderment. He searched his memory trying to remember when Paige had seemed this... what was the word? Engaged. That was it. Men weren't her focus. They never had been.

In high school, when her friends worried about boys and getting asked out on Saturday night, Paige preferred spending time with the horses. She had a social life. Boys, then men, naturally gravitated to Paige. She had a beauty not easily defined by the usual standards. Like her mother, Paige glowed from within, drawing admirers to her irresistible light.

Unlike her mother, Paige had no patience with silly flattery. Where Erin would soothe, smile, and charm, Paige batted away unwanted attention with the subtlety of a sledgehammer.

Erin used to say that Paige needed a man who wasn't afraid to give back as good as he got. The local boys had always been intimidated by her sharp tongue and keen intelligence. She didn't play games or hide her strengths to pump up their male egos.

Chuck had hoped that she would meet someone while away at college. Unfortunately, his daughter spent most of her time with her nose in a book. According to Erin, she dated. One time, his wife tried to assure him that Paige wasn't a virgin. Why she thought that was something he wanted to know, or would find reassuring, Chuck didn't know.

No father wanted to hear that his little girl was *that* grown up.

Since Paige's return to the Double C, she had turned down more dates than she had accepted. Lyle Wilson, the owner of the next ranch over, was the most persistent. He finally wore her down. They went out on a semi-regular basis. Usually, when Paige felt restless. Lyle was convenient. Easy going. And it was obvious he wanted much more than Paige was willing to give.

Chuck felt sorry for the man, but he knew Paige wasn't leading him on. She made it clear upfront that she wasn't interested in anything permanent. The fact that Lyle kept coming back was a testament to his determination. She hadn't wanted to date him, but she changed her mind. He figured it was only a matter of time before he had a ring on her finger.

It wasn't going to happen. As much as he would love a grandbaby to spoil, he knew Lyle Wilson was not the man for Paige. As his beloved Erin had said, their daughter needed a man who was her equal. Smart. Strong. Willing to let her be herself while not allowing her to run roughshod over him.

Lyle Wilson was pleasant. A little *too* pleasant. Chuck couldn't put his finger on the problem. Except for the fact that Lyle preferred running his ranch from the comfort of his office instead of getting his hands dirty, there was no reason for Chuck to object to the man's designs on Paige. It was her choice.

Deep down, he knew, as did Paige. Lyle Wilson was not the man for her.

He had begun to wonder if that man existed. Chuck gave Nate a considering look. It was early days. But maybe. Just maybe that man had finally arrived. Caleb Landis' son. Wouldn't that be something?

"You've been here a grand total of…" Paige looked at her watch. "Three hours and already you've decided I'm a smartass?"

"Better than a dumbass."

"Should I thank you for that distinction?"

"Sure." With Chuck behind him pouring a cup of coffee, Nate felt safe giving Paige a wink. "I never turn down a woman's gratitude."

When Paige rolled her eyes, Nate felt a zing in his stomach. She wasn't pissed off as she had been earlier. This was fun — for both of them. Something had changed.

When they met at the airport, Paige was all bristles and borderline resentment. The bristles were still there. Nate would be surprised, and a little disappointed if they weren't. The difference was in the temperature of the barbs she threw at him. No longer icy. The temperature had risen to a nice, comfortable level during the ride to the ranch.

As they sat drinking some of the best coffee he could remember, Nate felt another uptick in the heat index. He doubted Paige would have called it flirting. She was still under the misguided idea that he was interested in her friend Lottie. Being under no such delusions, Nate knew exactly what was going on.

This was a prelude. Not the dance itself. That would come later — if they decided to act on it. The attraction. The desire. The need. Call it what you wanted. Nate knew the signs. Right now, he was happy to play around the edges. All the reasons not to act were still there. However, Nate realized, if Paige gave him any encouragement, he would drop kick any obstacles without the slightest twinge of regret.

"The light will be good for another few hours. Why don't you take Nate on a mini-tour? I'll take care of dinner while you're gone."

"But... I mean, don't you want to talk?" When Nate and her father gave her blank looks, Paige sighed. "Hello. The movie? The reason Nate is here? I thought you would want to lay everything out right away."

"There's plenty of time for that."

"No, there isn't." Paige barely refrained from hitting her head on the hard, cherry wood table. "Shooting starts in two days."

"That soon?" Nate frowned. His father hadn't mentioned a timetable. Nate was under the impression this was still in the planning stages.

"I didn't see any reason to dilly dally." Chuck joined them, taking a seat next to Nate. "It's a small production. Digital, not film. I called in a few favors from my Hollywood days. Once I started, what I thought would be a slow rolling ball quickly picked up momentum."

"Meaning?"

"I'll explain everything at dinner." Chuck poured a dollop of cream into his cup, slowly stirring, with a benign smile on his weathered face. "Go. Stretch your legs. Between the two plane flights and the drive to the ranch, you must need to move around. Some fresh air will do you good."

"Dad..."

"Steaks!" Chuck slapped Nate on the back. "Thick and juicy. Our own beef, too. We still run about a hundred head. Prime, grass-fed Montana Angus. Once you taste it right off the grill, you'll weep every time you have to order that inferior crap most restaurants serve."

"Sounds good."

Nate looked at Paige and shrugged.

"Fine. Grab your jacket. It cools down early this time of year." As she passed her father, she leaned close. "This isn't over."

"Of course not, honey." Chuck smiled. "It's just beginning."

THE DOUBLE C never failed to impress.

Paige was proud of her home. The sweat and labor her parents put into it during the early days of their marriage was a tradition Paige happily carried on. It wasn't a sense of duty that made her keep the tack and saddles in the barn immaculately tended. Nothing forced her to muck out the stalls when she could easily have handed the job over to one of their day laborers.

It was love. Love for the land and every building on it. From the sheds to the main house. Paige grew up here. She crawled on the grass in the front yard. Toddled by her mother's side as she gathered the morning eggs. Learned to ride like the wind, her sturdy pre-teen legs gripping the sides of her horse — no saddle needed.

This was Paige's home.

If sometimes she yearned to know what was beyond the gently rolling fields, Paige shrugged off those feelings. In college, she had a small taste of something different. It was heady. Exciting. A world of endless possibilities.

If her mother hadn't gotten sick, who knew? Part of her always assumed she would end up back here.

After.

A few years of adventure before she had any serious obligations to anchor her in one place. Unknown places. Exotic. Heady. New. She had wanted to see them as only a young woman could. Unfettered by anything but the desire to taste a culture far different from her own.

That changed the day her father called with the news that her mother wouldn't see another year. In that instant, Paige left behind the girlish dreams and took on the mantle of an adult. It wasn't just her mother who needed her to be strong. Her father was lost without his Erin. Forgoing a few years of travel was a small price to pay.

There was still time for that. Nowhere was it written that she couldn't take time away from the ranch to see those far off places that littered her dreams.

Someday, she promised herself.

They walked in silence. It wasn't awkward. Neither felt the need to reach for unnecessary words. Nate was content to take it all in. Paige enjoyed the company. Which surprised her. One of the best things about her life was the time she had to simply think.

They were grand thoughts or troubling ones. Usually, she went over the endless list of things that needed doing. Fix the fence in the south pasture. Order feed. Replace the valves in her old truck.

What she did every day didn't shake the world. But it did keep her firmly on its axis.

"Do you love it here?"

An interesting question. But then, Nate was turning out to be an interesting man.

"When I went away to college, my new friends would ask how I could stand growing up in the middle of nowhere?"

"What was your answer?"

"I usually smiled and didn't say much. How can you explain Montana to someone who has never been here?"

Nate understood what she meant. Traveling extensively had taught him many things. One of the most important was that no two places were alike. A person growing up in a rural environment might think the city was the city. They would be wrong.

New York was no more like Paris than Montana was like Nebraska. Make a list. The differences would soon start to outweigh the similarities. Bright lights and traffic. A blanket of stars and uninterrupted fields. It was what the eye didn't see. The people. How they spoke. Thought. Lived their daily lives.

Until you walked on Montana soil, you could never understand.

Mountains to one side of the Double C and wide-open rolling fields on the other. The main house was painted a welcoming blue and white. Three stories. Not a box, though close, the sloping roof prevented it from resembling a large Christmas present without the bow.

It was large and welcoming with room for a family to grow. Paige was an only child. Nate wondered if that was by design or because Chuck and his wife weren't blessed with other children.

A ranch this size. Two people with plenty of love to share. When he factored all that in, Nate had his answer.

"I can't imagine growing up without my brothers. An only child. Way out here. It must have been lonely."

"I had Lottie. Though there were weeks during the winter when we only spoke on the phone." Paige stopped by the main corral. Two horses came over to nudge at her hand, hoping for a treat. She never left the house with her pockets empty. Half a carrot for each.

Rollie, the five-year-old sorrel mare finished first. She nipped at her companion, hoping Winter would drop his half-eaten carrot. The palomino gelding was as placid as they came. However, he wasn't a pushover. The horses were companions. Had been for a long time. He knew her tricks. Calmly, he chewed and swallowed. Then to show her what he thought of her, he turned away with a swish of his tail.

Paige laughed at their antics. Except for her parents and Lottie, animals had been her playmates during the first few years of her life. School widened her social circle. There were times when she preferred her company to be of the four-legged variety. Less drama.

"I have never been bored. Not a single day, hour, or minute."

Restless was different from bored. But that wasn't something she wanted to get into. Not with Nate.

"I get restless."

Paige's eyes shot to Nate. He looked at the mountains, not her. He wasn't reading her mind, simply stating a fact about himself. That was a relief. She didn't want him in her head, rooting out her thoughts.

Kindred spirit.

Paige heard the words spoken in her mother's voice. No, she didn't need Nate in her head. Between her own thoughts and her mother, it was crowded enough up there.

"Why?"

"Hmm?" Nate turned Paige's way, his blue eyes losing their faraway dreams to focus on her. It was disconcerting — and exciting.

"Why do you get restless?" Why do your eyes make my stomach flip over and make my mouth dry? "Your life is exciting."

Nate's eyebrow lifted, asking the question without words. *Nice trick*, Paige thought with a sigh.

"Google, Hollywood. It's what we common folk use to get information."

"What do you think we *non*-common folk use?"

"Minions." Paige's eyes twinkled, letting him know she wasn't completely serious.

"And they use—?"

"Google."

"Googling minions." Nate's lips twitched. "I don't think I've met any of those."

"Sure you have. You have an assistant."

It was a statement, not a question.

"Technically. Sure." Alice was essential when Nate worked on a movie. And when he wasn't.

"Does she… it is she, right?"

Nate nodded. Why did he suddenly feel defensive? One second, Paige made him smile; the next, he wanted to swat her smartass. For a man who was known as the easy-going Landis, the rollercoaster of emotions this woman elicited perplexed him.

"Naturally," Paige smirked. "Hence, Googling minion."

Nate wanted to wipe that smug little smile off Paige's mouth. Cliché as it might be, kissing her seemed like the perfect way. Since he had wanted to do it from the moment he saw her, it didn't take a lot of effort to talk himself into it.

Nate knew the kiss was coming, but somehow it ended up surprising him as much as it did her.

The feel of a woman in his arms. The touch of her lips. Her taste. Nate knew these things well. *Very* well. He might not know the number of women he had kissed since his first at the age of thirteen. That didn't mean he had lost his appreciation for the process.

Kissing was one of his favorite things. It wasn't just a prelude to sex.

To Nate, knowing the proper way to join his mouth to a woman's was an art. He wouldn't call himself a master. That connoted someone who knew it all. Nate considered himself an eager student. Proficient. Well versed. Yet always willing to learn.

On the job training of the best kind.

What Paige taught him in the first few seconds of the kiss was staggering. Her touch burned him. Her lips were beyond soft. Her taste? Addictive. Feeling her body next to his didn't give him the usual thrill. It overwhelmed, saturating his senses.

It wasn't a kiss.

It was *the* kiss.

The second the thought entered his brain, Nate felt a surge of panic. *No,* he quickly argued with himself. *Not ready.* The idea was so new, so unexpected, he shoved it out of his consciousness. He trailed his mouth along the sweet line of Paige's jaw, happy to concentrate on the physical — not the emotional. Analyzing the burst of feelings was for another day. Far, far in the future.

It became easier when Paige's arms stole around his waist, pulling him closer. He knew the moment she stopped fighting with herself and gave in to the kiss. Her body relaxed against him, her subtle curves fitting perfectly. Two parts of a puzzle. Shit. There it was again. The idea that this was how it was supposed to be. That everything until now led him to Paige.

Nate tore his mouth away, his breathing harsh — ragged. The idea was to break the connection that made his brain turn fuzzy and his heart beat in an odd, unfamiliar cadence. It was smart to stop before things got out of hand.

Nate didn't realize his arms were still around Paige. It felt so good to have her close. It never occurred to him that his heart wasn't going to stop trying to jump out of his chest as long as she pressed so near.

"Should I apologize?" *Please, don't ask me to apologize.*

"That would be silly."

Paige gently pried herself away. Not because she didn't like the feel of his arms around her. Because she liked it *too* much.

"Paige…"

"It was a kiss, Nate."

"No argument here."

"Wipe that grin off your face."

Paige almost smiled back. He was so damn charming. All he had to do was stand there, lips quirked, blue eyes bright as the clearest sky, and she wanted to forget why this was a bad idea. She struggled, searching. *Right. Lottie.* Best friend rules. She was already treading on thin ice. The cracks were getting bigger and bigger — moving closer with each passing second.

It wasn't fair that danger had to come wrapped in such a big, sexy package, but there it was. She needed to keep this professional. At best, friendly. Once more, she had to explain it to Nate. And while she was at it, it wouldn't hurt to remind herself why this thing between them would not go any further.

"I realize this isn't an original thought. You must have heard it a thousand times."

"Nate—"

"My mother assures me that compliments, as long as they are sincere, are a good thing."

"Nate—"

"You're so beautiful. You smell like honey and fresh air. And the way you taste! I could—"

"Nate!" Paige's shout was louder than necessary. Because she needed to stop herself as well as Nate. She liked his words. *Too much.*

"The kiss was…"

"Go on." Nate's smile widened. "Stroke my… ego."

Oh, boy. The man wasn't dangerous. He was lethal. Paige knew she was in trouble when she wanted to laugh at a line that would have made her cringe if delivered by anyone else.

The difference was easy to figure out. Nate's ego was very, very healthy. However, his ability to make fun of himself was just as pronounced. A sense of humor was the ultimate aphrodisiac for Paige. Life could destroy her if she couldn't laugh at it now and then. In her experience, finding a man who understood that was next to impossible. Combined with a mouthwatering package, it made Nate almost irresistible.

Almost.

"I liked it."

"Careful. Hold back on your gushing."

"*Very* nice."

"Weak," Nate sighed. "But I'll take it. For now."

"Once, Nate. It can't happen again."

"Can't? Or Won't?"

"Jesus." Paige tossed her hands in the air. "I thought you were a stuntman, not a lawyer. Forget the semantics. We kissed. I liked it."

"Me too."

"Now we have it out of our systems."

"We do?"

Nate didn't sound convinced. Paige tried to sound like she was.

"I don't want to clog things up, Nate. I'm still holding on to the hope you might be able to talk my father in off the-the proverbial ledge. Though that possibility is becoming more and more remote."

"I agree. But let's get back to that later. About that kiss. You liked it?"

"Now I am worried about your ego."

"I don't need the flattery, Paige." Nate moved closer, invading her space. The look she gave him was more exasperated than angry. He could work with that. "It was good. Better than good."

"*Too* good," Paige muttered.

"Maybe." Nate wasn't ready to deal with all the implications. He *was* ready to explore the possibilities. Whatever they were. "I can't stop with one, Paige. Who knows, the next kiss might suck. It happens. Like a movie that was a surprise hit. Everyone sees dollar signs so they make a sequel. It bombs. Turns out some things are better in sets of one."

"Like our kiss?"

"Like our kiss. What do you say?" Nate moved closer, his breath teasing her ear. "Want to find out?"

Paige already knew. The sequel would be better than the original. She swayed, just a little until Nate's lips touched her ear. For an instant, she considered turning her head. Mouth against mouth.

"You are the devil."

Chuckling, Nate stepped away. "No. Not even a disciple. Temptation isn't the devil's exclusive domain, Paige."

"Well, you're no angel." Paige gripped the rail of the pasture fence. She wanted to grab Nate. Knowing where it would lead, she kept her hands where they were.

"Thank God."

"Whatever you are, Nate, you aren't for me. Temporarily or otherwise. Let's head back to the house. Dad should have the barbecue ready for the steaks."

Paige wiped her palms on her jeans. Sweaty palms. Never a good sign when you were trying to convince yourself a certain man was just like any other. The words in her head, and the ones she said to Nate were one thing; her palms never lied.

"Is there a reason?" Nate fell in step with Paige. Her legs were long, but his were longer. He matched her stride for stride. "Boyfriend?"

"No. Girlfriend."

"Ah."

"Not that kind of girlfriend." Paige sighed. "Though sometimes I think it would be easier if I were a lesbian. Men are a mystery. And quite frankly, sometimes you give me a headache trying to figure you out."

"I've been assured by my gay friends that that is a myth." The cast gleamed white against his tanned skin. "Relationships are hard. A man and a woman. Two men. Two women. Add that element of sex, jealousy, and possessiveness. Once another person is your lover, all bets are off."

"I suppose." Paige hadn't thought of it like that. "What I have with Lottie is rock solid. Outside of my parents, she is the most important person I've ever had in my life. We've been best friends forever. In all that time, we have never competed over a man. She likes you. End of story. That kiss was as close to betraying her trust as I've ever come, Nate." Paige shook her head. "I won't cross that line again."

This was a new one for Nate. In all his years, he had never been turned down for a reason as convoluted, and noble as this one. It was obvious Paige wouldn't be swayed. One more thing to add to the growing list of things he liked about this woman. Loyalty. Fierce and true.

"Does my preference carry any weight in this?"

"Naturally." Paige glanced his way. "I'm flattered that you find me attractive, Nate."

"I believe the word I used was beautiful."

"So you did." Paige nodded. "And by the way? That isn't something I hear very often. I'm... attractive."

"The men you've met are certifiable idiots."

Paige felt that burst of warmth again. Damn, damn, damn. Why did he have to be so... She couldn't think of the word for him. Nate was unique. Maybe that was it. The question was why did he have to be so *Nate?*

"If I say something, will you promise not to take it the wrong way?"

"No."

Paige laughed. It had been a stupid question.

"I'll take my chances. I like that you find me beautiful."

Nate came to a halt, expecting her to do the same. Instead, Paige increased her pace, leaving him watching. Between her words and that fine, firm ass, she was killing him. He was only human. How much was he supposed to take?

"You're killing me, Paige." He quickened his pace, catching up. "If Lottie gives the go-ahead, will you kiss me again?"

"I'll kiss you now." Paige grazed his cheek with her lips. "Brother and sister." Her eyes lit up. "I hadn't thought of that. You can be the sibling I never had."

Nate stared at the screen door as it slammed behind Paige. *Was she out of her mind?* Friend he was fine with — for a start. But brother? Not in this lifetime. Nate entered the house. No one would ever accuse Nate Landis of backing down from a challenge. Whether Paige knew it or not, she had thrown down the sexual gauntlet and he had picked it up.

Whatever doubts or trepidation he felt earlier be damned. Once she made it clear that she wanted him, that was it.

Nate's smile was one his family would have recognized instantly.

Paige Chamberlin was about to discover no one told a Landis what he could and couldn't do. He had the family name to uphold. And a beautiful, stubborn, exciting woman to seduce.

Nate was enjoying Montana more and more by the second.

Chapter Five

"**N**O DOUBT ABOUT it, Chuck. That is the best steak I have ever eaten."

Nate slid another piece of succulent beef into his mouth, the juices bursting over his tongue. This was not something to be hurried. He chewed deliberately, savoring the moment.

"More beans, Nate?"

"Please." Nate held out his plate. "It's a treat to get something straight from the garden. There's nothing like it."

The meal was simple and delicious. From the meat to the baked potatoes, nothing came from the grocery store. Even the butter was hand-churned by the same woman who made the bread that Nate enjoyed his third piece of. First thing in the morning, he would go for a run. A few weeks eating like this, they would have to roll him out of Montana.

"I read about your accident." Chuck pointed his fork toward the cast on Nate's left arm. "Close call."

"I was lucky. A knock on my hard head and a broken bone. It's always a win when you walk away."

Nate didn't want to get into the details. An accident or sabotage. At this point, there was no proof either way. Besides, sharing the dangerous side of what he did was something he rarely engaged in. His mother didn't want to know. His father would listen, but Nate chose to spare him, too.

The only one who knew the down and dirty details was Garrett. His twin. Not exactly his other half. They weren't identical. The differences were as varied as the similarities. Nate was bigger. Broader. Faster. Garrett was built for endurance. His body lean. In a sprint, Nate won every time. Anything longer and Garrett would eventually take him down.

Garrett had a quick temper. He held on to a grudge. Nate was more of a slow burn. When he popped, stand back. It wasn't pretty, but it was fast. With a few exceptions, he couldn't stay mad. And once on Nate's good side, he would give the shirt off his back.

That trait went deep with every member of the Landis clan. Nate reminded himself of that several times on the trip here. Family first. Friends a close second. You didn't turn your back on either when they were in need.

"About this movie."

Chuck didn't need to be prodded. He launched into an enthusiastic monologue starting with the day he remembered Erin's script. He explained how the idea to fulfill its potential came to him fully formed. Chuck knew what to do and how to get it done. All those years in Hollywood would finally pay off.

Nate listened. Chuck's plan was impressive. He wasn't trying to make a blockbuster. He thought small from the very beginning. Smart for any first-time filmmaker. He gathered volunteers when possible. From what Chuck said, ninety-five percent of everyone involved had little or no experience.

That meant the budget would be almost nothing. It also meant a lot of mistakes and reshoots. There was no way they would finish in the timeframe Chuck laid out. Unless someone stepped in to help.

Nate took a deep breath. *Thanks, Dad,* he silently cursed his father.

You knew exactly what you were getting me into. A few weeks, my ass. Nate would be lucky if he got out of here by Thanksgiving.

"You have a crew lined up? Equipment? When did you do all this?" Paige asked, a perplexed frown on her face.

"It was mostly done on the phone," Chuck shrugged. "I'm sorry, honey. I know you're hurt that I didn't tell you about this sooner."

"Not hurt." Paige thought for a second. *Well, maybe a little.* "I'm worried that you're getting in over your head. You could lose the ranch, Dad."

"No," Chuck shook his head, his expression fierce. "I would never risk the Double C, Paige. I wouldn't do that to you."

"You think I'm worried about myself?" Paige laid a hand over her father's, squeezing gently. "You've spent half of your life building this place up. What would you do without it? It's your home."

Chuck looked like he was about to say something, and then changed his mind. Instead, he smiled, patting Paige on the shoulder.

"I've only committed money I could afford to lose."

"Dad." Paige looked at Nate. This was family business. What she had to say didn't involve their guest. "May I speak with you alone?"

"No problem." Nate stood. "I could use some air after that amazing meal."

"You don't have to go, Nate." Chuck began clearing the table. "There's nothing to be said that you can't hear."

Nate's eyes met Paige. He could tell from her expression that she didn't agree with her father.

"Call me if you need help with the dishes."

He grabbed his jacket before exiting the house. The gratitude he saw in Paige's eyes made him glad he followed his instincts. Family matters needed to stay in the family.

"I can't believe you drove our guest out of the house, Paige."

"He didn't seem to mind," Paige said. "Dad. Please, stop clearing the table and sit down."

Reluctantly, Chuck set the plates in the sink. With a sigh, he joined her.

"I know what you're going to say."

"Of course you do. That's why you didn't want Nate to leave. You thought I wouldn't bring the subject up with him in the room."

"I was right, wasn't I?"

"No. Nate being here wouldn't have stopped me." Paige shook her head. He didn't know her as well as he thought. "But I did think you would be more comfortable if we were alone before I started discussing money."

"There isn't anything to discuss."

Chuck gave her a determined smile. One she recognized. He was entrenched. Nothing she said would sway him. Knowing it was hopeless, Paige had to try, if only to make her father understand her worries.

"You and Mom worked so hard to become debt free."

"She would understand, Paige. I need to do this."

He was right. Her mother *would* have understood. Not because she was a pushover, but because her father wouldn't have done any of this without consulting Erin first. They had been a team. Paige always thought she was part of it. Now, for the first time in her life, she felt like an outsider.

"Why? What is really driving you, Dad? Help me understand."

For a second Paige thought he would answer. She leaned forward, hoping to finally hear an explanation that made sense.

Headlights and the sound of an approaching vehicle were Chuck's reprieve.

"Visitors."

Exasperated, Paige sat while her father jumped up with the enthusiasm of a child getting a highly anticipated treat. He was keeping something from her and that hurt. Her only consolation was the spark she saw in him. It went out when her mother died. Before, really. Now that it was back, she would be a poor daughter if she kept trying to put it out.

The first thing she would do was read her mother's script. She felt a moment of shame that she hadn't done so. Stubbornness. It was her friend — and her enemy. A two-sided coin. It was time to pull back — cautiously.

If this meant so much to her father, she would jump on board, all the time watching the bottom line. If she thought things were getting out of hand financially, Paige wouldn't keep it to herself. She didn't want to play the bad guy, but she wasn't afraid to be if necessary. For the good of her father, herself, and the ranch.

It might be fun, she assured herself. Learning something new. Working alongside her father. And Nate. Oh, boy. She couldn't forget Nate. He was the wild card in the equation. It was good that he was here. He had the experience — the know-how — that hopefully would keep the project on track.

The challenge would be to work closely every day — without getting *too* close. She could do that, right? Paige straightened her shoulders. Yes, she could. Absolutely. Well, maybe. Oh, crap. She had no idea.

Paige hoped she was good at playing it by ear. If not, she better learn how. Fast.

"Dad."

Chuck turned his head as he buttoned his jacket. As Paige rushed toward him, he smiled, opening his arms.

"I love you." Paige burrowed close, breathing in his familiar scent. Peppermint from the hard candies he always carried, and a touch of cedar. The closet in the master bedroom was lined with the wood.

"I love you too, honey." His baby. "It's going to be all right. I promise."

Chuck Chamberlin was the only man Paige believed when he said that. He had never given her reason to doubt him. She was determined to make sure, for both their sakes, that this time wouldn't be different.

NATE WALKED TO the barn, his way lit by the domed lights on the outside of all the buildings. Paige told him that they came on at dusk, staying lit until morning. Checking that the door was firmly latched, he moved on. Not that he had any idea what he was doing. The closest he had come to working on a ranch was a fictional one.

In his career, Nate had done four westerns. The first, *Ride the Lonesome Pine*, hadn't been great. Hell, calling it a piece of schlock would be kind.

At the time, he was young, inexperienced, and open to anything that came his way. He could have used the family name to get his foot in the door. If asked, his father would have made a few calls, set him up with enough jobs to keep him busy for decades.

Caleb Landis would have done that for all his sons. The fact that they didn't want him to made Caleb proud beyond words. Nate and his brothers wanted success. They wanted to be the best. They *did not* want to get there by riding the coattails of their famous parents.

Nate rattled the corral gate. Solid as a rock. Rollie, Winter, and whatever livestock might roam the enclosure, weren't going anywhere. He couldn't tell if they were out there. The lights didn't reach the back end of the corral. As he turned back toward the house, he heard a faint nicker followed by another. Nate opened his mouth, ready to answer before he stopped himself.

Was he crazy? Talking to animals? Chuckling, Nate looked around. There wasn't anyone to see him behaving foolishly. *Why not?*

"Hey, Winter. Hey, Rollie. How's it going?"

Not expecting an answer, Nate turned toward the house. Two nickers called out in the night. Without halting, Nate grinned. It seemed he had a couple of new friends. Four-legged or two, it didn't matter. A man could never have enough.

Lights suddenly appeared down the road heading in his direction. From the placement of the beams, Nate guessed it was a truck. He held his hand up to his eyes and waited. In Los Angeles, seven forty-five wasn't late to make a visit. He didn't know what was normal in Montana, but his guess was ranchers went to bed early.

The truck wasn't like Paige's. This one was bright penny new. The color was black. The size big. Almost obnoxiously so. The outside was all flash. An extended cab and oversized bed, it practically screamed *I have money — and I want you to know it.*

Nate hated to pre-judge someone, but in this case, he was willing to make an exception. Something told him that he and the driver were not going to be friends. When a tall, lean man wearing cowboy boots that didn't have a scuff in sight and pressed, creased blue jeans approached, Nate was certain of it. There was something wrong with jeans that looked like something out of *Urban Cowboy*. This was Montana, damn it. Not fake Texas.

"Evening."

"Hello." The man hesitated, just for an instant, before plastering a smile on his face. It was quick, but Nate saw the wariness before it was masked with friendly goodwill. He couldn't blame the guy. He came to visit the Chamberlins. Finding a very large, unsmiling stranger guarding the gate, so to speak, must have come as a surprise.

"I'm Nate."

Nate held out his hand. It was an innocent gesture. The look on his face wasn't. Why this guy had instantly gotten under his skin, Nate had no idea. The man cautiously took his hand. *Soft*, Nate thought. If he owned land around here, he didn't work it. Not personally.

Nate's lips quirked. It wasn't a smile. Not close.

"Lyle. Lyle Wilson. I live a few miles down the road."

"You're a neighbor?"

"The closest one." Lyle said it like it was some major accomplishment.

"Chuck and Paige are inside."

Nate almost laughed at himself. *Talk about bad dialogue, Landis.* Give the guy a break. Maybe he's here to borrow a cup of sugar.

"I'm here to see Paige."

Or maybe he wants me to punch those artificially white teeth down his throat. Nate's famous slow burn quickly heated up. It seemed he had discovered one of those rare buttons someone could push. *Paige.*

"Lyle. This is a pleasant surprise."

Maybe Nate looked for something that wasn't there, but Chuck's words were warmer in content than in delivery. Lyle Wilson was not Chuck's favorite person. The question was how did Paige feel about him? When he asked her earlier, she said she didn't have a boyfriend.

As Paige approached, Nate watched closely. Silently, he waited for her reaction.

"Hello, Lyle."

Pleasant. In the short time he had known Paige, she had been many things. Cautious. Annoying. Annoyed. Sexy as hell. But Pleasant. Definitely not. Nate hid his satisfied smile. The day she gave him pleasant, he would know his chances of getting her into bed were over. Flushed like the proverbial turd.

"Paige."

Lyle took her hand. Nate's eyes narrowed when he didn't let it go.

"Easy," Chuck whispered. "The man likes to touch her. But as far as I can tell, her hand is about as far as he's gotten."

"I know this is last minute, but I was hoping you would like to go for a drive. We could stop in at my place. I have some of that wine you like."

"I appreciate the offer, Lyle. But…"

"I know you get up with the sun." Lyle laughed. Why he thought it was funny Nate didn't know. The smile Paige gave him back put Nate's teeth on edge. *Really? Tell the guy he's an idiot and get in the house.*

"We'll be starting that project tomorrow, Paige. First thing."

Paige gave him a look that told him he should have kept his mouth shut. It was too late to take the words back. He would have to live with the consequences, whatever they were. She didn't make him wonder for long.

"There is no timetable, is there, Dad?"

"No, not exactly."

"And I'm not a school girl with a curfew." Paige gave Lyle another smile. This one wider and warmer. "I would love a glass of wine. I hope you don't mind work boots. I know how particular you are about those new hardwood floors."

"Not to worry. You can take your boots off before we enter the house."

Lyle escorted Paige to the truck, holding the door as she pulled herself into the cab. Scampering around to the driver's side, Lyle hopped in. The vehicle started and down the road they went in a flash as though he worried she might change her mind.

Nate watched the taillights disappear into the night. *What had just happened?*

"What happened?" Chuck asked.

"That's what I want to know."

"Not with Lyle. I know what happened there. You poked the bear, Nate."

"Paige being the bear."

It was an interesting analogy. She wasn't big and hairy. Quite the opposite. But she had a definite growl when provoked. It was sexy. Hell, everything about her was sexy.

Nate glanced at Chuck. Those were thoughts he should keep out of his head when he stood next to Paige's father.

"Paige likes to make up her own mind. If she feels like she's being pushed, she pushes back."

"In this case, that means leaving with faux-rancher."

Chuck let out a large belly laugh.

"Come on, let's head inside." He chuckled again. "Faux-rancher. I like that. How'd you pick up on it so fast?"

"He has hands like a man who sits behind a desk all day. Soft. Pampered."

Nate took Chuck's jacket, hanging it beside his own on the pegs by the door. When Chuck started loading the dishwasher, Nate automatically helped. He grew up with a full-time cook and housekeeper. However, he and his brothers had chores, their parents made sure of that. Doing dishes was something Nate was very familiar with.

"Mona at the hair salon in Basic says he gets a manicure every week."

"I used to do that."

"No kidding." Chuck took a long look at Nate's hands.

"There was this pretty manicurist who worked at the salon my mother went to."

"How pretty?"

"I was nineteen. I was in my very intense, and very brief, Dolly Parton stage."

"Now that paints a picture."

Nate grinned, remembering what an idiot he had made of himself. He had recently moved into his own place. It wasn't much. Determined to live on his salary, it was a shock to find out how expensive even a studio apartment was in Los Angeles. The last thing he should have been spending his money on was getting his cuticles trimmed and nails buffed.

The romance lasted all of a month. The sex was fine. Average. The moment Polli — she always introduced herself by telling him her name was spelled with an I — asked Nate to introduce her to his father, that was it. No more manicures. No more Polli with an I. The lesson had been expensive but invaluable.

On rare occasions, he still slept with women who wanted to use him to get ahead in Hollywood. *If* there was a strong physical attraction *and* they knew the score ahead of time. Nate made it clear from the beginning. He knew what they wanted, but sex was all they would get. Some stayed, some didn't. He did his best to make sure the ones who spent the night with him went away happy. The others? He imagined they went looking for another *benefactor*.

"It won't be easy."

Chuck handed Nate a dishtowel before he rinsed out the glasses Erin had always deemed too fragile for the dishwasher.

"I've dried dishes before. I think I can handle a few glasses."

"Don't be obtuse." Chuck put a crystal water goblet in the tray to drain. "You're interested in my Paige."

"I find her interesting," Nate said hesitantly. The last time he met a woman's father was in high school. The worry back then had been about ruining their baby's reputation. Since Nate tended to date *fast* girls, their reputations were already well established. The stories he could have told *dear old Dad* about their little girls would have aged them twenty years.

Chuck wasn't an anxious father of a teenage girl. That put this conversation on a level Nate wasn't prepared for. What did he say to a man who knew he wanted to sleep with his fully-grown adult daughter? Nate had no idea.

"She's a beautiful young woman."

"Yes." There was no arguing with that. Not that Nate wanted to. He waited with trepidation for Chuck to continue.

"Vibrant. Intelligent. She taught herself to read. Can you imagine?"

"You don't need to sell me, Chuck."

"That's what it sounds like, doesn't it." Chuck shook his head with a laugh. "*Here's my daughter. Prime stock, ready for market.* Paige wouldn't speak to me for a week if she heard me talking like that. Her mother would have ripped me a new one."

"Paige has a lot of her mother in her."

"Thank God." Chuck motioned to the framed picture on the wall. "She got the best of her mother. That down deep need to do things on her own is pure Erin."

Nate took a close look at the photograph. A smiling, bright-eyed woman with a short cap of honey-blond hair stood with her head resting on Chuck's shoulder. They looked... in love. Nate recognized it. He grew up with parents who never lost that glow of finding their soul mate.

Paige had her mother's hair. The shape of her face. The full mouth. Her height and slender build she inherited from her father along with his dark eyes. Their combined gene pool had done a fine job. In Paige, Nate could see Erin *and* Chuck.

"We always wanted more children." Chuck dried his hands. Unknowingly, he answered the question Nate had earlier wondered about. "For whatever reason, it never happened. I suppose we doted on Paige a bit more than we should have."

"That's natural. My parents indulged us. And kicked us in the ass when necessary."

"Erin was good at pulling Paige back." Chuck unconsciously traced his wife's face through the glass-covered frame. "Left to it, I let her run wild. She was something to see, Nate. Fearless. Still is. Except when it comes to men."

"Chuck…"

"Hear me out. Would you like some coffee? I think there's some brandy we got as a gift one Christmas."

"I'm good, thanks."

Chuck put a hand on Nate's shoulder, steering him to the living area that flowed out of the kitchen. Chuck took a seat in his usual easy chair. Nate sat opposite. The furniture was comfortable. Homey. The blues and browns of the upholstery broken up by the occasional splashes of color.

The kind of room a person could relax in. So that's what Nate did. He liked Chuck. And he was interested in hearing anything and everything about Paige. If the man harbored ideas about a blending of the Landis and Chamberlin families, he could think again. Nate was here to help make a movie. Not find a wife.

"Get that deer in the headlights look off your face, Nate." Chuck flipped the lever on the side of his chair. He sighed as the footrest popped up, elevating his legs. "I'm not a matchmaker."

"Good to know. What is this about, Chuck?" Not ready to relax like his host, Nate sat forward. "I've been here less than a day. I've had half a tour of the place and an excellent meal."

"All true."

"Let's not forget that Paige chose to *drink some wine* with your neighbor rather than spend another minute in my company."

"That annoys you, doesn't it?"

Deciding silence was the best defense, Nate shrugged.

"You aren't the first man to be dazzled, Nate."

Dazzled? Was that his problem? He certainly wasn't acting in a rational manner. Paige had gotten to him. Fast. He felt turned around and out of sorts. Nate didn't like the feeling. He was the even-keeled Landis. Women amused him. Aroused him. They were fun and sexy. He played for a while, and then moved on.

Paige wouldn't be any different. Would she?

"Since she's single and never been married." Nate raised his eyebrows. "Has she been married?"

"Nope. Not even close."

"Right." Why it mattered, Nate couldn't say. "Then what happened to all these dazzled men?"

"They tried to catch her eye. Some succeeded for a time."

"Like Lyle?"

"Like Lyle." Chuck rubbed his chin, his eyes pensive. "Mostly, Paige doesn't see the effect she has on men."

"Come on."

As a man who reluctantly, and silently, added himself to the list of the dazzled, Nate found Chuck's claim hard to believe. He wouldn't call Paige an all-out heartbreaker. Nothing that calculated. However, she had a healthy amount of flirt in her. She knew how to get a man's attention.

"Don't get me wrong. Paige knows she's attractive. But like her mother, she thinks of herself as average. Average looks, average appeal."

Nate snorted.

"We see; they don't." Chuck smiled. "My Paige has an ego. A big one. But it involves her brain. She tends to think she's the smartest person in the room."

"*That* I've noticed."

"The problem is she usually is."

"That would drive a lot of men away."

Chuck gave Nate a considering look. "You didn't argue."

"About her being smart? Why would I? I was raised by a woman with more innate intelligence that anyone I've ever met."

"Callie."

Nate nodded. "It drives my dad crazy that she always claims to be right."

"Because?"

"Because she is." Nate smiled at Chuck. "Ninety percent of the time."

"Let me guess. On those rare occasions, your dad lets it go."

"Are you kidding? Dad crows about it for days. Mom pretends to be annoyed. They make up quickly, which I suspect was the point all along. What they do behind the closed doors of their bedroom, I don't want to think about."

Nate loved that his parents were still hot for each other. Thankfully, they kept most of the details to themselves.

"Paige will never marry just for the sake of it."

"Isn't that a good thing? You want her to be happy."

"She's single-minded, Nate. The right man is likely to pass her by because she refuses to lose focus on her goals for the ranch. She needs to learn how to have some fun."

Chuck gave Nate a long, steady look.

"Me?" Nate asked. Surely, Paige's father wasn't pushing him to have a fling with his daughter? That would be... weird. "What are you saying?"

"Be her friend. Lottie is great; I love her like another daughter. But she's man crazy."

"I noticed."

"She's a sweet girl. She and Paige are fiercely loyal."

"I noticed that too." Paige took her loyalty a bit farther than necessary. At least, where Nate was concerned.

"Lottie means well, but her idea of having a good time is to drag Paige to the only bar in Basic. Saturday nights can get pretty rowdy."

"There's nothing wrong with that."

"Don't get me wrong," Chuck qualified. "I'm not criticizing Lottie. It simply isn't Paige's thing."

No, Nate couldn't imagine Paige going full-on *Coyote Ugly*. Though she would look fantastic in a pair of short shorts. Nate pulled his thoughts away from the image of Paige's long, bare legs.

"Friends?" Chuck didn't know what he asked. Nate had a lot of friends. He couldn't recall picturing any of them naked.

"I knew I could count on you." Chuck stood, stretching his arms over his head. "I think I'll go on up to bed. Is there anything you need? I know Paige put fresh towels in the guest bathroom."

"No, I'm fine."

"Good. Well then, I'll see you in the morning." Chuck had his foot on the stairs when he turned his head. "One more thing."

"Yes?"

Nate wasn't sure his brain could take anything else. As it was, he would be mulling this conversation over for some time. Between that and listening for Paige to return, he would be lucky if he got more than a couple hours sleep.

Chuck's parting words guaranteed his night would be sleepless.

"At some point, if you and Paige decide to become friends with benefits, don't you dare do it in my house."

DAMN NATE LANDIS. If it weren't for him, she would not be in the company of the dullest man ever put on the face of the earth. She only agreed to Lyle's invitation because she refused to let Nate dictate her actions. Yet, in the end, that was exactly what she had done.

Now she was stuck in Lyle's house, listening to him drone on about some hybrid beef that he planned to import from New Zealand. There was no blunting the pain with wine. After one sip of the foul-tasting brew, Paige couldn't bring herself to drink any more of it. She had no idea why he thought she liked it.

Lyle never listened. He liked the wine so he decided she liked it too. Typical.

Damn, Nate Landis.

"There is a meeting of like-minded cattlemen in Chicago next month. I'm going to use the time as a mini-vacation. I thought it would be the perfect chance for us to get away."

"Us?" When had they become *us*?

Lyle Wilson bought the land adjacent to the Double C while Paige was in college. The newly named Wild W Ranch was a combination of three properties, making it one of the largest privately owned spreads in western Montana.

As far as anyone could tell, it was a vanity project. Lyle Wilson came from money. A lot of money. Now thirty, he had inherited the bulk of his wealth in his early twenties. Since then, he increased his fortune by making savvy investments. He was smart. Charming. Attractive. The perfect package.

But the package didn't appeal to Paige.

They met soon after Paige returned from college to be with her mother. At first, Lyle offered nothing but friendship. When he dropped by the Double C, it was usually to bend her father's ear about ranching.

Not that Lyle took Chuck's advice. He had a fancy, Harvard-educated ranch manager who made all the big decisions. No. That wasn't true. The manager submitted a list of *options*. Lyle made all final decisions. That was an important point. Paige knew this because he emphasized it every time the subject came up. And like most things that involved Lyle, the subject came up repeatedly.

Paige had only herself to blame. She knew from the beginning that Lyle wasn't a man she would ever work up any interest in. However, they met when she was emotionally vulnerable. Lyle provided a distraction that Paige latched onto. Unlatching herself wasn't as easy. He was not a man easily discouraged.

Lyle would ask her out. Paige would say no. A few weeks would pass before he made his next pitch. Three times, he wore her down. Three times, she regretted it.

They had nothing in common beyond their zip code. No shared interests. She was open to any subject. Sports. Politics. Entertainment. He was open to one. Lyle. As soon as she figured out he was obsessed with himself, Paige knew they had no future. Romantic or otherwise.

For the life of her, she couldn't figure out why he was fixated on her. Most women would have switched places with her in a heartbeat. Wealthy bachelors didn't grow on trees, especially in Basic, Montana. Paige didn't care about that. Money was nice. She needed a man with whom she could carry on an intelligent conversation.

One thing she was certain of — Lyle Wilson was not in love with her. If there were a physical attraction, he hid it. A kiss on the cheek. Once. Not exactly the sign of a man overcome with passion.

Was he gay? Paige had no idea. He seemed almost asexual. Neutral. He simply wasn't interested.

It was time for Paige to make it clear, once and for all, that neither was she.

"What do you think?"

Paige's mind had wandered so far away, she had lost track of the conversation.

"I'm sorry? What was the question?"

For the first time, Paige thought she saw a flicker of real emotion behind Lyle's normally placid pale blue eyes. However, the slight sign of impatience disappeared as quickly as it came. The slow, calm smile that curved his lips was in place before she could decide if it had been her imagination.

"Chicago, dear." His tone was slightly condescending, as though he tried to get through to a child. Or a not too bright adult. "If you agree to accompany me."

One more strike against him. He never treated her as an equal. Everything was said with slow deliberation. Simple words. It was insulting. Not that she took it personally. Lyle spoke to everyone that way.

"What are we doing, Lyle?"

"Sharing some lovely wine."

Paige sighed. Everything was so literal with him. Fine. If he needed her to bash him with the edge of her blunt tongue, so be it. She should have done this after their first date.

"You are a very nice man, Lyle."

"And you are a very nice woman."

"Not really. I can be a bitch." Paige took her glass to the sink, pouring out the contents. Lyle's gasp made her roll her eyes. "You haven't seen that side of me because, the few times we've been alone, I never say anything. You do all the talking."

"I thought you were shy."

"That proves you don't know me. I'm a lot of things, Lyle. Shy isn't one of them."

"All the more reason for you to come to Chicago."

"No."

"But—"

"Just no, Lyle." This time, Paige wasn't leaving any doubt about how she felt. "I don't want to go to Chicago with you. Or Missoula. Or Basic."

"Is there a reason or is this a woman's thing?"

"You mean am I moody because it's that time of the month? The answer is no. I don't have my period. I told you, this is me. I can call on my inner bitch every day of the month. I don't need any excuses."

"There's no need to be crude." Lyle picked an imaginary piece of lint off his starched jeans.

"Fine. How about some honesty? Something I should have given you from the beginning." Paige slapped her hands down on the imported Italian marble that covered every inch of counter space. Lyle called the color 'enchanted moss.' Paige called it ugly. Like mucus with flecks of gold shot through it. "*I am not interested.*"

"It's that walking steroid, isn't it?"

"It's you and me, Lyle. It's the fact that we— Wait. Steroid? What are you talking about?"

"Muscle boy," Lyle sneered. "The guy guarding the house when I drove up? You should get a dog, Paige. They're easier to train."

"Nate? Nate Landis?"

Under other circumstances, Paige would have laughed. Steroids? She supposed to a man like Lyle who had a slightly underdeveloped physique, it might seem like Nate was muscle bound. To the eye of an appreciative woman, his body was perfection. Sex on a very long, gorgeous stick.

"Landis. Why does that sound familiar?"

"It's a common enough last name." Paige didn't want to get into the whole 'we're making a movie' thing with Lyle. She wanted to go home. Now. "I'm tired, Lyle and as you pointed out earlier, my day starts early."

"Of course."

Nothing ruffled Lyle. Paige could see that as an asset. If you were an air traffic controller. Or if you defused bombs for a living. In everyday life, it was damned annoying.

If there were ever a time to cut the small talk, this was it. Naturally, Lyle didn't get the memo. The ride back to the Double C seemed never ending as he went on and on about the fluctuating Asian market. Paige was so happy to see the front porch light she had the truck door open before they came to a full stop.

"Goodbye, Lyle. I—"

"I won't take what you said tonight to be the final word, Paige. Think about it for a few weeks. I'll call you when I get back from Chicago."

"There is nothing to think about. There is nothing between us, Lyle. You must feel the same. You've never even kissed me."

"Is that what this is about?" Paige saw Lyle's white teeth gleaming in the glow from the porch. "Why didn't you say so?"

When he started to get out of the truck, Paige jumped across the seat, grabbing at his arm. When he wanted to, Lyle moved quickly. Not wanting to be trapped, she slammed the passenger door. Before she could run up the steps to the safety of the house, Lyle was in front her, blocking her path.

"I don't want you to kiss me, Lyle."

"You'll change your mind. I've been told I'm very good."

"No."

"Relax." Lyle's hands closed around Paige's upper arms.

"And what? Think of England?"

"I don't know what that means."

"It means the lady doesn't want you mauling her."

Nate's arrival gave Paige the opportunity she needed. A quick twist of her body and an elbow to his midsection had his hands dropping away. She didn't stick around to enjoy the sight of him doubled over.

"Get in the house." Nate growled as Paige moved past him. She stopped long enough to take his hand.

"If you come with me."

"I'm right behind you."

Nate tugged at his hand, but Paige wasn't letting go. Their eyes met. No longer a warm ocean blue, there was ice in his gaze that made her more determined to get him away from Lyle.

"Please, Nate. I'm fine. Nothing happened. Besides, he's already gone."

While Paige waylaid Nate, Lyle wisely decided to get out of Dodge. A plume of dust and screeching tires signaled his hasty retreat.

"Fucking coward."

Paige pulled Nate along. With his cooperation, the task was a lot easier. He watched the taillights of Lyle's truck for a moment longer before following her into the house.

"Did he hurt you?"

Nate helped Paige off with her jacket. He lifted the edge of her sleeve, checking the skin.

"I'm fine." She tried moving away but when he gently held her still, she didn't put up a fight. It felt good to be fussed over. If only for a little while. "Nate, Lyle got the worst of the encounter. I jabbed him hard."

"You should have let me jab him harder."

"With this?" Paige took his hand in hers. "You could have shattered his jaw."

"Nah. I know how to throw a punch. I was thinking of a split lip. Painful and lots of blood."

Satisfied she wasn't going to bruise, Nate looked at Paige. The ice had melted, she thought with a sigh. Warm ocean blue.

"Thank you," she whispered. "Though I could have handled it on my own."

"I have no doubt."

Nate gently traced the ridge of her knuckles with his thumb.

"Bad idea."

"Hmm?" Nate smiled.

Damn that mouth. It gave a woman ideas. Bad, nasty, glorious ideas.

"I shouldn't be holding your hand."

Remembering his conversation with Chuck, Nate agreed. *Friends with benefits, my ass.* The warning had been clear as crystal. *Keep your hands off my daughter.* Nate planned on doing his best. At least in the house. However, Montana was a big state. If Paige could be persuaded, all bets were off outside these doors.

"You're sure he didn't hurt you?"

"Positive."

"Then he can keep breathing." Nate kissed the back of Paige's hand before letting it go. "Any chance he'll be back?"

"Not if he has a trace of self-preservation."

Paige wasn't thinking about what Nate would do to Lyle. If the jerk showed his face around here again, *she* would break his jaw.

"Good. We have an early start in the morning. Chuck has set up a meeting with everyone who will be working on the movie."

Paige shook her head. She was amazed at how much her father had gotten done without her knowledge.

"He isn't letting any grass grow under his feet."

Nate followed Paige up the stairs, stopping at her door. He wasn't going to look. He was better off not knowing what her bed looked like. Feeding his fertile imagination with images of how she would look, naked and ready for him, would only add fuel to the fire.

"Good night, Paige."

Inside her room, Paige listened to Nate's footsteps and the closing of his door. Thank God, her father was in the house. His and Nate's rooms shared a wall. That was all the deterrent Paige needed if she found herself tempted.

With a sigh, she flopped onto the bed, bouncing slightly. Nothing would happen between her and Nate. But oh, was she tempted.

For the second time that night, she cursed Nate Landis. The man was too good looking. Too sexy. Too… Everything. Why couldn't the man be a jerk? She could resist a gorgeous asshole. Unfortunately, Nate seemed to be one of the good guys.

Paige punched her pillow in frustration. Everyone had flaws. She was determined to find something, anything that would dampen the attraction.

Nate Landis could not be as perfect as he seemed.

Chapter Six

MORNINGS ON THE Double C carried a routine that seldom varied. Animals didn't care if you had a bad night or wanted twenty more minutes of sleep. They depended on you. Their well-being meant your needs came second.

Paige had always been an early riser. She liked watching the sun crest over the horizon as she tended the horses. It was something she missed when she went away to college.

It was a bonding time. For the past year, Paige had begun acquiring *problem* horses. Animals considered untrainable or had been badly abused. They were skittish around humans — rightfully so.

Neglect, beatings, starvation. She saw it all. These horses had no reason to trust her. It took time and patience. Things other people were not willing to give.

Paige knew the rewards. Seeing a beautiful animal restored to physical and mental health. On rare occasions, the horses were beyond her help. Calling the vet, having an animal put down, was the hardest part of her work. However, the rewards far outweighed the bad times.

When one of her horses found a new home with a carefully vetted owner, she knew it was all worth it. She had a growing collection of pictures on her office wall of smiling owners and the equally happy horses. Seeing the fruit of her labor made it all worthwhile.

"Hey, Rollie."

Paige scratched the horse's nose, feeding him a handful of oats. His constant companion nuzzled her hair, snorting his greeting.

"Winter." Paige laughed. The feel of his velvety muzzle against her cheek was familiar and welcome. "When have I ever forgotten you? Here you go."

The horses chewed contentedly. They were her favorites. Her first rescues. Looking at them now, it was hard to believe that they were the same half-starved animals that the local vet had delivered to her a year and a half ago.

They had been two racks of bones, their coats patches of mange and littered with fleas and puss-infested sores.

No one considered them worth saving. When Dr. Irene Mount contacted Paige, the horses were scheduled for euthanization the next day. Saving them was a long shot. Looking at Rollie and Winter now, she dared anyone to say it wasn't worth it. They weren't for sale. Never had been. Never would be. They would live their lives out on the Double C — pampered and content.

"I love you guys." Paige gave the animals one last pat. "Maybe we'll take Nate out for a ride one day soon."

Winter's ears twitched. He loved a good gallop through the fields. When Paige took him into the foothills of the Bitterroots, he could go for hours, exploring different paths.

Rollie wasn't as enthusiastic. He needed Winter to spur him on. If Paige took him out alone, he tended to plod, barely picking up his hooves. He would give a long-suffering snort, hanging his head with a heavy sigh. The only time he had any real energy was when he was turned toward home. With his comfortable corral as a goal, Rollie could move like the wind.

"You keep Rollie on his toes, don't you? He never lags when you're there to nip at his rump."

They were a perfect pair. Inseparable. Paige didn't know what they would do without each other. Luckily, neither of them would ever have to find out.

"You've had your breakfast. Now it's my turn."

Paige's thoughts turned back to Nate. That was nothing new. He had filled her head from the moment he stepped off the plane. *Had it only been yesterday?* How could one man become so important so quickly?

Because you've never met anyone like him.

It was true. Paige slowly walked across the barnyard toward the house. In less than twenty-four hours, Nate stirred up a variety of emotions. From lust to frustration and back to lust again. He made her laugh. He made her angry. Mostly, he made her want something she couldn't put her finger on. How could she want it if she didn't know what *it* was?

Why now? Her mother used to laugh that Paige skipped the worrisome teenage years, heading straight into adulthood. Her parents were never concerned about her becoming boy crazy. It wasn't going to happen. Not because she was mature beyond her years. There were times when Paige wished for nothing more than to temporarily go off the rails over a boy. Lottie did it every other week.

Paige would have gladly joined her if there had been anyone in Basic to get her hormones pumping. She remained a virgin until the grand old age of twenty-one.

As she did every morning, Paige used the side entrance to the house. Right off the kitchen, technically a mudroom, it was designed as a place to leave boots, coats, hats, and gloves that were loaded with muck from all over the ranch. Erin had made the rule before Paige was born. Work boots were not for the house.

Her mother might be gone, but Paige automatically toed off her boots. It never occurred to her not to.

"There you are. Perfect timing. I'm just dishing up the hotcakes."

"On a weekday?" Paige stopped, breathing in the aroma of hot coffee and bacon. "Did I miss the memo? This is holiday food."

"This morning felt special." Chuck filled a plate. "Sit. They're always better fresh off the griddle."

Having washed her hands in the mudroom, Paige didn't hesitate. She had been up long enough to work up an appetite.

"Milk?"

"Please."

Paige liked her hotcakes with plenty of butter and a dash of syrup. Her father liked his to swim in a pool of the dark liquid. Sweet maple soup with hotcake croutons. That was how her mother described it. Then she would kiss him, declaring she picked up enough syrup from Chuck's lips for her own serving.

It used to be a running joke. Paige hadn't thought about it in ages.

As he set the plate in front of her, Chuck looked at Paige. The smile he gave her was a touch sad but for the first time, she saw a spark of genuine humor in his gaze. The memories were easier to deal with. Especially the good ones.

"Where's our guest? Still in bed?" Paige took a sip of milk. "Hollywood hours won't cut it around here."

"Nate was up and out with me before you finished your shower." Chuck flipped the last hotcake. "We fed the herd down by the old barn and repaired a section of fence I wasn't aware was down. Nate noticed it on our way back."

"So there." Nate entered the kitchen, using his good hand to smooth back his slightly damp hair.

"Show off."

There was no heat in her words. Nate's willingness to jump in only added to her admiration. Why couldn't he be lazy? A slug-a-bed? She needed to find a reason to tamp down on the growing attraction she felt for him.

"Do you snore?"

Nate's blue eyes twinkled as he snatched a piece of bacon off her plate.

"I haven't heard any complaints."

I'll bet, Paige thought. A woman would put up with a lot if it meant having Nate in her bed.

"Hey," Paige slapped at his hand when he would have taken more food from her. "Dad practically cooked a whole pig." She pointed to the platter heaped with bacon. "Leave mine alone."

"Yours tastes better."

"Why is that?"

"Because it's yours."

Paige's eyes widened. Flirting when they were alone was one thing. But in front of her father?

"Coffee, Nate?"

"I'll get it, thanks."

Neither man acted as though anything odd had been said. It was as though this kind of thing was routine. A stranger was in their kitchen, drinking their coffee, eating food off her plate. That was not normal. Nor was Nate winking at her over the rim of his cup.

"Hollywood hours?" Nate asked before she could comment on his behavior. "What would those be, if you don't mind me asking?"

Paige thought about it for a second, and then laughed at her foolishness. "I have no idea."

Surprised and delighted by her response, Nate grinned.

"Let me give you a crash course on the subject. Unless you aren't interested."

"My mind is a sponge, professor. Consider me your willing pupil."

"Oh, I could teach you a thing or two." This time, Nate whispered. Flirting was one thing; all-out sexy talk was another. "All you have to do is say the word."

Paige's eyes met Nate's, silently pleading for him to keep quiet. Nate's smile widened. Apparently, he enjoyed her discomfort.

"Well?"

"Not going to happen."

"What isn't going to happen?" Chuck asked, joining them at the table.

"Nate wants to direct." Paige felt a burst of satisfaction when Nate choked on his coffee. "I told him it was your movie. You are the director."

"Is that true?" Chuck gave Nate his full attention, breakfast forgotten. "I know everyone in Hollywood has aspirations."

"Paige is right, Chuck. I wouldn't dream of stepping on your toes."

"You wouldn't be." Chuck sat back. He had the look of a man on death row, given a last minute reprieve. "I know it's a big job. I never would have asked. But if it's your dream. This is fantastic."

Chuck dug into his food with vigor. Between the relief of handing the responsibility of director over to Nate, and the dozen other things he needed to do, he missed the silent exchange between Paige and Nate.

I am going to kill you.

There was no misinterpreting that look. Trying her best not to laugh, Paige put a hand over her mouth, rubbing at the corners. A small cough covered the chuckle that slipped out.

Knowing she wouldn't be able to hold it together much longer, Paige jumped to her feet. Heading toward the mudroom, she called over her shoulder, "Leave the dishes. I'll do them when I get back."

"Where are you going?" Chuck called out. "Paige? Huh." He looked at Nate with a slight frown. "I wonder what that was all about?"

Not expecting an answer, Chuck poured half of the pitcher of syrup over his hotcakes.

Nate barely noticed. His mind was filled with one thought. He was stuck. For the life of him, he couldn't think of any way out. Garrett would bust a gut laughing when he heard. Wyatt and Colt would never let him live this down.

Directing a movie? Son of a bitch!

"Excuse me, Chuck. I'll be right back."

Nate rushed after Paige. She hadn't gone far. She was outside, leaning against the building. She had gotten her laughter under control and wiped the tears from her eyes. When she saw Nate, she almost lost it again.

"What the hell was that about?"

Paige cleared her throat. "Sorry." The look he gave her said he didn't believe it for a minute. "Honestly, Nate. I had no idea Dad would react like that."

"Why did you bring it up?"

"It's your fault."

"No."

"Yes."

Paige pushed away from the building. She was considered tall. Her boots had a two-inch heel. Yet she had to tip her head back to look Nate in the eyes. Happily, the journey was a scenic one. She started at his chest. Took in the strong curve of his neck. His alone was worth the price of admission — Paige considered herself lucky. She had a close up view — for free.

"What was I saying?" she asked, her eyes fixed on his mouth. Such a nice mouth.

"Has focusing always been a problem?" Nate moved closer. "Or has something, or someone, rattled your brain."

"There you go. That is why you're to blame. You don't just flirt. You F-L-I-R-T!" Paige put a hand on Nate's chest. Her intention was to push him away. Instead, she sighed, her hand rubbing ever so gently.

"Paige."

"Hmm?" Nate's chest was huge. Superhero huge. Swallowing, Paige tried to picture him without his shirt. It was easy. Too easy.

"Paige? Concentrate. You threw me under the bus. I don't want to direct. Not this movie. Not any movie."

"Really? I thought wanting to direct was the ubiquitous Hollywood dream."

"Not in my family. We have two producers, two actors, and one director."

"And a stuntman." Another piece of the Nate puzzle. "You like what you do, don't you? I bet you're good at it."

"I am."

"The best?"

"Top five."

Nate would never put himself at the top of any list. However, he knew his worth. In his corner of the entertainment universe, people respected the Landis name. *Nate* Landis. Nate liked where he was. *Who* he was. He wasn't an aspiring anything. He was a stuntman.

"Top five is good." Paige nodded. "Great."

"When it comes to other things?" Nate trapped Paige's wandering fingers, flattening her palm against his beating heart. "I'm number one. Want to hazard a guess what they are?"

"What is wrong with you?" Paige pulled at her hand. With a smile, Nate let her go. "You're always saying things that make my mind wander into dangerous territory."

"Sorry." Nate didn't sound contrite. Just the opposite.

"Lyle accused you of being on steroids."

"Asshole."

"My thought exactly."

"If you talk your dad into directing, I'll let you feel my ass. And anything else you want."

"If I don't?" Paige swallowed hard. In jeans, Nate's ass was amazing. Naked? She swallowed again. Her mouth watered at the thought.

"You know the answer. You want to touch any part of me?" This time, Nate's smile was slow and full of promises. "All you have to do is ask."

"This is dangerous territory."

"Only if you make it that way. There's nothing wrong with enjoying a kiss, Paige. Or a touch. Or…"

Hoping Nate would take the decision out of her hands, Paige felt a wave of disappointment when he backed away.

"Nate…"

"I'm not going to kiss you, Paige." Nate's eyes no longer held a teasing light. "After last night? If I pushed myself on you, even thinking you wanted me, I wouldn't be any better than your neighbor."

"You're nothing like Lyle."

"I like the woman in my arms to be willing." He shrugged; his voice dropped to a deep whisper. "Don't get me wrong. In bed?" Nate smiled when heard Paige sigh. "I can dominate with the best of them."

"Dominate?" Paige's eyes widened.

"I don't hit." Nate didn't want any misunderstandings between them. "A pat on the ass is as far as I go. Light bondage, if we're both in the mood."

"Oh, my."

"I'll leave the rest up to your imagination."

"Thanks a lot."

"You know what to do, Paige."

Nate gave her one last look, and then headed into the house.

"Now what?"

He paused, his hand on the doorknob. Looking over his shoulder, Nate sighed. He cocked his head toward the road where several cars traveled their way.

"Looks like we're making a movie."

Chapter Seven

CALLING THEM RAG-TAG would be kind.

Nate looked at the group assembled in the Double C barn. For a first-time director, this wouldn't be anyone's idea of a Dream Team. A few local theater members and a whole lot of enthusiastic greenhorns.

Chuck was one of them. Enthusiastic and inexperienced. The time he spent in Hollywood had prepared him for the basics. Setting things up was one thing. He had called some old friends and recruited some current ones. He knew what he needed to make a movie. However, when it came down to it, Chuck gladly handed control over to someone else.

That someone was Nate.

"Everyone?" Chuck raised his voice, getting the attention of the thirty-seven people who filled the barn. "First. Thank you. Taking time out from your busy lives to help us make this movie, well, it touches me to have friends like you. I can't promise you fame and riches." The crowd laughed. "I hope when we're done, we'll be better for the experience. And we'll all have a DVD we can bore our families with for years to come."

"If my kids want to inherit the *Wash and Go*, they'll have to show it every year on my birthday. I'm putting it in my will."

"You have three lines, Bert."

"My name will be in the credits, right?"

"Sure," Chuck nodded.

"Then they can damn well sit through the movie to see it. No fast forwarding."

Nate laughed, drawing the attention of the crowd. Chuck took the opportunity to make the introductions.

"Most of you have heard that we have been lucky enough to enlist the help of a man who knows the movie business. He learned at the knee of one of the greats and has years of personal experience. He has graciously agreed to direct the movie."

That announcement got the group talking.

"Everyone, say hello to Nate Landis."

This was it. He had two choices. Run for the hills. If he did that, he might as well keep running because he would never be able to face his father's disappointment. *You don't leave friends in the lurch.*

That left Nate with plan B. This movie was going to be made. He would do the best job possible. And, the most important thing, they would have some fun. This was his crew. Their experience level didn't matter.

From this point on, it was up to him to make the most of their abilities — whatever they were. If they saw that he believed in them, they would believe in themselves. That meant it was up to him to set the tone. Starting now.

Nate hopped onto a bale of hay, clapping his hands.

"Before we do anything else, let me introduce myself."

"We know who you are. You're Colton Landis' brother."

The speaker looked to be about sixteen. She and five girls quickly huddled together, giggling like... like teenage girls. Nate gave a resigned sigh. He was used to the reaction. His brother was a God to these girls and millions like them.

Colt reveled in the attention — most of the time. He had the perfect personality to be a movie star. Nate didn't.

What he did have was infinite patience. He smiled at the leader of the pack, signaling for her to step forward. The girl hesitated, but her friends, still laughing, pushed her toward Nate.

Not wanting to intimidate her, Nate stepped down. She still had to look up at him, way up. She might be used to strapping ranch hands, but she had never seen anyone like Nate Landis. The awe in her eyes made Nate smile. He was used to the reaction. He was a big, muscular man. To a girl who stood just over five feet tall and maybe weighed a hundred pounds, he must have looked like a mountain.

Wanting to help the girl feel at ease, Nate smiled. That was all it took. From that moment on, Nate had his first unofficial fan club. Colton Landis was gorgeous, but so was his brother. More importantly, Colton wasn't here, Nate was. Six teenage girls hadn't left Colton Landis behind; they simply added Nate and were now devoted to him. All it took was one dazzling smile.

"What's your name?"

"Jenna." The girl giggled, and then squealed excitedly when Nate put his hand on her shoulder. "I'm afraid Colt won't be making any surprise visits. You'll have to settle for me."

"Okay," Jenna sighed. "How tall are you?"

"Six-six."

Nate's answer was automatic. He didn't see anything unusual in the question. When the girls gave a collective sigh, he looked around. The men in the crowd seemed as perplexed as he was. Some of the women were smiling odd, knowing grins; a few made fanning motions with their hands.

He recognized the look on Paige's face. He'd seen it earlier. She tried not to laugh.

What? Nate asked her silently. She simply shook her head.

"First," Nate gently herded Jenna back to her friends. "I want you all to understand. I am not a director. My end of the business involves falling out of airplanes and jumping off cliffs. Most of the time I'm good at my job. Sometimes…" He held up his cast. "I got lucky."

"A broken arm is lucky?"

The question came from a middle-aged man toward the back. Nate needed to learn their names. But there was time for that.

Nate nodded. "Considering the alternative, I was damn lucky."

"I forget the lead actor isn't doing all those things. I guess that's the idea." An attractive woman in her early forties waved at Nate. "I'm Naomi Littlefield. This is my husband, Owen."

"Nice to meet you."

Nate shook Naomi's hand, then Owen's. It started the ball rolling. Soon everyone introduced themselves. The rush of names and faces might have been overwhelming, but Nate was used to a lot of people all at once. The first day on any set was like the first day at a new school. If you were lucky, you knew the main players. However, more often than not, Nate began each job acquainting himself with the cast and crew. Depending on the prevailing attitudes, it was sometimes easier said than done.

There was a pecking order on a movie set. The director was top dog. Stunt people were considered a necessary evil. When that was the attitude, it could make for an uncomfortable shoot.

Early in his career when jobs were at a premium, Nate put up with the attitude. Now that he could pick and choose, he passed on projects he knew would be more trouble than they were worth.

Nate didn't want to be a director. However, since there was no turning back, he wanted to start on the right foot. There was a fine line between maintaining the respect his position deserved and coming off like Pol Pot.

As his brother was fond of saying — director did not equal dictator. Nate considered himself lucky to have worked with and learned from one of the best in the business. Garrett Landis. His twin and his best friend.

Things quickly got out of hand. It wasn't enough to introduce themselves; everyone wanted to talk. About themselves. About Nate's family. They all loved his mother. Who could blame them? Nate was fond of her himself. Having Callie Flynn as a mother was nothing but a joy. Except when some guy would forget who he was talking to and proceed to make a salacious comment.

Nate couldn't think of anything as uncomfortable as hearing about how sexy his mother was. She was beautiful. Vibrant. Smart. Loving. A legendary screen goddess.

She was also the woman who gave birth to him. Some things a son shouldn't have to hear in relationship to his mom.

"Let's give Nate some room to breathe, folks," Chuck said after a few minutes. "He isn't going anywhere. You're coming at him all at once. I'll be surprised if he remembers his own name, let alone any of yours."

"My mom taught me a trick. She meets new people all the time and hates forgetting names." Nate deftly rattled everyone's names.

"That's impressive." Naomi Littlefield brushed up against him, seemingly unconcerned that her husband was two feet away. "I've been told that I had the looks to be in the movies. But I decided to get married instead. I suppose you see beautiful women every day."

"Hollywood has a never-ending supply."

Nate loved to flirt. He also knew when not to. Married women with wandering eyes were not his cup of tea. Whatever Naomi's game, she would have to find a different partner. He wasn't going to play.

"Nate?"

Chuck waved. Happy for the excuse, Nate crossed the barn.

"They're an interesting bunch."

Chuck nodded. "And green as grass. I'm sorry this morning has been so disorganized. It isn't exactly what you're used to."

"It's the first day, Chuck. No one knows what to expect. They're nervous and excited. Things will settle down."

"I can't tell you how happy I am to hear you say that." Chuck gave Nate a companionable pat on the back. "I thought this might have scared you back to Los Angeles."

"No. I'm not going anywhere."

As soon as he said the words, Nate knew it was true. Physically he was committed to this job. He had been resigned to making the best of it. Montana. He liked these people. He especially liked Chuck and his hardheaded daughter.

Nate looked around, his eyes lighting on Paige. She laughed with Lottie and two other women. The sound was happy and natural and it gave Nate a funny little jump in his gut. Pleasant — but decidedly odd.

When Paige caught him staring, he didn't look away. Neither did she. If anything, her smile got wider, her eyes warm. Nate didn't know what she was thinking, but whatever it was, he didn't want her to stop.

Chuck claimed his attention with a question about lighting and location. Reluctantly, Nate pulled his eyes away. He had plenty of time to look at her. The thought sent that feeling through his gut again. Odd, indeed.

PAIGE COULDN'T KEEP her eyes off Nate. The other women seemed to have the same reaction. He filled the room with his size and personality. People gravitated toward him. He was a big, sexy satellite drawing in the lesser bodies around him.

"I thought I might have exaggerated his yumminess in my mind." Lottie sighed. "He's even better than I remembered. How is that possible?"

"I've never seen anyone so…" Lisa Stanhope couldn't find the words. She worked at the library, though with her shoulder-length red hair and curvy body, she didn't look like the prototypical librarian

"Sex on a stick." Paige decided there was no harm in verbalizing what everyone thought.

"Yes," Lisa nodded. "Will I melt into a pile of female goo if I get too close? I didn't think men like that existed outside of the movies and my fantasies."

"Hold yourself together for a second and look at this."

Lottie scrolled through the pictures on her phone, and then held it out for the others to see.

"Four of them?" Lisa licked her lips.

"Four Landis brothers. The world knows about Colton. How have they kept the others under wraps?" Lottie pushed a few buttons, making the picture her screensaver.

"Who cares? We have them now."

"What do you think, Paige? Can you believe that gene pool?"

"It's impressive," Paige nodded. "Imagine how many women have gone swimming in that pool. Excuse me. Peter Minor is about to dump horse manure down Holly Lopez's shirt."

"She's awfully blasé." Lisa shook her head after Paige left. "If Nate Landis were staying in my house, I'd be over the moon. And a little sick to my stomach. I might dream about a man like that, but I'm not sure I would know what to do with him."

Lottie laughed. "Sweetie, a man like Nate Landis knows all the moves. All you would have to do is enjoy the ride."

"Where do I sign up?"

"Nope. To ride that one you have to be this tall." Lottie held her hand up several inches above her and Lisa's heads.

"What does that mean?"

"Paige."

"But—"

"Do you think I didn't make a play? My flirting had no effect on him. And you know that isn't something I admit easily."

"Because it never happens."

"True." It wasn't said with any ego. A fact was a fact. "He only has eyes for Paige."

"And Paige?"

"She's stubborn."

"True."

The women exchanged smiles. Loving someone didn't mean you overlooked their faults. Paige was a fierce and loyal friend. She also had a habit of digging her feet in when she didn't want to face the fact that she didn't always know what was best.

"I know that look," Lisa grinned. "You have a plan. What is it and how can I help."

"For the moment, I'm taking a wait and see approach." Lottie slung her arm over Lisa's shoulders. "Nate isn't going anywhere. I'm hoping he'll do his part. If the hungry wolf look he gave her yesterday is any indication, he will make his move. Soon."

Lisa sighed again. "What do think the chances are the other brothers will drop into Basic?"

"Slim to none." Lottie gave Lisa a commiserating look. "But there's always hope."

Chapter Eight

NATE DIDN'T BOTHER to look at the clock. It was early. Or late. It was all about your point of view.

After his day, he should have been dead to the world the second his head hit the pillow. However, an exhausted body did not always equal sleep. Nate knew that all too well. He turned onto his back, staring at the sliver of light that peeked through the curtains.

When he told Paige that he didn't sleep well alone, he hadn't been exaggerating. This was a lifelong problem. His mother said it was because he was a twin. Nate wasn't sure that nine months sharing a uterus with his brother equated to the need to have someone nearby when he slept, but it was as good a theory as any.

As boys, he and Garrett shared a room so he didn't know he had a problem until they were older and moved into their own. After a few weeks, the lack of sleep started to take its toll. He literally fell asleep in his cereal.

Never one to let the opportunity to rib his brother slip by, Garrett gave him all kinds of grief. Then, without a word, he moved his bed into Nate's room.

Over the years, Nate trained himself to sleep alone. A different woman every night was an exciting solution when he was younger, but that had lost its appeal long ago. His relationships never lasted longer than a few months. Partly because he traveled so much, mostly because he hadn't met a woman he could see himself with for a lifetime.

Nate loved his life. He had a great family. The job of his dreams. Plenty of money. Good friends.

Most nights he managed five or six solid hours of sleep. He still slept better when he wasn't alone, but for the most part, he could shut his mind and body down. Strange country. Strange bed. With a few exceptions, Nate found a way. Especially when he was worn out.

Nate rolled to his side, mind running over yesterday's events.

Once introductions and small talk had been taken care of, Nate decided it was time to set the tone for how they would move forward. His father always said, Make it clear from day one who was in charge. Confused leadership meant anarchy and was sure death to a movie.

It was a bit dramatic, but so was his father. Caleb Landis was bigger than life. Loud, brash. He could cut down a rival with one icy look from his laser sharp blue eyes. He lived life the way he wanted. No excuses. No compromises.

Nate's path was different from his father's, but that didn't mean he hadn't listened and learned. It was a good thing. He would need every bit of his father's wisdom. Chuck and his friends looked for him to make sure this movie was made.

Surprisingly, Nate didn't find leading the making of a movie that much different from leading his crew of stunt people. Solid ground rules were the key. The residents of Basic were not professionals, but they wanted to do a good job. That made it easier for him.

The first thing he did was make sure everyone had a script. Thanks to Chuck's foresight, that had been taken care of. The casting wasn't an issue. The movie had three main speaking parts. The male and female leads and their daughter.

Chuck seemed confident in his choices.

Wilt Adair and Edith Potter had played husband and wife half a dozen times at the Regency. The theater did a yearly production, usually a Christmas-themed play. It was the perfect time of year to ensure a big audience. School was out and the local ranchers and farmers had little to do except tend their livestock. A play was the perfect diversion during a cold, snowy December in Basic.

The part of the daughter was small, but pivotal. Chuck thought Maude Clancy, Edith's real life daughter, would be perfect for the part.

This was Chuck's baby. If he were happy with his choices, Nate wouldn't argue. He would keep his fingers crossed that the trio turned out to be decent actors.

Nate was impressed by the amount of preparation Chuck had done. Casting. Equipment. There was a long list of volunteers — more than necessary for such a small production. However, as Chuck pointed out, you never knew when an emergency would keep someone from showing up. These people had jobs and families. When life happened, the movie would take a backseat.

Nate would have to be diligent and keep them headed in one direction, but he believed he was up to the task. He wasn't nervous about taking on an unfamiliar job. In a way, he was more qualified than most first time directors. He grew up on movie sets. This was familiar territory.

His nerves weren't keeping him awake. It was old-fashioned sexual frustration. Paige wasn't caving and even if she did, he couldn't see sneaking out to the barn for a romp in the hay. Not with Chuck in the house.

When Nate wanted a woman, he usually had her. That wasn't ego talking; it was a bald-faced fact. This was unfamiliar territory and Nate wasn't sure how to handle it.

Telling Paige that she would have to make the next move was one thing. Wondering if she ever would was another. Factor in logistics and it was no wonder Nate couldn't sleep.

He glanced at the clock. Three o'clock. With the time difference, it would be an hour later in Los Angeles. Nate smiled. Garrett hated waking up earlier than absolutely necessary. Pissing off his brother was just the thing to take the edge off his frustration.

Grabbing his phone off the nightstand, Nate hit the top spot on his speed dial. Grinning with anticipation, Nate was surprised when Garrett picked up on the first ring. Even more, he was surprised by the chipper greeting.

"Nate. How's Montana?"

"Good. Beautiful, actually." Nate frowned. "Why the hell do you sound happy and wide awake? Have you looked at the clock?"

Garrett laughed. "I have to be on set at six and I have a gorgeous woman who likes to *get me up early,* if you know what I mean."

Nate knew exactly what Garrett meant and it did not help his mood.

"Fuck you," he muttered.

"Again, I have a gorgeous woman who takes care of that on a very regular basis."

"I should have made a play for Jade when I had the chance. Mom wanted me to ask her out."

"Mom didn't know that I'd already staked my claim," Garrett reminded him.

"I heard that," a female voice called out. "*Staked your claim?* Really?"

"Jade. Honey."

"Tell Nate hello for me. I'm going to take a shower. Alone."

"See what you've done." Garrett practically growled the words. "Morning showers with Jade are the best."

Now he felt better. Jade was one of Nate's favorite people. He thought of her as a sister. It was almost worth pissing her off if it meant depriving Garrett of a little sexual fun.

"You'll survive."

"True. Afternoon showers are just as good. Not to mention evening showers."

"I didn't call to hear about your sex life."

"No? Too bad. It is *spectacular.* Making love is so much better than having sex."

"Are you trying to rub it in?"

"Just a little." Nate could hear the smile in Garrett's voice. "I tried it with Colt, but he wasn't buying. According to little brother, sex is sex. Sometimes it's good. Sometimes it's off the charts. It's chemistry. Love has nothing to do with it."

"What did you say to that?"

"Not a thing. I put his words in the vault. When our resident Don Juan loses his heart, I'm going to pull them out and grind his nose in them."

"You're a good brother, Garrett."

"Damn straight. Now tell me about this movie, Nate. Or should I say, Mr. Director."

Nate was so surprised he almost dropped the phone.

"How the hell did you know about that?"

"A little thing called social media. Did you expect all of those people to keep it to themselves? Wyatt's assistant fielded calls all afternoon."

Nate frowned. "What kind of calls?"

"The usual. What do you think about your brother directing an independent movie? Will any other Landis be involved?"

Well, shit. It was stupid of him, but Nate hadn't thought about the internet. A group of people, with a smattering of teenagers. Why wouldn't they tweet, post, and Instagram the hell out of it? A movie was about to be made in Basic, Montana. Of course, they would let the world know about it in a hundred and forty characters or less.

"I always knew you secretly longed to be a director."

"Garrett…"

"All those years of denying it. How does it feel to be out of the closet?"

"I can still kick your ass, *little* brother."

"I'll let Sable defend me." Garrett referenced the woman who had acted as Jade's bodyguard when her crazy ex-husband had been on the loose. To prove her abilities, Sable used Nate for demonstration purposes. After the slender woman had taken him down, more than once, she got the job. "I have no problem standing behind a woman. How long did it take her to knock you on your ass?"

"About twenty seconds," Nate muttered. He still wasn't sure how it happened. Then happened again. Something about leverage.

"Seriously, Nate. How did you get roped into this? Dad sent you there to lend a hand. Directing is a big step up from supervising."

Nate spent the next few minutes filling Garrett in. He mentioned Paige in passing, but Garrett was his brother, his twin. It wasn't surprising that he picked up on something unusual.

"Now I get it." Garrett chuckled. "Your brain was scrambled by a beautiful woman. You've never been able to say no when a female bats her eyes at you, Nate."

Nate had no comeback for that. He was a sucker for a damsel in distress. However, Paige was neither a damsel nor in distress. She was a woman who insisted on taking care of herself. He told Garrett exactly that.

Garrett gave a silent whistle. No wonder Nate was intrigued. His brother was a born fixer. He couldn't walk away from anyone in need. It made sense that an independent woman with a stubborn streak would be the one to get under his skin. And in record time. Two strong personalities going head to head. Garrett couldn't wait to see how it played out.

"I wonder if I should tell you the rest of it."

Nate swallowed. He didn't like that touch of evil glee he heard in Garrett's voice.

"Do I want to know?"

"Probably not," Garrett conceded. "But this is too good to keep to myself."

"I could hang up."

"You think that would stop me?"

Nate sighed. "I know you too well, brother. I'll be inundated with texts, won't I?"

"And emails. And phone calls. I might even get Sally to send you some personalized GIFs. I know how much you love those."

Garrett's secretary was a whiz at anything computer-related. If he asked, she would send a dozen of those things in a heartbeat. Nate shuddered. He hated those things. Why they gave him the creeps, he didn't know. It was a personal phobia that he would just as soon not delve into.

"Fine." Nate prepared himself. "Give me your best shot."

"Take it easy," Garrett said in a reasonable voice that in no way reassured Nate. "A lot of men would be flattered. Think of it as a compliment."

"You love this way too much, so I know it has to be bad. Spill the beans, Garrett."

"I'll send you the link. Text me. I can't wait to know what you think."

Nate wanted to reach through the phone and give his brother a shake. The man reveled in teasing him. To be fair, he gave as good as he got. It was never as much fun to be on this end of it.

Nate was about to tell Garrett where he could shove it when he heard a sweet, breathy voice in the background.

"Garrett?"

The rest of Jade's words were too soft for Nate to hear, but if Garrett's groan was any indication, it was extremely personal and very welcome.

"Uh, Nate? I need to go. Jade needs my help."

Nate smiled. Garrett sounded distracted and who could blame him? His woman was wet and needy. His brother was a very lucky man.

"Go. Now."

"Call me if you need my help." Garrett wasn't teasing any longer. "Seriously, Nate. Twenty-four-seven. Anything you need, I'm here for you."

"I never doubted it, Garrett."

Nate ended the call, smiling. Garrett and Jade. On the surface, they seemed like an unlikely pair. However, if you looked a little deeper, they were perfect together.

She deserved all the happiness she could get after being raised by a father who was emotionally abusive and a husband who almost killed her. The fact that she came out the other side in one piece, and able to love Garrett as much as he loved her, spoke volumes. She was beautiful. Inside and out.

Nate stretched his long body. The bed was a surprisingly good fit. Before he reached his thirteenth birthday, his mother special ordered his mattresses. Garrett, Wyatt, and Colt were only a few inches shorter and his father not far behind them. She finally decided to re-fit every bedroom in the house. It made things easier to have standard bedding.

The first thing Nate did when he built his house in Laurel Canyon was to ask his mother for the name of the company she used. He had four bedrooms and four extra-large mattresses. If the day came that he started spending more than the occasional night there, everything was in place.

His home was brand new, fully furnished and decorated exactly to his taste. It seemed criminal that it sat empty most of the time. Garrett had a house close by, and until recently, it had suffered the same fate. Now that his brother was getting married, he and Jade planned to move in.

Right now, it was easier for Nate to bunk at his parents' house when he was in town. They loved having him and he loved the company. Not to mention the food was better than anything he made for himself.

The guest bedroom that Nate currently occupied was surprisingly roomy. His feet hung over the end, but that was easily fixed by moving his body so it lay diagonally.

No, nothing was wrong with the bed. The room was homey and comfortable. The connected bathroom was convenient, affording him some much-appreciated privacy.

Like the rest of the house, the room was a place where anyone would be able to relax. Anyone except Nate.

With a sigh, Nate rolled out of bed. He wasn't going to sleep so he might as well do something productive. They started shooting some exterior scenes today. The thought was to get everything done outside first. It was late September. The weather could hold for another month or they could get an early snow. Better safe than sorry.

Nate planned on having his part in this movie finished by the beginning of November. That meant sticking to a tight schedule. Shit happened, but if he was prepared, there was no reason to think that he wouldn't be back in Los Angeles in five or six weeks.

Quickly donning his running gear, Nate quietly slipped from his room. He didn't want to disturb Chuck or Paige so he stayed to the right as he descended the staircase, avoiding the squeaky sixth and third steps.

Funny, he thought as he let himself out of the house. Those steps were something Paige had pointed out when she showed him his room. Was that only the day before yesterday? He felt as though he had known her and Chuck much longer. There was an ease when he was around the older man. Nate liked him. Respected him.

The whole movie thing still struck him as a small slice of crazy. But who was he to judge? He made his living jumping out of forty-story buildings and rolling cars worth hundreds of thousands of dollars. Most people would think that was the height of lunacy.

Chuck had a vision. It wasn't hurting anyone. In spite of Paige's concerns, Chuck wasn't risking the ranch. Before Nate agreed to help, he had gone over the budget and cash layout. It was tight, but it wouldn't bankrupt the Chamberlins. As long as there were no major delays, Nate planned on getting this movie in early and under budget.

Nate paused, breathing deeply. There was no substitute for this. He loved Los Angeles. It was his home. But the air here was so clean it almost hurt his lungs. A man could get used to running in a smog-free environment. However, it might take a few days for his body to acclimate. Nate grinned, filling his lungs again. Oh, yeah. The rush made him a little lightheaded — in a good way.

Setting out at an easy pace, Nate decided to stick to the road. He was tempted by the wide, open fields but in spite of the bright, moonlit night, the countryside was littered with natural booby-traps. If he stepped in a gopher hole or tripped over a rock, he could break a leg — or worse. He could die before anyone found him. No, he would play it safe for once and run where there was little chance for disaster.

Nate started slowly. He liked to work the kinks out during the first mile, and then pick up the pace. Five or six miles at a time were his norm. He preferred running outside, but time and opportunity didn't always allow for it. He hated treadmills, but they served a purpose when he was stuck in Alaska in a blizzard or the wind blew so hard in South Carolina that even his sturdy body ran the risk of blowing away.

As he often did, Nate took the time while he ran to fine tune the project he was working on. That usually meant figuring out the intricacies of a stunt. Everything had to be perfect, from the equipment to the timing. Unconsciously, Nate scratched at the edge of his cast. Neither he nor the people counting on him could afford the slightest mix-up.

This morning, Nate wasn't thinking about exploding Ferraris or ducking punches; he ran the story over in his mind. Halfway through his second mile, it clicked. Erin Chamberlin wrote a simple story. Heartfelt and emotional, at the core, it was the story of a man and a woman. It took place over one week when a married couple had to decide if, after thirty years, they still belonged together.

Nate saw it clearly. A lot of close-ups. His leads had great faces. Wilt Adair and Edith Potter were in their fifties. Attractive and natural. That was how Nate would describe them. Perfect for their roles as people who had lived a hard life working on a farm that was barely surviving.

If he were lucky, they would be able to convey the everyday struggle that had brought them to the breaking point. It required a delicate balancing act that was difficult for seasoned actors. Nate knew what he wanted to put on film. Getting the performances to compliment his vision was another thing.

But if he pulled it off? Damn. Wouldn't that be something?

Going by the feel of his body, Nate figured he had run close to three miles. On the way back, he tried to clear his mind, concentrating on his breathing and the feel of the air on his face as he increased his pace. The moon was at his back, casting long shadows from where it cascaded over his body.

Scattered in front of him were images out of *A Nightmare Before Christmas*. Nate was fanciful enough to imagine Jack Skellington jumping up and jogging alongside him.

Nate laughed at the silly thought. *Nothing wrong with silly*, his mother would have reminded him. Nate agreed. However, there was a fine line between silly and looney. He debated the difference as he caught a slight movement out of the corner of his eye.

He didn't stop. Instead, Nate slowly jogged in a circle, his gaze fanning out around the area. It only took a few seconds for him to find what he was looking for. About five feet off the road was a burlap sack tied with a bit of rope. He hadn't seen it the first time he passed because a rock blocked the view from one side.

Nate approached with caution. He had no experience to draw upon, but what were the chances it would contain anything but trouble? A wild animal with sharp teeth came to mind. Or snakes. Nate shuddered at the thought.

The smart thing would be to keep going. Chuck would have a better idea how to handle it. At the very least, Nate could grab a flashlight and a pair of heavy gloves. Maybe a gun. Chuck must own a gun. This was a ranch in Montana. A rifle had to be mandatory.

Before Nate could decide his course of action, the occupant of the bag made his mind up for him. The whimper then sharp bark that hit his ears told him right away what he was dealing with. Without another second of hesitation, Nate knelt and untied the rope.

A cold, wet nose appeared, sniffing at Nate's hand. Apparently, it liked the smell because instantly, a head, pudgy body, and four large, clumsy feet followed.

"Hi."

On his knees, Nate picked up the puppy, laughing when it began to squirm. It had two goals. Get as close to Nate as possible and lick every piece of exposed skin it could reach.

Nate was happy to indulge his new friend. There was no way to tell how long the puppy had been in the bag, but it couldn't have been a pleasant experience. Freedom was sweet and apparently so was Nate.

"Or maybe it's salty you like," Nate said, cuddling the warm body close to his chest. The sweat produced from his run dried quickly, leaving a coating on his skin that suited the puppy just fine.

"What do you say we get you back to the house? There might be something tastier than me waiting for you."

Nate cradled the dog with his good arm before reaching for the empty sack.

"Easy," he crooned when the animal tried to burrow into his chest. "I promise; no one will ever put you in one of these again."

It only took a few minutes before Nate jogged up the porch steps. The light in the window told him someone was up and the smell of coffee that hit him when he opened the door was a welcome confirmation.

Paige. Her bright hair was pulled back into one long tail. It left her face free. Free of swinging hair. Free of makeup. Natural. *Damn*, Nate thought. Paige Chamberlin might be the most beautiful woman he had ever seen. Considering movie stars surrounded him every day of his life, and his mother was legendary for her face as well as her acting, that said something.

"Dad was certain you were still in bed," Paige held up the coffee pot. "Want a cup?"

"I'll take a gallon. Black."

"Bad night?" Paige was reaching into the cupboard when she spotted what Nate was carrying. "Where did you find the puppy?"

Forgetting the coffee, Paige rushed toward Nate. Seeing the smile on her face, Nate felt a twinge of jealousy. He wanted her to reach for him with the same enthusiasm.

"On my way back from my run I saw a bag on the side of the road. This cutie was in it."

"On our property?" Paige asked, visibly outraged. "Why would anyone do that? Who dumps a puppy? And on someone else's land?"

"We'll probably never know." Nate watched as Paige poured milk into a bowl before setting it and the dog on the floor. "Though I would love to find out."

"Me too. You could punch them out."

"Really?" Nate leaned against the counter. The puppy licked the bowl clean. Paige refilled it, but this time with water. "You want me to do it? I thought you would take care of it yourself."

Paige looked him up and down before her eyes met his. "I like the idea of scaring the person. I'd be happy to do the hitting, but I don't pack the same intimidation factor as you."

I don't know, Nate thought, *you scare me shitless.*

"What are you going to do with her?"

"Her?"

"The puppy?" Paige set a frying pan on the stove and proceeded to crack some eggs into in. "She's a sweetheart. It shouldn't be hard to find her a good home if you don't want her."

"I hadn't thought that far ahead. I've never had a dog. I travel so much it isn't practical. How about here at the Double C?"

"Mom adopted the sweetest mutt you could ever meet when I was about five years old. When he died, she couldn't bring herself to replace him. Having a dog around again would be nice."

Finished with her water, the puppy bounced over to Nate and promptly began chewing on his shoelaces. "None of that." He snatched her up. "Shoes are off limits, understand?"

Happily, she swiped her tongue across Nate's chin.

"I think she's decided who she loves."

"I have a way with women," Nate said.

It was the understatement of the year. Paige gave the eggs one last stir before plating them. She added some of the bacon that she had cooked while he was out and two slices of warm, buttered toast.

"Sit. Eat." Paige set the plate next to a fork and napkin. "Puppies and teenagers are right in your wheelhouse."

"I won't argue. However, women like me even better." Nate's smile was slow. "Want to know why?"

"Yes."

That threw him. Nate had expected her to counter with something snarky. Never one to look a gift horse in the mouth, he took an eager step in Paige's direction.

"But," she said quickly. "Not right now. Not today."

"When?" Nate asked. "Or is it a secret?"

"Why don't I pour you that coffee? Your new girl looks like she's ready for a nap."

"She's had a pretty traumatic time of it." Instead of setting her down, Nate took a seat, settling the puppy in his lap.

"There you go." Paige joined Nate at the table, a cup of coffee for him in one hand and hot tea for herself in the other.

"Thanks." Nate took a bite of the perfectly scrambled eggs then fed Beauty a small piece. Her whimper of happiness said it all. Warm food and Nate's lap. She was in doggy heaven.

Paige sipped her drink. "Nate."

Nate's blue eyes seemed to have an extra twinkle to them when they met hers. It made keeping her thoughts straight difficult.

"I like the way you say my name."

"Nathaniel."

Paige tried to sound like a repressed Victorian schoolmarm. By the smoldering look he gave her, she had failed. Miserably.

"Tell me what's on your mind, Paige. Beauty and I are eager to listen."

"I was thinking… Wait. Beauty?"

"Isn't she a Beauty?" The puppy's tail wagged. "She agrees. Sweet and pretty as a Montana morning."

"Goddamn you, Nate Landis."

"Watch the language in front of the baby." Nate pretended to cover Beauty's ears. "What did I do?"

"You're too…" *Edible?* No, it wasn't a good idea to tell him that. Nate didn't need any encouragement. Paige wanted to slow things down. Telling him how tasty he looked was not the way to do that.

"When you say things like *she's as pretty as a Montana morning,* how am I supposed to resist you?"

"That's easy," Nate shrugged. "You aren't."

The man was impossible. Deciding to change tactics, Paige came at him with logic.

"How long have we known each other?"

"I know where you're going with this, Paige. But…"

"Less than forty-eight hours."

Paige plowed ahead. Nate's argument, whatever it was going to be, would be tempting. She looked at his mouth and sighed. Too tempting. Especially when she knew how good he tasted. The man was a big sexy walking temptation. He might as well have a neon arrow flashing over his head that said, 'Mind-blowing Sex Guaranteed.'

"You need more time."

"I've never had sex with a man that I've known for less than three months."

"Say again?"

"You've slept with women you just met?"

"Once or twice." Or more.

Paige leveled a look at Nate.

"What can I say?"

"I don't want you to say anything, Nate." Paige absently ran her finger around the rim of her cup. "I don't care about that. I don't want to know who, what, where, when, or how many. Are you always safe?"

"Always," Nate said emphatically. No glove, no love was something his parents drilled into their sons' heads from an early age.

"And healthy?"

"I've never even had a cavity." Nate opened his mouth wide, showing her his perfect pearly whites.

"No need to show off," Paige laughed.

"I would never put you at risk, Paige."

Paige felt warmth steal over her. The tone of Nate's voice. The truth in his clear, blue eyes. He was such a good man. Sexy and sweet. Women who thought they liked the bad boy would change their tune in a flash if they got a load of Nate.

"That's all I needed to know. The rest is your business, Nate. I would prefer you keep it that way."

"Not a fan of kissing and telling?"

"God, no. Do you want to hear about my past sex life? Admittedly, it isn't as colorful or varied as yours, but it does exist."

Nate frowned at the thought. Hearing about someone else's sex life could be fun. Hearing about Paige's. No. No. And a big fat NO!

"How long do you need?" Nate was a fan of deadlines. When he had a goal in his sights, he became more determined. "A week? Two? There is a ticking clock, Paige. I won't be here forever."

It took a moment, but after a few seconds of silence, Nate realized he had hit on the problem. Or at least, a big stumbling block.

"I'm not a blushing virgin, Nate."

"Thank God. I don't know what I would do with one."

Paige laughed. "If you wanted her enough, you'd figure it out."

Nate pretended to contemplate the idea before smiling back. "I like a challenge."

"I'm not." Paige sighed. "A challenge. I'm not trying to be difficult. This isn't me being coy. I don't think I could if I wanted to."

"Paige." Nate put his hand over hers. He could feel the nerves vibrating through her. "Games can be fun. I played them when I was younger. I had more energy and a hell of a lot more patience back then. Now, I prefer straightforward. I want you."

"*I* want *you*."

"I'll be here six, maybe seven weeks."

"I know."

Nate looked directly into Paige's eyes. "I'm not looking for anything long-term."

Paige leaned closer, her gaze as steady as his. "Neither am I."

"So…?"

"So. We let nature take its course."

Paige turned her hand so her palm met his, curving her fingers. His hand was big and strong, calloused. She knew instinctively that she could trust him to keep her body safe. Fleetingly, she wondered about her heart.

"My nature says throw everything on the floor and have sex on the table."

The wild part of Paige's nature wanted to shout, *yes please*. The practical part reminded her where they were.

"My dad is feeding the horses. He could walk in at any moment."

Shit. Chuck. Nate had completely forgotten about Paige's father. It was a testament to her growing appeal. He knew better than to let his dick do the thinking. However, something about this woman made the world narrow. When he talked to her, she was all he saw. It was exciting and disconcerting all at once.

Nate fed Beauty the last bite of toast. She could barely keep her eyes open. Swallowing, she rested her head on her paws and sighed. She was warm, full, and knew with complete certainty that Nate would be there when she awoke. With that last thought, she slept.

"What is this?" Paige ran her thumb over the braided band that circled Nate's wrist. "I noticed it before."

"It's a buddy bracelet." Nate smiled. "A little boy who was very sick visited the set of a movie I worked on. He was in a wheelchair because he was too weak to walk, but his head was filled with dreams of being a stuntman."

"It isn't fair." Paige squeezed Nate's hand. "Children shouldn't get sick."

"No," Nate agreed emphatically. "I've worked with the foundation before. Seeing a child like that never gets easier."

"But you do it."

"Could you say no?" When Paige shook her head, Nate nodded. "I showed him and his parents around the set. God, he was bright, Paige. Everything interested him and he had a million questions. By the end of the day, he could barely hold his head up, but he left with a smile on his face. I received the bracelet in the mail a week later with a thank you note."

"What happened to the boy?" Paige's throat felt thick with the tears she wanted to cry for the little boy — for all the little boys and girls. She had to ask even as she dreaded the answer.

"Complete remission." Nate smiled. As good news went, it was about as good as you got. "This bracelet stays put."

"Are you superstitious, Nate?"

"No more than anyone else. However, why push my luck? Andy is playing soccer this year for the first time and I plan on going to a game. Hopefully, I'll get to go every year for a long, long time."

Later, Paige wondered what she would have said if her father hadn't chosen that moment to enter the kitchen. He broke the intense mood with the rush of fresh air and cheery greeting. Grabbing a cup, Chuck poured himself some coffee. He smiled at Paige but when he saw the puppy, he grinned.

"Who is that?"

Nate told Chuck the story while Paige cleaned up the breakfast dishes. Her back to the men, she let her mind wander.

It wasn't fair, she thought, stacking the plates in the dishwasher. The more she learned about Nate, the more she wanted to know. In her experience, men became *less* interesting the longer she was around them. Paige had the feeling that Nate Landis was a bottomless well of interesting. Uncovering the layers would take years. Decades. *A lifetime.*

Where had that come from? When she had told Nate that she wasn't looking for anything permanent, Paige had told him the truth. He didn't fit into her plans for so many reasons. Most importantly, Nate inhabited a different world. Not just geographically.

His family. The money. Paige didn't think he was a snob. However, she didn't know anything about Hollywood beyond the tabloid headlines and *Entertainment Tonight*. They were not a fit outside of the here and now. She would be a fool to think otherwise.

Paige knew what this was. Sex. Plain and simple. The attraction was off the charts. It had been from the moment she laid eyes on Nate. It was flattering to find out he felt the same. The important thing was to never forget. Their time together had a ticking clock attached. When the sand ran out of the hourglass, that was it.

No matter what, she would have to watch Nate walk out of her life. The last thing Paige wanted was a lifetime of regret because she didn't act on her desire. Her choice was simple. Take what Nate had to offer or turn her back on a passion she might never find again.

When put like that, the answer was amazingly easy. She would jump. Eyes wide open.

"I need a shower." Nate stood, cradling the sleeping puppy in his good arm. "This girl needs to see a veterinarian. Is there a good one in the area?"

"Dr. Mount," Chuck said over the rim of his cup. "Paige works with her rescuing horses and finding them homes. She specializes in large animals, but I'm sure she'll look at Beauty."

"I'll get her number later and set up an appointment. Right now, we have people arriving at eight. There is prep I want to go over with both of you."

"If that little lady will let me, I'll take her outside while you shower. We don't want her peeing in the house."

The transfer from Nate to Chuck went without any fuss. Beauty seemed content that she was in good hands, especially when Nate whispered to her that he wasn't going anywhere.

"Do you think she understood you?" Paige smiled.

"The words? No. I do think she knows the tone. She is a sweetheart. If I ever get my hands on the asshole that left her to die, he won't be eating solid food for a month."

Paige blinked in surprise. Nate came across as an easygoing guy. Quick to laugh. Someone who let things roll off his back with little worry. Yesterday was a perfect example. He had been thrown into the middle of her father's movie dreams and on top of that, had the directing job foisted onto him.

The way he handled the inexperienced cast and crew made Paige shake her head in wonder. He found a way to soothe nerves, tamp down some cases of robust enthusiasm, and charm everyone. Nate managed all this while somehow maintaining his role as leader and authority figure.

And Nate did all of that with good humor and charm.

That was why the steel in his eyes while he made the matter-of-fact threat to Beauty's previous owner sent a shiver down Paige's spine. *Holy shit.* Was it twisted that his alpha male chest pounding gave her a sexual thrill? She had no idea. Nor did she care. This was one of those layers she was peeling back and she liked what she saw. A lot.

"Nate?"

"Hmm?"

Paige moved closer. Then took one more step until she could feel the heat of his body. He smelled so good. Clean, male sweat. And Nate. It was a heady combination. She put her hands on his chest, smiling when she saw the spark her touch set off in his clear blue eyes.

"You said I would have to make the next move."

"I remember."

"Consider it made."

Paige felt a flutter around her heart an instant before her lips touched Nate's. Nerves? Excitement? Anticipation? All of the above? Plus that bit of the unknown. She was ninety-nine percent certain that this was a good idea. That one percent worried her. As Nate pulled her close, Paige had a fleeting thought.

What if my heart isn't safe?

She didn't have time to worry about it. What Paige had started, Nate had taken over.

This was no tentative 'let's try something' kiss. Now that Nate had her approval, he was all in.

"You taste like sweet honey," Nate growled the words into her ears.

Paige tipped her head, giving Nate access. She sighed. *When had that spot become so sensitive?* She hated having her neck slobbered on. However, what Nate did could never be called slobbering. Every touch of his tongue sent tiny sparks through her body.

Unable to stand it a second longer, Paige threaded her fingers through Nate's impossibly soft hair, tugging until his mouth returned to hers.

Paige felt as though she was discovering kissing for the first time. Whatever it was she had experienced before, it was nothing like this. Nate hadn't invented it. However, he put a new spin on the activity that put every other man to shame.

Not too hard. Firm. Commanding. Nate wasn't afraid to take what he wanted, yet he never made Paige feel like she wasn't a full participant.

"You make my head spin." Paige opened her eyes to find Nate looking at her. "You've had a lot of practice."

"I was twelve years old when Maisie Plumber gave me my first kiss. It's been a favorite pastime of mine ever since."

"Thank you, Maisie."

Paige's lips caught Nate's one last time before she reluctantly moved away. Touching him felt good. Too good. It wouldn't take much effort on his part to get her up those stairs and into her bedroom. Tempting. However, this wasn't the time or the place.

"That felt like an 'I've made up my mind' kiss." Nate smiled. He looked as happy about that as Paige felt. "What pushed you my way?"

"I like you. What?" Paige asked, laughing at the disgruntled expression on Nate's face.

"I hoped it was my overwhelming charisma and sexual magnetism."

"Don't be so needy." Paige gave Nate a playful punch on his rock hard abs. "You know your own appeal." It screamed from every inch of him.

"My turn. What is that expression about?"

"It's silly."

"I'm a fan of silly." Nate's eyebrows lifted. "Tell me."

Paige sighed. Nate was one of those people who wouldn't let something go.

"Let's get one thing straight. I'm asking you this out of curiosity. It isn't a come on."

"I thought I was curious before."

"Remember," Paige said.

"You aren't coming on to me. Got it."

God, this was embarrassing. Taking a deep breath, Paige plunged forward.

"Would you lift your shirt?"

"My shirt?" The look Nate gave her was confused — and a little intrigued.

"Please?"

"How can I say no when you ask so nicely? How's that?"

Paige wondered if she had drool on her chin. That bit of tanned skin that he exposed was better than she imagined it would be. She wanted to beg for more. *Rip the shirt off.* Then she could fall to her knees and lick every well-defined ridge.

"Paige?"

"Hmm?"

"Say the word and I'll show you every inch. Every long…"

Long? Paige's chest heaved.

"Hard…"

No fair. She couldn't remember the last time she had long *and* hard.

Nate's eyes lowered to his groin. Unable to resist, Paige's gaze followed.

"Very hard. Harder by the second."

"You are a mean, mean man."

"You started it," Nate unnecessarily reminded her.

"I'm not the one who has to suffer with that thing." Paige nodded toward the straining zipper on Nate's jeans.

Grinning, Nate shrugged. "I'll take care of it in the shower. Unless you would like to wash my… back?"

"Wait?" Paige held her hand to her ear. "Do you hear that? I think my father is calling. Bye."

The thought of Chuck was more effective than a bucket of ice. Nate heard the door slam, signaling Paige's exit. How the hell did that woman scramble his brains to the point he forgot the possibility that Chuck could interrupt them at any moment?

Lift your shirt. Nate knew what she was up to as soon as Paige asked. His body was his livelihood. It was up to him to keep it in tip-top working condition. It was his instrument. His tool. Sometimes, his weapon. His muscles had nothing to do with vanity and everything to do with giving himself every advantage when doing his job.

That said, Nate knew what he looked like. Good genes played a big part. He and his brothers hit the jackpot. A beautiful mother, a handsome father. Both sides had a history of long, healthy lives. Add that to his disciplined regimen of eating right and never missing a workout, Nate was what one lady friend had called catnip. A fact that he took advantage of at every opportunity.

Women liked him. And he liked women. It was a happy symbiosis. However, this was the first time he could remember reacting so strongly to a woman's appreciative gaze. With Paige, Nate lost all sense of time and place. He promised Chuck that nothing would happen in his house. One hot look from Paige and he almost forgot.

Nate reached past the shower curtain, turning the faucet on full blast. In spite of what he told Paige, he made the temperature on the cold side. Considering for a second, he shrugged and turned the hot water off. Before he could think better of it, Nate shed his clothes. *Damn dick,* he admonished his erect organ. *This will serve us both right.*

Taking a deep breath, Nate walked under the spray. The string of colorful and inventive curse words that spewed from his mouth was a testament to a childhood growing up on movie sets.

His mother tried to shield Nate and his brothers from the coarse language while his father shrugged it off. *Boys are expected to pick up curse words* he told their mother. *It would be different if they'd had girls.* Not the most enlightened attitude and one that got him a dirty look and a night in the guest room from his wife.

Callie Flynn insisted her sons curb their bad language whenever possible. It wasn't a problem — most of the time. However, icy water hitting an engorged cock seemed like a good time to call an exception. Nate's mother would have been appalled. His father would have been the first to sympathize.

The remedy didn't cure his problem; it simply reduced it. Nate stepped out of the cold shower. He should have jacked off — given himself some temporary relief. However, sometimes his hand was a poor substitute. Especially when having Paige was more than a possibility. Soon. Very soon, he hoped.

He could suffer until then. If he'd done his job properly, Paige pictured him in the shower. Naked. Touching himself. Misery loved company. He suffered and since she was the reason, he thought it only fair that she know a little of what he felt.

Nate slipped a towel around his waist and headed for his bedroom. Unlike when he left for his run, the sun streamed through the window. His bed was already made, no sign of his restless night remained.

Another thing he could thank his mother for. His parents expected them to keep their rooms neat and tidy. Picking up after himself was second nature.

He was about to grab some clothes from the dresser when his phone buzzed. Picking it up, Nate sighed. Great. A text from Garrett. It seemed his brother hadn't forgotten his promise. Or was it a threat. He supposed it depended on what was in the text.

Resigned, Nate looked. Then looked again. Staring in disbelief, Nate barely contained the impulse to smash his phone against the wall. Instead, he sat on the bed. He looked at the screen. Then looked again.

Somewhere, Garrett was laughing his ass off.

"Son of a bitch!"

Chapter Nine

NATE SETTLED EVERYONE into their roles with surprising ease.

Working the camera that Chuck borrowed was simple. Aim and shoot. That was it. The young grocery clerk assigned to the job seemed at ease with the piece of equipment. Homer Freed informed Nate that he was an amateur photographer. Nate patiently waited while Homer opened his iPad and scrolled through some of his photos.

Nice composition. Good lighting. Homer had a good eye for his subjects. Nate would keep an eye on the young man, but he believed Homer knew what he was doing. It appeared he had one less thing to worry about.

The call sheet for the morning, or rather the phone calls Chuck made last night, consisted of six people. Nate decided it would be best to work with small numbers as often as possible. It was an intimate story. Plus, the fewer people on set meant less chance for distractions and accidents.

Nate worried about someone getting hurt. It wasn't a huge concern.

The biggest, and only, stunt would come later when a pickup truck ran off the road and into a tree. It would require one person. Nate. The biggest problem was finding a vehicle to wreck. Chuck swore he had that taken care of so Nate put it out of his mind

Nate shook his head in amazement. Chuck was a wonder. He understood why the man had been in high demand when he worked in Hollywood. Between the equipment, the volunteers, and God knew what else, all that was left was for Nate to step in and make a movie.

"How did you get anyone to insure you?" Nate helped Chuck unload some cables from the back of Paige's truck.

"Wilt runs the local insurance office."

Nate gave a shout of laughter. Leave it to Chuck. To get the coverage he needed, he cast in the lead the man who could provide it. Genius.

"He *is* the best choice for the part," Chuck added with a smile.

"Undoubtedly." Nate slapped him on the back. "If you ever want to come back to Los Angeles, Chuck, you could make a fortune."

"I did fine when I was there." Chuck set down the box. Taking a deep breath, he looked around. "This is home, Nate. Everything I want is here. The only thing that would make it perfect would be my Erin."

"I'm sorry, Chuck. You must miss her."

"Every day." Chuck breathed in again. "She's with me, Nate. Someday, if you're lucky enough to have what Erin and I had, you'll understand. Her body was taken from me, but her memory, her soul, is right here on the Double C."

"Mom and Dad have that," Nate said.

"Then you do have an idea of what I mean. You've been lucky, son. You know what love looks like. You know how precious it is. When it happens to you, you won't make the mistake of letting it go; you understand that feelings like that are a gift. They don't come along every day."

"No, sir. They don't."

"Dad, there's a delivery that you need to sign for."

Nate watched as Paige walked toward them, her smile bright and easy. He tried to ignore the little ping he felt in the region of his heart. All this talk about love and forever. It was bound to send a man's thoughts in that direction. Enter a beautiful woman? It was only natural for him to feel… things.

When Nate told Paige he wasn't looking for anything long-term, he wasn't lying. He wanted what his parents had — what Chuck and his Erin were lucky enough to find. However, he didn't want it now. *Did he?* He gave Paige a longer look then shook his head. Nope. Not ready.

"I got a call from Dr. Mount."

"The vet?" Nate asked. Happy for the distraction, he fell in step with Paige.

"She has a horse at her place that she wants me to look at. The former owner is in jail on charges of animal cruelty. They had to put down all the horses but this one. Irene fought hard to save it. She wants me to give her a second opinion."

"It's a tough job. Life and death decisions can't be easy."

"No." Paige's eyes were sad when she looked at him. "Irene deals with it more than I do. When she *does* save an animal, the rest is worth it."

Nate made sure no one was watching before he took Paige's hand. The last thing either of them needed was gossip about a romance. Movie sets were tiny worlds often shut off for hours, days, sometimes months at a time. This one was smaller than most, *and* everyone already knew each other. Word would travel fast. To Basic and beyond. He didn't think Paige wanted to be the subject of tabloid gossip.

If he had half a brain, Nate would stop what was happening between them before they took the next step. He could slow down the gossip, but he couldn't prevent it. If he stepped back now, Paige's name and face would never hit the supermarket checkout lanes. She didn't deserve the notoriety that came with the Landis name. He chose to work in this business. Dragging Paige into it wasn't fair unless she knew what to expect.

"You know that I'm famous. Or rather, my family name is recognized all over the world. I'm a minor player, but when you're a Landis, you can't help but get sucked in now and then."

"Minor player?" Paige's eyes twinkled as she pulled out her phone. "I'd say you've made the big time."

Nate groaned when he saw what was on the screen.

"Don't teenage girls have better things to do with their time?"

Sometime after they had met, Jenna and her friends made a Facebook page devoted to Nate. And Instagram. And Twitter. And God knew how many others. The pictures were easy to come by. The internet was filled with them. However, seeing them all together, some with hearts drawn around his face, was more than Nate could stomach. He wasn't a movie star. Or a public figure. He was a hard-working grunt. And he liked it that way.

He knew it was a temporary blip. The minor excitement these girls generated would die down as soon as they found someone else to lift onto their wobbly, impermanent pedestals. He would survive with little, if any, damage.

He worried about Paige.

"You know I would never hurt you." Nate squeezed her hand. It was friendly. Comforting. Not the least bit sexual.

"Nothing that starts like that can end well," Paige said with a smile. Inside, her stomach wound into a mess of knots. Was it possible to dump someone when nothing had happened beyond a few kisses?

"I didn't think ahead of the here and now."

"I like the here and now. I thought we already agreed. This lasts as long as you're in Montana. What's changed?"

"That?" Nate pointed toward her phone. "The Landis name draws its own attention. I've managed to avoid the publicity circus — with a few exceptions."

"Like dating Nina Starr?"

Nate barely contained his wince.

"We didn't date. We…" How could he put it delicately?

"Screwed?"

Nate nodded. If he were honest, *screwed* was too nice a word. For one gloriously hedonistic month, he and the lead singer of *Wanderlust* fucked like overheated rabbits. Then it was over. No regrets. No recriminations.

By mutual agreement, they ended it as quickly as it began — walking away friends.

The press glommed onto them as the next hot couple, dubbing them N & N. One clever headline read *Landis sees his Starr rising*. He and Nina got a good laugh out of that. One of the reasons they remained on good terms was that neither wanted anything beyond what they'd had in the bedroom.

Nina was successful. She wasn't using his name in hopes of taking another step up the Hollywood ladder. Nate was his own man. He didn't need her money or the shine some men hoped would rub off on them when they spent time in the company of a famous woman.

"What are you afraid is going to happen, Nate?"

"The tabloids can be brutal." Nate frowned, his eyes a little sad. "I don't want you to have to duck cameras or nasty questions. If we do this."

"Sleep together?"

"Yes." Nate tapped her phone. "That seems harmless. Funny. And it is. When you see your face, with a not very flattering caption, you won't be laughing."

"I see." Paige pulled her hand from his. "You don't think much of me, do you?"

"I think about you all the time. That's the problem."

"No. I'm not talking about how your dick reacts to me." Paige's eyes weren't sad. They were angry, headed rapidly toward pissed off. "You think I'm weak? You see me as a woman who would crumble because of a little negative publicity?"

"Paige—"

"You're right. We need to stop. *I'm* no longer interested." Slowly, her gaze traveled up the length of Nate's body. "No matter how pretty the package."

"Damn it, Paige. That's not what I meant."

Ignoring him, Paige slid into the cab of her truck. "Go fuck yourself, Nate. I won't."

Nate stood with his mouth open, watching Paige drive away.

What the hell just happened?

"Hey, Nate." Chuck walked into the barn, his confused expression mirroring Nate's. "What sent Paige out of here with a bee in her bonnet? She was steaming worse than my Granny's teapot."

"You explain women to me, Chuck, and I'll tell you why she was mad."

"It's like that, is it?" Chuck grinned. "Paige's mother didn't lose her temper often, but when she did? Watch out. Most of the time I didn't know what I'd done."

"That's a big help." Nate's words dripped with sarcasm, mixed with a big dose of frustration.

"I'll share a secret. If you're interested."

"Jesus, Chuck. I have a movie to make and a woman who gets pissed off when I'm trying to be a good guy. Hell yes, I'm interested."

"It isn't a mystery. If you asked him, your dad would probably tell you the same thing."

"Should I call him or are you going to spill?"

Chuck laughed. Nate had the feeling the other man enjoyed this way too much.

"No need to bother him. Three words. *You. Are. Wrong.*"

"I'm wrong? *I'm* wrong?" Nate scrubbed a hand over his face. "What if I'm not?"

"Trust me. Ninety-nine times out of a hundred, you are."

"But—"

"Never mind about that one time. You're wrong ninety-nine times, son."

"I—"

"*Ninety-nine.*"

Nate didn't like those odds. Nor was he convinced it was true. He scoured his brain, remembering the times his parents argued. It was often. Oh, they had some spectacular blow-ups. Loud voices. Outrageous verbal exchanges.

Down to earth on most days, when Callie Flynn chose, she was the ultimate drama queen. Hand gestures that could knock an eye out if one didn't watch where he stood. She liked to recite Shakespeare. Lesser-known passages filled with fury and blood.

His father might be a producer by profession, but deep down a thespian longed to be heard. He gave as good as he got. She wanted to do Shakespeare? Caleb Landis countered with Marlowe. It was a sight to see.

It ended the same every time. In the bedroom. Confusing when you were seven. Embarrassing when you were thirteen. Now? Nate cheered his parents' unflagging libidos. He hoped he was still hot for his wife when he was in his sixties.

However, real, deep down fights were rare. Nate could count on one hand, with fingers to spare, the times his parents walked away from each other. Silence signaled true anger.

"Mom and Dad rarely fight."

"When they do?" Chuck prompted.

Nate pictured flowers. Big, over the top arrangements. Jewelry. His mother was a fan of emeralds. Some were given on her birthday. Or Christmas. The spectacularly large ones came after fights.

"Don't get me wrong, Nate. Women make mistakes. They blunder around. They say and do stupid things. The difference is, we do it more often. And when we do, we do it spectacularly."

"I'll take your word for it." Nate's head was swimming. He felt more confused than when he started. "How do I fix something when I don't know what I did? When I don't *think* I did anything?"

"Think about it," Chuck advised with a little too much good humor for the mood Nate was in. "If you don't figure it out, Paige will let you know. In her own good time. Oh, I almost forgot. Paige asked me to tell you. She took Beauty with her so the vet could check her out."

"She could have told me personally that she was taking my dog."

Laughing, Chuck grabbed a box and headed out of the barn.

The sound of a familiar ringtone had Nate snatching up his phone. A picture of his mother filled the screen. Not only was she a woman, but she was also the smartest person he knew. Hoping for a voice of reason, he answered.

"Mom. How do you always know when I need you?"

"EXCEPT FOR A bruise on her left rump, Beauty is in perfect condition."

"Do you think she fell?" Paige ran her hand over the puppy's head. It was meant to comfort, though whether it helped the dog or herself, she wasn't sure.

"My best guess is someone kicked her."

"Poor baby," Paige crooned.

Beauty cocked her head, as though sensing something was wrong. What, she had no idea. She couldn't be happier with all the attention. Even better, Paige smelled like Nate. To her, that meant he wasn't far away.

"She knows that she fell into a pot of jam when Nate Landis found her," Dr. Mount said, observing Beauty's vigorously wagging tail.

"It was love at first sight."

"Puppy love?"

Paige groaned.

"Really, Irene? How often do you pull out that old chestnut?"

"I work with large animals. I don't get many chances to make puppy puns. I figured I better jump at the opportunity."

Irene Mount was a strong, independent woman. Her mother swore she came out of the womb ready to take on the world. Born in Boston to an old-money family, she was expected to follow one of two paths. Marry into a family of equal wealth and status. Or go to college, work in an acceptable profession for a few years — then marry the man her parents handpicked.

Irene had known before she hit puberty that she wanted door number three.

Boys were great. Though she always went for the ones she couldn't introduce to her family. Not thugs or delinquents, but boys whose fathers' names didn't end with Roman numerals.

The one and only blow-up had occurred before Irene was supposed to come out. She thought it a ridiculous, arcane term. *Come out? What was she? A lesbian debutante?* It was meant as a joke. Unfortunately, her family had no sense of humor

The moment the words came out of her mouth, Irene's father raised his voice for the first time in her memory, the noise echoing through the normally silent mansion. Servants stopped in their tracks. Her mother had the vapors. Genuine, nineteenth century vapors. The family doctor was summoned. Smelling salts were applied. If Irene hadn't been in the middle of it, she would have found it anthropologically fascinating.

However, these were staunch, conservative Republicans. Homophobia ran rampant. Parents passed the affliction down from generation to generation along with stiff upper lips and snobbery.

There was only one known cure. Amputation. With a slight trace of regret, Irene cut off her family like a gangrenous limb. To this day, the pain lingered. However, she realized the second she walked out of those stifling walls that she hadn't breathed, really breathed, for the first eighteen years of her life.

The road she decided to go down hadn't been easy. She stumbled. A few times she fell. Hard. But not once had she been tempted to return to Boston or the life she left behind.

The cards she sent on birthdays and holidays were returned unopened. She made her choice — and so did her family.

Veterinary school came as a surprise. She needed a job. Working at the Chicago Zoo, cleaning cages wasn't glamorous, but it paid the bills while she took basic night school courses. She fell in love with the animals — and the man who looked after them.

He encouraged her to take a few classes in animal husbandry. Then a few more. She was on her way before she realized the destination. The love affair didn't work out. It seldom did when the man was married and never intended to leave his wife.

However, Irene found her passion. She worked hard to become one of the most respected large animal veterinarians in the country. She moved to Montana because she fell in love with it while vacationing with friends. They thought she was crazy when she announced she would leave Chicago for Basic.

Irene considered it one of the smartest things she had ever done. She and her practice thrived. Her reputation meant she consulted with other vets all over the world. When necessary, she flew where she was needed.

She knew the moment she saw the sleepy little town at the base of the Bitterroot Mountains. For the first time in her life, she was home.

Irene and Paige's friendship began soon after Paige returned from college. Her mother's illness made it difficult for her to work with her beloved horses. Despite the circumstances, taking over wasn't a hardship. Paige's love for the animals was inbred. Irene would drop by the ranch to visit Erin. That was when the subject of taking in rescue horses first arose.

It was a gradual process. Irene didn't want the horses placed with a novice who would lose interest, or worse, do more damage to the traumatized, neglected animals. It didn't take long for Irene to discover that Paige was a natural. She had a gentle touch and a firm belief in what they were doing.

Almost two years later, the women had a smooth working relationship and a strong friendship. It made segueing from the subject of Nate as Beauty's new owner, to him as her potential new lover, easier. Almost. Discussing her love life wasn't something Paige was comfortable doing. Not with Lottie. Not with Irene.

"I hear Nate Landis has made quite a stir with the young women of Basic." Irene calmly gave Beauty a shot in the rump. The puppy took it with good grace, licking Irene's hand in forgiveness. "All my patients should be so sweet. The last one I treated tried kicking me in the face."

"Lucky for us all you're quick on your feet."

Paige made light of it, but she knew there were dangers involved when working with any animal. The large ones that Irene specialized in didn't always understand that she was there to help them. Their instincts, especially when sick or injured, were to lash out. Irene was fortunate. She had sustained plenty of bruises and a few lacerations. Nothing worse.

Soft hands and soothing words helped. However, vigilance was the key. The moment she became distracted, that was when she opened herself to broken bones. A friend from college had died last year when he was kicked in the head. It wasn't something Irene liked to dwell on. She needed her mind clear and focused at all times.

Irene was good at her job because she cared. She loved what she did. It got her out of bed in the morning and sent her back happily exhausted every night. She knew what it was to let fear rule her life. That ended when she left Boston. Never again.

"Pilates and clean living keep these increasingly old bones spry."

"Oh, please," Paige scoffed. "Old? You?"

"Fifty next month."

"Since when is that old?" Paige wasn't being kind. She meant every word. Her father was pushing sixty and he hadn't lost a step. "You look fifteen years younger."

It was true. Irene was a slender woman. A few inches shorter than Paige, she stood tall and straight, her body strong. She wore her hair short, the dark strands cut in a flattering bob that skimmed just below her chin. Good bones and bright hazel eyes gave her face a classic quality. She drew a person's notice with a combination of vitality and intelligence. Pretty faded. What Irene had lasted a lifetime.

"I wasn't searching for compliments." Though she was pleased by Paige's words. "Now spill the info. Is Nate Landis as yummy in person as he is in all those pictures on his fan page?"

"Irene!" Paige was genuinely surprised. "Did you like his page?"

"Maybe. I'm only human, Paige." Irene smiled. "When I stopped by the diner for dinner last night, it was all anyone could talk about. My curiosity was aroused. And speaking of aroused. Wow! I quickly discovered why the women were buzzing like rabid bees."

"Do bees become rabid?"

"Smartass," Irene laughed. "You know what I meant."

"I do. And I can tell you he isn't thrilled by all the attention."

"He *is* a Landis, right?" Irene set Beauty on the scale, recording her weight. "Isn't he used to being in the spotlight?"

"According to Nate, that isn't his thing. He prefers being the anonymous Landis."

"With that big, tall, gorgeous body? How has he pulled that off?"

"You're looking at it from Basic, Montana. In Hollywood, every other guy looks like Nate."

The second the words came out of her mouth, Paige knew how crazy they were. No one looked like Nate. He stood out, even in a family of beautiful people.

"Okay," Paige conceded, returning Irene's grin. "He's unique. However, he's found a way to stay behind the scenes. Apparently, stuntmen are invisible."

"Interesting. There you go, Beauty." Irene set the puppy on the floor so she could explore and sniff out any interesting smell. The office was small and cleaned once a week, so there wasn't any mischief for her to get into.

"You still haven't answered my question. Does the man live up to his pictures?"

"Yes. And then some. Why don't you come over for dinner tonight and see for yourself? Dad put a pot of his world famous chili on to cook this morning. I know you're a fan. It's been too long since you stopped by."

"True." Irene had her reasons for avoiding the Double C. Or rather, the man who owned the ranch. It was a complicated story and not one she wanted to share with Paige. Luckily, she had a legitimate excuse. "Not tonight. I have a business meeting."

"Sometime this week?"

Friends. They were a blessing and a curse. She couldn't keep pushing Paige away. She was too important. "I'm free at the end of the week. Friday?"

"Perfect."

"Now that we've settled that. What's the problem, Paige? Why does Nate Landis have you so skittish?"

"He's... I don't know, Irene. I thought I understood what I felt. There's nothing wrong with good old-fashioned lust, is there?"

"I'm a big fan," Irene said. "As long as it doesn't hurt anyone. You're single. He's single?"

Paige nodded.

"The feeling is mutual?"

"Yes."

"Then lust away." Irene picked up Beauty, handing her to Paige. "Go and grab yourself a handful of sexy man."

"What was simple early this morning became complicated. Nate's flirted with me since he stepped off the plane. Though at first, I thought he was interested in Lottie."

"All men are interested in Lottie. She's a doll. Uncomplicated. Men like women who are easy to understand. Now, don't give me that look."

"What look?"

"The one you get when you think a loved one has been insulted." Irene patted Paige's hand. "You know I think the world of Lottie. She has a heart as big as Montana. What I meant was she lives for the moment. If she likes a man, she acts on it. You are a tougher nut to crack."

"So Lottie is a peanut and I'm what?"

"Macadamias have the hardest shell."

Paige loved Irene's mind. Brilliant in her profession, her brain was filled with endless trivial facts that she could pull out at a moment's notice.

"What is the second—"

"No," Irene vigorously shook her head. "You can't distract me. I can tell when you need to talk things through, Paige."

"You're right." Paige absently scratched Beauty behind her ear. "I planned on resisting his charm."

"How long did that last?"

"The big jerk kissed me, Irene. Without warning, he grabbed me and…"

"And?" Irene asked breathlessly.

"I've read about women melting. They feel like their bones have turned to goo."

"Mmm, I remember that feeling."

"I don't," Paige sighed. "I thought it was a bunch of crap. The overwrought romantic drivel that sold books and set women up for disappointment."

"Nate didn't disappoint?"

"*Nate* could write a book. *The* book. Throw out all the rest, that man should teach a Master Class."

"Oh, my." Irene fanned herself with her hand.

"Then he's all *the next move is yours.*"

"What does that mean?" Irene frowned.

Paige filled Irene in on what happened with Lyle, including Nate's insistence that he wouldn't exert his will on her — no matter how willing he thought she was.

"I've never cared for Lyle. He tried too hard to be smooth. For the first time, he let some rough edges show. Nate, on the other hand, sounds like one of the good ones, Paige."

"He is, Irene. Too good." Paige smiled when she saw that Beauty was sound asleep. It must be nice to drop off so easily without a care in the world to plague your thoughts.

"No one is *too* good, Paige. Take my advice. Pull him off that pedestal before it gets too high."

"That isn't the problem," Paige said ruefully. "One second, I want to rip his clothes off, the next I'm so pissed off I can barely speak. That is *not* a man you put on a pedestal."

"He sounds like a man I can't wait to meet."

"Watch out. He'll flirt with you before you're in the door."

"Is that it? Nate goes after every woman he meets?"

The question made Paige pause. It was so easy to forget how little she knew about Nate. Two days since they met. How was that possible? He didn't feel like a guest, it felt like he belonged. It was dangerous to think that way. When he left — and he *would* leave — Paige was afraid it would be much harder to get used to *not* having him around.

"You don't know him."

Paige smiled. Leave it to Irene. She knew how to cut to the heart of the matter.

"I can't answer questions about him, Irene. I can only go by my instincts."

"You have good ones. What do they tell you?"

138

"He doesn't lie," Paige said emphatically. "Nate told me that he likes women. Obviously, women like him. Why bother to hide the obvious? He's made it clear. He isn't looking for a long-term relationship. Whatever happens, it's temporary."

"Is *that* the problem?" Taking the long way around wasn't Paige's usual style. Nate Landis had her twisted into an increasingly intricate knot. Irene wanted to help — if she could find out what was wrong.

"I made it clear that I felt the same way." And she did. The important thing was to keep reminding herself. "We set the ground rules. No strings. I had my mouth set for a big bite of Nate. Then wham!"

"Wham?"

"The tabloids," Paige said with disgust.

"I'm aware of them. I need you to elaborate."

"Right. Sorry."

"Take a deep breath," Irene instructed. "Let it out. Now, start again. Tabloids?"

"Nate is convinced that between the movie, and his new status as the newest teen-dream, if we begin an affair, I will be fodder for the gossip rags."

"Isn't he right?"

"Probably," Paige conceded. "I'm a big girl. Isn't it up to me to decide if I'm willing to deal with the attention? Nate wants to backtrack. Friends and only friends. Not because he doesn't want me. It's for my own good."

"That's what he said? Final? No debate?"

"Yes."

"Paige...?"

"Okay." Paige sighed. "I don't remember. There is the slightest chance that I overreacted. All I heard was him taking my choices away from me. After that, I was out of there."

"That doesn't sound like you."

"It isn't. Nate has the ability to scramble my brain. I don't like it."

No. Paige wouldn't like it. But Irene did. Paige was focused. They had that in common. She knew that the ability to look toward your goal, allowing no distractions, was a curse as well as a blessing. Irene had success. Prestige. Her bank account was nicely padded. And she was alone.

Friends were nice. Better than nice. However, they weren't there to hold you on a long, cold Montana night. Lately, she had uncharacteristic moments of wistfulness. If she had taken the time to look around once or twice on her journey, she might have that someone to wake up with every morning.

Perhaps she was projecting her feelings onto Paige. Everyone was different. It wouldn't hurt her friend to remove her blinders. Straight ahead was great. However, it did make her miss out on a big chunk of the world. Irene had some regrets. That was a part of living. There was nothing wrong with helping Paige avoid some of them.

"You didn't give him a chance to explain?"

"No. I grabbed his puppy and ran."

"I'm flattered that you ran to me." Irene squeezed Paige's hand. "Would you like a piece of advice from someone who is older but not necessarily wiser?"

"Always."

"Grab that man and have your way with him."

"What if he's really changed his mind?"

"Then change it back."

Paige's eyes widened. "I hadn't thought of doing that. I'm not sure I could."

Irene laughed. "He's a man. He wants you. It isn't rocket science, Paige."

Paige carried Beauty to her truck, her mind racing. Letting the puppy take care of her personal business, she praised her before setting her on the seat and climbing into the cab.

Taking a deep breath, she started the engine.

"It isn't rocket science, Beauty."

As she pulled out of the driveway, her nerves starting to jangle. Science had never been her best subject. However, compared to getting Nate Landis into bed? It had been a piece of cake.

Chapter Ten

"I NEED THIS like I need a hole in the head."

"Your father always said that getting people interested in a project was half the battle."

Nate gave Chuck a rueful smile.

"My father never dealt with a fan club of adoring teenage girls. Showing up with no warning because they want to *help*? I open my mouth and they act as though every word is the most fascinating proclamation since Moses came down Mt. Sinai."

"You could tell them to go home."

Nate noticed Chuck's twitching lips. The man was lousy at hiding his amusement.

"I tried. It was like kicking a bunch of overly perfumed kittens."

"They are... what's the word? Fragrant?"

"That's a kind way of putting it. And an understatement."

Nate rubbed the back of his neck. Five days in and he had to admit, the shoot was going well. They had several scenes in the can. He wanted to start with some small, intimate moments that set the tone of the story.

On the surface, the dialogue was straightforward. It was up to the actors to convey the subtext of a couple struggling to hold together a decaying marriage.

Unlike newlyweds settling into a new life with all the adjustments that went with the first year, they were a middle-aged couple who had let the problems silently pile up. Chipping away. Eroding a once rock-solid foundation. Their children were grown and gone. The small farm had seen better days. When they looked at each other, they saw a mirror of themselves. Tired. Feeling the years. Wondering if there was anything left for which to fight.

The unexpected arrival of their youngest daughter sparks the first real emotion between them in years. Over the course of three weeks, they slowly rebuild what seemed irretrievable.

It was a gentle story mixed with moments of high emotion. A true character study. Going in, Nate had few expectations. However, the first scene had been an eye opener. His actors were raw and mostly untrained. They brought to their roles an honesty few seasoned veterans could achieve. Untainted honesty.

What surprised Nate was the depth and power. He became caught up in the scene, almost forgetting to call cut. Delighted, he held his breath to see if that first scene was a fluke. It wasn't. If they could maintain the quality, this was going to turn out better than he ever imagined.

"Wilt and Edith?"

"What about them?" Chuck asked, taking a bite out of his sandwich.

There was a table laid out with enough food to feed three film crews. Salads, desserts. Three kinds of sandwiches and a crockpot full of beef barley soup. Nate ladled a spoonful into his mouth, sighing with pleasure.

"They're talented."

"Surprised?"

"Do I sound like a snob if I say yes?"

"Nope." Chuck handed Nate a cup of steaming coffee. "I'm surprised, too. I've been to every play they've been in. Fifteen years, fifteen productions. Like I said before, they have talent. What I've seen this week is something else. I can't figure out where it's coming from."

Nate sipped from the mug. He knew the basics of directing. And he had Garrett on speed dial if he started to feel like he was getting in over his head. A master, like his brother, could draw performances from his actors. Nate had no illusions. Whatever was going on with Wilt and Edith, he had nothing to do with it.

"Do you believe in possession?"

"No." Nate laughed. "Not before now. Garrett says there have been times when nothing he does can fix a scene. For whatever reason, the actors can't get their heads around the material. Suddenly, boom." Nate snapped his fingers. "Magic. As though they channeled someone else."

"You think Katherine Hepburn pops down now and then — just to keep her hand in?"

"Why not?" Nate winked.

"On her way, she picked up Henry Fonda." Chuck seemed to like the idea.

"It's a colorful explanation." Knowing how this kind of thing could gain traction, Nate looked the other man in the eye. "Let's keep it to ourselves, okay?"

"Absolutely. Your newly formed fan club would be tweeting that we have ghosts before we could blink."

"Ghosts I could handle. If they asked *who is Katherine Hepburn?* I wouldn't be responsible for my actions. I wouldn't know whether to kick their texting butts off the set or cry for the state of today's youth."

Chuck laughed. He enjoyed Nate. He was smart and had a quick, dry wit.

"Nate?"

"My lovely leading lady."

Nate put a hand on Edith Potter's shoulder. Small in stature, the dark-haired woman had a big personality. Her brown eyes were sharp and intelligent with a bit of a twinkle. In many ways, she reminded him of his mother. She knew her mind and wasn't afraid to speak it.

"Anxious to check out the dailies?" Nate asked her. Like everything else, playing back footage of the day's shoot was not done in a traditional manner. Homer connected the camera to Chuck's TV and they gathered in the living room to watch.

"Every morning, I wake up thinking this has to be a dream," Edith said. "I barely knew what dailies were before we started. Now, watching them seems like the most natural thing in the world. Me. Starring in a movie? Who would have thought it possible?" The words were filled with pride and a touch of self-deprecation. Nate was already a little in love.

"Was there something you needed?"

Edith nodded. "It's Wilt." Then she threw her head back and laughed. "Oh, hell. I'm not sticking it all on him. I want to know, too."

"Know what?"

"Are we making asses of ourselves? This is bigger than anything we've done, Nate. Erin's script is good." She reached over to squeeze Chuck's hand. "Damn good. We want to do her proud."

"I won't lie, Edith." Nate met the woman's steady gaze with this own. "I didn't have a lot of faith in you or Wilt. I took a wait and see approach."

"Well," Edith demanded, her hands on her hips. "What do you see?"

"Talent. Bone deep. This week I've seen something that can't be taught. You and Wilt have a rhythm that comes from years of working together. You're comfortable."

"Like old socks."

Nate smiled. "Like people who have lived. I can't tell you why it's working, Edith. However, I do have one piece of advice."

"What's that?"

"Keep doing it. If you do, we are going to have something special."

"She'll be floating on your words for weeks. Months."

Nate watched Edith scamper back to her little group of friends. She whispered, making big gestures with her hands. Wilt Adair sat for a moment, his mouth agape. Then he silently punched the air before twirling Edith into an impromptu jig.

Laughing, Nate took another drink of his coffee. He had been on sets where directors withheld praise of any kind. The idea was to keep everyone on pins and needles, wondering if they were doing a good job. Happy actors meant complacency. Complacency led to a loss of tension.

Nate understood it — in theory. It was his experience a relaxed set yielded the same results without teeth gnashing and nail biting. Making a movie was a naturally stressful experience. Nate refused to add to it.

"The kitchen scene is short and easy. Unless something unforeseen occurs, we should get it in a few takes."

"Then we wrap for the day?"

Nate nodded. "Here is the shooting schedule for the rest of the week. If anyone can't make it, let me know. We'll work around them."

He doubted that this was the first movie ever made that catered to the actors' *day jobs*. However, until now, Nate had never encountered one. The good part was, everyone wanted to make it work. And somehow, they would.

"I'll take this in the house and run off some copies." Chuck picked up his plate and mug. "Nate?"

"Hmm?"

"I don't know what I would have done if you weren't here."

"You'd have managed."

"No." Chuck shook his head. "I thought I could do it. Watching you makes it clear I was living in a dream world. I'm going to call your father tonight and thank him for sending you. Paige didn't know it at the time, but writing him saved the movie."

Paige. She was avoiding him. Which wasn't easy considering they shared a house. However, she managed to keep her distance. They exchanged pleasantries at dinner, but he rarely saw her the rest of the time. With Chuck busy with the movie, she spent her time out on the ranch.

During the day, he was too busy to think about her. Though, if he were honest, she was never far from his thoughts.

Had he been wrong when he suggested putting on the breaks? He was thinking of her, not himself. A selfish man would have taken her to bed and damn the consequences. Why was taking her into consideration a bad thing?

"Any ideas?"

Beauty gave him the same adoring look she always wore when he was around. Why couldn't all relationships be this easy and uncomplicated?

"You think I'm perfect." Nate picked the puppy up. "Every man should have a woman like you in his life."

"Because human women expect more than a tummy rub and the occasional juicy bone." Lottie tilted her head to the side, her lips pursed in thought. "Check that. *All* women need an occasional juicy bone."

Lottie had been a surprise. One of the many volunteers, Nate expected her to lobby him to be on screen. She had the kind of face the camera loved. Beauty didn't always transfer to the big screen. A pretty face could come off as blank and one dimensional if the actor didn't have the personality to back it up. Lottie had vibrancy to burn. Her energy and enthusiasm were unflagging.

Surprisingly, Lottie was happy to stay behind the scenes. She helped wherever she was needed. Moving equipment. Setting out food. Running errands. All the while lightly flirting with every man in her path.

Everyone took Lottie for who she was. Friendly and, for the most part, harmless. She didn't make a play for other women's men. Nate appreciated that. Though he would have regretted it, if her flirting started causing friction, he wouldn't hesitate to ban Paige's best friend from the set.

"How are you today, Lottie?"

Smiling, Lottie stood before him, beckoning with her finger for him to lean down to her level. Curious, Nate set Beauty on the ground. Instead of standing to his full height, he stopped when his eyes met Lottie's. A second later, he was sorry. Sweet as can be, Lottie flicked her index finger against his forehead. Hard.

"Hey." Nate rubbed the area, surprised by the gesture and the pain it caused. "What the hell was that for?"

"Be glad I didn't box your ears." For good measure, Lottie stood on her toes and flicked him again. This time, she hit his nose.

"Do you want me to knock you on your ass, Lottie?"

"Please," Lottie scoffed. "You wouldn't raise a finger to a woman."

Nate frowned. He crossed his eyes, trying to see if the end of his nose was as red as it felt.

"What makes you so certain?" Now, he wasn't feeling terribly chivalrous.

"It's written all over your gorgeous face. Besides, if I thought you had it in you, I wouldn't have stepped aside for Paige."

"Stepped aside for...?" Nate shook his head in disbelief. "Let me make this perfectly clear, Lottie. I was never interested in you."

"You would have been." When Nate opened his mouth to protest, Lottie cut him off. "Be honest. If you had never met Paige, you would have taken me for a spin by now."

Probably, Nate thought. He gave Lottie the once over. Curvy. Pretty. Uncomplicated. Okay. Definitely. She was exactly his type. How many Lotties had there been in his life? Not that he regretted a single one.

Nate never played unless everyone knew the rules. In that way, he and Lottie were kindred spirits. They liked things light and easy.

Then there was Paige. It always came back to her. She filled his thoughts like no woman before her. She knew the rules. He made them clear up front. That was where the similarities ended. He planned on walking away from Paige. Easy? Somehow, Nate knew the answer to that. It was a big, fat no.

When Lottie raised her hand, Nate stepped back.

"I swear. Flick me again and I'll kick you off the set."

"No, you won't," Lottie said smugly.

"Don't make the mistake of thinking you know me, Lottie. I have a streak of mean in me. It takes a lot to get to it, but push me enough and I'm a ruthless bastard when I need to be." Nate scooped up Beauty and headed for the house.

"I'm sorry." Lottie hurried to keep up. "You want Paige. Paige wants you. What's the problem?"

"This is none of your business."

"Hello. Best friend here." Lottie was about to rap on his arm with her fist. The look he gave her made her think better of it. "Sorry. I have Paige's best interests at heart."

"What did Paige say when you asked her?"

"She was frustratingly evasive." Lottie stamped her foot in frustration. "She never keeps things from me so I know you did something."

Nate might have taken pity on her if the subject wasn't such a personal one. Paige chose to keep the details to herself. So did he.

"You're going to have to stay on the sidelines, Lottie. Whatever happens is between Paige and me until she decides otherwise. I have nothing to say. Except, you were right. I would never intentionally hurt her."

"What about unintentionally?"

Without another word, Nate entered the house. He took Beauty into the mudroom, setting her down by her food and water bowls. He poured some kibble from the bag. Leaning back against the washing machine, watching absently as she dug in.

Nate hadn't let Lottie in on his feelings. That didn't mean her words had no effect. Paige wasn't talking to her best friend? Why? Nothing had happened that warranted secrecy — not when it was someone with whom you always shared the major moments of your life.

Maybe he was making too much of this. Nate frowned. He wasn't keen on the idea. If Paige wasn't upset, that meant she didn't care. Was he in this alone? He cared? Paige didn't? Shit. How fucked up would that be?

"Nate?"

Nate looked up happy for the distraction. Homer hung on the mudroom door, half in, half out.

"What's up?"

"You better come. We have a problem."

"WHAT DID HE say?"

Lottie pulled herself into the cab of Paige's truck, adjusting the hem of her short flirty skirt. Paired with the eye-popping cleavage she displayed, any man would have a hard time carrying on a reasonable conversation. Nate hadn't glanced at her boobs. The man was either inhuman or so far gone he didn't see anyone but Paige. Lottie smiled. She knew the answer even if he didn't.

"You're smiling." Paige turned in her seat. "Why? What's going on?"

"I can't believe I let you talk me into that." Secretly, Lottie loved every second. However, there was no reason to let Paige know. "Sending your best friend to find out if a boy likes you? It is *so* high school. Except we never did that in high school. We were too cool for this kind of shit."

"I didn't ask you to do that," Paige exclaimed. "Please tell me you didn't ask him if he likes me?"

"I asked him why he wasn't screwing your brains out," Lottie said.

"Not using those exact words. Right? Lottie?"

"Relax. Boy, do you need to get laid. It does wonders for your nerves. And before you blow a gasket, I was much more circumspect."

Paige let out a relieved breath. "So?"

"He's a gentleman."

Paige wanted to scream. Lottie loved to draw out a story. Normally, Paige enjoyed the telling. Not today. She wanted details. Now!

"He's a gentleman. What does that mean?"

"What happens when his pants are off stays between him and his partner. Wait." Lottie thoughtfully tapped her chin. "You haven't seen him with his pants off."

"Because he decided to play the—" Paige groaned.

"Yes?" Lottie urged, her eyes twinkling.

"He decided to play the gentleman." Paige slapped her forehead. "Shit. Double shit. Shit on steroids."

"Exactly."

Five days. It had taken her that long to get it. Sleepless nights. Making sure she spent as little time with him as possible. Silently fuming. Except when she was alone with the horses. Man. If they could talk. Would that be embarrassing?

It took Lottie to dig out the answer.

"Thank you." Paige wrapped Lottie in a warm hug.

"Have sex." Lottie laughed, her arms squeezing Paige back. "We'll both be a lot happier. You get to bite into the tasty Nate Landis, and I get the juicy details."

"Up to a point."

"Fine." Lottie took out her lip-gloss. Like a good man in her bed, she hated to be without her peaches and cream. "Set me up with his brother and we'll call it even."

"Which brother?"

"I don't care. If his last name is Landis, I'm in."

"I still have the problem of how I'm going to get *this* Landis." Paige frowned. "There isn't anywhere on the ranch suitable. Except for a quickie. With all the people wandering around, I wouldn't take a chance on that."

"My place is free." Lottie closed her purse with a decisive snap. "Danny Floyd has been after me for months to spend the night."

"That's perfect. Wait." Paige suddenly remembered. "Irene is coming to dinner tonight. I have to be here."

"You have an extra key. When Irene leaves, grab Mr. Gorgeous and head to my place. It's only fifteen minutes away. You can play to your heart's content and be back before your father wakes up."

"It feels… I don't know. I understand the reason, but sneaking around? We're adults."

"You share a house with your father. What's the alternative?"

Exchanging smiles with Lottie, Paige nodded.

"Your place it is."

"THE EXTRA CAMERA is broken. This door is always locked, Nate. I swear."

"Easy, Homer." The young man wrung his hands, obviously

distressed. "I believe you. It looks like someone jimmied the doorknob."

"Why?" Homer leaned next to Nate. There were definite signs that a tool had been used to open the lock. "I can see stealing the equipment. You could sell it for some cash. A nice bit of change, if you know the right person. What reason could they have for destroying it?"

"That's what I need to find out."

Nate looked around the small room. This was his fault. Storing expensive equipment in the barn? What had he been thinking? He rattled the doorknob. The perpetrator wasn't an expert. Someone with any experience could have picked the lock without leaving the telltale signs. Unless they wanted him to know.

Nate shook his head. Christ. He didn't need to complicate matters. It was probably kids causing mischief. That was the least ominous explanation.

For now, Nate preferred to keep things simple. Local vandals. That's what he would tell the cast and crew. And it was the theory he would pitch to the police.

"Have you told anyone else?"

Homer shook his head. "I came to you as soon as I discovered it."

"Good. I'm going to fill in Chuck. He can call the cops."

Homer fell in beside him, his long legs matching Nate's stride step for step. "No one comes out here. I mean. There isn't any reason to. The stuff is extras. Lights. Cable. And the camera. If the cable I was using hadn't gone wonky, we might not have known about this for days. Maybe weeks."

Nate had thought of that. It lent weight to their theory. Random. It was scary. However, knowing someone was purposefully targeting the movie was worse. Much worse.

"You take the camera with you at night?"

"Well, sure." Homer swallowed nervously.

"I'm asking a simple question, Homer. This isn't a trap."

"Too many movies," the young man laughed.

"Join the club." Nate gave Homer's shoulder a friendly pat. "I grew up with them. Murder. Intrigue. My world was filled with it — depending on the kind of project my parents were making."

"Lucky," Homer sighed, his eyes filled with awe.

"Sounds great, doesn't it?"

"Yes."

"It was the best childhood imaginable."

"Montana doesn't compare," Homer said with a wistful sigh.

"Apples and oranges. Do you have good parents?"

"Sure. Mom and Dad are great."

"Then consider yourself lucky, Homer. You can pick any future you want. Stay in Montana. Move to Los Angles. Your choice. What you get as a child is a crap shoot." Nate turned, his blue eyes curious. "How did you do?"

"Sevens all the way."

"Good man. If you want to make your mom's day, tell her that when you get home."

"Geez, Nate," Homer kicked at the dirt. "Isn't that, you know, mushy?"

"Absolutely." Nate lightly punched Homer on the arm. "You're old enough to survive a little motherly mush. Trust me; you'll be glad you did it."

"Okay."

"And Homer?"

"What?"

"Leave the camera here from now on."

"But…" Homer started to protest.

"I trust you, Homer. It's for your safety. Until we know what's going on, I don't want someone breaking into your house to get the camera. Understand?"

Homer swallowed when all the possibilities rushed through his vivid imagination.

"Yes, sir."

"Good. I'll keep it safe." Nate gave him a reassuring smile. "And don't worry. This is a precaution. Nothing more."

Nate stopped in the kitchen, glancing at the clock. Everyone was gone for the day. Before he filled Chuck in on the vandalism, Nate wanted to speak with his father.

"Come on," Nate said to Beauty.

She trotted happily after him, taking the stairs one at a time like an old pro. Her rump still got stuck now and then, but she powered through, making it to the top. The first few times she tackled them was a different story. She struggled mightily. Patiently, Nate walked behind her, pushing her up to the next step when she faltered. For both their sakes, he always carried her on the way down. It wouldn't take long before she raced up and down the steps without a second thought. For now, he didn't want to take any chances on her tumbling headfirst.

"I know." Nate set the puppy on the neatly made bed. "You think that is yours. My mistake for letting you sleep there."

Beauty rolled on her back. She knew what would come. Nate was a pushover. Her faith was rewarded with a thorough tummy scratch. Her eyes closed, a whimper of happiness escaping her mouth.

Nate took out his iPad. As technology went, was there anything better than seeing your family when you spoke to them? For a man who spent so much time traveling, it was a godsend.

"There's my boy." Caleb Landis grinned.

In life, his father's personality filled a room. The small screen barely contained it.

"How's it going, Dad?"

"Good. Great. Your mother is having dinner with her co-stars."

"That's a trio that will draw a crowd." Nate could picture the paparazzi having a field day. Meryl Streep, Helen Mirren, *and* Callie Flynn. You didn't score like that every day. "Which restaurant hit the movie star jackpot?"

"Are you kidding? Callie organized a sleepover. I've been kicked out of my bedroom. Junk food and…? I have no idea. Pillow fights? I like pillow fights."

"Down, boy." Nate had no problem picturing his mother doing such a thing. Apparently, neither did his father. "I'm working with Dame Helen next year. Show some respect."

Caleb chuckled good-naturedly. "Garrett filled me in. How are you holding up?"

"I don't hate it."

"With that kind of enthusiasm, you must be a joy to work with."

This time, Nate laughed. "I know Chuck has been in touch. What does he say?"

"Fishing for compliments?"

"You found me out. My ego is now second only to Colton's."

"Hey," Caleb protested. "My ego is king in this family. Don't forget it."

"As if I could."

Nate loved this man. Ego and all.

"You look good. Rested." Caleb looked Nate over. A clear blue, they shared the color. Knowing his son, his gaze sharpened. "Who is she?"

"She." Shit, how could his father know? Lusting after his friend's daughter. Nate held his breath, waiting for the tongue-lashing he probably deserved.

"You never look that rested when you aren't at home. Unless you've found someone to share your bed. Tell me it isn't Paige."

Not yet. The way things were going, maybe not ever. Struggling with an answer, Nate found his reprieve when he felt a cold, damp nose nudging his hand.

"Dad, meet Beauty. She's been my bedmate for the last four nights."

"The name fits." Caleb grinned at the wiggling puppy. "She an upgrade. What was her name? Mistletoe? Eggnog?"

"Hollee."

"Right. Double E and Double D."

"Jesus, Dad."

"Hey, that was how she introduced herself." Caleb felt a wave of satisfaction when he saw Nate flush. "No one can say your taste isn't varied." His laughter rang out until he doubled over.

Rolling his eyes, Nate waited patiently.

"Finished?" he asked. His father nodded, wiping the tears from his face. "Good. Something happened today. I need your advice."

It didn't take long for Caleb's demeanor to change from teasing to serious. He listened as Nate explained about the break-in and the damaged camera.

"What does Chuck think?"

"I wanted to talk to you first. I need another camera and I don't want him to know you're sending me one until it's arrived."

"You think he'll balk?"

Nate shrugged. "I don't know, Dad. He put the movie together on his own. You wouldn't believe it. We have more volunteers than we can use. The equipment that he borrowed, or was donated, is top of the line. Chuck is a proud man."

"I agree. You can't go behind his back, Nate. No matter how good your intentions. Is he in the house?"

"In his office."

"What are you waiting for? Let's go."

His father was right, but that didn't make Nate feel any less like a chastised little boy. By the time he reached Chuck's office, he felt a little better. With a sigh, he knocked.

"Come in."

"Mind if I interrupt?"

"You aren't. I'm done for the day. Sit." Chuck motioned to the wing-backed chair opposite his desk.

"Chuck," Caleb called out. "Damn it, Nate, turn the screen."

"Caleb." Chuck took the tablet. "I hoped to see you soon, but I didn't expect it to be like this."

"There are days I would like to toss my cell phone in the ocean. But it allows me keep up with my family and friends. How can I complain about that?"

"It's a wonder."

The men exchanged pleasantries, giving Nate time to wander around the office. This was the first time he'd been in here for more than a few seconds. It was warm and welcoming. Like Chuck, himself.

Built-in bookshelves covered one wall. Pictures littered most of the area. Chuck and Erin. Years younger and grinning like fools at whoever was taking their picture. Nate's eyes sharpened. Paige. As a baby. Chubby — adorable. Older, proudly showing the gap left by her missing front teeth. The early teenage Paige, all legs, and elbows, but glowing with an unfinished beauty as she rested her head on her mother's shoulder.

The resemblance was remarkable. He wondered how Chuck felt when he looked at the picture. Did it make him miss his wife even more? Or did it give him comfort, knowing she lived on in their daughter? Nate imagined it was a little bit of both.

"I'll let Nate give you the rundown, Chuck. Something he should have done immediately." Nate took his seat when he heard his father's comment. "Then you can tell us what you want to do."

Chuck listened. It didn't take long because there wasn't much to say.

"I'm sorry, Chuck. Dad's right. Keeping this from you, no matter how good my intentions, was wrong."

Chuck shook his head, his eyes troubled. "The timing doesn't matter, Nate. I'm worried about the break-in. In all the years I've lived here, I can't recall more than a handful of similar incidents. And most of them involved drunks blowing off steam on a Saturday night."

"Security is a possibility. I can have some there first thing in the morning."

Rubbing his face, Chuck sighed. "I don't know, Caleb. If I thought anyone was in physical danger, I would shut the movie down."

"Let's not get ahead of ourselves."

Nate understood Chuck's concern. However, there was no need to go to extremes.

"Nate is right, Chuck. If it *is* local kids making mischief, engaging a security guard will scare them off."

"And if it's something more?"

"Better to find out right away," Nate said. "We're only five days in, Chuck. Let's wait and see. Chances are nothing else will happen."

"I hope you're right."

"Do you have a problem with me replacing the camera? Or hiring

156

some security?" Caleb grinned. "Call it an influx of capital from an enthusiastic investor."

"I'll call it what it is. A good friend lending a welcome hand." Chuck said with a slight catch in his voice. He cleared his throat. "You've already given me your son. How could I turn down this offer?"

"*Loaned* you my son," Caleb corrected with a wink. "I'm going to want him back. His mother will insist."

"Hmm. About that." Chuck looked at Nate, his smile a little *too* innocent. "Nate, would you go and check on Paige? We're having one more for dinner and I want to make sure she's on top of it."

"Sure. I'll call soon, Dad. Give Mom my love."

"Take care, son." There was a pause. "Nate?"

Nate leaned over the desk until he had a good view of his father. "Yes?"

"Watch yourself. Okay?"

Nate saw the concern and smiled.

"This has nothing to do with my accident, Dad. It's a smashed camera."

"Make sure *you* don't get smashed. What would I tell your—"

"Mother. I know. You can let Mom know that I'm watching my back," Nate finished. His father always used Callie when his overprotective instincts kicked in.

"Good. I love you, son. Now go on. Chuck and I have some reminiscing to do."

"I love you, too."

Leaving the office, Nate felt he was missing something. He gave Chuck one last look before closing the door.

"Is he gone?" Caleb asked.

"Yes."

"Then tell me what you couldn't say when Nate was in the room."

"How do you feel about playing matchmaker?"

"Nate and Paige?" Caleb sat up in his chair, an interested glint in his eyes. "You've seen a spark?"

"That would be putting it mildly. The interest was there right off. I gave Nate the concerned father speech."

"Nice." Caleb used to think it would be nice to have a daughter. However, when he thought about someone like Nate sniffing around, he decided he was better off with boys. Men were dogs. He should know. Until Callie, he was the worst of the lot.

"Did you scare him?"

Chuck shrugged. "Hell if I know. Something happened. The first night he was here, they made googly eyes. Nate chased off an unwanted suitor. I think that impressed her. Though I can never tell with Paige. Sometimes her feelings shine out of her. Sometimes she hides them behind a wall no one can penetrate. Nate, on the other hand…"

Caleb let out a delighted bark of laughter. "My boy is an open book. Tell me about your neighbor." Caleb leaned closer to the screen. "That sounds like a story worth hearing."

Caleb listened, nodding now and then or grinning, his blue eyes sharp with interest. A look Chuck recognized from his Hollywood days.

"You think there is something going on?"

"Mmm," Caleb rubbed his chin. "We can't push, Chuck. Nate is too smart for that. If he suspected you wanted to hear wedding bells, he'd jump back like a scalded cat."

"I didn't say anything about wedding bells."

"You didn't," Caleb asked, surprise in his voice. "What did you mean by *matchmaking*?"

Chuck sighed, his lips tilted to one side with a wry smile. "Am I coming off as a father desperate to marry off his daughter? Paige would kill me if she heard this conversation." His eyes widened. "She can never know about this, Caleb."

"Calm down," Caleb said in a calming voice. "Why should she?"

"She knows things."

"You mean she's psychic?"

"No. That isn't the right word. She knows when I'm up to something," Chuck frowned.

"She didn't know about the movie," Caleb pointed out.

"True."

"If Nate does his part, Paige will be too distracted to notice anything but him. He has a way with women."

"From what I read, all your boys do." That gave Chuck pause. "Will he break her heart, Caleb? She's never cared enough for that to happen."

"There are no guarantees, Chuck. Maybe Paige will be the heartbreaker."

"Oh, I don't think—"

"You start messing with human emotions and you never know what might happen."

Caleb unconsciously placed a hand over his heart. He had been lucky. The woman he gave his heart to had kept it safe for over thirty years. Not everyone found someone like his Callie. Or Chuck's Erin.

"We know what it is to love the perfect woman. Or at least, perfect for us."

"Yes." Chuck's smile was bittersweet.

"If Nate and Paige are the right fit, they'll figure it out. I wish I could be there to watch the bumps along the way."

"So you think I should orchestrate this?"

"Gently, my friend. With baby steps. Kid gloves. Plus, any other metaphor you can think of that fits the situation."

"I want Paige to be happy, Caleb. She deserves to have what I had with Erin."

"Everyone does."

Caleb thought of his oldest son. Wyatt's marriage had been a disaster from the beginning. Sometimes doing what you thought was the right thing, blows up in your face. Almost three years after its tragic end, Wyatt still dealt with the fallout.

"Paige goes through life pretending she's happy alone. I know the truth, Caleb. She wants love."

"Nate is tough as nails — on the outside. My boy has insides like a marshmallow. Women. Kids. That puppy he adopted." Caleb shook his head. "He can't walk away when someone is in trouble. Paige's neighbor stirred his protective instincts. If, as you say, the attraction is already there, Nate won't be able to resist her for long."

"I can't say the same for Paige. She's good at digging her heels in."

Caleb smiled. He had faith in his son. "Give her a little shove. Nate will take care of the rest."

"DO I SMELL chocolate?"

Paige felt her heartbeat flutter then kick into high gear. Nate had a way of causing her body to react in odd and interesting ways. None of which were unpleasant.

Planning a sexual encounter added a new layer of awareness. This would happen. Tonight. Paige wanted it. Oh, boy, did she want it. Being positive didn't stop her nerves from rearing their annoying heads.

Swallowing, she moved her lips into what she hoped resembled a natural smile and turned.

"My grandmother's famous chocolate cake."

Paige wiped her damp palms on the towel she always kept on her shoulder when she baked.

"Homemade?" Nate breathed in the heavenly aroma. "I'm impressed."

"Mom liked to cook, but she wasn't much of a baker." Paige shrugged. "When I was around eleven years old, I found these old, handwritten cookbooks in the attic. They were like a time machine into the past. Most of them came with notes and comments. After I had read a few, I had to make something. Turned out, I had the knack."

"No one in the Landis family bakes." Nate poured himself a cup of coffee before taking a seat at the kitchen table. "I take that back. Lorena does. She's been our cook since before Wyatt was born. We think of her as part of our family."

"That's nice."

"Your dad says you're expecting company." Nate winked. "Other than me."

Damn. Paige felt a mass influx of butterflies. He was so adorable. And sexy. And Gorgeous from top to bottom. No man in history filled out a pair of jeans like Nate Landis. And his arms? And chest? A t-shirt never looked better.

"Paige?"

"Hmm? Did you say something? I wondered if it was time to take out the cake."

Nice cover, Paige thought sarcastically. It was difficult not to let her mind wander. Lottie was right. She needed to get laid.

"Nothing important. I wondered if I should put Beauty in the mudroom during dinner." He smiled at the puppy who was nodding off at his feet. "She's a doll, but her manners are still a little sketchy."

"Irene won't mind."

"The vet?" Nate watched with appreciation as Paige leaned over the open oven door. "You have a nice ass."

Surprised by the matter-of-fact comment, Paige almost dropped one of the pans.

"Watch it, fella." Paige carefully put the cake on the cooling racks. "Throwing around remarks like that could result in ruined dessert. *And* burned hands."

"Are you hurt?"

Nate was in front of her before she could blink. Taking her hand, he turned it over, looking for a burn.

"I'm fine," Paige laughed. "I was kidding."

"It would be a shame to mar your skin." Nate raised her palm to his mouth. His lips gave it a warm caress. "You work hard on the ranch. How do you manage to have such smooth, soft skin?"

Paige's eyes met his. The blue was so deep she felt like she was drowning. She could feel his smile curve, followed by the light touch of his tongue. Mesmerized, she swayed toward him. She wanted to feel his touch on the rest of her body.

"Gloves," she finally answered. "And lotion. A lot of lotion."

"Just on your hands?" Nate's gaze slowly traveled the length of her body before returning. Heat radiated from him. She felt her temperature rise.

"*All* over. There are spots I have the hardest time reaching."

"If you ever need a hand…" Nate brought her other palm to his lips. "Or two? All you have to do is ask."

Paige licked her lips, the movement catching Nate's avid attention. "You could tempt a saint."

"I don't want to tempt anyone, but you."

Nate slowly closed his eyes, the breath rushing from his lungs.

"You aren't mad at me anymore?"

"Nope." She moved closer. The heat she had felt before wrapped around her like a big, soft blanket she couldn't wait to cuddle under. "There's the slightest chance that I may have overreacted."

"There's the slightest chance that I didn't do a very good job explaining myself."

They exchanged smiles.

"Having my face splashed across the tabloids doesn't worry me, Nate. In Basic, it would make me a celebrity. Free coffee at the diner for life."

"They can say some vicious things." Nate rested his forehead on hers. If her hormones hadn't been raging like a wildfire, Paige would have found the gesture sweet.

"Dad and Lottie won't care. Will you?"

"No. Of course not."

"There isn't anyone else in my life that matters."

"I matter?"

Nate whispered the words, his breath washing over her face. Clean. Coffee and mint. One more thing to like about him. The list grew by the day.

Paige chose her words carefully. She cared. Too much. Too fast. When Nate left, she had a feeling he would take a piece of her heart. She could live with that. Having Nate, if only for a short time, would be worth the risk.

For her sake, she couldn't let him know the way her feelings shifted. Nate would step back rather than engage a fraction of her heart. That was the last thing Paige wanted.

"Do you matter?" Paige reached for a light tone. "Certainly. What would Dad do without you? Stepping in as director saved the day."

"Director. Right."

Nate pulled back, though not away. His eyes held hers for a second. Paige didn't know what he saw but when he started to move, she put a hand on his arm.

"I need you, too."

"Why? For sex?"

"Yes," Paige nodded. "That was the deal. We have some fun until you leave in a few weeks."

"Paige—"

"I hope we can be friends, Nate." Paige interrupted him. She didn't want to know what he was about to say. If he changed his mind, too bad. While he was in Montana, he was stuck with her. "I know it sounds trite."

"It sounds lovely."

Paige sighed with relief. This time, she was the one to take his hand. Kissing the back, she rubbed her thumb along his. So strong. So gentle. It was a heady mix.

"Would you like to go for a drive after dinner?"

"The two of us? Alone?" Nate grinned. "Seeing a woman who lives with her father makes intimacy a challenge."

"I know." Paige smiled back. "Since I've been back home, the men I've dated lived alone. You staying here makes for a unique problem."

"The last time I had sex in a car was…" Nate thought hard. "Never! Damn. How did I miss out on that rite of passage?"

"You and me both, fella. I had something else in mind for tonight, but if you'd rather use my truck, we can do that."

"Does your option have a mattress?"

Paige nodded.

"I want to see you. All of you." Nate ran a finger down the side of her face, stopping at her mouth. Slowly, he traced the curve of her bottom lip. "We have weeks to take advantage of that truck. We'll lose our virginity together."

The sound of her father descending the staircase was the only thing that stopped Paige from sliding her fingers into Nate's hair and kissing him like there was no tomorrow.

Pushing Nate into his chair, Paige checked the casserole, hoping her father would blame her red cheeks on the heat of the oven.

"Chocolate cake. Paige makes the best dessert. You're in for a treat, Nate."

Nate coughed into his coffee, spilling the contents over the rim. He quickly wiped his mouth with his hand, trying his best to cover his smile.

Paige knew what he was thinking. She shot him a dirty look. *This is my father, you ass.*

Clearing his throat, Nate scooped up Beauty.

"This little lady needs some fresh air." As he passed Paige, he whispered so only she could hear, "And so do I."

As much as she adored Irene, Paige wished she wasn't joining them for dinner. Not tonight. Rushing her father through the meal would have been much easier if it were just the three of them. Now, she had to play hostess while trying to keep her mind off Nate.

Taking the offset spatula from the drawer, she began frosting the cake. This was going to seem like the longest meal in history.

Chapter Eleven

DINNER WAS AWKWARD. Each of the four people around the table had their reasons. Reasons they had no intention of sharing.

Paige kept looking at the clock, wishing the minutes away. Naturally, instead of speeding up, time slowed down to a crawl. Her father was to her right. The man she hoped would soon be her lover, on her left. This wasn't awkward. It was… Honestly? She didn't know what it was. But Freud would have had a field day with the thoughts pinging through her brain.

Thank God for Irene. Her bright small talk was the only thing keeping the evening from being a complete disaster. Paige was so wrapped in her own drama she didn't notice the tension between her friend and her father.

"Nate. Are you enjoying directing? I understand this isn't how you normally spend your days."

Smiling, Nate shook his head.

"It's interesting, Irene. However, this will be my debut and my swan song. Garrett is the director in the family. I'm happy to leave it in his capable hands."

Unlike Paige, Nate sensed the friction between Irene and Chuck. It was obvious the veterinarian tried to put on a happy veneer. Perhaps it took an outsider to see the stiffness in Chuck's shoulders or the too-bright smile on Irene's face.

Whatever was going on, Nate wanted to ease the edge of emotions he felt swirling around the table. Irene gave him the perfect solution. He was proud of his family — every one of them. When it came to their accomplishments, he could go on for hours.

"I loved *Time Zone*. When it's on TV, I get sucked in every time."

"That was an early one." Nate's grin widened. "Lord, what a time he had with that movie. Bad weather and a younger brother who was a little too full of himself."

"Was Colton in *Time Zone*? I don't remember seeing him."

Those were the most words Chuck had spoken since they sat down to eat. Like Irene, it was obvious he wasn't comfortable. He seemed genuinely interested in what Nate said. Without realizing it, he started to relax.

Irene caught on to what Nate was doing and sent him a grateful smile. When he gave her a quick wink, she felt a little flutter in her stomach. *Oh, my*. Nate Landis was a dangerous man. Charm radiated off him even when he wasn't trying. One little wink. One glimpse into what it would feel like to be the center of his attention and Irene understood Paige's dilemma.

How could you resist him? Why would you want to?

"That's an interesting story, Chuck." Thinking about it, Nate laughed. "Colt has a level head on his shoulders. With all the attention and adulation he's received in the last few years, he could have become an egomaniacal asshole. Pardon my language."

Irene blinked. She couldn't remember the last time a man apologized for using colorful language. This was Basic. Asshole was mild in comparison to what she heard on a daily basis. With that simple apology, Nate raised another notch in her estimation.

"What about Colt and the movie?"

Caught up in the story, Paige put her elbow on the table, her chin resting in her hand. Nate had no problem with being the center of attention. It wasn't something he sought out, but this was different. These were friends. The entertainer side of his Landis blood kicked in. The actor in him didn't surface often, but when it did, he showed a certain flair that would have made his mother proud.

"Baby brother was a newbie. The part in *Time Zone* was small. Garrett had cast him before *Our Waving Flags* was released."

"I haven't seen that one," Irene said.

"It is *so* good. Colt plays a young man who joins the Army to honor his father's memory. Lottie and I cried buckets," Paige sighed. Her eyes brightened. "Then he takes his clothes off."

"All of them?" Irene's eyes widened with interest.

"Every stitch."

"Oh, my. Is it available on Netflix?"

"Women." Chuck sat back shaking his head. "Why do they insist on drooling over an image on a screen?"

"This from the man who watched *Be Mine* how many times?" Paige crossed her arms, waiting for her father to respond.

"I…" Chuck blushed, unable to meet Nate's amused gaze. "It's a good movie. Excellent, as a matter of fact."

"Mom has that effect on a lot of men, Chuck. I'm used to it."

"I'd rather you didn't mention this to your father."

The red on Chuck's face rapidly spread down his neck. Three sets of eyes watched with interest as the bright color melded with the collar of his shirt.

"Dad has lived with this for over thirty years. Mom is a beautiful woman. Somehow, she gets more beautiful every year. Trust me, he would understand."

"Still…"

Noting Chuck's distress, Nate let him off the hook.

"Your secret is safe. Right, ladies?"

"I was teasing, Dad." Paige patted his hand. "My lips are now sealed on the subject."

Smiling at the exchange, Irene was surprised when Chuck gave her an inquiring look.

"What?" She shrugged. "Who would I tell? The bull I'm treating for prostate problems?"

"Bulls have prostate problems?" Paige didn't know if it was funny or strange. From the grimace on her father's face, she decided to rule out funny.

"We have wandered off track. You were telling us about Colt?"

"And Garrett, Chuck. He puts up with a lot when it comes to family. However, if it affects his work, he isn't as lenient."

Nate took a sip of the excellent red wine. According to Paige, it had been a gift from some friends who ran a vineyard in Washington. Years of travel and good food had developed his palate. He knew a good vintage when he tasted it. He had to remember to get the name. His mother loved wine. A case of this would be the perfect gift for Christmas.

"As I said before, Colt rode the wave of his first success as an actor. Unfortunately, his head had swelled a bit as a result. He thought he should have a more important part in Garrett's film."

"I take it Garrett didn't agree." Paige smiled, sipping her wine.

"Give the little lady a cigar."

Nate weaved the rest of the tale, easily holding the interest of a rapt audience. It wasn't difficult. Not only was it a good story, he had lived through it. He was able to add a personal perspective, drawing the others in with humor and a brother's love.

Our Waving Flags was his breakout role. One he earned through hard work.

It was natural for him to want bigger and better parts. Garrett agreed. However, not in his movie. He had his actors. When Colt took the small role, he had been happy to get it. If he didn't want to honor his commitment, fine. Plenty of actors would be happy for the chance.

"What happened?" Irene demanded, her eyes wide with anticipation.

"He showed up. Reluctantly."

"Your dad talked him into it?" Chuck asked, sure of the answer.

"No." Nate shook his head. "Mom and Dad stayed out of it. They refused to get in the middle."

"Smart."

"Four competitive sons, Irene. They decided early on not to take sides or step into a problem unless absolutely necessary. Most of the time we find our own solutions."

"How much blood was shed?" Chuck grew up with brothers. Fighting came with the territory — no matter how close you were.

"When we were kids? Not much." Nate chuckled. "We became very good at directing our punches away from the face. Mom wasn't big on seeing blood all over her sons' faces. One broken nose. The way she went on, you would have thought I killed him."

"Who?"

"Wyatt. He borrowed my Jedi action figure. I wanted it back."

"Easy as that?" Paige was amused by his matter-of-fact tone.

"It was *my* Jedi. *And*, he didn't ask. There's a code of behavior for that kind of thing. I was well within my rights. Besides, Wyatt needed taking down a peg or two. He was in a particularly obnoxious *older brother* phase. He never completely outgrew it, but he isn't as obnoxious." Nate shrugged with a smile. "Most of the time."

Paige could hear the love and affection in Nate's voice. It was there when he spoke of his family. *All* of his family. She loved her father unconditionally. The fights and disagreements never lasted long. It seemed Nate was lucky enough to have the same kind of relationship with his parents and brothers. The knowledge gave her a warm feeling inside.

"Finish the story," Irene urged. "What happened between Colt and Garrett?"

"They were professional during the shoot. Though, according to Garrett, Colt pushed the boundaries of the term as often as possible. He was never late — but he cut it close. He would arrive with seconds to spare. Garrett hates that. He's known for bringing his movies in ahead of schedule."

Colt told a different story. He complained that Garrett was dictatorial. Overbearing. He couldn't stand to be on the set a second longer than necessary.

This war of wills continued longer than the family expected, spilling over into their private lives. Callie would have stepped in if Caleb hadn't reminded her that they only had to work together for two weeks. This would blow over.

"Did it?" Chuck took a sip from his wine glass, surprised to find it empty. He had been so caught up in Nate's narrative he hadn't realized he'd drunk the contents. Reaching for the bottle, he asked around if anyone wanted a refill. Everyone declined. He poured himself half a glass, and then sat back, ready for the conclusion of the story.

"Colt cooled down as soon as he signed on for his next movie. A juicy script and a nice paycheck can smooth over your temper fast. On the other hand, Garrett wasn't ready to forgive. And trust me. Garrett never forgets."

His brother could go for months, sometimes years, before he had his revenge. Some people might say that was maniacal, but they were wrong. Garrett didn't obsess. He didn't stew over every wrong done to him. However, if he saw his opportunity to even the score, he took it.

Colt paid the price faster than most. Looking around the table at the expectant faces, Nate gave them what they had been waiting for.

"Garrett cut him out of the movie."

"No," Irene gasped.

"Wow! That is cold." Paige's eyes were round with disbelief.

"Sounds fair to me."

"Dad!" Paige gaped at her father. "You don't mean that. Colt is Garrett's brother. How can you think it's right for him to do that?"

"Paige, honey, you don't understand the movie business. Colt was screwing with Garrett's livelihood. His reputation. Brother or no brother. That can't be tolerated."

"But—"

"It was brilliant," Nate declared. "Garrett accomplished two things. He taught Colt a much-needed lesson in humility. And, he showed the industry that you don't mess with Garrett Landis. If he was willing to do that to his own brother, imagine what he would do to a non-family member."

"Like I said," Chuck nodded, voice filled with admiration. "Brilliant."

"I want to know how Colt handled it. He couldn't have been happy."

"He ranted and raved — long distance. He was on location in the wilds of Canada."

"That was it?" After everything Nate had told them, Paige couldn't believe Colt would leave it at that.

"Pretty much," Nate said, a twinkle in his blue eyes. "Oh, did I mention that Colt hired two guys to fill Garrett's Maserati with spaghetti and meatballs? Plus sauce. Gallons and gallons of sauce?"

Everyone burst out laughing. Nate painted a vivid picture of revenge. The red spaghetti sauce symbolic of an effective, yet bloodless revenge. Once they calmed down, they all wiped the moisture from their eyes.

"Garrett couldn't have let that go."

"What would you have done?" Smiling at Paige, Nate raised a questioning eyebrow.

"Strangled him. I mean a Maserati. Those can go for…"

"A lot." Chuck provided when he saw Nate wasn't going to name a specific amount.

"Deciding to end the war, Garrett let Colt off."

"Scott free?"

"Not exactly. He had to get the car detailed so it could be donated to charity. Then he purchased Garrett the car of his choice. Since the spaghetti incident put him off Maserati, he chose a Lamborghini. Loaded."

"That's getting off easy?" Paige exchanged amazed looks with Irene. "Yikes. Talk about an expensive lesson."

"Colt knew he deserved it. He's never taken any part for granted since then. No matter how big or small, he treats them all the same."

"The world you live in, Nate, is beyond my comprehension," Irene said with a sigh. The she grinned. "Entertaining as hell, though. Now, didn't I see a chocolate cake on the counter? To hell with my no sugar pledge. I want a slice. A big one."

"With ice cream?" Paige asked as she cleared away the dinner dishes.

"Chocolate or vanilla?"

"Both?"

"In for a penny. Bring it on."

The conversation during dessert was easy and relaxed. Picking up the last crumb with her fork, Irene sat back, full and satisfied. For a meal she dreaded all week, it had turned out to be the nicest evening she'd had in a long time. She would have loved to linger over another cup of coffee, but she had a flight to catch in the morning.

The prize mare of an Arabian Sheik was due to foal any day. Acting like a nervous father, he insisted she be attended by a doctor he trusted. Irene wasn't one to argue with someone who paid so well. He lived in California so she wouldn't be gone long. And she felt the need for a few days away.

Irene's gaze shifted to Chuck. However, before she went, she needed to clear up some unfinished business.

"That was a wonderful meal, Paige. As always. And wonderful company." Pushing her chair back, she smiled at Nate. "If you ever decide to give up stunt work, you could hire yourself out to parties. You had us enthralled."

Nate quickly got up, helping Irene to her feet. "When you have a colorful family, the stories write themselves."

"But it takes a certain knack to relay those stories so entertainingly."

"Do you have to go so soon?" Paige looked at the clock. Ten o'clock? How was that possible? Nate and his stories. She would have to thank him. Smiling, she pondered the possibilities. Once she had him naked, she would thank him – repeatedly.

"I have an early flight. I'll be gone for most of the week, but Dr. Langston is on call in case of an emergency."

Hooking her arm through Irene's, Paige walked her to the door.

"Maybe the Sheik will ask you to marry him. Again."

"What?" Chuck's head jerked around from where he stacked the dessert plates. "When did this happen?" Paige didn't notice the harsh tone of Chuck's voice. Irene did. Intrigued by the reaction, so did Nate.

"Ahmed has been proposing for years." Irene donned the coat that Nate held for her. "He would have a heart attack if I said yes. His three wives wouldn't be very happy, either. It's a little harmless flirting."

"Marriage isn't something to joke about," Chuck muttered as he carried the plate to the sink.

"Oh, Dad," Paige playfully admonished. "It's harmless. He *is* awfully handsome. And with all that money? You could retire and become his California wife."

"I'll give it some thought in January when I'm shoveling five feet of snow out of my driveway."

"Travel safe." Paige gave Irene a warm hug.

"I will." Irene turned to Nate. "Well? Aren't you going to kiss me good night? How often do I get the opportunity to be this close to an honest to goodness internet sensation?"

Nate groaned but happily complied, kissing Irene's cheek.

"I could have gone all night without that subject coming up."

"Sorry. I held in the impulse as long as I could."

"Your restraint was admirable." Nate opened the door. "Let me walk you to your car."

"I swear. You are from another era. Thank you, but I have something that I forgot to bring in."

"I'll be happy to get it for you."

"That's sweet of you." Irene laid a hand on Nate's arm when he would have accompanied her out of the house. "It's for Chuck. Would you mind?"

"Me?" Chuck looked slightly panicked. "Um. Sure." He wiped his hands on a dishtowel. "I'd be glad to."

He didn't look glad. Nate thought he looked like a man walking his last mile. No, that wasn't right. Chuck looked. Nervous. But this was something else. Anticipation? Excitement?

Well, well, well. Chuck's Erin had been gone for over two years. It looked like the grief was lessening and his libido kicking into gear. He might be reluctant. However, once that ice cracked, Chuck would have a hard time stopping the thaw.

Unaware of the undercurrents swirling around her, Paige watched the door close behind her father. She opened the dishwasher. She paused when she became aware of Nate's gaze, a slow smile forming on her lips.

Speaking of libidos. Nate's had been working fine for years. However, something about Paige took it to another level. That smile alone made him want to fall to his knees and beg for a taste. One sip.

Hell, who was he trying to fool? A sip wouldn't be enough. Tonight would be the beginning of a long feast. The first course.

"How soon can we leave?"

Paige didn't have to ask what Nate meant. Her thoughts were right there with his.

"Forty-five minutes. An hour at the most." Paige looked at the puppy who watched from her pillow by the fireplace. "What about Beauty? She's gotten used to having you near at night."

Nate patted his leg. Happily, Beauty jumped up. Her still growing body lost control for a second, paws splaying in four different directions. Undeterred, she righted herself before trotting over to Nate.

"You are the sweetest thing, aren't you?" Nate picked Beauty up. He scratched the spot behind her ears that had her eyes closing in happiness. "Come on. You need to take care of business for the night."

"And then?" Paige asked. She couldn't decide who was more adorable. The puppy or the man. When he touched his nose to Beauty's, she decided to call it a draw.

"I'll put her on my bed for the night. She'll be fine until we get back."

She enjoyed the view of Nate's ass as he left the room. With a silent whistle of appreciation, Paige sped up her task. The sooner the dishes were done the sooner they could head out to Lottie's place. The sooner they were at Lottie's the sooner she could rip Nate's clothes off. Naked Nate. Soon to become her favorite thing ever.

"WHAT DO YOU have for me?"

Irene watched with amazement as Chuck circled her car, peering into the window.

174

"Is it in the trunk?"

"Don't be an idiot. No, strike that. You're already an idiot. Don't compound it."

Chuck swallowed nervously, his hand rubbing the back of his neck. A gesture Irene recognized. He was upset and confused. She felt her indignation begin to melt until she remembered. *She* was upset and confused. No one gave her any slack. Especially Chuck.

"Irene—"

"No. I'm going to talk. You listen." With each word, she poked a finger into his chest for emphasis. "It was a kiss. One kiss. A very nice kiss."

"But—"

"I loved Erin, too."

"I know."

"Not once while she was alive did I harbor any thoughts about you except as a friend."

"No." For the first time all evening, Chuck looked directly into Irene's eyes. The sadness he saw made his heart clench. "I never dreamed otherwise."

"Good," Irene nodded. "Because there is something you need to understand."

This was hard, but it needed to be said. Whatever happened, she couldn't lose Chuck. He was one of the first friends she made when she moved to Montana. She didn't know if something romantic was possible with him. As she had said, thinking of him that way was new. And scary. There was Erin's memory. It was over two years since her death, but Irene knew that Chuck still grieved for his wife every day.

She wasn't going to tell him that Erin would want him to move on. It was a cliché, even if it were true. Chuck knew that, above all else, Erin would want him to be happy. It was up to Chuck to decide what that meant. Irene couldn't tell him.

The kiss had come as a surprise to both of them. If Irene had seen it in a movie, she would have rolled her eyes. Chuck stopped by her office to pick up some ointment for one of the horses. They bent at the same time to pick up a file she had dropped. As they stood, it happened. No warning. Chuck pulled her into his arms and kissed her. To her amazement, Irene kissed him back.

It left her breathless and a little lightheaded. By the glazed look in his eyes, she was certain Chuck felt the same. It took about ten seconds for the implications to sink in and less than that for him to rush out the door. Two weeks later, this was the first time she had gotten him alone.

"I like you, Chuck. I can't tell you when I started to want more than just your friendship, but there it is. I would like us to be lovers."

Chuck's eyes widened. Irene waited for him to say something, but when he opened his mouth, all that came out was air. Like a slowly deflating balloon.

It appeared Chuck wouldn't make this easier. With a sigh, Irene plowed forward.

"The Genie is out of the bottle, Chuck." She shook her head, frowning. "You know what? Forget the stupid metaphors. We're adults. Let's act like it. I've told you what I want. If you decide you'd like it too, that's fine. If not, I still want to be your friend."

"I want that too." Chuck found his voice. It sounded raspy and rough, but it was there. "The friend part." Chuck sighed. "I always want us to be friends, Irene."

"And the rest?"

"I don't know."

At least it was honest. A little part of her had hoped for more, but at heart, she was a pragmatic woman. Chuck needed time to process what was happening between them. In his mind, he was still married to Erin. Thinking of Irene as anything but a friend would be cheating. Until he moved past that, there was nothing more she could say.

"Can we talk when you get back?"

"Of course." Irene gave him a sympathetic smile. "I wish I could tell you not to beat yourself up over this, but that's your decision." Before getting into her car, she hesitated, and then gently squeezed his hand. "Friends first and always."

Chuck watched Irene's car drive into the night. *Friends first and always.* Did he want more? Was he capable of more? He closed his eyes, waiting for Erin to give him the advice he so desperately needed.

Nothing. A wave of panic washed over him. *Where was she? Where was the voice that had kept him sane? His link. His lifeline.* Then he heard it. Faint but clear.

It's time, my love.

His head fell back. Looking into the clear, star-filled night, Chuck felt a deep sadness crash over him. He wasn't ready.

Then, the panic lifted. Calmness settled into his bones. The sadness — his loss was still there. However, for the first time in forever, there wasn't a weight on his heart.

Chuck brushed at something on his cheek. Tears. Taking a breath, he let them fall.

I will never stop loving you, Erin.

Walking back to the house, Chuck wasn't thinking about loss. His mind was on the future. The possibilities. The smile of a lovely woman and the kiss that no longer seemed like a betrayal.

Taking a deep breath, Chuck let the clean Montana air fill his lungs. Then with one last look at the stars, he entered the house.

Chapter Twelve

THE ROOM WAS quiet. The only sound coming from the old grandfather clock that stood in the corner.

Chuck was in bed. He went to his room as soon as he returned from walking Irene to her car. Nate found it interesting that he wasn't carrying anything. Whatever Irene wanted to give him, it was either small enough to fit in his pocket, or it had been an excuse to get him alone.

By the introspective look on Chuck's face, Nate guessed it was the latter.

He helped Paige finish the dishes before putting Beauty in the mudroom. After discussing it with Paige, he decided she, and his bedding, would be better off in a room where she couldn't get into any mischief.

Nate checked the mudroom thoroughly, making certain all the cleaning supplies were out of reach. He filled her bowls with food and water. Then he settled her onto her pillow. Crouching down, he placed her new chew toy nearby.

"Chuck is going to install a doggy door in the morning. For now, if you can't hold it, don't be embarrassed. Puppies have less control. I'll clean it up if you make a mess and promise to keep it between the two of us."

Beauty cocked her head, blinking twice. It didn't matter that his words were meaningless to her. His tone was what mattered. She knew she was safe and loved. Wasn't that what everyone, person or dog, wanted?

"Is she going to be okay?"

"She'll be fine." Nate gently closed the mudroom door. "I turned on the dryer. The sound should soothe her until she falls asleep."

"How do you know so much about puppies?" Paige asked.

Her smile widened when Nate moved closer. He took her hand, linking their fingers. Paige's fingers were long, tapering to nails that she kept short and unvarnished. Turning her hand, he gave the back a lingering kiss. His reward, besides the feel of her soft skin against his lips, was the flair of awareness in her deep, brown eyes.

A man would fight any battle to have a woman like Paige look at him that way. And here she was — offering herself freely. No battles. No strings. No expectations. Nate was a lucky bastard.

"I read a lot when I travel. Delays are part of the game. I pick up magazines people have discarded. You learn some interesting things that way."

Paige was learning more and more about Nate. In this day of handheld technology, he chose to read magazines rather than spend all his time bent over his smartphone. He read articles about puppy care when he didn't own a dog. And the touch of his lips on her hand sent her pulse racing.

Nate Landis was infinitely sweet and surprisingly complex.

"I like it when you smile. Want to share what's on your mind?"

"I hope it's the same thing that's on yours."

"Mmm." Nate eased her arm around his waist. He anchored Paige's hips with his cast. "It's a sure bet. Are you ready to go? Anything you need to get?"

"I put a bag in the truck before dinner. How about you?"

Everything Nate needed was in his jacket hanging by the front door. Condoms and a toothbrush. He could still hear the edict his father gave to each of his sons. Never leave home without protection. And always, always use one. Nate treated his father's words as the Gospel.

As for the toothbrush? Nate liked his teeth. They were strong and white. And he planned to keep them that way.

"I'm set."

Nate helped Paige on with her jacket, and then took her hand, leading her out of the house. He waited while she locked the door.

"You're going to open the truck door and help me in, aren't you?"

Surprised by the question, Nate frowned.

"Does that bother you?"

"At this point, I would be disappointed if you didn't do it." Paige took his proffered hand, walking down the steps. "I don't think admitting that means I have to turn in my liberated woman card. It's sweet. Old-fashioned."

"I'll tell my mom that you approve. She didn't harp on us about it. When Dad would open a door for her, or help her on with her coat, she would say, 'See boys. This is how you show a woman respect.' It stuck."

Paige started the truck. As soon as Nate was in the cab, she hit the gas. It was after ten. She wanted to get going before any more of the night slipped away.

"Are you nervous?"

Nate asked the question after several minutes of silence.

"Sure. A little." She shot him a look before returning her eyes to the road. "Are you?"

"No. Not nervous. Anxious would be a better word. I want to make this as good for you as possible."

"I want the same thing." She chuckled. "In reverse. You have a lot more experience, Nate. I don't want to disappoint you."

"I'm a guy, Paige. We're easy to please." He leaned as close as his seatbelt allowed, taking a deep breath.

"Vanilla and wildflowers. Plus that elusive bit that comes from you.

Your scent makes my mouth water. The touch of your hand on mine makes me hard. Want to feel?"

Hitting the brakes, Paige swerved to the side of the road. Her hands gripped the steering wheel so hard her knuckles turned white.

"I didn't mean to upset you." Nate hit the latch on his seatbelt. "I'm sorry, Paige. Let me—"

"No. Let me. Please, let me."

Paige launched herself at Nate with no thought except touching him. She sighed with satisfaction when he caught her easily with his good arm. His strength made her melt inside.

"Remind me. What was your question?"

Nate buried his face in Paige's long blond hair, his lips curving.

"Want to feel?"

"Yes, please."

Paige adjusted her body, her long, jean-clad leg hooking over Nate's muscular thigh.

"I'm going to kiss you. *And* touch you. Okay?"

Nate waited until Paige's lips were a breath away before he growled deeply, "Yes. Please."

Paige wasn't in the mood to tease. Not that Nate would have let her. Their mouths met in a rush of mutual desperation.

"So sweet." Nate's tongue teased her bottom lip. "Like wild cherries. Open for me."

Nate didn't have to ask twice. Her tongue met his. The glide was heated. Intense. They couldn't get enough of each other, going back for taste after taste. The sound of their breathing filled the cab, steaming the windows.

Running her hand over his chest, Paige sighed with pleasure. Nate had a body meant to be enjoyed. His chest was like iron. She opened his shirt, cursing the buttons. Snaps. The man should invest in shirts with easier access. She gave a sigh of pleasure when her fingers touched his heated skin.

"Perfect."

"I'm glad you think so."

"Mmm." Paige's hand wandered lower, her mouth following behind with a trail of kisses, bringing a groan of pleasure from Nate. The groan turned into a gasp when she lightly bit the ridge of his defined abs. Paige smiled. If he liked that, wait until she...

"Jesus, Paige." Nate's hips jerked once, then twice. "I said feel. If you keep squeezing me like that, I'm going to go off like a firecracker."

Gently, Nate removed her hand from between his legs. He brought it to his mouth, kissing her palm.

"I didn't realize you would be so..."

"Easy?" Nate laughed.

"Big."

Paige swallowed. Nate was a large man. Very large. It hadn't occurred to her that he would be big *all over*. It was a little daunting. The men she had been with had run from average to on the small side. It was quite a leap to go up not one size, but several.

"Paige. I've never had a problem *getting in*, so to speak. I'll take it slow."

"I'm not worried," Paige assured him. "Honestly."

"This is new." Nate tipped her chin so he could look into her eyes. "Not sex, but sex with each other. We decided to do this on a bed. Remember? I got a little carried away."

"Me too." Paige's gaze wandered to Nate's straining zipper.

"Move over. Put your seatbelt on and drive to Lottie's place."

"Maybe if I got a sneak peek." She reached for the button closure on the waistband of Nate's jeans.

"No." Nate pushed her across the bench seat. He placed her hands on the wheel before buckling her in. "I am not riding with my dick hanging out. Drive."

"Fine." Paige did what he asked. "I don't think I was asking too much."

"What if I asked you to whip off your shirt and bra? Would you mind driving with your breasts out there for anyone to see? I know there isn't a lot of traffic around here. Would you want to take a chance on another rig driving by and getting an eyeful?"

"It isn't a fair comparison." Paige tried not to laugh, but the situation had gone from overheated to ridiculous so quickly, she couldn't hold it in. "No one would be able to see what you had on display. And, you've strayed from the original point."

"What was the original point?"

"Size?" Paige nodded toward his prominent erection. "I wanted to see what I will be getting into."

"Or rather, what will be getting into you?"

Paige snorted. "Funny. You should take your act on the road. The size of your dick is a matter of comfort. My comfort. The size of my breasts is, well, to tell the truth, I don't know why that matters. Unless you have a thing for mammoth hooters. If that's the case, you are out of luck."

"I like all breasts," Nate declared. "Give me a woman with her shirt off and I'm a happy man."

"I'll tuck that away for future reference."

Nate was so unabashedly honest. He liked women. He liked naked women. Why that didn't bother her, Paige couldn't say. Nothing about Nate bothered her. She was afraid that might end up being a problem. For now, she was going to enjoy him. She would worry about her vulnerable heart another time.

"Here we are."

Paige pulled to a stop. Last month, Lottie had moved out of the house she grew up in. Her father passed away two years ago and she moved back to help her mother. It was a reasonably amicable arrangement until Aunt Phyllis came to visit — and never left. Her mother's sister did not approve of Lottie. As soon as the word tramp passed her aunt's lips, Lottie was gone.

She visited her mother whenever she was certain Aunt Phyllis was out.

Lottie rented a small house on the outskirts of Basic. It wasn't fancy, but the lawn was green and freshly mowed. A line of marigolds bordered the walkway, the yellow warm and welcoming. Paige knew that Lottie hated getting dirty. She wondered who her friend had charmed into doing the yard work.

"I like the color."

"Mmm. Lottie batted her eyes and her landlord repainted the entire place. Inside and out." Patiently, Paige waited for Nate to open her door.

"Lottie can get more done with her fluttering eyelashes than anyone I've ever met."

"It's a talent she was born with."

They walked hand in hand to the front door. Paige took the key from her pocket. Once inside, she waited until Nate turned the lock.

"Now. Drop your pants."

"Just like that? No foreplay?"

"What do you think we've been doing since you arrived? And in the truck? It's been one big, frustrating pile of foreplay."

"I can't argue with that."

Paige leaned against the pale lavender wall, her arms crossed, and waited.

"You want a show?" Nate unbuttoned his jeans, and then unzipped them. "Slow? Fast? You pick."

"Why don't I give you a hand?" Paige straightened. She closed the distance between them in three long strides. "That cast will slow things down."

"Paige. Slowing things down might be a good idea."

Easing to her knees, Paige smiled up at Nate. Her eyes sparkled with anticipation as she tugged at the denim that stubbornly clung to his hips.

"You don't like me down here?" Paige touched his leg just below his sexy black briefs.

"That's a loaded question."

"Loaded," Paige said the word slowly, making it sound provocative. "Like you."

With her eyes glued to his erection, she reached out to unwrap her present. Nate almost let her. It was tempting. Unlike Paige, he knew what would happen if she touched him again.

Nate was a man who prided himself on his control. It wasn't that he insisted on ladies first. Paige would be taken care of. Again and again.

He worried about coming the second she touched him. That hadn't happened since he was an untried teenager under the bleachers with Adrienne Wolstein. Paige had him on edge. The way he felt, the touch of her sweet, warm breath might be enough to set him off.

"What?" Paige asked when Nate moved her hands.

"Why don't you stand up?" Nate tugged, urging her to rise. "We'll get you undressed."

"I like it where I am." Paige smiled, feeling uncharacteristically smug. "You're in a bad way, aren't you?"

"Paige... Don't poke the bear. Not when he's dealing with a raging hard-on."

"I don't want to poke you. I want to kiss and make it better."

"I haven't had sex in over a month." Nate knew the smart thing to do would be to back away. However, the closer her mouth came to his dick, the more he felt rooted to the spot.

"Me neither." It was more like a year, but Nate didn't need to know that. "What's your excuse?"

Nate lightly tapped his cast against her shoulder. "Recovery from a concussion. A hovering mother. *And* an unplanned trip to Montana. It became the perfect storm. I haven't been celibate this long since... It had to be in my teens."

"I can count on one hand the number of men I've been with and you're worried about a month without sex? Poor baby."

The sarcastic teasing in Paige's voice made Nate smile. Until she made a sneak attack. The kiss she gave his cloth-covered dick put an end to the debate. No more fooling around. Things were about to get serious. Seriously good.

"You've had your fun. Now it's my turn."

"Fun? I'm still waiting for some naked — Nate!"

Nate swung Paige up against his chest. His cast made it impossible for him to carry her in his arms, but this was better. He held her around the waist, pressing her body against his chest. Eye to eye. Nate grinning. Paige gasping with surprise.

"You want naked Nate? I want naked Paige. Sound good?"

He didn't give her time to do more than nod. Paige's lips were right there. How could he resist? Nate covered her mouth with his. He toed off his boots, kicking away his jeans at the same time.

"Which way to the bedroom?"

Realizing her arms dangled like branches flapping in the wind, Paige wrapped them around Nate's shoulders.

"You're so strong."

As soon as the words left her mouth, Paige groaned.

"What?"

"I sound like one of your teenage groupies. Oh, Nate. You have such big muscles. Can I feel one?"

"The last time I let a teenager feel my muscles, I *was* a teenager." Nate kissed her again, hard and fast. "You sound like a woman who appreciates her partner. Bedroom?"

"End of the hall."

Lottie's taste ran toward pastel frilly. Lace and satin covered the bed and the windows. The hardwood floor was covered with a candy pink shag rug.

Nate shuddered.

"It looks like it was decorated by a demented five year old."

"Lottie's parents didn't believe in happy colors. Brown on brown, accented with brown was the motif. She's making up for lost time."

"It doesn't matter." Nate tossed her on the bed. "All I'm going to look at is you."

"I like that idea."

"Then let's get those clothes off you. I've been fantasizing about your long legs since the moment I saw you."

Nate grabbed one of Paige's boots with his good hand. Bracing his foot on the bed, he pulled it off, and then did the same with the other. Paige unsnapped her jeans. She shimmied the material down her hips, letting Nate take care of the rest.

"Smooth and strong." Nate started at her ankle, running his hand up her calf. "I want these wrapped around my waist while I'm deep inside of you."

"You still have on your shorts."

Nate grinned. He caressed Paige's thigh, stopping an inch from her silky red panties.

"You still have yours on."

"Nate…"

"I know. You asked first."

Paige licked her lips. Her eyes narrowed the focus on his thumb as he lowered the waistband. Lower. Lower. It took some maneuvering. He was one-handed and his erection wasn't making it easy.

"Holy…" Paige breathed in. "Is there a saint I should thank?"

"You like what you see?" Nate asked with an indulgent smile. "Not scared?"

"Beautiful."

"Mmm. If you say so." Nate joined her on the bed, divesting her of her shirt. "It takes care of business."

"I'll bet it does."

"No."

"I want to touch."

Nate unhooked Paige's bra, blindly tossing it across the room.

"Later. Now this," he cupped her breast, savoring the soft, smooth skin. "This is beautiful."

"It's all in the eye of the beholder."

"I behold perfection."

Leaning close, Nate took her nipple between his teeth, biting with just the right amount of pressure. Paige's head fell back. It felt like a shot of hot electricity jolted from her breast to between her legs. That was new and so erotic she wanted to scream for him to do it again. Reading her mind, Nate moved to her other breast, this time his teeth felt sharper, eliciting a sensation so intense it felt like a mini-orgasm.

Was that possible?

"Is what possible?"

She hadn't meant to say it aloud. Nate's heavy-lidded gaze held hers, his thumb rubbing — soothing — her nipple.

"Paige? Did I hurt you?"

"No," she cried out. "God, no. I liked it. I didn't know I would like something like that. I…"

"Don't be embarrassed." Nate rolled over, taking Paige with him. He settled her on his chest. Smoothing back her long blond hair, he gently kissed her lips. "Tell me what you felt."

"I know it isn't possible." Paige met his blue-eyed gaze. He told her not to be embarrassed. And she wasn't. However, sex was one thing. Talking about it was another.

"You liked when I bit your nipple?"

"Yes." She felt her cheeks heat. "It's crazy, but it felt like I…" she lowered her voice, "came."

Nate didn't laugh. His smile was gentle. Understanding. A little wicked. "That's a good thing. Isn't it? If it makes you feel good, I say bring it on."

"We are really doing this."

"What?"

"Pausing during sex — to talk about sex. Is this usual for you?"

"I like to be verbal, but no, I can't recall this particular situation." With ease, Nate reversed their positions. "It's good. I was on edge. Talking has slowed things down. I want to make this good for you, Paige."

"You already have. You are."

"Good. I'm going to play a little. You keep on talking."

Paige gasped when Nate's teeth tugged on her earlobe. Lord, the man loved using his teeth. Apparently, she was fine with that. *More* than fine.

"What do you want me to say?"

Nate didn't answer. Instead, he trailed a path of kisses down her neck. Paige tilted her head, giving him better access.

"Nate? What should I talk about?"

"There isn't a script." He breathed the words against her skin, the moist heat sending a shiver of pleasure through her body. "Let it flow naturally."

"What if I…"

"Paige." Nate slipped his fingers into her hair, massaging her scalp. His eyes were an intense blue. The look he gave her was so raw, so passionate it took her breath away. "You don't have to say a word. All I ask is that you be here with me."

"I am," Paige frowned.

"Physically, yes. I mean I want you here." He tapped her temple. "I thought talking might relax you. The suggestion seems to have had the opposite effect."

"I'm relaxed."

Nate smiled but didn't respond.

She sighed. "I don't know what happened."

"You were feeling good," Nate prompted. "You—"

"That's it!" she exclaimed. Paige framed Nate's face with her hands, her eyes on his. "You make me feel too much."

"Is that possible?" Nate seemed to think about it for a second before shaking his head. "Nope. Sex, if done properly, should make your body sing from the tip of your toes," he rubbed his foot against hers. "To the top of your head." Bending, he kissed her on the forehead.

"Then I've been doing it wrong. Sex is nice."

"Nice?" Nate sputtered. "If all you feel with me is *nice*, shoot me now."

"That's just it. With you, I feel..."

"Yes?" Nate kissed her, making stars shoot before her eyes. "What do you feel?"

"Everything."

That single word felt like a confession. Not of guilt. It was fear. For the first time in her life, she laid herself bare. Holding back had always been easy — natural. She could enjoy sex and walk away pleasantly satisfied. She never longed for a man because she always remained detached. Until Nate, no one had ever asked for more.

Be with me. It seemed like such a simple request. However, when Nate asked it of her, he made a request she wasn't sure she wanted to give to him.

189

It had never been an issue before. No one had ever asked. If they had, it wouldn't have mattered. She felt close to Nate. It made her feel free — and vulnerable. Could she open up to him without losing part of herself?

Paige didn't have a choice. She wanted Nate. Getting up and walking away was not going to happen. Nate wanted full participation. He insisted. Nate wasn't getting past her defenses with brute force. His touch — his kisses melted her walls like warm water pouring over spun sugar.

Relentless, yet somehow gentle. Inevitable. From the moment he stepped off that plane, everything had been leading to this. He was a gift. And she would be a fool not to welcome him with open arms.

"I don't want to talk anymore." Paige smoothed her hands across his face, her thumb rubbing over his lower lip.

"No? Tell me what you want, Paige."

The twinkle in his eyes said he already knew the answer — he needed her to say it.

"You. I want you."

"How difficult was that?" Nate nuzzled her ear. "Hold on. I'm not going to last long, and I'm taking you with me."

Paige didn't have time to worry. He leaned to the side, the arm with the cast supporting his weight. With the other hand, he took hold of his erection.

"Condom," she gasped as he began to enter her.

"All done."

When? It was her last cohesive thought. Nate took his time, easing in, giving her body time to adjust. Slow. Excruciatingly so. The fit was tight, but oh so perfect. Just right, as though her body had been made for this moment. Made for Nate.

"So wet. Like a hot, slick glove." The veins on Nate's neck stood out with the effort he exerted to take it slow. "Good?"

"Yes." Paige wrapped her legs around his hips, trying to pull him closer. "More. Now!"

"I don't want to hurt you."

Frustrated, she gripped his hair with her hands, kissing him with everything she had. "Do I look like I'm in pain?" she panted.

That was all Nate needed. He pushed into her, burying himself in her tight passage. He reveled in the feeling.

"So good."

"Move, Nate. Don't make me beg."

"I want you to beg," Nate growled. "Later. Right now all I want is this."

The stars that had been floating before Paige's eyes exploded into a red-hot kaleidoscope of colors, blinding her. Nate's first thrust was followed by another, then another. Each more powerful than the last. Each taking her higher and higher.

The air seemed thinner, her senses keener. Paige urged him on. They were not making love, but it was more than sex. The connection was too real. Almost too much.

"Look at me, Paige," Nate commanded. "Let me see your eyes."

Paige didn't know what Nate saw when she complied. However, she saw a blue so beautiful she wanted to jump in. No hesitation. No fear of drowning. She knew he would keep her safe. Safe. Yes, she was right where she belonged. That was the push she needed. Paige let go and fell.

"Nate!" she cried out.

"Take me in. Take all of me."

Paige's hands gripped his waist, the last few thrusts shooting her up again, ever so briefly. Every muscle in her body felt limp. Her legs fell to the mattress. The weight of Nate's body felt wonderfully heavy. She wanted to stay like this forever. His face pressed into the crook of her neck. The brush of his hair against her chin. His breathing slowing — matching the rhythm of hers.

Nothing outside this moment mattered. This was where she wanted to be. Right now. Right here. Perfect.

"I'm glad you didn't want Lottie."

"Lottie who?"

"Good answer." Paige caressed the damp skin of Nate's back.

"I should move."

When his weight started to shift, Paige's hand flattened at the base of his spine.

"Stay. Please. Just for a little while longer."

"I'm too heavy." Nate eased away.

"But—"

"Condom."

Paige rolled to her side, watching as Nate walked to the bathroom. It was a nice view. She knew his ass would be spectacular. She decided right then that naked Nate from the back was the best view in the world. That lasted until he came toward her. He looked even better coming than going.

"I like you naked."

"I like *you* naked."

Nate slid into bed. Paige expected him to take her into his arms. A little post-coital cuddling seemed appropriate. Instead, he disappeared under the covers. Frowning, Paige lifted the sheet.

"Hey, fella. What's going on down there?"

"Shh." Nate settled between her legs. Considering what they had just done, it was silly to feel shy. However, there was a big difference between him looking her in the eye while they had sex and him looking *at her sex.*

"But I want to know what you plan on doing down there."

"You know."

"Now?" Paige tried to close her legs. An impossible feat with two hundred and twenty-five pounds of big, muscular male blocking her movement.

"Now."

The first touch of his mouth had Paige clutching the headboard.

"Oh. My. God"

She heard Nate's familiar chuckle.

"You were saying?"

"Oh, my God. If you stop, I will never forgive you."

"I wouldn't want that."

If asked, Paige would have said she wasn't a fan of oral sex. The experience had always been more embarrassing than pleasurable and she always felt guilty for not enjoying it. With a few swipes of his very talented tongue, Nate turned her beliefs upside down.

Embarrassing? Not at all. Pleasurable? Hell yes. Oral sex? Best. Thing. Ever.

"You taste so damn sweet."

Was she supposed to answer? The best she could manage was a long, gasping moan. It seemed to be enough for Nate. He took another taste. When he added one finger, then two, Paige almost passed out.

"I can feel how close you are. Do you want to come?"

"Mmm."

Nate pushed the cover aside. The cool air did nothing to ease the heat that raged through her. Paige reached for him, trying to pull him back so he could finish what he started. But Nate had other ideas.

"You want me to beg?"

"Yes."

Paige couldn't believe that he would get her so close only to play such a wicked game. Nate shot her a cocky grin. Damn him. He held all the power. She would give him what he wanted. She would get her orgasm. Then she would make him pay.

"Please, Nate. I'll do anything. Anything."

"I only want one thing." Nate's mouth hovered over her.

"What?"

"To hear you scream my name."

Paige got what she wanted and so did Nate.

"Happy?"

Nate pulled the covers over them, and then gathered Paige into his arms.

"You have no idea."

She felt boneless. It was the best feeling in the world. Paige savored the feeling for a few minutes. Then, when she felt ready, she slid her hand down Nate's stomach. Not surprisingly, she found him rock hard.

"That feels fantastic," Nate sighed. His hips moved, encouraging her caresses.

"Nate?"

"Hmm."

Paige slid between his legs.

"Get ready to beg."

"THE CLOCK. THAT can't be right."

Nate squinted at the glowing numbers. Groaning, he turned onto his side, away from the glare. With little effort, he pulled Paige around until her back was to him, his arm holding her close.

"Don't look," he sighed. Happily, he buried his face in her soft, fragrant hair. "It doesn't count if you can't see it."

"But we already saw it." Paige let herself enjoy the moment. Snuggling with Nate was something she could get used to.

"My eyes weren't focused."

"It's a quarter after four."

"Ten minutes." Nate cupped Paige's breast. It was more intimate than sexual. One lover touching another. Paige sighed. Not better than sex — but good. Damn good.

"Dad never sleeps past five."

"I can't move. You drained me with your insatiable woman ways."

"My what?"

Nate smiled, his lips moving to her neck.

"It's a line from this crapfest of a movie I made when I was just starting out. I don't know why I remember it."

"Neither do I. Come on. We have to get moving."

"I haven't slept that well in months."

"When did you sleep? You were either in me or preparing to get in me for the last five hours." Lifting his hand, she kissed the back. "Not that I'm complaining."

"I know how to power nap. For me, ten minutes is like seven solid hours for someone else." Nate circled her nipple. Behind her, she was amazed to feel the stirring of his penis. "I'm big on time management. Let me show you what I can do in five minutes."

Laughing, Paige pushed his hand away. She sat up, the chill of the room reminding her how much better it felt wrapped up next to Nate.

"We don't have five minutes." Scrambling away, Paige jumped to her feet. "Nathaniel… what is your middle name?"

"Erasmus."

"Seriously?"

Nate stretched. It was not a bed made for a man his size. Curled up with Paige was one thing. Full length, half of his legs hung off the end.

"Family name." He yawned.

Erasmus. Interesting. Paige flipped on the overhead light. Her clothing was strewn in every direction. Shirt on the chair. Panties near the dresser. It didn't help that her legs felt like limp spaghetti. Not that she was complaining. Nate wore her out, but there was a grin on her face.

"Done. Let's go."

Paige whirled around. Nate stood by the door, fully dressed. There was an energetic buzz to him. *What the hell?*

"How did you do that?"

"Do what?" Nate handed Paige a sock that had somehow ended up on Lottie's bureau behind the bottle of *White Diamonds* that Paige gave her last Christmas.

"Go from groggy to bushy-tailed in three seconds flat?" Paige grumbled, hopping on one foot as she pulled on her boot.

"Seven hours sleep will do that."

"Asshole." Paige batted at Nate's hands. "I'm able to zip my own jeans."

"But it's so much fun to help."

"Nate. Or should I call you Erasmus."

"I wouldn't."

Paige's face lit up.

"What?"

"Nothing." She swung on her jacket. Taking a clip from the pocket, she twisted her hair into a quick bun. "You're a bit sensitive about your middle name."

195

"And that makes you happy."

"Strangely, yes." Paige jumped into Nate's arms, her mouth covering his. "It makes you human."

Following Paige from the room, Nate frowned.

"I wasn't human before?"

"You never put a foot wrong." Paige waited while Nate locked the door. "It's nice to know you a have a foible."

"I have dozens of flaws, Paige."

"I'm sorry." At the top of the porch steps, Paige stopped, putting her arms around his waist. "I didn't mean it as an insult."

"I don't want you to have the wrong idea about me. Pedestals are difficult things to live on. The fall can be brutal — for everyone involved."

Paige looked him in the eye, the porch light showing the surprise on her face. Then, she burst out laughing.

Nate closed his eyes, his head falling back.

"First she grins, then she laughs in my face. Do I dare ask?"

"Pedestal?" Paige shook her head. "That is the last place I would put you. I want you right here. On the ground, with me."

"There you go. That is exactly what I wanted to hear."

Nate gathered Paige close. His mouth was a hair's breadth away from hers when the world exploded.

Chapter Thirteen

PAIGE'S EARS WERE ringing. It felt as though someone had hit her with a ton of bricks, and then dumped them on her chest for good measure.

Light filled the darkness. Not steady, but flickering to her right, the shadows jumping around in front of her eyes.

Nate. *Jesus, Nate!* He had shielded her with his body. They were sprawled on the porch. Paige tried to shift, but she couldn't budge his weight. *Dead* weight. Desperate, she pushed at Nate's shoulder, shaking it. She needed a response. Any response.

"Paige? Are you all right?"

"Are you?"

Nate rolled to the side, but he kept Paige close.

"I had the wind knocked out of me, that's all." He patted her arms and legs, checking for injuries. "Do you feel any pain? Cuts? Burns?"

"I'm fine," she assured him.

Now that she was certain Nate was in one piece, Paige's attention turned to the driveway.

"What the hell?" Paige surged to her feet. "Is that my truck?"

"I'm afraid so."

Going with her first instinct, Paige tried to run to the burning vehicle. If Nate hadn't grabbed her arm, she would have jumped off the porch. What she thought she would have accomplished, she couldn't have said. It was a goner. Fire engulfed it front to back. Shattered glass from the windows littered the lawn; tiny shards nestled in the row of once cheery yellow flowers.

Lottie's sweetly groomed yard was no more. The marigolds and green lawn nearest the truck were singed black. Thankfully, the road leading to the house and most of the driveway had several layers of fresh gravel covering them. It prevented the spread of the fire beyond the truck.

"That's right. The truck exploded. No one was hurt. That's right." Nate turned to Paige, his face grim. "The fire department is on the way. Do you know if Lottie has an extinguisher?"

Paige nodded. "In the garage. I'll get it."

"I can find it." Nate pulled her close.

"Nate—"

"Shh. Let me hold you. Just for a second."

Paige was fine with that. She felt a little shaky. It was somehow comforting to know that Nate felt the same.

"Call your dad." Nate kissed her temple. "I'll be right back."

In the distance, Paige heard the wail of a siren. Basic had one fire truck. The noise it made was distinct — different from the two police cars. The station was located on the opposite end of town. The vehicle speeding down the main street, lights flashing, would bring everyone out, curious to see where it headed. Not the best way to start your day. It wouldn't take long for a crowd to gather and word to spread.

Nate was right. She needed to call her father.

Paige took her phone from her pocket. She stopped and took a deep breath. She didn't want to sound weepy and desperate. Her father would be worried enough without her crying.

"Hello?" Chuck's voice had the sound of a man who had been awakened from a sound sleep. "Paige? What's wrong?"

"I'm fine. But I'm afraid I can't say the same about Grandpa's truck."

DEALING WITH THE aftermath of the explosion didn't turn out to be as complicated as Paige thought it would be.

The firemen doused the truck with water though Nate had most of the blaze put out before they arrived.

"Here, take this. You're shivering."

Paige took the steaming cup of coffee from Lottie with a smile.

"I'm sorry about your lawn."

"Lawns can be replaced." She placed her arm around Paige's waist. "Best friends can't. Thank God you and Nate weren't in the truck."

The thought had occurred to Paige. Which was why she shivered. A few more seconds and her father would be dealing with a tragedy instead of a hollowed out pickup.

Lottie arrived with Danny Floyd. The man she had spent the night with was also the town sheriff. Lottie was there when he received the call. Naturally, she insisted on riding along. It was her house and her best friend. Nothing would have kept her away.

As Paige predicted, spectators began to arrive shortly after the fire department. Half the town seemed to be parked in the once empty field behind the house. Some of them brought thermoses of coffee, gathering in varying sizes of cliques.

"Pretty soon, Mavis Branch is going to show up and start selling breakfast rolls from the trunk of her car." Lottie frowned at the growing crowd.

"Speak of the devil." Paige nodded toward the dark brown station wagon pulling to a stop across the road.

"Unbelievable."

"Entertainment is at a premium in Basic, Lottie. Cut them some slack."

"I can't believe you're so calm. I would be quivering like a bowl of strawberry Jell-O."

"No, you wouldn't. You'd be yelling for the police to find the idiot who burned your pretty lawn." Paige turned her head. "Why strawberry? You hate the stuff."

"Exactly. Remember that stuff Mom made for every church potluck, or town get-together?" Lottie shuddered. "Foul. There was always one spoonful missing at the end of the evening."

Paige nodded. "Some poor soul who hadn't tried it before. Why did she finally stop making it?"

"One day, after twenty-five years, she finally figured out no one liked her Strawberry Surprise."

"Is that what she called it?" This was new to her. "What was the surprise?"

"That it was made with Jell-O. Mom thought that nobody knew. Bless her heart."

Paige laid her head on Lottie's shoulder. The silly, inconsequential talk helped. Between that and the coffee, she felt some heat seeping back into her bones.

"Not a great end to your night." Lottie wrinkled her nose when a puff of acrid smoke drifted over them. "Come on inside. The air is better."

Gratefully, Paige let Lottie lead her into the living room. She took a seat on the light green sofa. She set down her cup, and then leaned back, closing her eyes.

"I feel like I could sleep for a week. I don't know why I'm so worn out."

"I hope it has something to do with the hottie in the kitchen."

Paige opened her eyes. Nate. His head was bent toward Danny Floyd, nodding at whatever the police chief said.

"Oh. Right."

"Well?"

"Hmm?" she answered absently.

"Tell me how it was? How *he* was." Lottie joined her on the sofa. "You look worn out, he doesn't. Is that good or bad? Bad. It means he made you do all the work. Damn. I would have bet the bank that he was a giver. He has sex god written all over him."

It was true. Nate didn't look like a man operating on almost no sleep. He radiated a vitality that Paige envied. All she wanted to do was take a hot shower and go to bed. Nate looked like he could go all day without breaking a sweat. Maybe there was something to his power naps. Or maybe Nate Landis wasn't human.

Remembering the hours before her truck exploded, Paige smiled. Nate was human, all right. *Superhuman.*

"You're smiling." Lottie bounced with excitement. "I need details. And lots of them."

"No."

Lottie fell back, her eyes wide. "That good? You always share a little. If you want to keep it to yourself, Nate Landis must have been spectacular."

Paige's grin widened.

"I need something. Anything." Glancing around to see if anyone was near, Lottie whispered, "At least answer this. How big is he?"

"None of your business."

Lottie's eyes became as big as saucers. "That big! And if that dreaming expression you're wearing is any indication, he knows how to use it."

Again, Paige only smiled.

"Paige, honey, if you weren't my best friend, I would hate your guts. However, as per the unwritten gal-pal code, I couldn't be happier. You deserve some fun. Promise me one thing."

"What's that?"

"Don't fall in love with him."

"I won't."

"Well, crap." Lottie sighed, her eyes filled with concern. "You've had sex before and never fallen in love. I should have known that Nate Landis would be trouble."

"I'm not in love with him, Lottie." *Not yet.* "I like him. We're having fun — nothing more. That was established right at the beginning."

"Ground rules are good," Lottie nodded. "Until they aren't."

"What does that mean?" She was tired and on edge. The last thing she needed was one of Lottie's riddles.

"Nate is different. True?"

"Nate is… a good guy."

"That makes him different." Lottie liked men. She dated. A lot. She had sex when she wanted to, though not as often as people thought. Paige grew up with Chuck Chamberlin — the original good guy — as her father. Her friend didn't realize that men like that didn't grow on trees. In Basic, any man was hard to come by, the good ones — down deep good — were almost non-existent.

"Doesn't not wanting to fall in love with him count?"

"If you're worried about it, I'm afraid it's too late."

"Don't say that." Paige grabbed Lottie's hand. "I can stop this. I won't be alone with him."

"Oh, Paige," Lottie patted her hand. "The ball is rolling down a very steep hill."

"Couldn't you put that differently? Balls crash. It's inevitable."

Lottie heard the panic in Paige's voice and wanted to kick herself. There was nothing wrong with falling in love. Most people dreamed of finding *the one*. Maybe Nate would turn out to be that for Paige, maybe he wouldn't. If he broke her heart, Paige would recover. Right?

"You know what? Forget what I said. What do I know about love?"

"You are the most loving person I know," Paige said with fierce certainty.

"You see me that way because you love me." Lottie hugged Paige. "Don't ever stop believing. Okay?"

"Promise."

"Paige?" Nate came into the room. "The sheriff wants to get your statement."

"Go on," Lottie said. "I'm going to take a shower and get ready for work."

"Your dad didn't stay long."

"He wanted to make sure we were okay, and then he had to get back and feed the animals." The chores needed to be done every day. They relied on them for their survival. The horses didn't care about exploding trucks. "He didn't talk to you before he left?"

"No. Should that worry me?"

"He doesn't blame you for this mess, Nate."

No, he thought, *but maybe he should.*

"I was thinking of what we were doing before your pickup was destroyed."

"Oh, God. Do you think he knows what we were doing?" Paige felt her cheeks heat. "That never occurred to me."

Nate cupped Paige's cheek. She looked ready to drop. He wished he could take her home, but the sheriff insisted on talking to them now. Nate figured it was best to get it over with and done with. The problem was he didn't think it was over. Not if his theory was correct.

"I'm sure he's put two and two together by now." Nate guided her into the kitchen. "We'll deal with that later."

"Morning, Paige."

"Danny."

Paige had known Danny Floyd all of her life. They went to school together — first through twelfth grades. He had been her first crush and her first kiss. They had been eleven. It was awkward and a little sweet.

She later found out he did it on a dare. Paige wanted to crawl into a hole and die. Lottie marched up to him after school and knocked him on his ass. From that day forward, Danny was in love.

Despite the unfortunate kiss, Danny was one of the rare good guys that Lottie had mentioned. He started out as deputy, and then elected sheriff when old Paul Trainor retired. The man had good husband and father written all over him. Unfortunately for Danny, Lottie refused to see him as more than a friend and a part-time lover. He wanted more but the few times he tried to push her, Lottie stopped seeing him.

He was tall and slender with wavy brown hair. Danny had a nice face. Even features that most people would call handsome. He was a catch by every definition of the word. Everyone in Basic knew how he felt — everyone but Lottie.

"The EMT guys said you checked out fine. How are you feeling?"

"Wrung out."

"We'll get this over with as quickly as possible."

Nate pulled out a chair at the table, seating Paige. He poured them both a cup of freshly brewed coffee, and then joined her.

"You left the house just after four."

"That's right. I wanted to get back to the ranch before…" Paige's eyes darted away from Danny's.

"Is it necessary to discuss the whys and wherefores, Sheriff? Paige and I spent the night here. We were on the porch when the truck exploded."

"Right." Danny made a few notes. "Any idea who would do such a thing?"

"No," Paige shook her head, frowning. "It doesn't make any sense. That wasn't a prank. We could have been killed."

"Nate?"

"How would he know? Nate has only been here a few weeks, Danny."

"I don't know who did it, but I'm pretty sure it was because of me."

Paige listened with growing horror while Nate told them about what happened during his last stunt.

"You said your broken arm was the result of an accident." Without thought, Paige laid a hand on his cast. "Are you saying somebody tried to kill you?"

"There's no proof. A witness came forward. He tried to scam me out of some money. It turned out he didn't know anything."

"You think this is related?" Danny stirred a spoonful of sugar into his coffee.

Normally, Paige would have appreciated his calm, professional attitude. Under the circumstances, she wanted to slap him upside the head.

"I can't think of any other explanation."

"You don't have a name? A lead? Anything?"

"I have some friends who are investigating." Jack's last report had been like all the others. Nothing new. "I wish I could tell you more."

"I don't like the idea of a killer running around my town." Danny looked grim. "I'd like to talk to these friends of yours. The more they can tell me the better."

"I'll give you the contact information for H&W Security. However, this won't be your problem for long, Sheriff."

"Why is that?"

"Because I'm leaving as soon as I can make the arrangements."

"What?" Paige couldn't believe her ears.

"If I'd thought I was putting anyone else in danger, I never would have come, Paige. If I stay, this could happen again. And whoever is nearby might not be as lucky as we were."

"No."

"He's right, Paige."

"What about Dad? He's counting on you to help him make Mom's movie." Paige knew she sounded desperate, but she didn't care. She refused to let Nate walk out of her life so soon. She knew it was inevitable. Just not right now.

"When I explain, he'll understand. He'll probably pack my bag and drive me to the airport."

"I don't believe that. There has to be another solution." Jumping to her feet, she waved a finger in front of Nate's face. "You agreed to do a job and you aren't leaving until it's finished."

"Paige."

Nate watched her storm out of the room. He knew why she was upset. Did she think he wanted to leave her? After last night? He wanted more. His plan had been to spend the next few weeks making love with Paige again and again. It wasn't easy knowing their first time together might have been their last.

JAMES CRANSHAW WAS not a brave man. He was a weasel. Hiding in holes. Coming out at night where he could slip into the shadows — undetected.

He made his living by taking jobs from people who wanted bad things done but didn't want to get their hands dirty. James Cranshaw didn't mind. The pay was good and he liked the thrill of ruining lives while knowing he would never have to pay the consequences.

His specialty was fire. James shivered. Watching flames engulf a building — especially if someone was inside — turned him on like nothing else. Women were a dime a dozen. Give him a roaring blaze any day.

Mistakes were rare. However, they did happen. Which was why he always insisted on half of his fee upfront. Clients didn't like sloppy work. On occasion, they refused to pay — even after he rectified the situation. That wasn't the proper way to do business. Being a man who hated confrontation, he slinked back into the shadows without his money.

Not that he allowed his client to get off that easily. A month, maybe two, later, a fire destroyed something the client loved. A fancy car. A beachside retreat. A spouse.

Lesson learned.

Anonymity was the key to his success. It made him a rich man and kept him breathing. Never meet. Never give your name. He kept over two hundred post office boxes all over the United States. Small towns. Large cities. From Florida to Hawaii. James liked to travel — though never under his real name.

Even James Cranshaw was an alias. That person ceased to exist thirty years ago. After his first fire. Bye-bye, Mom and Dad. The backwater police assumed he died with them. No one questioned the notion. That night he walked into the shadows. And that was where he had stayed. Until two years ago.

It was his own fault. He liked to drink. He called it his second love. Fire and alcohol. In the wrong hands, they could be a lethal combination. James knew how to handle both without getting burned.

He didn't know how Michael found him. A casual comment exchanged in a liquor store. A mutual love of aged whiskey. James made three mistakes that night. Going out when he had already consumed the last half of a bottle in his apartment. Striking up a conversation with a stranger. And not watching his back.

He woke the next morning with a bump on his head and a brand new burner phone, and a new *friend*. Not Michael — if that was really his name. He worked for someone. A man who was as anonymous as James used to be.

The first call came while James packed his few possessions. The plan was to be gone before whatever shit was about to hit the fan, landed on him. He would lay low for a few months. He didn't want to move his money. The accounts were safe. But he wasn't going to take a chance on his activities being traced. He had a secret stash that would hold him over.

James almost didn't answer when the phone rang. No one who went to this much trouble would let him get away that easily. Screwing up his small supply of courage, James took a deep breath.

"Hello."

"Mr. Cranshaw."

The voice was smooth. Educated. It sent a shot of ice through James' veins.

"Who is this?"

"Call me your… friend. Yes. I like that. This is your friend, James. Your *best* friend." The man's laugh was the least jolly thing James had ever heard.

"I doubt that."

"But it's true, James. I'm about to give you the greatest gift any friend can give another."

"What is that?" James held his breath.

"Why, the gift of life. You do what I tell you, and you get to live."

James sank onto the beat-up sofa that came with the apartment. High-end booze was the only thing he spent his money on. His pleasure came from knowing it was there — and the memories of how he acquired it.

For the first time, he wished he had splurged now and then. A new car. Nicer clothes. He was going to die, and damn it, unless he could swallow every cent, there was no way to take it with him.

"Relax, James. I don't want to end your life. I have spent too much time looking for you."

"Me?"

"Naturally, I don't mean you in particular." His tone was slightly chastising. "I meant someone with your unique skill set."

James didn't answer. What could he say to that? Thank you?

"To get what I want, from time to time, people need to die. You are going to take care of that, James. I will be happy. You will live. And as an added bonus, I'm going to pay you your usual fee."

"Why not hire me? Why bother with all of this?"

"That is a very good question, James. What do you think is the answer?"

James heard a match striking and the familiar puffing sound that accompanied the lighting of a cigar. James' father loved a good smoke. He used one to set his childhood home on fire.

"You want control over me."

"Very good. I never do anything unless I know I'm pulling all the strings. Hmm. That makes me the Puppet Master. I like that."

"How will this work?"

"Whenever I need a favor, a disposable phone will be delivered. The next day, a text will be sent. There will be a name and a location. The rest will be up to you. And James?"

James swallowed. "Yes?"

"I do not tolerate failure."

That was how the unholy alliance began. James had no illusions about himself. He lit fires. Sometimes people died. Simple and clean. Working for the Puppet Master changed that. He was no longer his own man. His new *boss* insisted on exclusivity. No freelancing. No exceptions.

He received a monthly payment — automatically deposited into one of his three offshore accounts. When he completed a job, a bonus amount was added.

James kept to the agreement — he was afraid not to. The two times he tried to disappear, he paid the price. A broken nose. Then a broken arm. He didn't want to find out what would be next. He didn't tolerate pain well.

He did what he was told and he did it right — the first time. No screw-ups. Clean. Easy. Never a trace left behind. No witnesses. No messes to clean up.

Until now.

The truck had been a mistake. Miscommunication. The Puppet Master wouldn't tolerate that excuse. He would know the real reason James screwed up.

Single malt whiskey.

Damn it. It wasn't his fault. He was in the middle of nowhere. Fucking Montana. Why would anyone choose to live here? Miles and miles of nothing. After that? More nothing.

When the command came in for him to get his ass to Basic, James assumed he would be in and out. A quick job. Easy. What could there be to keep him busy in such a backwater hole?

Two weeks later, he had his answer. *Nothing.* There was nothing for him to do. *Break a camera? Really?* It had been so far below his skill level, he almost protested. *Almost.* Instead, James drank. He brought five bottles of the good stuff with him. More than enough. Or so he thought. He was down to one bottle. Half of which he had been consuming when the text came in.

Last minute instructions issued at two in the morning? How could he be at his best? Blurry, bloodshot eyes didn't focus well in the middle of the night. A line that read, *get rid of him,* wavered into, get rid of *them.* Anyone could have made that mistake.

The only thing that might save him was the fact that he hadn't succeeded. *Who was he kidding? He was a dead man.*

James didn't go back to his hotel room. The only things there were some dirty underwear and a death sentence. He headed out of town in the old Chevy he had purchased for this journey into oblivion. As he literally drove for his life, he went over the mistakes of the evening.

He should have waited until some of the alcohol had worn off. He knew better than to do a job when the booze was freshly singing in his veins. It made him reckless. One of the main reasons he drank. It was the only time he was released from the weight of his fears.

Whiskey made him stand tall. It also made him dumber than a sack of rocks.

The house should have been his target. It was small. A few charges strategically placed and boom. Blame it on a gas leak. End of story.

The size of the house made him go for the truck. His hands weren't steady. He worried about being heard. Normally, he would be in and out. Slick. Silent. However, his head started to pound. He had been convinced the entire town could hear the thunder of his footsteps. He couldn't risk being caught. So he skipped the house and put a remote-controlled detonator under the gas tank of the truck. As soon as the man and woman were inside, he would hit the switch.

Any halfway-decent investigator would determine it wasn't an accident. But so what? No one would trace it back to him — or the Puppet Master.

The plan would have worked. Except he fell asleep. Something woke him. The sound of the front door closing? Whatever it was, James sat up with a start, panicked that his targets were getting away. Without thinking, he reached for the remote and set off the charge. For a second, he forgot his pounding head and the inch-thick coating of fuzz on his tongue. The night was ablaze. Fire. The surge of excitement was familiar — welcome. He let the feeling rush through him. Until he saw something moving on the porch. One body. No two.

Holy Fuck. They were alive.

James didn't think twice. He started the car and drove. Three hours later, the panic hadn't worn off. He kept running his mistakes over and over in his mind. One piled on top of the other. He was well and truly trapped beneath a shit-pile of his own making. His head was clear enough to realize there was no digging out. So he did the only thing he could. He kept driving. North. To Canada.

Luck wasn't his friend. Not that it ever had been. The SUV ran him off the road and into a tree. The crap car was old. Too old for airbags. Goddamn it. His face was smashed up. He could taste the metallic bite of his own blood.

"I fucked up."

"Yes. You did."

Michael. From the liquor store. One bullet to the brain. James had one last thought before his life ended.

Fucking Montana.

Chapter Fourteen

NATE WONDERED IF he was the only sensible person left in the world. Or maybe he was on caffeine overload. He was certain the words coming out of his mouth were intelligible. Logical. Yet instead of agreeing, Chuck, the cast, the crew, and even the horses, acted as though nothing had changed.

Lottie had driven Nate and Paige home. It was a bit of a detour on her way to work, but she said she felt better personally seeing that they were dropped off safe and sound.

The trip was uneventful — and silent. Paige wasn't speaking to him. Lottie — in solidarity — for once kept her thoughts to herself. Nate hated the chill that had settled between him and Paige, but there was nothing to say. He was leaving. Not because he wanted to. It was for her safety. For the safety of her father and her friends.

As they approached the house, he was surprised to see so many vehicles in the driveway. Surely, Chuck had canceled today's shoot. Word of the explosion would have reached everyone long before now. What reason could they have for being here?

"Looks like a party." Lottie eased her car to a stop. "I'm sorry I have to miss it."

"Thanks for the ride." Paige gave her friend a hug. "Call me later. I could use a girl's night out."

"Really?" Lottie glanced at Nate. He shook his head before getting out of the backseat. "After everything? Let's wait a few days. After…"

"He's determined to leave, Lottie." Paige sighed. Her eyes carried a resigned sadness. "I would rather go out with you than sit home and mope."

"Drinks it is."

Lottie hated to see her friend defeated. Paige was a fighter. But how did you fight for a man who wasn't yours and now, never would be? It was her job as best friend to help ease the pain. Tequila shots, loud music on the jukebox, and a sympathetic ear. Lottie would be there to make sure Paige didn't do anything stupid. Too much to drink? Yes. Rebound sex? Absolutely not.

"It looks like everyone is gathered in the barn." Paige started to walk in that direction. When Nate didn't join her, she turned. "Come on. You might as well get this over with. It will be easier to explain yourself to the group. It will save Dad having to do it."

Nate couldn't argue. Nor did he want to. He brought this mess with him. It was up to him to clean it up. That meant making those people who had put their trust in him understand that he wasn't abandoning them. The movie would get made. However, someone else would be stepping in as director.

Nate decided what to say when his phone rang. Wyatt. He looked up to see Paige waiting for him.

"It's my brother."

Paige nodded. "I'll let everyone know you're coming."

"What's up, Wyatt?"

"You tell me."

Nate could picture his oldest brother. It was after nine. That meant Wyatt was in full producer mode. Italian suit — tailored to perfection. Crisp white shirt. His tie would be straight as a pin. He looked like the perfect young executive. And in many ways, that's what he was.

"You heard." Shit. The first call Nate made after the police should have been to his parents. "I'll call Mom and Dad right away."

"That can wait a few more minutes. Chuck spoke with Dad a few hours ago. He assured him that you were fine. Mom tried calling, but she got your voicemail. You can imagine how that went over. If Dad hadn't stopped her, she would be halfway to Montana by now."

"I turned my phone off while we were giving our statements. I didn't think to check my messages when I turned it on."

"The *we* being you and Paige Chamberlin?"

"That's right."

There was a long pause. Nate knew this game. Wyatt was a master of it. He asked a question then waited until the other person spilled their guts. More than once, Nate had caved under the pressure of the excruciating silence.

Not this time. Paige was none of Wyatt's business.

Nate wasn't certain, but he thought he heard Wyatt chuckle. Before he could decide his brother dropped some news Nate could have done without.

"My assistant has been fielding questions from the press."

"Well, shit."

"I know you hate publicity, but—"

"Goddamn it, Wyatt."

"Hear me out. Jesus." Wyatt sighed. "I have three brothers, each more frustrating than the last. You, Nathaniel, have been generating a lot of interest. Over the past few months, you have slowly been losing anonymity."

"Not by choice." Nate ran a hand through his hair. He noticed Rollie, her head seeming to beckon him. He walked to the corral and scratched her nose. Silly, but he felt calmer with the horse rubbing her muzzle against his hand.

"I know." Wyatt's voice softened. "I wish I could tell you it will go away. You know it would be a lie. First, the accident on the set of your last film. By the way, the theory that it *wasn't* an accident is gaining traction."

"Is that good or bad?" Nate had the feeling he already knew the answer.

"The crazies are coming out of the woodwork. According to one person, what happened to you ties into the Kennedy assassination, Watergate, and Iran-Contra."

"What time machine did that guy step out of? Hello. Restrict your conspiracy theories to events from the twenty-first century."

"I had an intern set up a tip-line."

"It's gotten that bad?"

Nate exchanged looks with the horse. She seemed as annoyed as he was. It was nice to know she was on his side.

"Yes." Wyatt didn't like to mince words. "You are the current social media darling, Nate."

"That's a bit of an exaggeration."

"Check out the numbers. You have almost one hundred thousand likes on Facebook alone."

Groaning, Nate rested his forehead on Rollie's neck. The horse nickered. Sympathy? Nate didn't care. That was his interpretation.

"Now you understand why this morning's news has caused such a stir. The Landis name plus everything else? You need to get ahead of this."

"I should give an interview."

"One," Wyatt said before Nate could protest. "We pick the time, the place, and the person. You know how it works. Get the facts out there, diminish the interest."

"The facts?"

"The ones you want to share. The rest you can gloss over. If you want, I can have a press release made up. All you will need to do is be charming and smile, and the world will be happy."

"Nothing is released without my approval, Wyatt."

"Jesus, Nate. Really? This is your brother. You think I'm going to screw you over?"

Shit. Nate felt Wyatt's slap-down from here. He deserved it — and worse.

"I'm sorry. This has knocked me for a loop."

"Almost getting blown up will do that." There was an edge to Wyatt's voice. "I don't like the idea of losing my brother."

"I'm with you," Nate said. "I'm leaving as soon as I can. Set up the interview. I'll be back in Los Angeles in a day or two. After I check in with the family, I'll head out again."

"Where?"

"I don't know yet. Someplace where I don't have to worry about anyone else getting hurt."

"We'll talk about that when you get here."

"My mind is made up, Wyatt."

"We'll see."

Nate wasn't going to argue. He knew what Wyatt thought. The family would gang up on him and convince him not to leave. They could try, but there was no way he would put them in danger. He had almost cost Paige her life. He wasn't taking any more chances with the people he loved.

Nate froze. *People he loved? Paige?* It was a slip. His brain was as tired as the rest of him. That was the only explanation.

Rollie gave him a knowing look.

"Keep your thoughts to yourself."

"What?" Wyatt asked.

"Nothing." Nate frowned at the horse before turning away. "I need to explain things to the movie crew, Wyatt. Tell Mom and Dad I will call them in a few hours."

"Will do. And Nate?"

"Yes?"

"Watch your back."

Nate put away his phone, thinking back to the day he arrived in Montana. Jack Winston had given him the same advice. At the time, it hadn't occurred to him that someone would try anything this drastic. How did one prepare for this kind of attack? How could he protect himself, or anyone else, from a bomb?

There was only one answer. *Get as far away from civilization as possible.*

"Nate." The sobbing call of his name greeted him the second he stepped into the barn.

"Oh, Nate." A sobbing Jenna threw herself at Nate.

"Calm down." Awkwardly, he patted the girl's back. "I'm fine."

As gently as possible, Nate peeled Jenna's arms from around his waist and handed her over to her equally distraught friends.

"Cut the blubbering," Homer said with disgust.

"Oh, shut up, Homer." Jenna wiped at her eyes, careful not to mess up her mascara. "Go play with your camera."

"Enough." Chuck gave the youngsters a warning look. "Nate. Why don't you take a seat? You look done in."

"Thanks, Chuck, but I'm fine."

Nate looked around the room. It appeared that almost everyone was here. Beauty scampered to a halt at his feet, her eyes filled with unconditional adoration. He picked her up, smoothing a hand over her head. Happy to be in her favorite place, with her favorite person, she relaxed with a huge puppy sigh.

"We know the shoot was canceled." Edith Potter offered Nate a cup of coffee. There was a table filled with the usual assortment of pastries and beverages. When Nate shook his head, she smiled. "Coffeed out?"

Nate nodded. He searched for Paige, finding her in the back. A few of the women stood by her, but her eyes were on him. Nate held her gaze, trying to see past the exhaustion etched on her face. She looked like a warrior returned from battle. It was a fanciful thought, but somehow accurate. His heart twisted. He knew she was angry. And hurt. And he knew he was the reason. The knowledge killed him. The sooner he got away from her, the better.

"We wanted to see for ourselves that you and Paige were all right."

"I appreciate it, Edith. I'm sure Paige feels the same."

"Oh, Paige filled us in while you were on the phone. I can't believe something like that happened here in Basic. Thank God you walked away unharmed."

"I'm glad you're all here." Keeping his gaze off Paige, Nate took a

216

deep breath. He hadn't realized this would be so difficult. In a short time, he had grown fond of these people. No matter how good the reasons, he hated letting them down.

"I want you to know how much working with all of you has meant to me."

"Why does it sound like there is a 'but' coming after that statement?"

Nate gave Edith a weary smile.

"Because there is. I'm heading back to Los Angeles first thing in the morning. I have a friend who has agreed to take over. He has a lot more experience so you don't have to worry. The production will continue."

Nate had expected a few protests. The eruption of angry voices had his eyes widening in surprise.

"We refuse to accept your resignation."

"Edith—"

"I mean it, Nate. I think I speak for everyone when I say it won't work with anyone else. You know us. You understand what Erin wanted." Edith looked around the barn, her eyes coming to rest on Chuck. "Ask him."

"Chuck. Do you want to risk these people?" Nate shook his head. "Paige could have died today."

"This isn't about me, Nate. Not anymore." As Edith did, he looked around the room. "I'll admit, when I first started, I wasn't thinking past my wants. My needs. It was selfish and I'm sorry, Paige."

"Oh, Dad." Paige crossed the barn, her arms slipping around her father's waist. "You weren't selfish."

Chuck snorted, making Paige laugh.

"Maybe a little selfish. Why is that a bad thing?" She met his gaze. Brown eyes, so alike, the emotions mirrored. "Mom would love this. Somewhere I believe she is cheering you on."

"Cheering us on." Chuck kissed Paige on the forehead. "You see, Nate. You have too many people who want you to stay. Including Erin."

Nate wondered if the combination of too much coffee and too little sleep was making him a little crazy. His argument was sound. Sensible.

Hell, every person here should be pushing him out the door as quickly as possible.

Instead, they used every trick in the book to make him stay. Guilt and sentiment topping the list.

The problem was Nate didn't want to leave. To his ever-growing surprise, he was having a blast directing the movie. It didn't signal a new calling for him. However, it was interesting to see things from the other side of the camera. He was getting a little insight into Garrett's professional life. And maybe, just maybe, he would be more sympathetic the next time a director drove him crazy with unreasonable demands.

And then there was Paige. She was his biggest reason to leave. Her safety. His heart. *Shit.* There it was again. If he left, his heart would be safe. That made him a selfish bastard — and a coward.

If he stayed, he risked everything. The lives of people he had come to care for. And falling hard for Paige. Correction. Falling *harder* for Paige. He was on the precipice. Nate watched as she gave her father another hug. The ground beneath his feet was crumbling — inch by inch. The smart thing would be to jump back before he tumbled all the way. When Paige smiled, her eyes meeting his, Nate gave a mental sigh.

Stupid or not, it looked like he had made his decision.

"If I do this—"

Homer let out a whoop of excitement.

Nate pinned him with his best steely gaze. Homer sat down, chastised but still grinning.

"I have to insist on a few things."

"Name it."

For the first time in hours, Nate felt like laughing. Homer was all in, the look on his face a lot like the one Beauty had given him. Puppy love. Hero worship. Who knew they were so similar?

"Number one. And this is non-negotiable. Everyone under the age of eighteen? I'm sorry, but the movie set is off limits."

"But Nate!"

"I'm not trying to punish you and your friends, Jenna. Your safety is my priority."

"Because you care about me?" Jenna's friend Wynona jabbed her in the ribs. "I meant us." Jenna shot her friend a warning look before turning back to Nate. "You care about us?"

"Of course I do." Nate held his arms open. Five girls rushed in for a group hug. "When this is over and the bastar—" Nate cleared his throat. "I mean the jerk responsible is behind bars, you can come back." Nate stepped back. "In the meantime, what if I get Colt to send you some autographed swag?"

They squealed, leaving the way they always traveled — bunched together.

"Homer. Will you give the young ladies a ride home?"

"But—"

"We pick up the day after tomorrow. Bright and early."

"Fine." With a sigh, Homer waved a hand toward the barn door. "Come on."

"Poor Homer." Chuck smiled at the retreating teens.

"Poor me. One mention of my brother and my adoring fan club jumps off my bandwagon." Nate meant it jokingly. However, he had enough of an ego to feel a bit of a twinge.

"Don't be so sure." Edith gathered her purse and jacket. She gave Beauty a pat on the head, sending the puppy's tail wagging. "They adore you. Trust me; they won't desert you that easily."

After that, the barn cleared out quickly. Nate waved as the last car drove away. Then in the distance, a black SUV appeared. Chuck and Paige stood on either side of him as the vehicle came to a stop.

"Mr. Landis?" A man with a military haircut and arms the size of tree stumps stepped out. Tattoos covered every inch of exposed skin. He was tall. Almost matching Nate.

"Yes."

"Travis Marshall." He smiled, softening his chiseled features. "Jack Winston sent me."

Setting Beauty down, Nate shook the man's hand. "Travis. This is Chuck Chamberlin and his daughter Paige."

"Pleased to meet you." There was a touch of the South in his voice.

"Georgia?" Nate asked.

"Tupelo, Mississippi. Best honey in the world."

"I can't argue. I spent a very pleasant spring down South. Biscuits and honey every morning."

"And grits." Travis sighed. "Don't forget the grits."

"You're making my mouth water," Chuck smiled. "You want to come in the house? I can't promise a Southern breakfast, but I have a pot of corn chowder on the stove. Do you like cornbread?"

"Yes, sir."

Gesturing to Travis, Nate held back as Chuck and Paige headed inside.

"I haven't had a chance to call Jack."

Grinning at the puppy sniffing his boots, Travis bent down to introduce himself. "Is there a problem?"

"You could say that. We need to increase the security."

Travis stood up straight, the good old Southern boy quickly replaced by a man who meant business.

"When you say increase, how many do you mean?"

"I'm not sure." Nate rubbed the back of his neck.

"Let's call Alex," Travis said. "He handles this kind of thing every day. You can fill us both in. He'll get you what you need."

"Let's take this inside." Nate started up the front steps. "Chuck and Paige should hear this."

"This is their ranch, right? They need to sign off on bringing in more security?"

"That won't be a problem."

Nate held the door for Travis. Whatever it took to keep Paige, Chuck, and everyone safe. He would brook no arguments. If it took a hundred men to lock this place down, so be it.

Beauty sat, waiting patiently.

"I won't let anything happen to them. This is between us." He scooped her up. "If I don't think I can keep them safe, we are out of here. You and me. Understand?"

Beauty gave him what looked like a nod. Nate knew she didn't understand his words. However, he swore the look in her eyes said, "What about Paige? Can't she come?"

It was his own conscience talking. And maybe his heart. Nate rubbed his chest, right above that beating organ. Nope, Paige didn't belong with him and his nomad lifestyle. She belonged here. With her father. With her horses. This was her home.

Nate took a long look at the ranch and the mountains that bordered it. He knew he would miss this. Most of all, he knew he would miss Paige.

Chapter Fifteen

HER FATHER HADN'T blinked an eye when Nate declared he was bringing in more security. On speakerphone with Travis' boss, Alex Fleming, Chuck laid out the logistics of the ranch and number of people who worked on the movie at any given time. Once they had everything worked out, the speed in which it was set into motion made her head spin.

H&W Security gathered their crew and had them on a plane to Montana in record time. This Alex Fleming knew how to get things done.

Travis had explained that Alex was ex-Army. He said it with a touch of reverence that made Paige curious about what the man's job had been. When she asked, Travis shrugged. Alex was the best, he said. That was it. The subject was closed.

The best? The best what? Sniper? Code Breaker? Spy? She quickly realized that she had seen too many movies. Travis and Nate trusted Alex. That was all Paige needed, or wanted, to know.

The house couldn't accommodate fifteen large men and the equipment they brought with them. Luckily, the weather was holding.

Early October could turn cold — fast. However, it seemed this year they were in for a mild, seasonably warm month. The barn, in addition to housing the movie paraphernalia, was now a makeshift barracks.

"It won't be very comfortable," Paige said as she watched the men remove cots and sleeping bags from a large, black van.

"This is a five-star hotel compared to some of the places we've slept," Travis informed her.

The group worked like a well-oiled machine. There was no need for conversation. They were trained to be ready for last minute assignments and knew how to hit the ground running.

The rest of the day was a blur of activity that often looked like barely contained chaos. Paige watched the show with admiration and a touch of awe. Motion sensitive cameras. Flood lights. Alarms. She lost track of everything they installed.

The men spoke in a kind of shorthand that was confusing at first, but the longer she listened, the easier it was to decipher. There was no question about what was going on when one of the men reported that the house had been swept. It was clean. No listening devices, cameras, or other foreign objects found

Alarmed, she asked Travis why he thought someone would bug the house.

"It's routine for us to check," he assured her.

Paige was relieved. She was still working on reassured.

On top of everything else, the men had brought along portable gas stoves and an upscale version of K rations. It was an impressive setup.

When she asked her father what all this was costing, he told her that Nate was handling it.

"You're letting Nate foot the bill?" Paige couldn't believe her ears. Her father was a stickler about paying his way. There was no way they could afford one of these men, let alone fifteen of them. And the equipment? It boggled the mind.

"You heard him, Paige. All of this," he motioned to the bodies at work, "is the only way he would agree to stay. Do you want him to leave?"

"You know I don't."

They hadn't discussed the reason that she and Nate had been at Lottie's house, and Paige didn't expect they ever would. However, Chuck wasn't a fool. He knew her relationship with Nate had taken a more intimate turn.

"I'm signing over all rights to the movie."

"Dad! You can't do that."

"I wanted Erin's story to be told. It was never about making money. Now," Chuck shrugged. "I'm not fooling myself. If the movie turns a profit, it will be a miracle, but it's the only thing I have to offer. Nate would never agree to take part of the ranch."

"Damn straight."

Paige took in the sight of Nate. There was nothing for him to do. Every man had a job. He would be in the way if he offered to help. However, there was no doubt who was in charge. Travis orchestrated the action, but he consulted with Nate every step of the way. It wasn't because he footed the bill. Nate was a born leader. He was the man one would gravitate toward in any crisis — confident that he would find a way out.

Paige understood. She believed in standing on her own two feet. Making her own way. Solving her problems with no outside help. Yet all she wanted to do was curl up in his arms and let him take care of everything. That impulse made her keep her hands firmly anchored to her sides.

"This is your ranch, Chuck. Yours and Paige's. The same goes for the movie."

"I can't let you do all this without paying you back. I know the movie isn't worth anything, but it's all I have to offer." Paige recognized the stubborn set of her father's chin. Her brown eyes weren't the only thing she inherited from him.

"My mess, my responsibility."

"You're here because of me," Chuck reasoned.

"Technically, I'm here because of Paige. Isn't that right?"

Paige nodded. She didn't trust herself to speak. Too many emotions that she hadn't found names for.

"Fine." Chuck crossed his arms. "You agreed to stay because my people guilted you into it. That shifted the responsibility back to me."

Fascinated by the game of testosterone ping-pong, Paige waited to see how Nate would respond now that the ball sailed back his way.

"I hold all the cards, Chuck."

Nate's stance was deceptively relaxed. Even with her father between them, she could feel the coiled energy radiating from him. Nate looked like he didn't have a care in the world. Paige wouldn't want to be the person who made the mistake of testing that theory.

"Damn it, Nate." Paige knew her father was out of arguments. And so did he.

"One more thing." Nate's gaze landed on her, then shifted to Chuck. The deep blue color intense. "That is the last time I want to hear you say that the movie isn't worth anything. I've never been privileged to work on a project that meant more than this one. You can't measure it in dollars and cents. The sense of accomplishment and pride I see in the cast and crew. The way you are honoring Erin's memory. It's priceless, Chuck. Never forget that."

"He's the most arrogant person I have ever met," Chuck said with a huff as they watched Nate walk over to where Travis was making notes.

"Yes," Paige agreed.

"Frustrating."

"Absolutely."

"Pig-headed."

"No argument here."

"Admirable." Chuck's tone softened.

Paige smiled, nodding her head.

"A man like that is a rare thing."

Once in a lifetime, Paige thought. *If you were lucky.*

"Lottie called him a good man."

"Mmm. She hit it on the head." Chuck put an arm around her shoulders. "You're in love with him."

"I…" Paige shook her head. "I barely know him, Dad. People don't fall in love this fast."

"I fell for your mother the second I saw her. I opened the front door and saw my future wrapped up in a coat that made her look like the Michelin Man. The heart has no sense of time, Paige."

"I don't know what I'm feeling." Paige couldn't tell her father something when she didn't know the answer. "Nate has me tied in knots, Dad."

"That's okay. Knots aren't always a bad thing."

"In this case, they are. Nate and I are on two separate paths that have briefly intersected. In a few weeks, he'll be off to who knows where. I'm fine with that."

"Oh, Paige."

"What?"

"Earlier, you gave him hell when you thought he was leaving."

"No one wanted him to leave. Don't laugh." Paige smiled in spite of herself. "My reasons may be a bit more personal than everyone else's."

"Just a bit." Chuck tucked her arm through his and began walking toward the house. "You may believe it will be okay, Paige. But when the time comes, letting him go won't be easy."

"No." That much she would admit. "I won't make a scene or beg him to stay."

"You forget one thing."

"What's that?"

"This love thing can work both ways. When the time comes, Nate might not want to give *you* up."

Hours later, her father's words stuck with her, like little whispers of hope that she couldn't shake off. Closing her eyes, Paige rolled her head in a slow circle. Right now, all she wanted was a good night's sleep. It had been crazy to think she would be in any condition to go out. When Lottie had called, Paige yawned through the conversation as she filled her friend in.

Mentioning the addition of the security force had not been a good idea. She blamed it on a fuzzy brain. Lottie's first reaction was a squeal of excitement. Fresh blood. It was all Paige could do to keep her from jumping in her car and racing over. The men were not here for Lottie's enjoyment. They had a job to do.

"They take breaks, don't they?" Lottie asked slyly.

"Yes. What's your plan? Sit around and pick them off one by one? Five minutes here? Five minutes there?" Paige had to smile. She knew Lottie better than anyone. If she thought it would work, she would do exactly that.

"I hoped for a little longer." There was a pause. "Five minutes? I can work with that."

"Down, girl. You don't want to be the cause of a man losing his job."

"Fine." Lottie heaved a huge sigh of disappointment. "Fifteen of them?"

"Fifteen," Paige confirmed.

"What a waste."

"You'll survive," Paige teased.

"I suppose." Lottie laughed. "It's a good thing they don't know what they're missing. Those men would be eating their hearts out."

They hung up with a promise to get together as soon as things returned to normal.

PAIGE HAD LONG ago passed exhausted. Sometime during the day, there had come a point where her eyeballs began to feel like they were glued open. Add to it the rollercoaster of emotions, and it was a wonder she functioned on *any* level.

She stood in front of the bathroom mirror, brushing her teeth with slow, deliberate motions. It was just after nine o'clock. At this time last night, she had been bouncing around, anxious for her night with Nate to begin. The only thing on her mind had been how good the sex would be. The answer was great. Fantastic. Earth shattering.

Since then, her world had turned upside down and spun around in the span of a few short hours.

The explosion. Nate's decision to leave. His decision to stay. Not to mention the influx of strangers whose job it would be to keep the ranch and everyone on it safe.

Paige pulled the band from her hair, running her fingers through the long tresses. As with brushing her teeth, washing her face was a nightly routine she refused to skip no matter how tired she was. A touch of moisturizer and she was done. She shut off the light and headed down the hall.

Travis and two of his men shared the bedroom on the first floor. She refused to worry about those big bodies trying to fit onto a couple of twin beds and an old love seat. They insisted they would be fine, and she took them at their word. She made sure they had clean sheets and towels and knew where the bathroom was. The rest was up to them.

At the end of the hall, her father's door was closed. There was no telltale sliver of light underneath signaling that he was still awake. He was as worn out as the rest of them. The early night would do them all good.

Without a second thought, Paige walked past her door, instead entering the bedroom farthest from the stairs. Removing her robe, she slid under the covers.

"What are you doing?" Nate's voice rumbled. The room was dark, but Paige had no problem finding him. She snuggled up against his back, her arm reaching around his waist.

"Going to bed."

Paige laughed quietly when she felt a wet tongue lick the back of her hand.

"Beauty is happy to see me."

"She's a sweetheart. She's happy to see everyone." Nate took her hand, rubbing the damp spot.

"I'd like to think I'm a little bit special."

"You have no idea."

Paige smiled, her lips touching Nate's warm back. No shirt. Being good, she didn't check to see if he had anything on below the waist. Her nightgown provided enough of a barrier to keep this visit G-rated.

"I made a promise to your father, Paige."

"You are an honorable man, Nathaniel." Paige rested her head on the pillow, her eyes drooping.

"Paige?"

"Hmm?"

"We can't do this."

"What?" Having Nate close by was all the extra push Paige needed. Sleep was blissfully close. If only he would stop talking.

"No sex. I promised."

That caught her full attention.

"No sex? What would you call what we did last night?"

"That was at Lottie's. We can't do it here. In this house. I promised." Nate made no effort to move away. He *was* honorable. He was also a man. He asked her to leave before he broke a promise he considered sacred.

Relieved, Paige relaxed. Sex was still a go. Letting her eyes drift shut, she reassured Nate.

"I want to sleep with you. *Just* sleep. I don't want to be alone."

Nate understood. It felt good to have her with him. It felt right. He closed his eyes and took a deep breath, letting it out slowly. His body settled into the mattress, his limbs heavy.

"Good night, Paige."

She didn't answer. Nate felt the warmth of her even breathing against his back.

I could get used to this. Nate waited for the feeling of panic. When it didn't come, he knew something had changed. However, he was too tired to figure out what it was.

Lacing his fingers with Paige's, Nate drifted off. No more worries. Not tonight.

"TELL ME WHAT'S going on."

He hated being left in the dark. It was one of the reasons he hired others to be his eyes. Information was power.

He had his enemies watched — constantly. Any weakness. A tiny chink in their armor could be invaluable. One never knew when a seemingly innocuous fact would be the one to give him the leverage he needed.

The devil is in the details. That had been his father's favorite saying.

Overlook nothing, he would tell his son. Sloppy people lose. Be meticulous in everything and one could conquer the world.

The world didn't interest him. What would he do with it? No, his focus had always been much more localized. A block of buildings. A chain of stores. A racehorse. He never wanted what he could easily buy. He wanted the unattainable.

To get it, he destroyed anyone who stood in his way. That was where the fun lay. The more he hurt the person who stood in his way, the better. The problem was the pleasure was fleeting. The luster quickly wore off his shiny new toys leaving him dissatisfied and looking for the next thrill.

He had been working toward his current goal for some time. The chase was sweet. His prey, elusive. Now that he could see the end in sight, he would not let anything stand in his way.

"The place is swarming with armed security. They spent most of the day installing surveillance equipment."

"Can you get around it?" He swirled the expensive brandy, warming it through the crystal. The finest of everything. Some would say there was no difference between a bottle that cost four thousand dollars and one that was a thousand more. It wasn't true. He tasted it on his tongue. In the back of his throat. The difference was exclusivity. The more expensive the item meant fewer people could afford it. *That* made it better.

"I can't get close enough to tell what they're using. I thought some of the men might leave once they were finished, but they are patrolling the area. Half a dozen at a time. Every few hours they—"

"I don't give a shit what the guards are doing." He threw the expensive crystal glass across the room, spilling the precious liquid in every direction. "Tell me what is going on inside."

"My ears are down." He referred to the remote listening device he had used during the first few hours after the security crew's arrival. "Something is blocking the signal."

"Then unblock it."

"It will take some time."

"You have until tomorrow. Understood?"

"Yes, sir."

He sat back in his chair. Opening the top drawer of his desk, he took out a framed picture. Paige Chamberlin. The moment he saw her, he knew she was what he had been looking for.

Beautiful. Elusive. Her blond hair gleamed in the sunlight. Natural. He made certain she didn't get those highlights from a bottle. Everything about her called to him. Refined and wild at the same time. Educated. Well spoken.

Paige hadn't been spoiled like so many attractive women were. Women like her friend who used her looks to get what she wanted. Paige worked hard, never asking for handouts. He admired that.

Soon she would have anything she wanted. He would see to that.

He ran a finger across the glass, imagining it was her skin. He wouldn't grow tired of Paige. She would amuse him for months. Perhaps years.

When the time came for him to find a new toy, he would regret getting rid of her.

Chapter Sixteen

"GREAT JOB. THAT is a wrap for the day."

Eight solid hours. Nate considered that a triumph. All the drama hadn't slowed them down or disrupted their rhythm. If anything, everyone seemed more focused and intent on making the best movie possible.

"Same time tomorrow?" Wilt asked.

"I want to get some exterior shots." Nate walked the man to his car. "The forecast is calling for rain next week so Homer and I are going to take advantage of the sunshine while it lasts."

"Need any help?"

"Enjoy the time off," Nate said. "You and Edith have some heavy scenes coming up. I want to tackle the plate throwing fight on Monday."

"Think you can churn up the rage?" Edith teased Wilt. "When was the last time you were mad? Really mad?"

"That's easy. The time you deliberately dropped a bowling ball on my foot. The memory of two broken toes should do the trick."

"Dare I ask?" Nate enjoyed the banter between Wilt and Edith. It was done with the ease of long-time friends. "Why did you drop a bowling ball on Wilt's foot?"

"To rile him up, naturally." Edith had the good grace to look contrite. "It was an impulsive decision. I didn't take the time to think it out."

"It was two weeks before I could walk without a limp. Luckily, we were doing a production of The Man Who Came to Dinner. That wheelchair was more than just a prop."

"Now you can thank me."

"I beg your pardon?"

Edith gave Wilt a big, innocent smile. "I was preparing you for this part. If I hadn't broken your toes, you wouldn't have anything to draw upon for our fight scene."

"Thank you? Thank you?"

"You're welcome."

Nate laughed as his leading man and lady continued to argue as they got into his car and drove off.

"They could take that act on the road."

"No need. They have a standing room only crowd every time they perform in Basic," Nate told Travis.

The man had acted as his shadow all day. Not an ideal situation. When Nate sent for reinforcements, he wasn't thinking about himself, but after speaking with his parents that morning, Nate was resigned to it. Callie had given her enthusiastic seal of approval. She felt better knowing someone had his back.

His mother would worry. She said it was part of the job. Therefore, if it relieved her mind to have him saddled with a glorified babysitter, so be it.

"Small towns can be the best. And the worst." Travis shrugged. "I left Mississippi behind because I wanted to see the world. I thought the Army was my fastest way out. What I saw I wouldn't wish on anyone."

Nate couldn't begin to understand what Travis had been through. He seemed well adjusted, but he learned from his brother's fiancée that outward appearances could be deceiving. You never knew what another person was going through.

Between Garrett and a professional counselor, Jade said when she was able to talk about what happened to her, she finally began to heal. Nate hoped that Travis had someone to confide in.

"I can't imagine going back to Tupelo. It's been ten years. I'm not the same kid who left looking for adventure. Excuse me."

Nate waited while Travis listened as one of his men checked in. The Bluetooth headset kept the men connected no matter where they were on the ranch. Now, Chuck had an escort while he checked fences. Paige worked with one of her horses. She was in the corral by the barn, making it easy for Nate to keep an eye on her. Two men from the crew had her in their sights at all times, but he liked checking for himself that she was safe.

The sun gleamed off her long, honey-blond hair. Nate knew that it was as soft as it appeared. Waking up with Paige in his arms, he had run his fingers through the thick, silky tresses. Having her so close, warm, and sweet, it had taken all his willpower not to make love to her. She was temptation personified and he had never been a man to turn away from a willing woman.

Surprisingly, he found there was something to be said for simply holding someone as the first ray of sunlight streamed through the bedroom window. No. Not someone. Paige. The moment was special because she was the woman. Because *she* was special.

As though she sensed his scrutiny, Paige looked his way. Her smile was slow, followed by a wink before she returned to brushing the dappled horse's coat.

"She's amazing."

"I can't fault you for noticing." Nate turned his head, giving the other man an even stare.

"Impressive," Travis said with a grin. "I had a drill sergeant who could knock a recruit down to size with one look. You could give him a run for his money."

"Just making sure you know that Paige is not available."

As soon as the words were out of his mouth, Nate knew it was the truth. Paige was his. Simple as that. He waited for his stomach to clench with panic. It didn't happen. He felt calm even though his heart raced. He felt grounded and light at the same time.

"Ah," Travis nodded. "You've staked your claim."

"I guess I have."

"Does Paige know that?"

"No. But she will," Nate said emphatically.

"Maybe she won't want you. Maybe she would like another option."

"You?"

"Maybe."

Nate couldn't believe the nerve of the man. He had the nerve to stand there, practically throwing a challenge in his face. Was he crazy or suicidal? Luckily, Nate caught the twitching of Travis' lips.

"You have a dangerous sense of humor." Nate shook his head. "Try grinning with a broken jaw. I could have hurt you."

"You could have tried." Travis gave Nate a measuring look. "I'd say your chances would be fifty-fifty."

"Idiot."

"Hey," Travis shrugged. He was still smiling, but his eyes were serious. "I have a younger sister. I wouldn't want a guy fooling with her if his intentions weren't honorable."

"Honorable?" Nate laughed. "Jesus, do people still talk like that?"

"They do in Tupelo. I doubt that Basic is much different." Travis tapped the device in his ear. "Copy that. I'll be right there."

"Trouble?"

"Probably nothing." Seeing the worried frown on Nate's face, Travis patted his shoulder. "Colin, our tech geek, found a hiccup."

"What does that translate to in non-geek speak?"

"Every morning, Colin does a check of the monitoring from the previous day. The system is set up to alert us when there is any kind of breach. Most of the time it turns out to be nothing."

"Breach?" Nate didn't like the sound of that.

"Come with me." Travis headed toward the van that housed the monitoring equipment. The vehicle was parked by the side of the barn where the satellite feed was the strongest. "Colin can explain it to us at the same time."

Nate had been inside the van. Travis showed him the setup yesterday when it arrived. It wasn't what he had expected. Instead of banks of flashing lights and multiple computer screens, the equipment only took up one wall. The rest of the interior looked like a luxurious dorm room. A coffee pot, a microwave oven, and a mid-sized built-in refrigerator on one side. A bed on the other. Colin spent a lot of time cooped up in here, Travis had told him. H&W wanted him to be comfortable.

"What's up?" Travis hopped in the back. Nate stayed outside by the door. The van was luxurious, but it wasn't meant to accommodate three adult males.

"Could be nothing."

"But…" Travis prompted. He knew how Colin operated. Under the gun, the man was the fastest tech he knew. However, he loved to draw out moments like this one.

"We are still in catch-up mode so I was late doing the usual morning run-through. Man, there are a lot of deer in this area. If Jack and Drew hadn't given the system that *wildlife* upgrade, the alarms would be going off constantly."

"Colin, you're wandering." Travis rolled his eyes at Nate. "Circle back to the point."

"Right."

Colin's fingers moved over the keyboard at sonic speed. For someone who spent much of his time in a small, enclosed space, he had the look of a man in prime condition. It was a requirement when you worked at H&W Security. No matter what your job was, you stayed field fit.

"There," Colin pointed to the screen.

Nate leaned closer. "What are we looking at?" All he could see were a bunch of lines.

"Right there." When Nate shook his head, Colin hit two keys, increasing the size of the lines. "There is a jump — it looks like a little wave."

Reaching between the men, Nate tapped the screen. "That?"

"I wouldn't have called you in for one jump. They happen. Even with beyond state of the art equipment like this." Colin moved the line along. "This is what got my attention."

"Another jump." Travis frowned at the screen.

"One I can justify. Two means an attempted breach."

"Someone tried to listen in," Travis explained to Nate. "A long range device. They can be effective. But it would easily be blocked by our stuff."

"They wouldn't get anything but static. They tried at eight o'clock and again at nine."

"That was it? Just a second." Travis tapped his earphone. "Go." He listened then turned to Nate. "There is a Dr. Mount at the first checkpoint. She's on the approved list, but we like to double check first-time visitors."

"Irene is a friend of the family. Let her in."

"Roger that."

"I can't trace this after the fact," Colin sat back in his chair. He took a drink of coffee before continuing. "If I caught the person in the act, I could pinpoint where the signal came from. I have set up an internal watchdog. I'll be alerted if it happens again."

"They know they're being blocked," Nate said. "It would be stupid to try again."

"Luckily for us, stupid is more common than you think." Travis hopped out of the van. "We make a lot of hay on the stupidity of would-be criminals."

"I don't want to keep Chuck and Paige out of the loop. Is this something we should be worried about?"

"It's worrisome," Travis admitted. "On a scale of one to ten, I'd call it a three. We have the advantage because we know it happened. The who and the why is still up in the air. Maybe it was a reporter trying to get a scoop. You're hot news right now."

"That makes sense." Nate's gaze automatically wandered to Paige. "If it hadn't been for the explosion, it would be the only logical explanation. Of course, if it weren't for the explosion, you and your crew wouldn't be here and we wouldn't know about the would-be eavesdropper."

"I would tell you to relax and let us handle it, but I don't suppose you can do that."

"Not in the DNA."

"Mmm. It's a common trait in my circle of acquaintances." Travis slapped Nate on the back. "If worrying keeps you on your toes, that's a good thing. Don't let it consume you." He nodded toward Paige. "Let yourself enjoy the first blush of love."

"When did I mention love?" Nate hadn't used the word. Not yet. He found it disconcerting to hear it from Travis before he admitted it to himself.

"Denial isn't just a river in Egypt." Travis walked away, laughing at his witticisms.

"That one is as old as the trees," Nate called out.

"Old but accurate," Travis replied, not turning around.

Nate opened his mouth, but the retort he had planned didn't materialize. He wasn't in denial. He was being... cautious. Yes, he thought of Paige as his. Yes, he began to envision a future beyond his time in Montana.

Nate always pictured himself finding what his parents had. He wanted to be in love. He wanted a woman to share his life — have his children. Someone who was a friend. A lover. A mate in the truest sense of the word.

He had been fortunate to see firsthand what that looked like. It was a hard standard to match, but Nate knew the right woman was out there.

"Hi." Paige appeared before him, her smile bright as sunshine. "I'm done for the day."

"Me too."

Nate took her hand, carrying it to his lips. Beautiful Paige. The right woman. After all his travels, who could have guessed that he would find her on a ranch just outside a place called Basic, Montana.

"I like when you do that." Paige's eyes were a warm, chocolate brown.

"You like my lips on your hand?" Nate kissed her again, lingering on her soft skin. "Where else do you like them?"

"I like them everywhere. Anywhere. If we weren't in plain sight with I don't know how many eyes watching, we could play show and tell." Paige's voice lowered. "I tell you where to kiss me..."

"And I show you how good I can make you feel."

Paige closed her eyes. Looking at Nate made her want things. Hot, sexy things that right now, weren't possible.

"We need to be alone."

Nate's mouth was close to her ear, the touch of his breath on her sensitive skin sent a shiver down Paige's spine.

"Yes." Her mind raced. "The tack room. It's private and you won't be breaking the 'no sex in the house' rule."

"You go first." Nate moved away, trying to look like a man who wasn't arranging a sexual rendezvous. "I'll follow in a few minutes. Wait." Nate fished the key out of his pocket. Since the smashed camera incident, he and Chuck were the only ones with keys.

"Crap," Paige's attention moved to something over Nate's right shoulder. "Keep the key. It was a nice thought."

"What?" Nate frowned, turning to see what Paige was looking at. He sighed. Irene Mount was getting out of her car.

"Irene," Paige called out.

Nate saw the frustration he felt mirrored in Paige's eyes as she turned to greet her friend. With a sigh, he ran a hand through his hair. He was pushing thirty. At this point in his life, sex wasn't supposed to be this complicated. Between Paige's father, exploding trucks, and friends who dropped by without notice, getting her naked was more of a challenge than he liked.

The sound of laughter drifted over him. Sweet and sexy at the same time. The happy sound reached into Nate's heart. It was difficult to hold onto any resentment when Irene was responsible for putting a smile like that on Paige's face.

"Nate." Paige beckoned him over. "Come see the picture of the foal Irene delivered."

"Starlight's Promise. His mother was a champion in her day."

Irene beamed like a proud parent as she passed her phone to Nate. The gangly newborn stood by his mother. If a horse could look arrogant, this one found a way. He seemed to know his place was rarefied. He would be pampered and catered to. And if his genes held true, he would run like the wind. In time, he would be put out to stud. The circle of life.

"Is your father around?"

Irene looked around, feeling a bit nervous. After their last encounter, she wasn't sure what to expect. On the drive from the airport, she tried to give herself a pep talk. Yes, she had put her cards on the table. Yes, when she drove off after suggesting that she and Chuck become lovers, his expression had been one of shock, not pleasure. And yes, she knew it had been the right thing to do.

Irene wondered if being right was worth the risk of losing a good friend.

"Dad should be back soon," Paige said, blissfully unaware of what was going on in Irene's head. "Come in and tell me about the Sheik. What was your room like? Did he pay you a midnight visit?"

"That's a good question. Did he?"

"Hello, Chuck." Irene was amazed that her voice sounded so normal. Her mouth was so dry the words should have stuck to her tongue on the way out.

"I didn't know you were back," Paige said with a smile. "Isn't this a wonderful surprise? The foal didn't want to wait. He arrived only a few hours after Irene got there so her trip took less time than expected."

"I…" Irene swallowed, trying to find the right words. There weren't any that seemed to fit the situation, so she winged it. "Basic made the national news."

"According to Lottie, there has been an influx of new blood." Paige understood that Nate's last name drew a lot of attention. *He* drew attention. Still, it was hard to imagine why anyone would travel so far out of their way on the off chance they might catch a glimpse of a celebrity.

"Reporters and looky-loos from what I hear," Chuck said.

"They want a statement. I have a satellite interview scheduled for tomorrow morning. I'll give a statement and answer a few questions. Hopefully, that will be enough to dampen the interest."

Nate frowned. He hated this part of being in the public eye. Hopefully, it would soon die down and his life, and the lives of everyone connected with him, would return to normal.

"All that security," Irene had counted seven men, including the one who stopped her as she drove up to the Double C. "Is it necessary?"

"Come in for a cup of coffee. I'll fill you in."

"Okay."

Puzzled, Paige watched her father and Irene disappear into the house.

"Something seemed off between them. Now that I think about it, there was some tension at dinner the other night. I wonder what's going on."

"Do you really want to know?"

"Yes." Paige turned to Nate. "Of course I want to know what's bothering my father and one of my dearest friends. The question is how do you know? Did he say something?"

"I have keen powers of observation."

"So? Spill."

"It's sexual tension. If you weren't Chuck's daughter, you could have noticed. It's obvious."

Paige stared at Nate for a second, her mouth opening, and then closing. She blinked before releasing a burst of laughter.

"Get out of here. Dad? And Irene? That's crazy."

"Why?" Nate asked, crossing his arms.

"Because they — I don't know. Because they're friends."

"Friends who have realized there could be more." Nate rested a comforting hand on her shoulder. "I know this is difficult, Paige. Remember, no matter what happens Chuck will never stop loving your mother."

"I'm an idiot." Paige slapped her hand against her forehead. "For months I've been racking my brain, trying to think of a woman to fix him up with. And there she was, right under my nose."

With a laugh, Paige twirled in a circle.

"You aren't upset?" Nate took her into his arms.

"I'm thrilled." She laid her head on Nate's chest, snuggling close. "Best of all, *Mom* would be thrilled. She loved them both. I hope she can see this. I hope she's smiling."

"CHUCK," IRENE NERVOUSLY walked across the floor, stopping with her back to him. "About what I said the other day. I don't want to lose you as a friend."

"Why would you?"

Irene jumped at the nearness of his voice. She turned to find him less than a foot away.

"We can be both, can't we? Friends and lovers." Chuck lightly kissed Irene's cheek. Her eyes fluttered shut.

"Yes," she breathed. "Please."

"Then that's what we'll do."

"Chuck." Irene sighed his name. "You don't have to worry. I know how much you loved Erin. How much you still love her."

"Yes."

Irene's smile was a little sad. What was it like to be loved that much? By a man as wonderful as Chuck? She sighed. It didn't seem to be in the cards for her to find out.

"I have enough love to go around, Irene."

"What?" Her eyes grew round, not sure what he was saying.

"Love." Chuck cupped her chin, his thumb wiping away the tears she hadn't realized she had shed. "I have loved you as a friend for a long time."

"Friends." Irene nodded. "Of course."

"I think I could love you the way a man loves a woman."

"You do?"

"I thought if I moved on — if I opened myself up to someone else, it would mean leaving Erin behind. Now I realize. Love doesn't get cut in half if you share it — it multiplies." Smiling, Chuck looked deep into Irene's eyes. "I will always love Erin. I wouldn't want to stop."

"I would hate it if you did." The emotion Irene felt was so new, so big. "Would you mind sharing that love?"

"With Erin? Never."

Chapter Seventeen

"A FTER YEARS OF being the *anonymous* Landis brother, how
does it feel to be the hottest thing going?"

Nate smiled at the woman doing the live interview. The only saving
grace was that she was in a studio in Los Angeles and he was in Chuck's
office, hundreds of miles away. The second she made air quotes around
the word anonymous, Nate almost lost it. This was the most watched
entertainment reporter on the internet? He would have to trust Wyatt
on that one.

Anyone watching would see exactly what Nate wanted them to see.
He seemed relaxed. His demeanor was gracious — personable.

Inside was a different matter. He wanted this over. Interviews were
a pain in the ass he avoided like the plague. The attention it garnered
was bad enough. Why was this woman treating him like God's latest gift
to the entertainment world? It was embarrassing and irritating.

Just a few more minutes, Nate reminded himself. His smile
widened. *Did it look as fake as it felt?* At this point, he couldn't have cared
less.

"I'm riding the wave. When it dies down, as it is bound to do, I will be happy to return to being a stuntman. You know how it is, Amanda." Nate deliberately used the reporter's name. He could see her eyes soften. When he wanted, Nate knew how to pour on the Landis charm.

"Tell me about this movie you're directing. It's a small, intimate project. How did it come to your attention?"

When the subject switched from him to the movie, Nate felt himself relax. He enthusiastically shared the story of Erin's screenplay and her husband's dream of honoring her by getting it produced.

By the time he was finished, Amanda was close to tears.

"That is beautiful, Nate. You sound passionate about this project."

"I am. I can honestly say this has been one of the greatest experiences of my life. Everyone involved has put their blood and sweat into it. The lead actors, Edith Potter, and Wilt Adair are giving two of the most honest performances I have ever seen."

"Are you predicting Oscar nominations, Nate?"

"From your mouth to the Academy's ears, Amanda." Nate waited for her to finish giggling. He had hoped for a laugh, but it wasn't that funny. "Naturally, this isn't about awards. This is a labor of love."

"Is it true that the cast and crew are volunteers? Including yourself?"

"Basic is a close-knit community, Amanda. When they found out what Chuck Chamberlin needed, they came out to help. I was amazed at the turnout."

"That's wonderful." Amanda put on her serious reporter face. "However, it hasn't been smooth sailing all the way, has it, Nate? The entertainment world was shocked when we heard the reports of an explosion. On the heels of the accident you had on the set of your last movie, I have to ask. How are you doing? And are the incidents related?"

"Thank you for your concern, Amanda." Nate's smile was grim. "I'm happy to report that no one was injured by the explosion. My cast," he held up his arm so the audience could see, "will be coming off next week. That accident, and the explosion, are ongoing investigations. I can't say anything more."

"Well," Amanda sighed dramatically. "I think I speak for everyone when I say how relieved I am that you, and your friends in Basic, Montana, are doing well."

"Thank you, Amanda. I appreciate your good wishes."

"Before I let you go, I know I'm not alone in wondering. Have you caught the directing bug? After years of claiming you had no ambitions past being a stuntman, are we going to see a shift in careers?"

It was all Nate could do not to roll his eyes over the way she said stuntman like it was a dirty word.

"There is only one director in the Landis family, Amanda. When I finish this project, I will happily hand the mantle back to my brother Garrett."

"No sibling rivalry?" Amanda prodded. "Garrett Landis isn't just your brother. You're twins. That must make for a unique professional — and personal — dynamic."

Nate almost laughed. He knew what Amanda was doing. She wanted him to give her something. A morsel of a soundbite that she could run with. The backbiting Landis twins. Wouldn't that be a scoop?

Sorry, lady. Not going to happen.

"The only problem I have with Garrett is when he grabs the last drumstick at Thanksgiving."

Disappointed but resigned, Amanda smiled good-naturedly and quickly wrapped things up. Nate made the obligatory post-interview chitchat before shutting down the Skype feed.

From start to finish, about an hour and a half. Not bad. Nate stood, stretching his back. When his phone rang, he answered immediately.

"What did you think?" he asked Wyatt. He knew his brother would call as soon as the interview concluded.

"You looked good. Who did your makeup?"

"Fuck you, too."

"Nice mouth. Apologize to your mother."

Shit. Nate hadn't realized his mother would be watching with Wyatt. A head's up would have been nice.

"Sorry, Mom."

"Please tell me you aren't using language like that around Chuck and his daughter."

"Absolutely not."

Nate searched his memory. Chances were good he had slipped once or twice around Paige. Then there was the dirty talk. But what was said in the throes of passion, that didn't count. And you certainly didn't mention it to your mother.

"That's my sweet boy," Callie laughed. "You looked so handsome, Nathaniel. I've missed seeing you."

"I've missed you too. I was going to fly back to get my cast taken off, but with everything that's happening here, I've decided to drive over to Missoula instead."

"I don't want you taking any chances, Nate. Dr. Gunderson is the best orthopedic specialist in the country. He put the cast on; he should be the one to take it off."

Callie Flynn was not a worrier. With four sons, she had learned early on to let boys be boys. That meant a lot of scrapes, bruises, and bloody noses. However, she made certain her men were well cared for. A broken bone was nothing to take chances with.

"I love you, Mom." Nate never took for granted how lucky he was to have this woman as his mother. "I spoke with Dr. Gunderson. He's the one who recommended the woman I'm going to see."

"Stop fussing, Callie."

"Hey, Dad." Nate loved speakerphones. Especially when his family gathered around. "Who else is there?"

"Colton is the only M.I.A."

"Please tell me Jade is there. She is so much prettier than the man she's saddled herself with."

"That's what you should have said to the reporter. It would have made her day." Garrett chimed in. "And stop hitting on my woman."

"You have one job. Keep Jade happy. I'm in Montana, dipshit. Sorry, Mom. If my charm reaches her from this distance, you must be slacking off."

"Kiss my—"

"Enough," Callie cried out, laughing in spite of herself. "I want to know the truth, Nate. What is going on? Your father keeps telling me not to worry. Like that's going to happen."

"I wish I had something new to tell you, Mom."

"If the broken camera and the explosion are connected, that seems like a huge escalation."

Nate agreed with his father. "At this point, all we can do is wait and hope the aftermath scared the bomber off. Between the local police and the security we have set up here, no one will be able to sneeze or move without getting noticed."

"Promise me you won't take any chances."

"I promise, Mom. I won't risk myself, or anyone here."

"Tell me about Paige."

Nate swore he heard laughter in the background. His mother's next words confirmed his suspicions.

"Go away, Garrett. And you too, Wyatt."

"Me? What did I do?"

"You egg your brother on. All of you leave so I can talk to Nate alone."

The sound of bodies exiting the room filled the next few seconds. The next time his mother spoke, she was alone.

"There's nothing to tell you, Mom." Nate decided to get out ahead of her. He should have known better.

"Paige Chamberlin. Is she the one?"

"You weren't this blunt with Garrett. If I recall, you let nature take its course, so to speak."

"Garrett and Jade were in my backyard. Literally. I can't see you, sweetheart. And I've never met Paige. Is she good enough for my boy?"

Nate couldn't hold out against his mother. It was foolish to try. Besides, he felt the need for some motherly advice. And *his* mother gave the best.

"I'm not sure I'm good enough for her."

"Oh, baby." Callie caught her breath. "She *is* the one. When can I meet her? You have to bring her home as soon as you wrap the picture. We'll get the whole family together and…"

"Yes?" Nate waited patiently for her to wind down.

"I may have gotten a little ahead of myself. And you."

"Just a little." He loved her enthusiasm. It made Callie, Callie. "It's so much, so soon, Mom. I've been at full speed ahead from the moment I saw Paige. I think she is going at a slower pace. She might never catch up."

It was a terrifying thought. One that made his stomach roll.

"Not love my Nate? You have me worrying about this young woman's intelligence."

"After you, Paige is the smartest woman I've ever met."

Callie felt ready to cry. Of all her boys, Nate had the tenderest heart. People didn't realize it because he hid it well. *And* when they looked at him, all they saw was the outer shell. Big. Strong. Indestructible. She had always known that when it finally happened — when he fell — Nate would fall hard.

Paige Chamberlin was a very lucky woman. Callie hoped she knew just how lucky.

"I wish I could tell you that love is easy."

"You and Dad have made it work."

"We've had our bumps."

"Really?" Nate frowned. He thought of his parents as rock solid. He couldn't remember any serious fights. Arguments, yes. But bumps? "You made it through."

"Because we never forgot the love. I've never told anyone this. Not even your father. Every day when I get up, I ask myself a question."

"What's that?" Unconsciously, Nate leaned forward, as though his mother was in the room with him.

"Am I still in love with him? The answer has always been yes, Nathaniel. At my angriest, the answer has always been the same. I saw my mother and father drift apart." Callie's voice was tinged with sadness. "They stayed married but they began leading separate lives. They became roommates instead of lovers. I swore that would never happen to me."

"Thank you."

"For what, baby?"

"For having an infinite capacity for love."

"Are you trying to make me cry?" Callie wiped the tears from her face. Happy tears.

"Never." Nate knew she enjoyed a good cry now and then, so he didn't feel too guilty. "I love you, Mom."

"I love you. Take care of yourself. And take care of Paige. If she's half as smart as you say, her heart will soon catch up with yours."

Nate hung up, his mind on his mother's words. Paige's heart. Was she falling in love with him? Time wasn't on his side. There was only one thing to do. He had to spend as much time with her as possible.

Paige would fall in love with him. Or become so sick of his face, she would be ready to toss him on the next plane south.

"NO. WILT, I understand that hitting a woman goes against everything you are. But right now, you aren't yourself. This man, at this time, slaps his wife across the face. If you don't make it convincing, the scene won't work."

"Can't I give her a hard push instead?"

"Wilt—"

"Let me, Nate." Edith stood, hands on hips. "Damn it, Wilton Montauk Adair."

"Montauk?"

Wilt shot Nate an embarrassed look. "It's where I was, you know, conceived." Wilt whispered the last word.

"Oh, for Pete's sake." Edith threw her hands up in the air. "You are the father of five. I hope you didn't blush when you told them the facts of life."

"Denise took care of that."

"Seriously?"

"Well, I—"

"I don't care!" Nate shouted.

That got everyone's attention. Nate didn't raise his voice. Not when things went bad. Not when he had every reason to be frustrated. He kept his cool and managed to inspire and lead. To hear him lose it — even briefly — raised some eyebrows.

"Can you do this, Wilt? Or do I need to change the tone of the scene?"

"It's powerful, isn't it?"

"Yes." Taking the edge off his voice, Nate gripped Wilt's shoulder. "This is the turning point in the story — in the relationship. You slap your wife. Not because you hate her, but because you feel how close she is to slipping away for good. This is frustration, Wilt. We've all felt it. Add on desperation. And a bone-deep fear that you are about to lose the only woman you have ever loved."

"When you put it like that, *I* want to slap me."

Wilt laughed and Nate knew he had him. Edith broke the tension with her quip. He could feel that his leading man was ready.

The scene wasn't smooth. Nate didn't want it to be. He wanted one take — beginning to end. The words exchanged were raw. Hurtful. Passionate. The crack of his hand against her cheek. The shock. The tears. And finally, the embrace.

Nate chose to film the last scene when he felt the energy and confidence of his actors were at their peak. This was the moment the audience would be waiting for. The build. It had to be right or the moviegoers would be left feeling flat. He needed everything Wilt and Edith had.

Holding his breath, Nate watched the scene unfold. When the slap came, Wilt didn't hesitate. Neither did Edith. Nate knew he witnessed something special.

"Cut."

Breathing hard, Wilt and Edith kept their arms around each other for several more seconds.

"That was unbelievable." Edith smiled gratefully when Wilt escorted her to a chair and handed her a bottle of water. Without a word, he collapsed next to her.

"You humble me."

"Oh, Nate…" Wilt blushed.

"Get used to taking a compliment, Wilt." Nate smiled at the blush spreading over the other man's face. "I won't be the last to tell you that you two are amazing."

"You took us there, Nate." Edith sailed on an acting high like she had never dreamed existed. She wanted to savor it as long as possible.

"It was in you, Edith. In Wilt. I'm not taking credit for any of it."

"Say what you like, Nathaniel. You, my boy, are the heart of this production. We won't ever let you forget it."

Now Nate felt like blushing. Shaking his head, he took Homer to the side, giving him instructions.

"It's later than usual. We'll wait and look at the footage tomorrow when we have fresh eyes. Great job today. You always get the shot. It means a lot to know I have you running the camera."

Edith wasn't the only one riding a high. Nate felt wound up — bursting with energy. Sexual energy. He made it through his end of the day's routine. Actors and crew sent on their way. One last look around to make sure the equipment was stored and locked up.

It took an hour. By the time he was finished, Nate felt ready to explode.

"Hey. Good day?" Paige walked into the barn looking impossibly fresh and sweet.

"One second. Travis!"

"What?" Hand on his holstered gun, Travis came barreling through the barn door. He looked around expecting disaster. When he saw Nate and Paige — perfectly safe — he threw his hands up. "I thought someone was dying. Next time save the wear and tear on my heart. A simple, *Hey Travis. Will you come here*, will suffice."

"I'd tell you I'm sorry, but I hate to lie."

"Great. What's the emergency?"

"I need you to keep everyone out of the barn."

"That's it?" Travis exclaimed.

"Nate." Paige shrugged at Travis. "What—"

"Come with me."

Nate grabbed her hand, tugging her along toward the tack room. He fished the key out on the way and had the door open in record time.

"You want me to stand guard?" Travis chuckled, finally understanding.

"Yes," Nate called out.

"No," Paige yelled, dragging her heels. She knew what Nate wanted and she was happy to oblige. However, she was not having sex with Travis outside the door.

"Fine." Nate took Paige by the waist, throwing her over his shoulder. "Travis?"

"Yes?"

"Outside. You," he slapped Paige on the butt. "Inside. And stop squirming."

Shaking his head, Travis closed the barn door. He crossed the driveway.

"Colin," he said into his headset.

"Yo."

"Spread the word. The barn is off limits until further notice."

"What's up?"

"Just do what I ask without any questions. For once."

"Roger that, you old grouch."

Travis sat on the porch. He figured it was far enough away to suit Paige while close enough to keep watch.

God, he envied Nate. Not that he wanted Paige. More and more she felt like a little sister. No, he envied the sex. Period. It had been too long.

He needed a vacation. First thing when he was back in Harper Falls, he was going ask Alex for a week off. A sandy beach where women wore as little as possible. If he couldn't get lucky where the weather was hot and drinks plentiful, the world was a cruel and unjust place.

Travis leaned back and admired the star-filled Montana sky. Fiji, he thought with a sigh. Definitely Fiji.

Chapter Eighteen

NATE KICKED THE door shut. Unceremoniously, he dumped Paige onto a pile of blankets.

"Take your clothes off. Now." He had already dispensed with his jacket and was toeing off his boots.

"What set you off?" Paige sat up, enjoying the show. Nate stripping. Women would pay good money to see this and she had a free ringside seat. Yes, please.

"I haven't had more than a sweet, good morning kiss in months." Nate tossed his shirt to the side.

"Two days," she said with a laugh. Though she knew what he meant. Watching his clothes fly, Paige's mouth watered.

"Two days. Two months. It's been forever since I've tasted you. Why are you not naked?"

"You distracted me." Feigning a pout, Paige held out her foot. "Want to give me a hand?"

Nate paused, his jeans halfway down his hips.

"I'll give you a hand. Right to your backside."

Paige knew he was teasing. But she knew what a little swat felt like. She wasn't taking any chances.

"I'm undressing." Paige shrugged out of her jacket and quickly pulled off her t-shirt. Triumphantly, she held it out. "See?"

"Keep going," he growled.

Boots, socks. Paige unbuttoned her jeans as Nate's bare feet came into view. Slowly, enjoying the anticipation, her eyes traveled upward. Long, hair-roughened legs. Oh, yes. She remembered how they felt as she gripped them with her softer, smoother limbs.

"Paige?"

"Hmm?"

"Why have you stopped?"

"I love wrapping my legs around yours while you're moving inside of me."

"Well, shit."

"What?" Paige raised her eyes. His hard cock was right there. Mouth level. Beautiful. Mesmerized, she reached out, wanting to feel his heat in her hand.

"No." Nate stopped her, grasping her hand with his own. "First you casually mention me being in you."

"There was nothing casual about it."

"Then you go for my dick. I don't want to end this party before it gets started. Do you?"

Unzipping her jeans, Nate grabbed the waistband with his good hand and pulled.

"But it's so pretty." Paige obligingly lifted her hips. "I wanted to see if it was as hot as it looked."

"Give me a second and I'll show you. Lose the bra, Paige."

"Fine but…" Paige slowly unfastened her bra, but her attention was on Nate. "Can I do that?"

"You want to put the condom on me?" Nate asked incredulously. "Are you trying to kill me? I wouldn't let you touch me. What do you think would happen if you rolled this sucker on?"

"Why don't we find out?"

"Bad, bad girl." Nate sidestepped her hands. "Why didn't I know you were so bad?"

With rapid efficiency, he took care of the condom. Before Paige could blink, he had her pinned under his body. Happily, she adjusted her legs to cradle him between them.

"I'm not bad. I was just—"

"Drawn that way." Nate grinned. "I love a woman who is able to quote a movie when I am about to do this."

Paige's eyes met Nate's. Slowly, he entered her. She felt every inch of him. The heat. Oh, yes, there was heat. It was intense. Hotter than she imagined. It felt like the sun at its zenith on a July day. She wanted to bask. She never wanted summer to end.

"You are perfect."

Nate kissed her, his lips surprisingly tender. The urgency was still there, growing as the kiss deepened. Paige pulled him closer, her hands gripping his hips — urging him closer.

"Easy." Nate bit Paige's jaw. "I'm setting the pace. Put your legs around me. That's right. Does it feel as good as you remember?"

"Better." Paige ran one foot along his thigh. So strong. She could feel muscles bunching, ready to spring. "This tickles." She moved her foot. "In a very, very good way."

"Let me make it better." Nate pulled his hips back. "Much, much better."

Paige saw stars. Beautiful and infinitely bright. Every thrust Nate made brought them closer to exploding. No. Not the stars. She was the one who was going to explode. She felt her skin begin to tingle. That white hot intensity that started in her center and stretched throughout her body.

Paige reached. Reached for an ending all the while wishing it would never end.

"Are you with me?"

Nate's words returned her focus to him — to his face. His expression. The need. The passion. Etched forever into her memory. This gorgeous man. Mine. She cried out silently. All mine.

"Take me with you, Nate. I'm ready. Make me fly."

Nate took her at her word. She flew into a million sparkling pieces.

"How will I ever find them all?" Paige whispered.

Nate's breath was harsh, his face pressed into her neck. He kissed her damp skin.

"I'll help. What are you looking for?"

Me. Paige weakly lifted her hand, focusing on her moving fingers. Solid. Whole. Puzzled, she wondered how that was possible. Was it Nate? Had he held her together?

Paige felt a shift inside of herself. It was new and a little scary. For so long she had kept her heart safe. It wasn't difficult. She had never met a man she could trust to keep it safe. Now, with so many questions still unanswered, she gave it to Nate.

He might break it. Yes. When Nate left. When he returned to his life in Hollywood, Paige knew her heart would never be the same. However, she knew that Nate's actions would never be deliberately malicious or cruel. He would regret leaving her.

Nate stated his intentions from the very beginning. Some fun. No strings. No future. Paige went into this with her eyes wide open. He didn't try to make her fall in love with him. It wasn't his fault that of all the men she had met, he turned out to be the one with the key to unlocking her heart.

Any pain. Any sense of loss would be on her. It was up to her not to let him know. She didn't want to saddle him with guilt. When Nate left, Paige wanted him to leave with nothing but good memories. When he thought of her — if he thought of her — she wanted him to think of her with a smile.

"Hey." Nate pushed up on one elbow. "You didn't answer. What are you looking for?"

"Never mind." Paige smoothed back the hair from his forehead. "I already found it."

NATE WAS SNAPPING his jeans when there was a discreet knock at the door.

"Nate?" Travis called out. "Sorry to disturb you. There is a man insisting on coming to the house. When I say insisting, I mean insanely obnoxious. Do you want my guy to clear in Lyle Wilson?"

"No."

"Nate." Paige laughed. She pulled on her boot, and then unlocked the door. "Let him in, Travis."

"Have you already forgotten your last encounter with that—"

"Neighbor? Whatever my personal feelings, Lyle has the ranch next to ours. Dad has to deal with him. I don't want to make it difficult."

"That makes sense." Nate frowned. He helped Paige on with her jacket, kissing her softly. "I hate that."

"Sense can be annoying," she admitted. "Listen. I will never date Lyle again. Or be alone with him. He crossed a line and there is no going back. That doesn't mean I have to be unfriendly."

"You are a better person than I am, Paige. I would kick him to the curb without a second thought."

"No, you wouldn't." Paige took his hand. "Not if your father's best interests were at stake."

"Again, I hate it when you make sense."

They exited the barn just as Lyle's truck rolled to a stop. He was out of the cab and in front of Paige with more speed than Nate would have thought him capable.

"Paige. Darling. I just arrived home and what was the first thing I hear? An explosion involving your truck? Please tell me you weren't injured."

Lyle took her hands, trapping them between his. Nate let out a low growl. Shaking her head at him, Paige tugged until she was able to free her hands then quickly clasped them behind her back. Lyle looked like he wanted to grab at them so she wasn't taking any chances.

"I'm fine, Lyle. We both are." Paige stepped closer to Nate. "Thank you for your concern."

Lyle barely gave Nate a glance, his focus on Paige.

"Has there been an investigation? Do the police know anything? And why is the entrance to the ranch being guarded like a top-secret weapons facility?"

Paige answered the slew of questions in order.

"There is an ongoing investigation. No news on that front. As for the guards?"

"I brought them in." Nate casually slipped an arm around Paige's shoulders.

The message was clear. *Mine. Back off.* Lyle's eyes narrowed, but he didn't comment, choosing to ignore the gesture — and Nate.

"I'm relieved, Paige. I was sick with worry." He looked around the driveway. "What are you using to get around? It isn't practical to have only one vehicle. I'll have one delivered first thing in the morning."

"It's already been taken care of," Nate stated matter-of-factly.

"It has?" Paige asked. She had arranged to meet with an agent from her insurance company, but that wasn't until the end of the week.

"Yes."

"Okay." Paige shot him a look, but he did his best stoic man impression. "Thank you for the offer, Lyle. It was very generous."

"Not that you would have accepted." Nate pulled her closer.

"Exactly. I thought that was obvious." As soon as they were alone, Paige was going to stick her elbow in his ribs. Nate was acting like a possessive caveman. It wasn't a good look on him.

"To you. And to me. I think Lyle needed it spelled out."

"Nate—"

"Never mind, Paige. I dropped by to assure myself that you were doing well." Lyle reached for Paige, quickly drawing back his hand when Nate pinned him with his sharp, blue eyes.

"That was very neighborly of you, Lyle. I'll tell Dad you were here."

Paige shrugged off Nate's arm the second Lyle's truck was out of sight.

"What the hell, Nate?"

"I was being protective."

"Protective is one thing. Neanderthal Nate is another. Any second I expect you to pound your chest. Me Nate. You Paige."

"That's Tarzan. You're mixing your references."

"And here's another. *I want to be alone.*"

"No you don't." Nate fell in step with her.

"Yes. I do." Making good on her mental threat, Paige jabbed him in the side. It was like hitting an iron wall. She poked again. "What are you made of?"

"Snips and snails and puppy dogs' tails?"

Damn, he was cute! She couldn't stay annoyed when he said things like that.

"You went a little overboard, Nate." Paige took his hand, lacing her fingers with his. "Lyle got the picture when you put your arm around me. Was the rest necessary?"

"Necessary? No. But it felt good." Nate slowed the pace to a stroll. "Lyle Wilson is a leach, Paige. He attaches himself and won't let go. It takes more than a gentle hint with a man like that."

"Maybe." Paige squeezed his hand. "Hey. What was all that about a new truck? I didn't order one?"

"I told you, I did."

"It better be for you. Lyle isn't the only one who can't get away with something like that. It's too much, Nate."

"Fine. You can use it while I'm here. I'll sell it when I leave."

When he leaves. Paige felt it again. That sting near her heart. *In* her heart. She didn't have much time left with him. She planned to enjoy every minute.

"That I can live with."

"Are you sleeping with me tonight?"

"Yes."

"Good. Who knew torture could feel so amazing?"

Nate took her in his arms. His kiss held the promise of more to come. Not tonight. Not in his bed. But soon. Often.

Paige molded herself to him. She would take what she could get. For as long as she could get it.

LYLE WILSON SLAMMED the laptop onto the floor.

"I have no desire to watch Nate Landis do anything. Let alone give a vanity interview. The man is a pumped-up heathen. *Why can't we kill him?*"

Michael wisely refrained from pointing out that Lyle didn't kill anyone. He paid other people to do that for him. Taking his iPad from his case, he pulled up the interview. He heard the screen on the laptop break. He would salvage the information from the hard drive and buy a new one tomorrow.

"He's too high profile. If you want to wait a few months, it can be taken care of when he's in California."

"Oh, I want." Lyle paced his office. "I want him to suffer. I want you to film it."

Michael let his employer rant. There was no way in hell he would film anything. However, Lyle didn't need to know that.

"He touched her."

"You already knew they were lovers."

Lyle plugged his ears. "No, no, no." He stamped his foot. "I don't know that. You don't know that. Nothing is certain. Like me, Paige has particular tastes. If that idiot hadn't screwed up, Landis would already be dead. Why isn't he dead?"

Michael sighed. It was like dealing with a petulant two year old. Only he could send a child to his room. Lyle had too much money and too volatile a temper to send him anywhere he didn't want to go.

"This interview gives us the perfect way to get Nate Landis to pull the security team and let down his guard. You want Paige Chamberlin?"

"Oh, yes. I do."

"Have a little patience. From all reports, the movie is ahead of schedule. Landis won't stick around after they finish."

"How long?"

"Two. Three weeks tops."

"But—"

Michael held his breath, expecting an argument. Lyle Wilson rarely took advice. He didn't like any idea but his own. If the money wasn't so good… Michael didn't bother to finish the thought. The money *was* good. He couldn't retire on what he had saved. One day he would have enough tucked away and he would simply disappear. Until then, he did what he was told.

"Paige will be vulnerable." Lyle smiled. "She will need someone sympathetic. Understanding."

"Exactly."

"I will take her on a vacation." Lyle poured himself a glass of brandy. He didn't offer Michael a drink. It never occurred to him. "While we're gone, we'll get married. A long honeymoon, I think."

Michael knew what that meant. He would force Paige to go away with him. Force her to marry him. Force her to stay away. If Paige Chamberlin ever saw Montana again, Michael would be very surprised.

"Tell me about the interview."

"You don't want to watch it?"

"Didn't I already say that?"

Michael put away the iPad.

"Landis' broken arm happened during a stunt on his last movie."

"Stuntman." Lyle spit out the words.

"There has been speculation that it wasn't an accident. Landis reiterates this in the interview. It was suggested the accident and the explosion could be related."

"Which means?"

"If the person responsible for the accident came forward and admitted to blowing up the truck…" Michael let the sentence hang. He would let Lyle finish. And take credit for the idea.

"Problem solved. There wouldn't be any need for security. They would clear out and you could resume keeping tabs on Paige."

"Brilliant, Mr. Wilson."

"Yes. I like it. Where do we find someone willing to confess? Someone who won't screw it up."

"Leave that up to me," Michael said. "The right amount of money can buy you anyone." He should know.

Chapter Nineteen

"YOU LOOK HAPPY."

"My world is good," Paige told Lottie.

"If you can forget the security crew prowling around your property. And why they're here."

"I keep that out of my thoughts." Most of the time. It wasn't always easy. Someone wanted to hurt Nate. Wanted him dead. She could never forget that. "You met a few of the guys. Tell me. Aren't they sweethearts?"

"That wasn't the word I would use."

"Don't say it."

"Prime beef."

Paige sighed. "You never do what I ask."

"Excuse me." Lottie set out some plates. Since Paige was restricted to the ranch, she decided to come to lunch. "Beef. All lined up. And you have turned me into a vegetarian."

Paige took the casserole out of the oven. She waved it under Lottie's nose. "Beef enchiladas. Eat up."

"I thought I wanted you to take a ride on the Nate-mobile. It is an upside down universe when you are having sex and I'm not."

"What about Danny? He's always happy to be of service. So to speak."

"Do not mention that name." Lottie put a dollop of sour cream on her enchilada. Then added another for good measure. "He's on strike."

"What does that mean?"

"Mmm." Nate came in through the mudroom, Beauty trotting at his heels. "What smells so good? Mexican?"

"I thought you were eating with the crew."

"It's crowded. Travis and half of his gang are scarfing up lasagna like they haven't eaten in days. Wilt is grilling Colin on the latest cyber whatever. Every woman in there is flirting like mad. I thought I would take a break and eat with you."

"They can flirt, but I can't?"

Paige laughed. "You want to flirt? Go flirt." When Lottie started to stand, Paige said, "Where is the fun when you're doing it out of spite?"

"Spite?" Nate took three enchiladas and half of the bowl of guacamole.

"She's mad at Danny for his one-man version of *Lysistrata*."

"That isn't funny," Lottie flopped down in her chair. "Or accurate. Danny isn't trying to stop me from going to war."

"He wants to be your one and only."

"So he's withholding sex?" Nate asked. "Interesting strategy."

"One that won't work. I've gone without his brand before."

"That was when you knew you could get it with the crook of your little finger." Paige hid her smile behind her napkin. "Giving something up voluntarily is a lot different than being forced because the brand was discontinued."

"He's not... Shit. Enough of the roundabout references. Danny is giving me the cold shoulder. I. Don't. Care."

"Fine. Would you like some refried beans, Nate?"

"Are those homemade?"

"Fresh this morning."

"Load me up."

"Are you listening to me?" Lottie attacked her food with a vengeance. "Danny is out of my life. He may have started this brief war, but I'm ending it. Bloodless. No casualties. We are done. End of discussion."

"I like Danny," Nate said.

"Everybody likes Danny." Taking pity on her best friend, Paige leaned over and gave her a hug. "Lottie likes Danny. Don't you?"

"Sure. He is sweet. And great in bed. He's one of the good…" Lottie swallowed, her eyes round with shock. She looked at Paige. "Danny is one of the good guys, isn't he?"

"Yes, he is, honey."

"They don't come around very often."

"No. So what are you going to do about it?"

"Crap. I need to go."

Lottie grabbed her purse and sprinted out the door.

"What did I miss?"

"Lottie has seen the proverbial light."

Paige slid from her chair into Nate's lap. Laughing, she peppered his face with kisses.

"Whatever happened, I'm all for it. More kisses please."

Paige gave Nate a long, hard kiss.

"A spring wedding."

"What?" Nate's hands stilled on Paige's waist.

"For Lottie and Danny. His mother will be over the moon. So will Lottie's."

"My brother is getting married in May."

"That's nice." Paige gave Nate a final kiss on the cheek before moving to get him a glass from the cupboard. "Tea or water?"

"Milk. Paige."

"Such a good boy. Your mother would be proud."

Paige set the glass in front of him. Before she could clear away Lottie's plate, he took her hand.

"Paige."

Tipping her head to the side, she gave him a puzzled look. "What?"

"Have you ever thought about when you would like to get married?"

Paige pulled her hand from Nate's. Palms suddenly felt damp. Why would he ask her about marriage? Nervously, she rubbed her hands on the legs of her jeans.

"No." Paige frowned. "I mean, naturally I've thought about getting married. Who doesn't? I always thought we would have it here, on the ranch. The time of year didn't matter. That was before my mother died. It hasn't crossed my mind since."

Which was a lie. She thought of marriage. With Nate. However, she couldn't tell *him* that.

"Your dad would like grandchildren."

"Sure." Paige took the dishes to the sink. It was easier to have the conversation with her back to him. "Someday." She took a deep breath. "How about your parents? Are they after you," she quickly added, "and your brothers to give them grandkids?"

"They don't push, but I know they want some. Wyatt was married. But his wife was a mess. It was probably for the best that she didn't have a baby."

"Now there's Garrett."

"And Jade." Nate smiled.

Hearing the affection in his voice, Paige glanced over her shoulder. "You like her."

"I do. She went through a lot. Abuse. She's strong. Resilient. And she loves my brother with all her heart. How could I not like that?"

"You would have to be an idiot. And you are not that."

Please. Paige closed her eyes, making a silent plea. *Do not tell me I'll find someone.* The last thing she wanted to hear was Nate placating her with predictions of her future. She wanted to yell at him to shut up. Instead, filled with dread, she clutched the counter and waited.

"The reason I asked—"

"I do like those young men." Chuck entered the kitchen laughing. "They are hardworking and dedicated. Admirable, especially in this day and age."

266

"I should get back to work."

"Did I interrupt something?" Chuck asked, frowning at the door Nate so hastily exited.

"No," Paige shook her head. "Your timing couldn't have been better."

"HOW MANY DAYS shooting do you think we have left?"

"Another week. Are you looking forward to getting back to your regular routine?"

Nate already knew the answer to his question. Homer had taken to movie making like a duck to water. It was going to be hard to keep him here in Montana now that he'd had a small taste of the business. If he decided to give Hollywood a go, Nate planned on making sure the young man had a job and a place to stay waiting for him. Homer had a good head on his shoulders, but it was easy to be seduced by the glitz and glamor — especially when he was new to it. He felt a sense of obligation. If Homer had caught the fever, Nate was the carrier.

"I like this routine a lot better." Homer carefully lowered the camera into its case. "Nate—"

"Hmm?" Nate scrolled through the messages on his phone. Most were from Wyatt. Big brother's team had been fielding offers ever since Nate's interview aired. It was an interesting and strange mixed bag. If he chose, he could host a reality show to find the next great stuntman or pose nude in Playgirl. It was a big hell no on every offer. When Homer didn't answer, Nate put the phone away and looked at the young man.

"Is there a problem?"

"No." Homer ran his hand over the camera case. "I have a lot to learn about filmmaking." He turned to Nate, an intense longing in his eyes. "I want to learn it all, Nate."

"Think long and hard, Homer. Hollywood can chew you up and spit you out in the blink of an eye."

"I won't change my mind."

"I didn't think you would. Give me your phone." Taking it, Nate entered his number. "Give me a few weeks. Then call me. If you're willing to start at the bottom and work hard, I know you have a bright future."

"Wow!" Homer stared at Nate. "Wow! I'll work my ass off, Nate. I promise."

"I know you will. One more thing," Nate called out when Homer was halfway to his car.

Skidding to a halt, Homer turned around. "What?"

"That number is for your eyes only. If I start getting phone calls from giggling teenagers, it will be your ass in a sling. Understood?"

"Yes, sir. I'll secure the number right away." Homer grinned. "I can't trust my mom. The other day I caught her watching some clips on YouTube. Did you know there's a channel devoted to you?"

Nate groaned. "I knew," he informed Homer. "Drive safe."

Shaking his head, Nate picked up the camera case and headed toward the house.

Homer's mother. Jesus.

NATE JUMPED IN the cab of the spiffy new Ford F-150. The Supercrew was similar to the one he had recently purchased back in Los Angeles. It had all the bells and whistles, including the aluminum body and twin-turbocharged Eco Boost V-6 engine. It was a dream to drive and if Paige knew it was in her name, she would blow a gasket.

He would cross that bridge when he came to it. For now, he had the memory of Paige's eyes lighting up when the truck was delivered. When he dangled the keys in front of her, he could tell she wanted to snatch them out of his hand. Paige, being Paige, reiterated that the truck was his. She would use it because it was there and he was kind enough to offer, but when he left, so did the truck.

Nate simply nodded, failing to correct her on two important points. The truck was Paige's. Fully paid for. Fully insured. And he wasn't leaving unless she came with him. That was something they would work out. However, Nate's mind was made up.

Paige was his future. In Montana. In Los Angeles. In Timbuktu. He loved her. He ran a hand over his chest — over his heart. It felt good to admit it, even if it was only to himself. He was almost certain she loved him. The rest was window dressing, as his father liked to say. Easily torn down and rearranged. If you had love, nothing else mattered.

"Ready to go?" Nate asked his passengers.

"I am," Travis said, buckling his seatbelt. "Beauty is already out like a light."

Nate looked behind his seat. Curled up on her blanket, Beauty let out a noise that was somewhere between a snort and a sigh.

"She slept all the way here and she'll sleep all the way back."

"I don't doubt it. I walked her around while you were with the doctor. Or should I say, she walked me."

"She isn't used to a lead," Nate defended. "We'll take a few classes when we get to Los Angeles."

"She's smart. It won't take her long to learn."

Nate pulled out of the parking lot, merging into traffic. He flexed his left hand. It was a relief to have the cast gone. He liked Dr. Sanders. In her early sixties, she was professional while keeping a twinkle in her eyes. Her desk was littered with pictures of her family. A husband of forty years, three children, and seven grandchildren. Her first great-grandchild was due in January.

After examining his hand and ordering x-rays, she declared the break healed. She gave him a rubber ball to squeeze and a set of daily exercises to help regain strength and flexibility.

"My nurse has been in a tizzy ever since you made your appointment, Mr. Landis. Would you mind taking a picture with her? I know you must get tired of being asked."

"Putting my arm around a beautiful woman? Why would that get old?"

Before he was finished, Nate posed for six pictures and signed as many autographs. Even Dr. Sanders got in on the action.

"As long as everyone else is doing it," she said with a blush. "My granddaughter Sadie will be jealous. You are her screensaver on all her devices."

Either he was getting used to the attention, or Dr. Sanders and her associates were somehow the exceptions. Nate found it easy to be gracious — even enjoying their excitement. When he volunteered to leave a voicemail message for Sadie, Dr. Sanders swore that the girl would be floating off the ground for weeks.

They had been traveling south about twenty minutes when Nate's phone rang. Not taking his eyes off the road, he handed it to Travis.

"Who is it?"

"Jack."

"Put it on speaker."

"Jack," Nate said. "Tell me you have good news."

"Hello to you too."

"Hello, and kiss my ass."

"Now was that so difficult?" Jack chuckled. "Good manners cost nothing, you know."

"I'll send you a thank you note as soon as I get home, jerk. What's up?"

"Who is with you?"

"Hey, Jack."

"Travis." Jack instantly turned serious. "Good. I can fill you in at the same time. Nate? Do you know Bernie Renshaw?"

"The name sounds familiar." Nate searched his brain. "I can't place it."

"That director you sent to the hospital with a broken jaw? Bernie Renshaw was his personal assistant. He turned himself into the LAPD this morning. He confessed to everything. The failed stunt and the explosion."

Nate didn't know what to say. Yes, he did.

"Why? That incident happened over a year ago. Todd Winesap didn't press charges because he didn't want the publicity. He's a lousy director and a worse human being, but I can't imagine him being behind this."

"Renshaw claims he acted on his own." Nate could hear the doubt in Jack's voice. "Winesap's stock fell pretty fast after that crap he pulled with your crew. Add in bad box office returns on his last two films and you have a man scraping the bottom of the directing barrel. Infomercials don't pay a lot. Winesap fired Renshaw a few months ago. He got a job as the assistant to the second unit director on your last movie."

"Why does this smell of bullshit?"

Nate wanted to believe it was over. He would love to tell Paige and Chuck that the threat was over — that they could get back to their normal routines. Ones that didn't include twenty-four-hour surveillance and bodyguards.

"We smell it too, Nate. We listened to a recording of Renshaw's confession and we have a transcript. Everything he says meshes with the facts. He claims he wanted you to pay and when he saw his opportunity, he took it. The first attempt on your life was simply taking advantage of the situation. It wasn't premeditated. When it didn't work, he became obsessed with the idea of killing you."

"He followed me to Montana and decided to blow up a truck I wasn't in?" Nate asked. The facts might mesh, but it didn't make sense. "Does he have a background in explosives?"

"He claims he got the information off the internet. And before you ask, we can't check his computer. Renshaw says he destroyed it. It's in the ocean somewhere between Los Angeles and Catalina."

"Right." Frustrated, Nate ran a hand through his hair. "What do the police think?"

"Are you kidding? They're over the moon. This is a high profile case and as far as they are concerned, it is now closed. The D.A. is already using the story for his re-election run. He's been on every news program, local and national, touting the amazing job his people did to bring this dangerous criminal to justice." Jack's voice dripped with sarcasm. "The asshole has conveniently forgotten that until Renshaw confessed, they treated the failed stunt as an accident."

"Whoever is behind this wants me to let down my guard."

"I knew you weren't just a pretty face."

"What's our next move, Jack?"

"You keep doing what you're doing. I could increase security, but I don't think that's necessary. Stay as close to the ranch as possible and don't go anywhere alone."

Nate looked out the window at nothing but open space. He couldn't be more alone. However, he wasn't going to tell Jack that.

"I should be wrapping the movie in about a week. Once I'm gone, Chuck and Paige can get their lives back."

Nate realized his plan to ask Paige to go with him would have to wait. He couldn't risk her life. She would be safe here in Montana while he found out who was behind the attempts on his life.

"There is another option, but you won't like it."

"At this point, I'm open to any suggestion."

"We pull the security. Or at least, we make it look that way. If this is about getting you to let down your guard, it naturally follows that another attempt on your life will be made."

"Absolutely not, Jack." Nate shuddered at the thought of putting Paige, and everyone else, in that kind of danger.

"That's what I thought you would say." Jack paused. "This confession has to be about money. Nobody gives themselves up unless they are crazy or being handsomely compensated. From all reports, Renshaw comes across as rational."

"Can you find a money trail?"

Jack's laugh held no humor. "If it's there, we'll find it."

"Good." Nate drummed his fingers on the steering wheel. "I need a place, Jack. Somewhere remote where a man who has been under a lot of pressure would go to be alone."

Jack caught on fast. "A place where a would-be killer could track this man down and finish the job?"

"Exactly. Could you find me such a place?"

"In about a week?" Nate could practically hear the wheels in Jack's brain turning. "That will give us plenty of time to set up a band of security. You will look like a sitting duck, but we'll drop the net before the killer gets within shouting distance."

"What about the crew and me? Are we staying after Nate leaves?"

"I don't want Paige and her father left alone." Nate didn't know how long it would take to flush out his enemy. He didn't want Paige and Chuck vulnerable.

"If they agree, two of the crew will stay behind."

"They'll agree." Nate wouldn't give them a choice.

"You sound awfully confident. If Paige is anything like the women in my life, she doesn't appreciate having decisions made for her."

"Paige has a stubborn streak, Jack." This came from Travis. "She and Rose would get along just fine."

"Like Rose," Nate interjected, "Paige is smart. She'll listen to reason."

"Mmm. If you say so." Jack didn't sound convinced. "I'll leave that up to you. Keep your plans under wraps, Nate. When it's time for you to leave, we'll *leak* your location. Until then, the fewer people who know, the better."

"Jack is right, Nate." Travis hung up. "I know it will be difficult to lie to Paige."

Nate wanted Paige safe. He wished he could tell her everything. But it wouldn't change what he would do. All it would do was give her sleepless nights worrying. He wanted to spare her that.

"Popular guy," Travis laughed when the phone rang. "Ah, the lovely Paige. Want me to speaker it?"

"Yes, but keep your comments to yourself." Nate shot him a warning glance. "Paige."

"Are you cast-free?"

"Thank God. That thing itched for weeks. The second it was gone, so was the itch."

"Psychosomatic."

"Gesundheit."

Travis snorted. "Really? No one will accuse you of having a rapier wit."

Nate flashed him a middle finger.

"Tell Travis hello for me."

"Hi, Paige."

"Hi. Nate, would you mind stopping in Basic and picking up a few things? I meant to have Lottie do some grocery shopping for me, but I forgot."

"No problem. What do you need?"

"Flour. Salt. We usually get our eggs from a local farmer, but we've been going through so many, we need to supplement. Organic if they have them. Then—"

"Honey." Nate chuckled. "Send me a text. I'll get whatever you need."

"Okay. And Nate?"

Nate straightened. Recognized the tone in Paige's voice. Husky and filled with promise.

"Travis can hear you."

"I know," Paige's voice lowered, sending a shot of heat to his dick. "I wondered if we could go for a drive after dinner. We need to christen your truck. That big back seat should do nicely." With a sultry laugh, she hung up.

"Son of a bitch," he muttered. Aware of Travis sitting next to him, Nate tried not to squirm.

"Something wrong?" Travis asked.

He sounded a little too happy. Nate decided to ruin his day.

"Nope. I have a sexy woman waiting for me. What do you have?" Nate seemed to contemplate the question. "Oh, that's right. A bunch of smelly, hairy men. I wonder which of us is going to have the better evening? The one in the truck with the gorgeous woman? Or the one watching from a discreet distance?"

"And everyone thinks you're such a nice guy," Travis grumbled. "You have a mean streak, Nate Landis. A mile wide and just as deep."

"I went to Beverly Hills High. There is nothing more destructive than a pack of over-privileged trust fund brats."

"Come on," Travis scoffed in disbelief.

"Laugh if you want. By the time we graduated, half my class battled either an eating disorder or drug addiction. Or both. I was lucky."

"What saved you?"

"Three brothers who had my back. And," Nate smiled, "I had

amazing parents. They weren't about to let any of us head down a dark path. When we stumbled, they were always there to catch us before we could fall."

"That sounds like more than luck," Travis said, smiling back.

Luck, Nate thought, *and two secret weapons named Caleb Landis and Callie Flynn.*

"THAT'S A FEW things?" Travis asked, looking at the grocery list Paige had texted. "Who is she feeding, an army?"

"You know she likes to bake. How many cookies have you eaten? Or pieces of cake?"

"I ate half of an apple pie yesterday," Travis said with a happy sigh. "I see what you mean. I'll grab a shopping cart."

"What is the difference between bleached and unbleached flour?"

This was the second aisle they had been down. The choices were mind-boggling, even in the small *Basic Market*. Nate didn't shop for food. He either ate at his parents' house, ordered in or went out. He tried to picture the contents of his brand new stainless steel Sub-Zero refrigerator. Water? Some kind of fruit that by this time was either wizened or moldy. Probably both.

Nate quickly realized he was way out of his depth. He hoped Travis knew something about this stuff. If not, he would have to call Paige. Nope. Too embarrassing. It was either Travis or the lady stocking the shelves.

"Go for unbleached. That's what my mom buys."

"Good man." Nate grabbed a ten-pound bag. "Is that enough? Paige didn't say how much she wanted."

"I gave you my one bit of knowledge," Travis said. "You are on your own."

"Two it is." He looked at the list. "Salt. How hard can that be?"

Kosher. Table. Sea salt, Nate groaned. He gained a new appreciation for anyone who did this on a regular basis. Table salt sounded generic. Hoping for the best, he grabbed a box.

"She called last night."

Two men stopped a few feet away. They wore similarly lined jean jackets that failed to cover stomachs that protruded over the sagging waistband of grease-stained jeans. With an automatic glance, Nate noticed their cart contained beer and frozen pizza. If those were the basic staples of their diets, it was no wonder they couldn't pull up their pants. When one of them reached for a can of confetti frosting, Nate shuddered.

"No kidding? It's been over a month. Was she begging you to take her back?"

"Bitch knows better than to try that," the taller one sneered. "She wanted the dog. Can you believe it? She begged me to get her that puppy. Something to keep her company while I was at work. Then she runs off with a car salesman from Billings. It felt good to tell her what I did to her precious Cocoa. I said, *I threw the bitch in a bag and booted her out of the truck. Just like I should have done to you.*"

"What did she say?"

"Fuck. She cried so hard, I hung up so I wouldn't have to listen. Come on. I want to get home before the game starts."

"Stop!" Nate barked.

The tall one looked around. "Are you talking to me, asshole?"

"That's right."

"Fuck you, pretty boy. Why don't you and your fag boyfriend fuck off?"

Travis moved so he could keep an eye on the two men, his body blocking Nate from going after them. "I know what you're thinking."

"Do you?" Nate's voice was even — seemingly calm. One look at the storm brewing in his eyes and Travis knew there was nothing calm about him.

"You want to tear the idiot in half for what he did to Beauty."

"That sounds about right."

"Beauty?" The tall one snickered. "Who the hell is Beauty? Is that his pet name for you?"

"If you hit him, what good will it do?" Travis put a hand on Nate's arm. He knew it wouldn't do much good if Nate were determined. However, he had to try.

"Move your hand, Travis."

Nate didn't look at Travis. Unblinkingly, Nate stared at the idiot who continued to run his mouth off. Travis doubted the man had a death wish. He was simply too stupid to understand how close he was to drinking his meals through a straw for the next few months.

"Let's go, Harv."

"Smart," Travis said. "You take your friend and go. I won't be able to hold Nate back much longer."

"Are you holding me back?" Nate raised an eyebrow but his stare didn't waver.

Jesus, Travis thought. *The man was a scary son of a bitch when he wanted to be.*

"Shut up, Leroy." Harv shoved the cart at his friend. Full of himself, and half a dozen beers, he raised his fists. "Bring it on, faggot."

"Really?" *Maybe the guy was suicidal.* Travis stepped aside. "It's your funeral."

What happened next couldn't be called a fight. If you blinked, you missed it.

Harv threw a sloppy punch that Nate easily sidestepped. Nate aimed at the man's nose. The sound was unmistakable. The bone didn't break. It shattered.

Without a backward glance, Nate wheeled the shopping cart down the aisle away from the screaming Harv.

"Oranges." Nate checked Paige's list. "How many should we get?"

Chapter Twenty

WHEN PAIGE WAS a little girl, the days were long. As with most children, she wished her time away, waiting for milestones and special occasions. Christmas couldn't come soon enough. If only she were sixteen and could get her driver's license. High school graduation.

All she could see was the next thing. Why would she want to live in the present when the future held the promise of excitement — the lure of the unknown.

She sat on the steps of her home, watching as they filmed the last scene of her mother's movie and all she could do was wonder — where had the time gone?

"I can't go back and slow the clock, Beauty." Paige smoothed her hand over the puppy's head. Happy, Beauty snuggled deeper into Paige's lap. "You've been here as long as Nate has. Five weeks. Is it wrong for me to wish for five more? I would settle for one."

Today would end Nate's reason for being on the Double C Ranch. The cast and crew gathered around, watching as Wilt and Edith played out the ending. A simple shot. Few words — so many emotions. After the struggles, the decision had been easy. Love won out. They would face the future — whatever it brought — together.

It was a lovely ending. Two people. Hand in hand. Their backs to the camera as they looked out over their land. The sun wasn't rising or setting. It was straight overhead — bright. Hopeful.

It was ridiculous, but Paige found herself envying that fictional couple. They had love. Years and years of it. With more to come. A lifetime together. She was going to lose the love of her life. Five weeks. That was all she'd had.

"I want more, Beauty," Paige whispered. "*I want a lifetime.*"

"And cut," Nate called out. "That's a wrap."

Applause broke out. Hugs and handshakes exchanged. Paige watched as everyone gravitated toward Nate. He stood out — not just because of his size. He had taken control from day one, steering the production with sure, steady hands. Nate always spoke of the team, but they knew he was the reason they made it through.

"I understand we're having a party," Nate said, his arm around Edith.

"Damn straight," Wilt called out. His wife was by his side, holding his hand, her eyes filled with love and pride. "We've earned a little shindig."

"Emphasis on little," Edith clarified. "We want to celebrate. We started out friends and neighbors. Thanks to you, Nate, we are now a family."

Paige could see how touched Nate was by Edith's words.

"Does that make me everyone's father?" Nate asked with a grin.

"Well, Daddy." Edith pushed Nate out of the barn. "You go rest your old bones while we youngsters set up the party."

Paige knew Nate wasn't ready to rest. There were details that needed his attention. While he consulted with Homer, she lifted Beauty and headed into the house.

"I know you would like to run around and play," Paige told the puppy when she tried to get down. "There are a lot of big people with big feet out there. I don't want anyone trampling you."

She set Beauty on the floor. Paige looked around, momentarily at a loss. *Cookies.* That was the answer. Baking always made her feel better. Chocolate chip could be a nice addition to the party. Paige started pulling out the ingredients. She had plenty of everything, thanks to Nate and Travis' trip to the store.

"He was your hero, wasn't he?" Paige asked Beauty. "You might not understand, but you know he loves you. He took care of that nasty creep who dumped you on our property."

The incident in the store had been witnessed by half a dozen people, adding to Nate's popularity — in Basic and beyond. The story buzzed across social media before the police arrived. Harv tried to shift the blame, claiming Nate sucker-punched him. He expected his friend to back him up. However, in the face of so many witnesses, Leroy caved like a house of cards.

Nate walked out of the market a bigger sensation than when he went in. And Paige had enough pantry staples to last her the rest of the year.

"Sometimes things do work out." Paige measured the flour into a bowl. "You found a better home. You will be loved and cared for the rest of your life."

As for Paige, she could make these cookies with her eyes closed. Instead of distracting her, she had too much time to dwell on what life would be like without Nate. Sick of her self-pity, she added a cup of chocolate chips. Then for good measure, she shoved a handful into her mouth.

She was taking the last batch out of the oven when Lottie burst into the house.

"Where's the fire?" Paige paused, spatula and cookie in mid-air. "Oh, God. Please tell me nothing is on fire."

"Way more exciting without the destruction." Lottie put a hand to her chest, her breathing ragged. "Outside. You have to come."

"I've been outside, Lottie." Paige continued transferring cookies to the cooling rack. "You'll have to do better than that if you want me to drop everything."

"Nate's parents are here." Lottie sighed. "Nate comes by his good looks honestly. His mother is more gorgeous in person than in her movies. And his father? Hubba hubba."

Paige blinked once, then twice. She couldn't have heard correctly.

"Callie Flynn and Caleb Landis? Here? Now?"

"Yes," Lottie cried.

"No."

"Yes. And before you say no again? Yes, a million times. Now do you believe me?"

"Yes."

With deliberate care, Paige removed her apron, hung it up, and headed for the back door.

"Hey, what are you doing? You're headed the wrong way."

"Nate's parents are out there?" Paige tipped her head toward the barn.

"Right."

"Then this isn't the wrong way."

"Oh, no you don't." Lottie jumped in front of her, blocking her path. "Running away? My best friend? Since when?"

"I'm a mess." Paige grasped the easiest excuse. It helped that it was true. "This morning I was working with the horses. Then I made cookies."

"I can tell." Lottie wiped the corner of Paige's mouth. "Chocolate chip?"

Paige rushed past Lottie into the mudroom. Looking in the mirror, she groaned. God, it was worse than she thought. She looked like a bag of chips had melted down her chin.

"I understand why you're nervous." After Paige had washed her face, Lottie handed her a tube of lip-gloss. "I've known Danny's folks all my life. Now that he and I are officially dating, my stomach was in knots the first time he took me over there for dinner. Guess what, I survived. His mother and I are having lunch next week."

"That's nice, Lottie," Paige said. She was happy for her friend. This was different. "I'm a mess."

"You're beautiful." When Paige tried to protest, Lottie stopped her.

"I know what you mean. Things are up in the air with Nate. The idiot hasn't told you he loves you."

"He doesn't."

"He does." Lottie gave Paige's hair a quick fluff. *Blond perfection*, Lottie thought, without a twinge of envy. "Not that it would hurt for you to say it first."

"I'm not saying it to you before I've said it to him. And I'm *not* saying it to him."

"Then—?"

"No." Paige looped her arm through Lottie's. "Nate is leaving Montana. He's never said differently."

"You could go with him." Lottie's smile was a little sad. "I would miss the hell out of you but it would give me an excuse to visit Los Angeles. Maybe I'll be discovered."

When Lottie struck an exaggerated glamour pose, Paige laughed in spite of herself.

"What they'll discover is what a goofball you are."

"True. Paige—"

"Nate is leaving. I'm staying. We had fun." Paige shut her eyes and took a deep breath. "He isn't going to break my heart, Lottie. If it's a little bent, I'm to blame, not him."

Lottie rested her head on Paige's shoulder in silent support. Words weren't necessary. She knew her best friend better than anyone. It wouldn't help to point out that she was lying to herself. *Bent heart, my ass.* Lottie could hear it cracking. The second Nate Landis drove away, Paige's hearts would break into a million pieces. And Lottie would be here to help pick up the pieces.

"Am I presentable?"

Paige turned in a circle. She had a smile on her face that almost reached her eyes.

"Like I said. You are beautiful. Ready to meet some honest to goodness Hollywood royalty?"

Royalty. Paige could handle that. Nate's parents? That was another matter. Squaring her shoulders, she nodded and opened the door.

"I CAN'T BELIEVE you're here!" Nate swung his mother around in a circle. Her laughter filled his heart. It was the happiest sound in the world.

"Since it was on our way, we decided to stop by."

"I thought you were on your way to New Orleans to finish your movie." Frowning, Nate looked at his father. Caleb shrugged.

"In Callie's world, Montana is on the way to Louisiana."

"But—"

"Nate, are you arguing with your mother's logic?"

Grinning, he hugged his father. "No, sir. It's good to see you. Both of you."

"Chuck," Caleb stuck out his hand. "It's been too long."

"Thirty years too long." Chuck greeted Callie with a kiss on the cheek. "Though looking at this lovely lady, I would think it was yesterday. Then I look at you…"

Caleb's deep laugh ran out. "It's true. Callie stays forever young. I don't know how she does it."

"Pure thoughts and plenty of sunscreen," Callie said, her famous gray eyes twinkling.

"Pure thoughts my—"

"Caleb," Callie shot her husband a warning look. Then she winked and their fascinated audience sighed with delight. "Hello." Callie beamed, waving at the people gathered around. "Chuck, why don't you introduce Caleb to your friends? Nate and I will be there in a minute."

Callie waited until they were alone to pick up Nate's left hand, kissing the back.

"All better?" she asked.

"It was just waiting for your blessing." Nate tipped her chin with his finger until he could look into her eyes. "So Montana was on your way?"

"I could play dumb."

"You? Never."

"I *am* an actress." Callie took his arm. "I don't see your Paige."

"How do you know?" Nate looked around. There were several young, attractive women in the crowd.

"Call it intuition. I thought it might be the brunette who ran in the house as we arrived. But you didn't take any notice."

"Why would I?"

"Because, when…" Seeing Nate's attention shift over her shoulder, Callie turned her head. *Ah. There she is.* Not the curvy brunette. The leggy blonde.

"What?" Nate's eyes returned to his mother. "What were you saying?"

"It doesn't matter." Callie took his arm. "Introduce me to Paige."

"How did you know?" Nate led his mother toward the house. "You're a witch, Callie Flynn."

"No, Nathaniel. I'm a mother."

"SEE YOU LATER."

"Wait." Paige grabbed at Lottie's arm, her eyes darting to Callie Flynn. "She's coming this way."

"I know. Introduce me later. I'm going to drool over Nate's father. I love a yummy older man."

"What about Danny?" Paige called out as Lottie skipped away.

"I'm fully committed. But I'm not dead. There are no rules against looking."

"This must be the famous Beauty."

Nate grinned. He loved how his mother picked up the puppy all the while keeping her eyes on Paige.

"Hello." Callie smiled, holding out her hand, gently grasping Paige's. "I'm Callie."

"I know." For all the butterflies in her stomach, Paige couldn't help smiling back. "Welcome to Montana."

"Why, thank you." Callie handed the squirming dog to Nate. "I've never been here before." Keeping the young woman's hand, she looked around before her eyes settled on Paige. "I can see why Nate has enjoyed his time here."

"Mom—"

"Is that punch everyone is drinking? Be a love and get Paige and me a cup."

There was no use arguing, not that he would try. His mother was a force of nature — one the men in her life rarely challenged. On those rare occasions they did, she knew it had to be important. She would listen carefully, and weigh their opinions. And sometimes, let them think they won.

Hugging Callie, Nate whispered, "Be good."

"Such a darling." Callie let loose her mega-watt smile. "Would you mind giving me the mini-tour?"

Paige felt torn between good manners and the urge to bolt into the house. Two things kept her where she was. Lottie's voice reminding her she didn't run from anything — and the kindness she saw in Callie's eyes. The color was different, but when she looked closer, she realized it was the same quality she would often see in Nate's.

It calmed her. Centered her. It allowed her to return Callie's smile warmly instead of stiffly and artificially.

"Would you like to meet two of my rescue horses? Rollie and Winter are fixtures around here. Don't tell him I know, but Nate talks to them on a regular basis."

"Really?" Delighted, Callie strolled alongside Paige. "You could tell them anything without fear of judgment."

Surprised that Callie understood, Paige nodded. "I admit they've heard a few of my problems. When my mother died, I would brush their coats and talk for hours. They are very good listeners."

Callie felt for Paige's loss. It was obvious she still felt the loss of her mother deeply. As they walked, Paige told her about how rewarding the work she did with horses was when they were healed and ready to be placed with owners who cared for them properly.

"You have a kind and gentle heart, Paige — filled with love and compassion."

Callie's compliment touched Paige. "I'm no different than everyone else."

"Yes, you are," Callie assured her. "It takes a special person to give life back to these wonderful animals."

"Thank you, Callie. But I don't think of myself that way."

Callie smiled. *That is one of the things that make you so special.* It was what her Nate saw, Callie was certain. It was why he loved this young woman. Being attractive on the outside would never be enough. Nate needed someone whose beauty ran deep.

Tears filled Callie's eyes. She came to Montana to decide if Paige was good enough for Nate — and she had her answer.

"Is something wrong?" Paige asked in alarm.

"No, sweet girl." Callie's smile lit up her face. "Everything is just as it should be."

THEY GATHERED IN the living room. The cast and crew had partied until late, hating for the experience to end. Not wanting to get anyone's hopes up, Nate didn't point out that this wasn't over. If things went the way he envisioned, there would be a premiere. Interviews. Publicity. Basic, Montana and its citizens would be getting more attention than they could have imagined.

However, before any of that, Nate had wanted his parents' opinions. With just them, Chuck and Paige, he ran the raw footage. He was too close to be a fair judge anymore. He thought it was good. Very good. Now, he needed fresh eyes. Who better to tell him what he needed to know than the two people he admired most. When the last scene ended, he held his breath.

"Oh, Nathaniel," Callie sighed.

"Well done, son."

Nate closed his eyes, the emotions too big. His mother and father were over the top personalities. They could be loud and boisterous. Life was to be enjoyed — savored. They never held back their feelings or their love.

When Caleb and Callie scaled it down to a few words, Nate knew they were deeply touched by what they saw. Sometimes quiet meant more than exuberance. This was one of those times.

"It's good, isn't it?" Chuck's voice was thick, his feelings clogging his throat.

"I'll tell you how good," Callie said, squeezing his hand. "I'm jealous that I wasn't the lead."

Caleb laughed. "That's the highest praise she can give a movie, Chuck. My wife, the ham."

"Look who's talking. You'll want to handle distribution."

"Naturally."

"Whoa." Nate held up a hand. "I'm thrilled by your reaction, but this is a long way from finished."

"Which is good." Caleb's brain was already five steps ahead. "This should be a slow build. Grassroots. We get our tech people to start chatting it up. It will be up to you how much you want to be involved."

"Before I started I would have said not at all." Nate gave a self-deprecating laugh. "Like it or not, my recent rise in popularity will be a boost to the movie. Use me if you have to but, please—"

"I know," Caleb said. "We'll schedule as few interviews as possible until the movie is ready to release. How about you, Chuck?"

Chuck looked surprised. "What about me?"

"Nate is a big part of the selling point, but ultimately, this is your story. Yours and Erin's. As with Nate, we can work around it if you aren't comfortable stepping out in front of the media."

"I hadn't thought about it." Chuck scratched his chin, a perplexed smile on his lips. "I wanted to honor Erin. Getting the movie made was always my endgame. Nate took it to another level. Now we're talking about publicity and movie premieres. It's all a little much."

"That's understandable." Callie patted his hand. "Nothing has to be decided tonight. Think about it. Talk it over with Paige."

"I'm on board with whatever Dad wants. If it had been up to me, the movie never would have been made."

Paige felt torn. Part of her was embarrassed by her lack of faith in her father. However, if she hadn't contacted Caleb asking for help, she never would have met Nate. No matter what, she would never regret that.

"You brought Nate to us," Chuck said, echoing part of her thoughts. "I don't know what we would have done without him."

"You can always count on Nate," Callie agreed. "Ever since he was a little boy he has—"

"Okay." Nate jumped to his feet. "When Mom starts telling stories about *little Nate*, I know it's time to call it a night."

"I agree," Caleb said, smiling at his wife.

"Fine." Good naturedly, Callie let Caleb pull her to her feet. "Paige, anytime you want to hear about Nate's pre-pubescent adventures, give me a call."

Paige didn't answer. She didn't think she would be speaking to Callie very much after tomorrow. She and Caleb would continue on to New Orleans. And Nate? Wherever he went, it wouldn't have anything to do with her.

"Need some help with the dishes?" Nate asked. He played with the ends of her hair, his eyes warm.

"There are only a few coffee cups. Take Beauty out for her nightly walk. Dad and I will take care of the cleanup."

Nate waited until his parents were out of earshot and Chuck was in the kitchen. "Will you join me later?"

"After everyone is down for the night." Paige wasn't passing up the chance to sleep next to Nate. This might be the last time. She wanted to stockpile all the memories she could.

Nate lightly touched her cheek, and then called Beauty. She watched until the door closed behind them before picking up the last two cups and joining her father.

"Aren't Caleb and Callie everything I said they were?"

"And more." She stacked the cups in the dishwasher. "Dad?"

"Hmm?"

"Why didn't you invite Irene to stay after the party wound down?"

Chuck paused. Paige thought he looked slightly uncomfortable. That was the last thing she wanted.

"I know you've been spending time at her place. When you go out to visit friends, you're going to see Irene, aren't you?"

"Yes." Chuck put down the dishtowel. When he turned, his eyes were shadowed with concern. "Irene and I are…" He hesitated. "I don't know what you call it at our age. Dating doesn't seem right."

"Do you love her?"

"Paige—"

"It's okay, Dad." Paige took his hand. "I hope you love her. She's a wonderful person. Why wouldn't I want two of my favorite people to be happy — together?"

"Thank you." Chuck hugged her. His baby. He was proud she had become such a generous, loving woman. "I will never stop loving your mother, Paige."

"I know that." Paige let the tears fall. "Loving Irene is honoring Mom's memory. She would want this for you. *I* want this for you." She wiped her cheeks. "Now, it isn't too late. Why don't you pay her a visit? If you do it right, you can be back for breakfast and our guests will never know you were gone."

"Paige!" Chuck felt his face heat. Then he looked at his watch. "I'll give Irene a call. She might have an early appointment."

"Either way, I don't think she'll object to some company."

Ten minutes later, Chuck drove away, his bodyguard trailing behind at a discreet distance.

PAIGE DIDN'T TRY to sleep. She was in Nate's arms and she wanted to savor the too rapidly waning moments. If this was all there was, she wasn't going to miss any of it.

Nate's steady breathing. The feel of his heartbeat under her hand. Beauty having puppy dreams at the foot of the bed. Paige felt warm. Safe. This was home.

That was it. This was where she belonged, with the man she loved. If she didn't tell him now, she would regret it for the rest of her life. Wasn't rejection better than not knowing? If there were the slightest chance she could go to sleep every night and wake up every morning lying close to Nate Landis, she would risk finding out he didn't want the same thing.

Paige pushed her hair back. Resting on her elbow, her eyes took in Nate's face. As it always did, the sight made her breath catch and her heart skip a beat before thumping wildly.

So beautiful. It might not be a word he would appreciate, but it fit.

Now that she had met his parents, she understood why he was more than just a pretty face. Callie and Caleb were amazing people. They had given Nate a foundation of love and strong moral compasses to follow. They didn't just talk the talk. They followed through on their beliefs.

Nate could have coasted on his family name. The money. The fame. It was all there for him to exploit to his benefit. Instead, he built his own niche. His reputation — professionally and personally — was earned the old-fashioned way. Through hard work and dedication.

How could she not love him? The surprise would be if she didn't fall — hard.

"Nate?" Paige whispered his name. Lightly, she kissed him and chuckled. He was her sleeping beauty.

Ah, he wakes.

"Hello," she said, kissing him again.

Nate's lips curved, the sleep slowly clearing from his blue eyes.

"Is it time to get up already?" Nate shifted, looking toward the window. "I don't see the sun. Let's cuddle for a few more minutes."

"It's still early." Happily, Paige rested her head on his chest. "I wanted to talk."

"Cuddle and talk. Sounds good."

Now that the moment was at hand, Paige felt the words stick in her throat. *I love you.* Why was it so hard to say? Because Nate's response would shape the rest of her life. This was big. Colossal. She didn't take this moment — or the words, lightly.

"Make love with me."

Not let's have sex. Or let's screw. Or fuck. *Make love with me.* It was the first time she had used those words and silently she urged Nate to understand the difference.

"I promised your father. Wait. Did you say make love?"

"I didn't promise, Dad. And yes. I said make love."

Paige didn't wait for his answer. She didn't want him to say anything that would ruin this moment. She slid under the covers, kissing her way down his chest. He tried to push her away, but Paige was determined. Lifting the sheet, she smiled.

"If it will make you feel better, lie back, and let me do all the work. If you don't actively participate, you won't technically be breaking your word."

"That is the slippery kind of logic that can get a person into a hell of a lot of trouble."

"No trouble," Paige assured him. "Lift your hips." Surprised when he complied so quickly, she removed his shorts, not wanting to press her luck. Her hand reached between his legs. Long, hard, and ready. She licked her lips. "Now, I'm going to enjoy this early morning treat. Close your eyes and think of England."

England, my ass, Nate thought. Gripping the headboard, he closed his eyes and thought of Paige. Nothing but Paige.

"I've never tasted you at this time of day. Are you sweeter this early? Or spicier." Paige swiped her tongue over the tip. "Mmm. Both. Very nice."

"Nice?" Nate let out a long breath.

"We'll start with nice. Then there is only one way to go. Up."

Starting at the base of his erection, Paige licked every inch. When she reached the top, she paused, letting them both savor the anticipation. Finally, needing more, she took him into her mouth using her teeth to lightly scrape as she followed the same path, this time going down. And down.

"I don't want to come in your mouth." Nate's words were ragged. "I want to come in — holy shit. What was that?"

"A little trick I picked up off the internet. You liked it?"

Nate saw stars. And fireworks. And God. "I will never curse modern technology again. Come up here."

"But I'm not done. There was this little thing the woman did with her tongue that I want to try."

"Another time. Right now, I need to be inside you."

Another time? Will there be another time? Paige wanted to ask.

"Oh, dear," Paige said with exaggerated regret. "No condom."

Before she could slide down the mattress, Nate pushed her onto her back.

"What part of another time don't you understand?" Grinning, Nate kissed her hard and fast. "Stay. I'll be right back."

With a sigh, Paige watched Nate get out of bed. When he picked up Beauty, she gasped. Poor puppy.

"I forgot she was there."

"Me too," Nate admitted ruefully. "Sorry, baby girl. We got carried away."

Paige waited while Nate put the dog in the bathroom, shutting the door.

"Will she be okay in there?"

"She has water and a soft place to curl up." Opening the top dresser drawer, he took out several foil packets.

"Someone is feeling ambitious."

Nate tossed the extra condoms on the end table. "Better safe than sorry. I would rather not have to get up again."

"Let me?" When Nate hesitated, Paige teased, "All the nights we've slept together, you've managed to keep your hands to yourself. Where's that self-control now?"

"All those nights you kept your mouth off my dick."

"True." Paige gave him a self-satisfied smile. "I guess I was the one with the self-control."

"Here." Nate handed Paige the condom. "Have you done this before?"

"Mmm." Paige contemplated Nate's erection like an artist presented with a blank canvas. Beautiful in its simplicity and so many possibilities for someone with the right kind of imagination.

Paige ran a finger over the taut, heated skin. She knew exactly what she wanted to do with it.

"Tear open the packet, Paige."

"It seems a shame to cover it."

"Do you want to get pregnant?"

"No." Paige shook her head. *Someday.* With Nate as the father, she could easily picture it. But not now.

"Then get the condom on me or I'll do it myself."

Not wanting to miss her chance, Paige quickly ripped the foil, removing the condom.

"I could try putting it on using my mouth."

"YouTube?"

"Yes."

"Let's save that for another time."

"Your loss," Paige said with a flutter of her lashes.

"Have you ever had your ass spanked?" Nate ground out the words through clenched teeth.

"No. I was a perfectly behaved child."

"Sure you were." When Paige rolled the condom onto his cock, Nate's head fell back, his eyes closing. "That's right. Slowly."

"Shouldn't you watch to make sure I'm doing it right?"

"I'll check it when you're done. Right now, it's better if I don't look."

Paige understood his dilemma. Putting a condom on a man was extremely intimate — and erotic. She felt flushed and unbearably aroused. By the feel of him. The heat. The pulsing veins. Nate was ready to burst. Hands down, he won the self-control prize.

"Done," Paige said with a sense of pride. She sat back to admire her work, a teasing light in her eyes. "Not bad for my first time. Maybe I should take a picture and post it on Instagram. Your fans would go wild."

Without a word, Nate checked the condom. The look he gave her told Paige playtime was over. He was suited up and ready for business.

Paige scrambled to the center of the bed, thrilled when he followed. Big and dangerous, Nate took the hem of her nightshirt, pulling it off in one fluid motion.

"You aren't wearing panties."

"I never wear them to bed."

"Why didn't I know that?" With one hand, he anchored her wrist above her head.

"Because you've been so good." Paige took a deep breath when he lightly bit her neck. "No touching below the waist."

"Paige."

"Mmm?"

"Look at me." Languidly, she raised her lids. The sharp blue intensity in his eyes made her gasp. "No more good guy."

Nate lowered himself over her until his body covered hers. Heated flesh to heated flesh. Paige sighed. Finally. She wrapped her legs around his waist, urging him closer.

"I think I'm going to like Bad Nate," Paige said. She felt an intense thrill rush through her at his next words.

"I know you are."

From there it was like being on a long, winding rollercoaster. Nate took over, dictating where the ride took her. One moment fast and breathtaking, then he would execute a gentle turn only to shoot her back up.

Paige gripped his shoulders as he spun her around until she was on top, yet even then, he was in control. Nate took her hips, guiding her — showing her the pace he wanted. Easy, like a gentle wave taking her along. He kept her close to ecstasy, but wouldn't let her reach the peak.

"Faster," she begged.

"Not yet." Nate kissed her breasts, taking the hard, aching point between his teeth. The bite was just right, bringing pleasure and pain in equal measure. "Don't you want the ride to last?"

Nate bit her again, and then gently bathed the spot with his tongue. God, what was he doing to her? She didn't care. She wanted this. All of it. More and more. And then she wanted it again.

"Never let it end, Nate. Promise me it will never end."

"Forever, Paige." Nate threaded his hands into her hair, cupping her head. His lips were a breath away from hers. "Forever."

It was a promise that went straight to her heart. Paige returned Nate's kiss. Love blended with passion. Intense. Impossibly beautiful. When the orgasm hit, she tumbled over and over, reveling in the moment. She let herself fall, unconcerned about hitting the earth. She knew Nate's arms would keep her safe.

When her head stopped spinning, Paige opened her eyes. She smiled when she found Nate looking satisfied and pleased with himself.

"Bad Nate," she laughed. Wondering where she found the strength, raised her hand, patting the side of his face. "Bad, bad Nate."

Nate captured her hand. He kissed the palm before holding it on his chest. She wondered if he realized their hands were clasped over his heart.

Say it, she silently urged him. She took his free hand, laying it over her heart. *Say you love me.*

All she heard was his breathing. Bucking up her courage, Paige formed the words. *I love you.*

"Your parents are leaving after breakfast?" *Coward!*

"On to New Orleans."

"You're leaving too."

"Jack is flying in to pick me up."

"I see." Paige flopped onto her back. "I guess that's that."

"Paige," Nate leaned over her. "I'm coming back."

"When?"

Nate hesitated. "I can't say for certain."

Paige didn't know whether to laugh or cry. Was she supposed to wait around on the off chance he decided to honor her with his presence?

"Great. You're good in bed. Stop by when you're in the neighborhood and we'll do it again."

"Hey." Paige slapped at him when he stopped her from leaving. "Paige. Don't fight. I'm afraid I'll hurt you."

"You already have!" She shouted. She wasn't going to laugh or cry. She was too angry. "Let go of me, Nathaniel. You had your fuck. I'm going back to my own bed."

"Jesus." Nate held her down, waiting for her to stop struggling. It took longer than he expected, but finally, she quieted. "Finished?"

"Are you?" She tried to move her arm. Frustrated, she growled, "You're a big bully, you know that?"

"Bully? Fuck that." Nate rolled away.

Seizing her opportunity, Paige headed for the door, only pausing to pick up her nightshirt.

"I'm coming back."

Struggling to untangle the garment, Paige snorted, "Right. I won't hold my breath."

"I'm coming back because I love you."

"Well, why didn't you say so?"

Paige blindly tossed her nightshirt across the room and jumped into Nate's waiting arms. His kiss felt different. Deeper. Richer. Sweeter. Or maybe it was her. Love, when freely expressed, did make a difference. All the difference in the world.

"Isn't there something you would like to say?"

Paige floated. Every part of her felt lighter than air. She wanted Nate with her. Taking his face between her hands, she met his gaze. Blue as the Montana sky.

"I love you."

"That's good." He turned his head, kissing one hand, then the other. "These now hold my heart. It's only fair that you give me yours in exchange."

"I promise to keep your heart safe, Nate."

"Forever?"

"That's a good place to start."

Chapter Twenty-One

"NOW THAT WE'VE had a wonderful breakfast and everyone is feeling relaxed, why don't you tell us your plan."

Surprised, Nate's gaze shot to his father.

"Plan?" It was an inane response, but when his father looked at him like that, he felt like he was twelve. He and his brothers called it the *magic stare*. Something about it had them spilling their guts no matter how hard they tried not to.

"You think I don't know what you're up to?"

"No," Nate muttered. "But a man can dream."

"You have a threat hanging over your head. If it were me, I would go on the offensive," Caleb shrugged. However, there was nothing casual in his tone. "I assume Jack is taking you somewhere so you can flush this person out."

Nate's smile was ironic. They were alike in so many ways. It made sense his father would glean his plan.

"What?" Paige exclaimed. "I thought you had business to take care of." As soon as the words left her mouth, she realized catching his would-be killer *was* his business.

"I don't like it." Callie put her mug down with a thud. "And I don't like that you kept this to yourself."

Caleb rubbed her shoulder. "I didn't think of it until last night after you had fallen asleep. There was no point in saying anything this morning until Nate confirmed my suspicions."

Chuck circled the table, refilling cups with the pot of coffee he carried.

"None for me, Dad." Paige's stomach couldn't take anything acidic when it was slowly turning into a knotted mess.

"After last night, you were going to leave without telling me any of this?"

"Paige…"

"What happened last night?" Callie asked Nate.

"Are there no secrets in this family?"

"Secrets erode, Nathaniel," Callie stated. "However, if this is something private between you and Paige, I won't pry."

"Not private." Nate smiled at Paige. "New. I told her I loved her."

"Oh, Nate." Callie's famous eyes filled with tears. The color was a misty gray when they turned to Paige. "And you?"

Paige took Nate's hand. "I love him with all my heart."

"I have to end this." Everyone heard the words but he said them to Paige. "We can't live with bodyguards and who knows how many layers of security. As long as a threat looms, we can't move ahead."

Nate outlined the plan. There was nothing complicated. Jack supplied the house and the security.

"And you play sitting duck." The knots in Paige's stomach tightened by the second. "How is that a good plan?"

"It's a great plan," Caleb said. "If it didn't involve my son."

"You're certain this is the only way?" Callie surprised Nate with her even, resigned tone. He nodded and she surprised him even more. "Then you have to do it."

"You could use a decoy," Caleb said. "But you would never do that. Not if it meant putting someone else in danger."

"I am your son."

Caleb's eyes misted. "Keep that in mind. I will be royally pissed if you don't take care of yourself."

Less than an hour later, Callie and Caleb were packed and ready to be on their way.

"I'll call you next week," Caleb told Chuck as they shook hands.

"We'll come again soon." Callie kissed Chuck's cheek, whispering, "I think Paige would like to be married here, don't you?"

"Yes." Chuck knew Erin would be watching. "Before that, Christmas is beautiful here. You could bring the whole family."

"Christmas." Callie's face lit up at the thought. "That sounds lovely."

"Nate." Caleb hugged his son. "Keep in touch."

"I will."

"Keep my baby safe." Callie held back the tears. This wasn't the time. She would save them for when this was over. Then she would weep with relief while Caleb held her close.

"And you." Callie opened her arms to Paige. "Welcome, sweet girl. I'm so happy to know my son's heart is in good hands."

"TAKE ME WITH you."

Paige kept her hands tightly clasped behind her back as Nate loaded his bags into the van. Most of the security crew had already left. It was amazing how quickly they shut things down and packed everything up. They were on their way to the airport. The plane that Jack Winston piloted would carry them as well as Nate to Harper Falls. From there, Nate would travel to an undisclosed location.

It didn't matter how many times Nate reassured her, Paige could not stop worrying. However, if she were with him, she would see for herself that he was safe.

"You know that isn't going to happen."

"I could hide on the plane."

"No, you couldn't. Besides, who would take care of Beauty if you're with me?"

"Dad could—"

"Please." That was all Nate said. In the end, it was all that was necessary. Paige walked into his arms.

"I'll never forgive you if you don't come back."

"I could promise there won't be a scratch on me. However…"

"As long as you're breathing, I'll take you any way I can get you."

Nate lowered his mouth to hers, needing another taste. She was always with him, no matter where he went. The feel of her skin. The touch of her hands. Her scent. Her laugh. In his mind. In his heart. His Paige.

"EVERYTHING IS SET up. I want to go over the plan. Nothing will be left to chance. You can spend the night then leave in the morning. The cabin is about an hour's drive from Harper Falls."

"I'm counting on you and your people, Jack. I have someone waiting for me and I can't let her down."

"The lovely blonde?" Jack asked with a grin. "Paige, right?"

"Good memory."

"I remember the way you looked at her. I guess you spent the last few weeks doing more than making a movie."

He handed Nate a headset before putting on his own. They were in the cockpit, making the final checks before takeoff. Nate watched, mentally running through the familiar routine. He was about to ask Jack if he would mind turning over the controls for takeoff when his phone rang. A second later, Jack pulled his phone from his pocket.

"I'll take my call outside."

Nate looked at his screen. Alan Strand. He had known the man for several years and used him regularly on his stunt crew.

"Alan. Good to hear from you. How is the job in Singapore going?" Nate made sure everyone on his crew had jobs while he was out of commission. Alan and several others worked on the latest Tom Cruise film.

"Nate. I have to tell you. I did it."

"Hey. Have you been drinking?" Nate frowned. He had a strict rule.

No alcohol during a shoot. Technically, Alan didn't answer to him this time, but he didn't like to think Alan broke that rule even if he wasn't there to enforce it.

"I had a few. Dutch courage." Nate could hear Alan take a deep breath. "I need you to know. I should have told you right away."

"Told me what?"

"I fucked up the stunt. I almost killed you. It was an accident. When you walked away, I figured I dodged a bullet. Then I heard someone confessed. It was me, Nate. I need you to forgive me."

Nate reeled, trying to figure out the implications. The botched stunt had been an accident. No one tried to kill him. Then what about the explosion? The two weren't connected. Did that mean he wasn't the target? Paige's truck. *Paige*. Son of a bitch.

"Nate?" Alan called out. "Are you still there?"

"Sober up, asshole." Nate tore off his seat belt. "And stay away from me."

"Nate." Jack came barreling into the cockpit, barely missing knocking his head into Nate's.

"Call Travis." Nate was trying to shove past. "There's something wrong."

"No shit." Jack followed on his heels. "That was Alex on the phone. It took some digging, but the money trail leads from Bernie Renshaw to a dummy company."

Nate jumped from the plane. Next came Jack and the security crew. They checked their guns.

"Who is it?"

"Lyle Wilson."

"Fuck! Goddamn it." Nate scrolled through the numbers on his phone. "I'm calling Paige. What about Travis?"

"He isn't answering."

"Paige's phone went straight to voicemail."

"Calm down. No." Jack pushed Nate toward the passenger side of the van. "I'll drive. Call her father. Then her friends. Try not to panic anyone."

"How the hell am I supposed to do that?"

Jack waited until the back of the van was filled with men, and then hit the gas.

"Breathe. You've only been gone an hour, Nate. I'm sure Paige is fine."

It was bullshit and they both knew it. Disaster could strike in a heartbeat. An hour was a lifetime. Nate had one hope. Whatever Lyle Wilson wanted, it involved keeping Paige alive. He needed to get to her before Wilson changed his mind.

PAIGE DECIDED TO take Beauty for a walk.

The puppy was happy to romp across the fields and she felt like being alone with her thoughts. Or as alone as a woman could be who had a very large bodyguard trailing behind her.

"I know you won't stay home."

"Nope." Travis held her jacket out for her. The weather had taken a cold turn and she needed the extra layer.

"Then walk beside me. I feel odd having someone's eyes on my ass."

"I don't watch your ass." Travis fell into step beside her. "Much."

Paige laughed. It was impossible to get Nate off her mind, but she liked Travis and she appreciated his humor. He had become a friend and she didn't feel like she needed to keep up a running dialogue. They walked for several minutes in a companionable silence.

"I'm sorry you had to stay behind. You'll miss all the action. Did you draw the short straw?"

"I volunteered."

"Why?"

Surprised, Paige glanced at him. He really was handsome. Not as handsome as Nate. However, if she were honest, she could be a trifle biased.

"Nate needs to stay focused. He'll rest easier knowing I have your back."

"I hate this." Damn. She was not going to cry.

"Promise me a dance at your wedding?"

Paige knew what Travis was doing. Shifting the conversation from serious to light. Since she needed the distraction, she went along.

"Nate hasn't asked me to marry him."

"He will." Travis picked up a stick, tossing it for a delighted Beauty to chase. She hadn't mastered the return part yet, but she was terrific at fetching. "Or you'll ask him. Either way, you two are getting hi— Hey, isn't that your neighbor?"

Glancing across the field, Paige frowned. The black truck headed their way was indeed Lyle's. It seemed odd for him to be out here where there was no road. He never drove in the fields because he didn't like wear and tear on his vehicle.

"Paige. I called the Double C and your father said you had headed this way. I hoped you would come by my place. I've decided to redecorate and I would love your opinion."

"Me? I don't think we have the same taste, Lyle." Paige knew it for a fact.

"Perhaps." Lyle laughed, but there was an edge to it. "It was really just an excuse. I heard that Nate Landis left and I thought you might need a friend. I know the two of you became close while he was here. I know you must be missing him. Come for a drink." When Paige hesitated, he added, "Please. Nothing romantic. Let me be a good neighbor. Your friend and the dog are welcome, too."

Paige felt a wave of sadness. Mixed with her fear and worry over Nate, it made her vulnerable to Lyle's sympathy.

That was how she found herself in Lyle's living room. She knew the moment she climbed into his truck, it was a mistake. When they reached the house, she saw the relief on Lyle's face when Travis said he would wait outside with Beauty. If they left now, they could cut across the fields and make it home in time for her to start dinner.

"One glass of wine. It's the kind you like." Lyle handed her a glass. "Then I'll drive you home."

Paige wondered at what point trying to be polite morphed into idiotic. She hated this wine. She wasn't going to drink it simply to make

Lyle feel better. With a smile, she raised the glass to her lips. She only wet her lips, but that was bad enough. God, she hated this stuff. It made her lips tingle. That was odd. She didn't remember it doing that before.

"I need to get going, Lyle."

"One more sip." Lyle looked eager, his eyes strangely intense.

"I don't want any more." Paige set the glass down near the offensive bottle of wine. Before she had taken two steps, Lyle grabbed her arm.

"Drink the wine, Paige."

"Are you out of your mind?" Paige tried to pull away. For a man with scrawny arms, he was surprisingly strong. "Why are you obsessed with me drinking that stupid wine?"

"Because." His voice was low and calm. "It's drugged. It will be much easier to get you on the plane if you are unconscious."

Paige felt a shot of panic. Lyle was crazy. Why hadn't she seen it before? His eyes looked almost feverish. His tongue kept darting out, wetting his lips. She had to get away.

Travis. Paige felt a wave of relief. Help was only a scream away.

"Your friend won't be of any help," Lyle said as if reading her mind. Paige jumped when a gunshot rang out. "There. End of problem. Now, my dear, you have a choice. Come with me of your own free will. Or drink the wine."

"I pick door number three."

"What?" Lyle looked genuinely confused. "Door? What door?"

"This one, motherfucker."

In a flash, Paige grabbed the wine bottle from the bar and swung at Lyle's head with all her might. It was almost comical the way he crumpled into a heap.

"What door?" he mumbled, grasping his head.

"My mistake. I meant bottle."

"What?"

"She said bottle, asshole."

"Nate!" Paige didn't care where he had come from or if she was hallucinating. He looked solid and that was all that mattered. She threw herself into his arms, swearing to herself that she would let never go.

Nate held Paige close, happy to breathe in her welcome scent.

Chapter Twenty-Two

NATE DIDN'T WANT to let go of Paige. Hell broke out all around them. Men with guns rushed in. Lights flashed in the driveway. Lyle Wilson was dragged away in handcuffs still muttering about door number three.

All Nate cared about was holding Paige and reassuring himself that she was all right. The hell with the chaos around them. She clung to him for dear life — shaking. He soothed her with whispered words and soft kisses.

"Travis," Paige tried to pull back. For the first time, tears began to flow. "I heard a gunshot, Nate."

"Shh," Nate gently wiped her cheeks. "There he is. Safe and sound."

Nate pointed across the room to where Travis conferred with Danny Floyd and Jack Winston.

"What happened, Nate?" Paige laid her head on his chest, her body burrowing as close as possible.

"We'll sort it out. Right now, just hold on. You're safe. That's all that matters."

THE NEXT MORNING they sat around the dining room table at the Double C, drinking coffee with friends and family. From the outside, it looked like any other gathering. The subject matter changed the complexion completely.

"Lyle Wilson started singing, or should I say squawking, before his lawyer arrived. And continued. The lawyer couldn't shut him up."

Jack Winston looked like a man who hadn't slept in days. And that wasn't far from the truth. Though he had no official capacity, the local police had let him witness the interrogation of Lyle Wilson.

"Why?" It was all Paige could think to ask.

Like Jack, none of them had slept. After giving her statement, Nate took her home. Chuck was with them, having arrived at Lyle Wilson's house minutes after Paige called him to let him know what had happened.

Once they were back at the ranch, Paige curled up next to Nate and Beauty on the couch, her father nearby, and insisted Nate fill in some of the blanks.

Nate told them about the phone calls he and Jack had received.

"After that, Jack drove like a maniac and I called Chuck. When we got to the ranch, he showed us the direction you and Travis took. We drove until we hit Wilson's place. We heard the gunshot just as we arrived."

Nate shuddered when he remembered the terror he felt when he heard that sound. If Jack hadn't stopped him, he would have jumped from the truck before it stopped.

"The first thing we saw was a man on the ground and Travis with his gun drawn. Beauty wisely hid behind Travis."

They had to wait for the rest of the story. Around ten in the morning, Jack and Travis drove up. They were rumpled and tired but ready to fill everyone in.

"I thought you had been shot," Paige hugged Travis, happy to see her bodyguard looking none the worse for wear.

"I might have been if it weren't for Beauty. I tossed the stick for her when she suddenly stopped in her tracks, whining like crazy. I'd never heard her make that noise and it sent a shiver up my spine. I pulled my gun and hit the ground. The bullet missed me by inches. I played dead until I saw a pair of wingtips by my head. I knocked his feet out from under him and that was when the cavalry arrived." He smiled at the sleeping dog. "I owe her steak for life."

"Now it's your turn," Nate said to Jack. "Wilson spilled his guts?"

"He was outraged that Paige hadn't been arrested for assault."

"What?" Paige couldn't believe her ears.

"When that didn't play, the air went out of him fast. He started crying and everything poured out. His obsession with Paige. The attempt on Nate's life was a mistake. His paid assassin, the guy that shot at Travis, killed the bomber and others over the years. Once Wilson started, his confession covered years of shit no one would have thought to link to him."

"He was crazy." Paige would remember Lyle's eyes for the rest of her life.

"Yes," Jack agreed. "The longer he talked, the prouder he became. He wanted to brag about his imagined accomplishments."

"And me? What was I supposed to be?" Paige hated to ask but she needed to know.

"His playmate." Jack shrugged knowing it sounded ridiculous. "He became bored easily. Something about his *superior intelligence*. He saw you as his match. He liked that you didn't fall into his lap. You were a challenge. When Nate came along, he thought getting rid of him was the answer. Then it was decided. Nate was too high profile to kill. They would wait until he was gone and take Paige out of the country where no one would find you."

"And then?" Paige knew there was more.

"When you no longer amused him, you would disappear for good."

"Jesus Christ." Chuck had turned white. "Right next door. I could have lost you."

"But you didn't," Paige hugged her father.

"Thanks to Paige's bravery and ingenuity." Nate's eyes filled with pride and love.

Paige smiled back. "Thanks to a lousy bottle of wine."

"I FEEL NORMAL."

"That's good." Nate kissed her bare shoulder. "Normal is good."

"After the last few days, I agree."

They were in Nate's bed. Beauty slept soundly at their feet. It could have been like any other night. However, everything had changed. The danger that had hung over them was gone. They no longer doubted how the other felt. Love. It freed them in so many ways.

"Best of all," Nate said, cupping Paige's bare breast. "No nightshirt."

Paige shivered when Nate rubbed his thumb over her hardening nipple. "And no underwear."

"Watch the roaming hands," he warned her when she caressed his butt. "I have things to say. Then you can have your way with me."

"Look who's talking about roaming hands."

"Want me to move it?" Nate gave her breast a gentle squeeze.

"No. Do you want me to move?"

Nate smiled when Paige squeezed his ass, none too gently.

"No."

"I love you, Nathaniel."

"I love you." He waited for a beat. "We haven't had time to talk about the future."

"Will we be together?"

"Forever."

"In Los Angeles."

It wasn't a question. "Is that really what you want? What about the ranch? Your father? Your horses?"

"I love the ranch. Before my mother died, I had plans to see the world. I put that dream aside — happily." Paige turned to face him. She laced her fingers with his. "Dad already hires extra hands to help out. And he has Irene."

"That is a good fit."

"Perfect," Paige agreed. "As for my horses. Rollie and Winter have a home here for life. I hope we will visit. Often?"

"Yes."

"Montana isn't the only place that has horses that need rescuing. You mentioned that big place of yours in Laurel Canyon."

"I'll set up a meeting with my architect. You tell him what you need, we'll build it."

Paige kissed him. Sweet, with the promise of heat.

"We'll need a kennel. I want to expand the rescues to dogs. Not every puppy is as lucky as Beauty."

Nate kissed the back of her hand. He was the lucky one. A stupid accident. A broken arm. They had led him to Montana. Here he found his heart. His love. His life. His Paige.

Epilogue

MOVIE PREMIERES WERE a pain in the ass. Dealing with logistics, the press. Dressing up in a suit and tie.

Nate would have skipped the last bit if Paige hadn't pointed out that at least for tonight, he wasn't a stuntman. He was a director. *The* director of *Erin's Dream*. Besides, according to his fiancée, he looked sexy in a custom-tailored suit. How was a man supposed to argue with that?

Erin's Dream. All through production, they had referred to the movie as *the production*. There was no title because Erin never gave it one. Chuck hadn't thought far enough ahead to consider a finished movie that would be released to the public.

The title worked on every level. Originally, the female lead was named Marjory. Chuck changed it to Erin. When Nate suggested calling the film *Erin's Dream*, Chuck was overcome with emotion. The perfect tribute to his beloved wife. The perfect way to move on with Irene while never forgetting Erin.

"She's a natural." Callie slipped her hand through Nate's arm. "Paige has charmed everyone here. Look at that old gasbag, Myron Potts. She has the toughest critic in Hollywood eating out of her hand."

"Who can blame him? She's the perfect package. Brains and beauty."

Paige glowed. Her blond hair cascaded down her back like a streak of honeyed sunshine. The dress that Callie helped her choose showed off her long, lean body to perfection. His mother informed him the color was summer peach. It made Paige's skin appear creamy and soft — and he was the only man in the room lucky enough to know she felt better than she looked.

"You were worried about her."

Leave it to my mother, Nate thought affectionately.

"Not worried. I know Paige can handle any situation. I was afraid she would take one look at this circus and regret leaving Montana. I find it a lot to take in and I'm used to it."

"She's happier with her animals."

"Yes."

Paige had accomplished miracles in only a few months. The new buildings around the Laurel Canyon property already housed two horses and three dogs. She had homes for the dogs and expected more to arrive next week. The horses would take more time, but Nate knew with Paige's loving touch, they would recover and live long, happy lives.

"Go." Callie smiled, pushing Nate toward Paige. "Rescue her before that man bores her ears off."

"I can't remember the last time a movie moved me so much." Myron Potts waved his hands, wildly emphasizing every word. "The raw emotion was startling."

"Paige's mother wrote an amazing story."

"Nate took it and turned it into an amazing movie."

Taking her outstretched hand, Nate's blue eyes lingered on hers. He would never grow tired of seeing the love shining for him. He planned on treasuring it for the rest of his life.

"I know you've stated publicly that *Erin's Dream* doesn't signal a change in careers. With the overwhelmingly enthusiastic response, you must be reconsidering." Myron leaned closer, hoping for an exclusive scoop.

"Nate is a stuntman."

"But surely—"

"You heard Paige. I'm a stuntman. Excuse us." He gripped Paige's hand and started to walk away. Then he turned back, unable to resist. "And don't call me Shirley."

"I love that you did that." Paige was still laughing when Nate pulled her onto the dance floor. "By the look on Myron's face, I'm not sure he got the reference."

"Then shame on him. He can look it up."

Nate danced with an easy grace, leading her with a sure touch. He didn't do this often, but having Paige made him consider making it a regular thing. Date night. After their unconventional courtship, they enjoyed going out. Dinner and dancing would be a nice addition.

"Your dad was beaming all evening."

"He loved every minute. I know he's never going to forget seeing Mom's movie on that big screen. Thank you."

"Thank you, Paige."

"Me?" Paige laughed. "What did I do?"

"You gave me something I didn't know I was missing. Your heart."

"And you gave me yours. Promise me something? Never ask for it back."

"Never."

Nate lowered his mouth to hers. Cameras clicked. Within seconds, Nate's fans all over the world sighed with envy, dreaming they were in his arms.

Nate no longer cared. Paige was his dream come true. And he never had to close his eyes.

Coming Soon

MAY
Dreaming Of Your Love
(Hollywood Legends Book Three)

JULY
Dreaming Again
(Hollywood Legends Book Four)

DECEMBER
Dreaming Of A White Christmas
(Hollywood Legends Book Five)

How to Get in Touch

Please visit me at these sites, sign up for my newsletter, or leave a message.

http://www.maryjwilliams.net/home.html
https://www.facebook.com/pages/Mary-J-Williams/1561851657385417
https://twitter.com/maryjwilliams05
https://www.pinterest.com/maryj0675/
https://www.goodreads.com/author/show/5648619.Mary_J_Williams

www.ingramcontent.com/pod-product-compliance
Lightning Source LLC
Chambersburg PA
CBHW071101250626
47159CB00002B/543